AUG 1 3 2010

Y0-BDP-384

WITHDRAWN

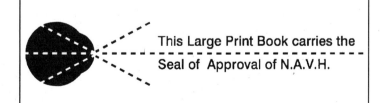

This Large Print Book carries the
Seal of Approval of N.A.V.H.

THE 13TH HOUR

THE 13TH HOUR

RICHARD DOETSCH

THORNDIKE PRESS
A part of Gale, Cengage Learning

ELISHA D. SMITH PUBLIC LIBRARY
MENASHA, WISCONSIN

GALE
CENGAGE Learning

Detroit • New York • San Francisco • New Haven, Conn • Waterville, Maine • London

GALE
CENGAGE Learning™

Copyright © 2009 by Richard Doetsch.
Thorndike Press, a part of Gale, Cengage Learning.

ALL RIGHTS RESERVED
This book is a work of fiction. Names, characters, places, and incidents either are products of the author's imagination or are used fictitiously. Any resemblance to actual events or locales or persons living or dead is entirely coincidental.
Thorndike Press® Large Print Thriller.
The text of this Large Print edition is unabridged.
Other aspects of the book may vary from the original edition.
Set in 16 pt. Plantin.

LIBRARY OF CONGRESS CATALOGING-IN-PUBLICATION DATA

Doetsch, Richard.
    The 13th hour : a thriller / by Richard Doetsch. — Large print ed.
        p. cm. — (Thorndike Press large print thriller)
    ISBN-13: 978-1-4104-2600-0 (alk. paper)
    ISBN-10: 1-4104-2600-9 (alk. paper)
    1. Prisoners—Fiction. 2. Murder—Fiction. 3. Time travel—Fiction. 4. Large type books. I. Title. II. Title: Thirteenth hour.
PS3604.O343A617 2010
813'.6—dc22   2010004294

Published in 2010 by arrangement with Atria Books, a division of Simon & Schuster, Inc.

Printed in the United States of America
1 2 3 4 5 6 7 14 13 12 11 10

For Virginia,
my best friend.
I love you with all my heart.

You cannot kill time without injuring eternity.

— HENRY DAVID THOREAU

All my possessions for a moment of time.

— QUEEN ELIZABETH

I should have become a watchmaker.

— ALBERT EINSTEIN

AUTHOR'S NOTE

You are not mistaken as you turn to the next page and find Chapter 12.

The chapters of this book are in reverse order and are to be read that way for reasons that will become evident upon your journey.

CHAPTER 12

July 28,
9:22 P.M.

The dark-haired man slid the exotic, custom-made Peacemaker across the table. With a frame of polished bronze with gold accents, its ivory grip inlaid with precious stones, it was unlike any other weapon produced in the nineteenth century, a six-shooter crafted in 1872 that had been lost to time, forgotten by history, spoken of in collectors' circles as myth.

As with many of the finest pistols of the day, intricate etchings appeared along the stock and seven-and-a-half-inch barrel. But these etchings were unique — religious texts drawn from the Bible, the Koran, and the Torah, expertly rendered in an elegant calligraphy: *The gate that leads to damnation is wide — To hell you shall be gathered together — Yet ye bring wrath — Darkness which may be felt — Whoever offers violence to you, of-*

fer you the like violence to him. The sayings were rendered in English, Latin, and Arabic, as if the gun were a weapon of God designed to strike down the sinner.

Crafted for Murad V, the thirty-seventh sultan of the Ottoman Empire, it had supposedly disappeared from existence in August 1876 when he was deposed for insanity after only ninety-three days of rule.

"Dual action," the man said as he picked up the weapon in his gloved hand. "You don't see many like this. In fact, I would dare to say this is one of a kind."

Ethan Dance handled the gun with reverence, as if it were a newborn baby. His sleepy, bloodshot eyes scanned the intricacies of the weapon, his latex-encased finger running about the gunmetal and gold in appreciation of the Colt pistol's craftsmanship. He finally laid it down and reached into the pocket of his wrinkled blue blazer.

"Looks like the same religious fervor was scratched into the ammunition." Dance laid a bullet on the table, silver, forty-five caliber. It, too, was etched, the casing wrapped in a flowing Arabic script. "There were five left in the cylinder. They're silver, you know, not sure why, its not like there were werewolves running around Istanbul in 1876. Then again, the pistol was designed for a madman."

Nicholas Quinn sat across from Dance, silently looking at the weapon. He could smell the fresh oil on its workings, a hint of sulfur residue in its chamber.

"What does something like this cost? Fifty, one hundred thousand?" Dance picked it up again, rolled out the cylinder, spinning it like a western lawman. "This gun was just a rumor, no record of ownership for 130 years. Where do you find something like this? On the antique market, black market, the hush-hush just-between-us market?"

Nick sat there in silence, his mind spinning.

The door opened, and a gray-haired man in a blue suit poked his head in. "Need you for a second, Dance."

Dance threw up his hands. "Kind of got some stuff going on."

"Well, life sucks out loud. With the plane crash, it's the two of us, Shannon, and Manz for the whole place. So unless you want to get back down to that field and start sorting through mangled bodies of women and children, you'll get your ass out here."

Dance slammed the cylinder back up into the gun, spun it once for effect, and held it up, looking down the barrel as if he were aiming at an imaginary target.

He laid the gun back in front of Nick and looked at him a moment before grabbing the lone silver bullet.

"Don't go away," Dance said as he walked out, closing the steel door behind him.

Nicholas Quinn finally inhaled, as if he were taking his first breath in three hours. He did everything he could to hold back his emotions, tucking the news in the farthest corner of his mind, knowing that if he let it run about it would eat him from the inside out.

He was dressed in the muted blue and gray Zegna sport jacket Julia had given him two weeks earlier for his thirty-second birthday, freshly pressed, looking as if it had just come from the tailor. He wore it over a light green polo shirt with his jeans, pretty much his uniform for casual Friday. Nick's dark blond hair was on the long side, in need of a cut, one that he had been promising Julia he would get for the last three weeks. His strong face was handsome and unreadable, a trait that had proven invaluable in business and poker. No one could see through his eyes to the truth in his heart, except for Julia, who could always read his thoughts from just the curve of his lip.

Nick looked around the small, confined

room, a space clearly designed for the purpose of creating anxiety. There was the single metal table, the ornate, bejeweled gun upon its lime-green Formica surface; four extremely uncomfortable thick metal chairs, his ass already numb after fifteen minutes; a white wire-caged clock hung by the door, the time approaching 9:30. The walls were bare but for a giant white board on the near wall, three colored markers hanging from a tattered shoelace off a corner. On the opposite side of the room sat a two-way mirror, which not only allowed observation by whoever stood on the other side but also created a feeling of paranoia for whoever sat in this room wondering how many people were watching, assessing, convicting you before a plea had even been entered.

An intense agony began to strangle Nick's heart. Everything in his world had stopped. His emotions had been wrung dry over the two hours before he got here. A swirl of questions and confusion dominated his thoughts.

For the briefest of seconds, he thought he could smell her, Julia's essence, as if it somehow lingered upon his soul.

Nick had gotten home at three this morning after a four-day whirlwind business trip around the Southwest, so exhausted he didn't even remember getting into bed. But he did remember waking up.

As he had drifted into consciousness, he looked directly into Julia's blue eyes, which were filled with love. She had been gently kissing him, drawing him up from whatever dream held him tight, coaxing him back into the world.

She wore nothing but an Eric Clapton T-shirt, which remained on for only three more seconds, tossed to the floor to reveal a perfect body. She was nearly as fit at thirty-one as she had been at sixteen, her breasts firm, her belly tight with just a hint of a six-pack. Her forever long legs were tan and lithe. She was of Spanish, Irish, and Scottish descent, and there was a classic beauty to her face, her high cheekbones and full lips turning the heads of most men when she walked into a room. Her large blue eyes always grew more alluring during the summer when her skin tanned to a light golden hue, with a hint of freckles rising up on her nose.

Julia straddled Nick, leaning down to lightly kiss his lips awake. Becoming lost in her tangle of long blond hair, the smell of lavender and her natural essence filling his mind, Nick's dream of moments earlier was coming to life.

They made love with the heat and excitement of first love, lost in each other's arms, hands roaming each other's bodies, kisses and warm breaths trailing skin. Their passion had rarely waned, even after sixteen years. And it was never merely sex, despite the preternatural lust they felt for each other, there was always the selfless abandonment, each delaying fulfillment in deference to the other, each concerned with the other's pleasure above his or her own, it was always making love.

And as they lay entwined, in the afterglow of the moment, the sheets in a ball at their feet, they both lost sense of time, of where they were, of whatever worries they faced in the coming day, taking comfort in each other's embrace.

With the sunlight dancing upon the white pillows, Nick finally rose from the bed, stretching his toned body to full alertness, and caught sight of the small table on their porch.

Despite her own lack of sleep from too many hours at the office, Julia had risen to prepare breakfast and set the wrought-iron table on the private, second-floor deck just off the sitting room. There was bacon, eggs, fresh-squeezed orange juice, and skillet cake, all fixed and silently carried up from the kitchen as he'd slept.

In nothing but underwear and T-shirts they ate as the sun began its climb in the summer morning sky.

"Special occasion?" Nick asked, alluding to the meal.

"Can't I just welcome you home?"

Nick smiled. "After that first course, a dry bagel would have been more than enough."

Julia smiled back, her look warm and caring, but there was something else there, a hesitation in her eyes.

"What did you do?" Nick asked with a chuckle.

"Nothing." But her voice and the slight dimple rising on her cheek said otherwise.

"Julia . . . ?"

"We have dinner with the Mullers tonight at Valhalla," Julia said quickly.

Nick stopped eating as he looked up. "I thought we agreed we were staying home."

"They're not so horrible." Julia smiled a disarming smile. "I really like Fran. And come on, Tom's not that bad."

"When he stops talking about himself. If I hear one more word about how much money he makes, or what kind of car he just bought —"

"— He's just insecure. Think of it as a

compliment."

"How could I possibly think of his yammering as a compliment?"

"He's trying to impress you; he obviously cares about your opinion."

"All he cares about is himself." Nick cleared his plate, placing it on the large serving tray. Julia grabbed the remaining dishes, stacking them atop his.

"I thought we made plans together, not for each other," Nick said.

"Nick." Julia grimaced. "We couldn't get reservations until 9:00."

The moment was suddenly lost as a tension grew between them.

Julia picked up the tray and walked to the door. "It's Friday night; I just wanted to go out."

And she slipped back inside the house, leaving Nick standing there alone.

Nick walked inside, through the sitting room and into his bathroom, shutting the door, turning on the shower. He stepped in, hoping the cool water would wash away his suddenly foul mood. He hated wasting time with superficial friends, those whose thoughts never ran deeper than the menu.

Fifteen minutes later he was dressed in his favorite Levi's and a polo shirt and walked back into the room to find Julia

19

dressed and heading for the door. She had transformed from his sexy wife to a businesswoman in a black skirt, Tory Burch shoes, and a white silk blouse. She picked up her purse, throwing it on her shoulder, and looked at him.

"I think we should cancel," Nick said calmly, in an almost pleading voice. "I really just want to be home."

"You'll be home all day," she said.

"Yeah, in my office working, trying to finish my report," Nick said a little too quickly.

"Why don't you work out? Go for a run. Relieve some of that stress. I really want to go out tonight. It will only be two hours, we can even skip dessert."

"Like that will make the evening any more bearable." His dismissive tone came out as a challenge.

"Just do it for me," Julia said as she walked to the door. "You never know, it might turn out to be a good time."

"What about me? I've been on too many planes to count, and we both know how much I love flying. I'm lucky to know what state I'm in."

"Nine o'clock."

"I don't want to."

"Nine o'clock." The anger was beginning to show in her voice as she walked out. "I'm late for work."

"Fine," Nick exploded, his voice echoing through the room and down the hall.

Her only response came ten seconds later with the slamming of the back door, the thud shaking the whole house.

It was the first time in months that a morning had ended badly. The days were always supposed to start with hope and optimism before being pulled into an abyss by the trials and tribulations of work.

And all at once he regretted his rage, regretted parting at odds over something so trivial as a dinner date. There was always tomorrow, there was always Sunday. He tried her on her cell phone but there was no answer, and rightly so.

The lights of the interrogation room flickered on and off, the windowless space falling in and out of a pitch-black dark before the overhead fluorescent light settled back into its pale dim glow.

"Sorry about that," Dance said. "The generator's been running over nine hours now. It's seen better days."

He settled back in his chair and tilted his head. "You a Yankees or Mets fan?"

Nick just stared at him, amazed that he would ask such a question, considering everything going on.

"Jeter just hit a grand slam in the bottom of the ninth to beat the Red Sox, six to five." Dance shook his head, seeing Nick's lack of interest, and reached into his pocket.

A second man had joined them and had yet to say a word. His chair was tipped back against the wall as he pushed a few strands of out-of-place hair from his face. Detective Robert Shannon was an unfortunate stereotype, his muscled body crammed into a black short-sleeved shirt two sizes too small, accentuating his arms and chest. His black Irish hair was slicked back, and there was a small scar on his chin. His slate-blue eyes were angry, accusatory. He was spinning an old-fashioned billy club in his hand, tossing it back and forth like a miniature baseball bat, as if he were some beat cop out of 1950s New York. Nick couldn't help thinking the guy was already convinced of his guilt.

Dance pulled a small Dictaphone from his pocket, held it out, and hit play.

"Nine-one-one emergency?" a woman's voice sang out.

"My name is Julia Quinn," Julia's whispered voice said. "Five Townsend Court, Byram Hills. You have to hurry, my husband and —"

The phone clicked off. "Hello," the operator said, "Hello, ma'am?"

And Dance clicked off the recorder.

"She made that call at 6:42," Dance said. "May I ask where you were?"

Nick remained silent. Not out of defensiveness but because he was afraid that if he spoke he would break down. Hearing Julia's voice only magnified his pain, the suffering that infused his heart.

He knew exactly where he'd been at 6:42; he was still in his library working, he had been there most of the day except for grabbing a few Cokes and Oreos from the kitchen.

The gunshot had startled him from his concentration, his hearing grew suddenly acute, and, as if he had been on some delay, he finally bolted up from his chair. He ran out through the living room, through the kitchen, to the mudroom, where the back door to the garage hung wide open.

He couldn't understand why Julia had left the door open again. He saw her purse on the floor by the coat hooks where it usually hung, its contents scattered on the floor. And as he crouched to pick it up he finally saw the blood dripping down the white wainscoting, his eyes trailing it down to see her black skirt, her long leg, her foot in its yellow Tory Burch shoe sticking out by the back stairs, her body, her face concealed by the lowest steps.

And in that moment, all the air left his lungs as he collapsed to the floor. Shaking uncontrollably, he rubbed her leg, calling to her, whispering her name, knowing she would never answer him again.

After a minute, his heart all but dead, he finally looked up, to see his best friend standing over them with tear-streaked eyes. Nick released her leg and rose to his feet. Marcus laid his hands upon Nick's shoulders, holding him back from advancing toward Julia's upper body, putting all 220 pounds of what was once muscle into keeping him from a sight that would haunt him till the end of days.

As Nick fought his best friend to get near his wife, a scream of anguish finally poured forth, filling the small room before dissolving to silent tears, the sounds of the world falling away to nothing as the reality of the moment set in.

They waited at Marcus's house next door, silently sitting on the front steps for over an hour before they heard the sirens announcing to the neighborhood that something horrible had happened. It was a sound that would be with Nick forever, for it was the sound track to his tragic loss and the prelude to the unthinkable nightmare of accusations that were about to begin.

The gray-haired man stuck his head into the room, again. "His attorney's here."

"That was fast," Dance said.

"The wealthy don't wait," Shannon said, speaking for the first time, as he tipped his chair forward and stood up. His eyes bore into Nick as he headed for the door.

"Let's go." The gray-haired man waved his hand, ushering the two policemen out.

The door closed with a loud clang behind them but reopened not thirty seconds later; Nick's heart hadn't even had a moment to slow.

The man walked in as if he owned the room, tall, polished, with an air of wisdom and calm that displaced some of the terror that had enveloped Nick for much of the last several hours. His hair was dark, flecked with gray, silver highlights at the temple; his eyes were sharp and focused. His face was weathered from life, character lines etching the tanned skin about his eyes and forehead. He was dressed in a double-breasted blue blazer and sharply creased linen pants, his yellow silk tie set off against a pale blue shirt, all of it combining to display a man of refinement and taste. He even smelled rich.

"They already took most of you, eh?" the man said in a deep European-sounding voice as he pulled out a metal chair and took a seat across from Nick.

Nick stared at the man, confusion filling his eyes.

"Your wallet, keys, cell phone, even your watch," the man said, looking at the pale stripe on Nick's bare wrist. "They slowly strip your identity, then they take away your heart, and finally your soul, until you'll say whatever they want you to say."

"Who are you?" Nick asked, the first words he had spoken inside the confines of these walls. "Did Mitch send you?"

"No." The man paused, looking about the room, assessing it and Nick at the same time. "With the case they have against you, an attorney is the last thing you need. He'll charge six hundred an hour, give you a bill for half a million, and make you feel like you owe him as you sit in your prison cell doing twenty-five to life."

Nick stared at the elegant man, even more confused. "Mitch is on his way. I've got nothing to say to you."

The man nodded, exuding calm, as he laid his arms upon the table and leaned forward.

"I understand the crippling grief you must be feeling. It's horrible that they don't even allow you a moment of mourning before they start trying to steer you into a confession." The man paused. "When did justice start to become about winning and losing, an us-against-them mentality, instead of the revelation and uncovering of truth?"

Nick looked the man up and down.

"Have you seen the file on you, their case?" the man said. "It's detailed; I doubt they'll even offer you a plea deal."

"I didn't kill my wife," Nick finally said.

"I know, but that's not how they see it. They see motive, the weapon," the man said, casting his eyes at the gun sitting in the middle of the table. "They're hoping for a confession to avoid the extra paperwork."

"How do you know?"

"They'll spend twelve hours slowly wearing you down getting you to confess to avoid the weeks of meeting with the DA for months of trial preparation." The man paused. "You'll be convicted, spend the rest of your days in prison, mourning the death of your wife, always wondering what really happened."

"So, if you're not an attorney, why are you here?"

The man's warm eyes remained fixed on Nick as he took a deep breath, his chest expanding before finally exhaling.

"You can still save her."

Nick stared back at the man, the words not making sense. He leaned closer for clarity. "What?"

"If you could get out of here, if you could save her, would you?"

"She's dead," Nick said with confusion, as if the man were unaware of the fact.

"Are you sure?" the man said, looking more closely at Nick. "Things aren't always what they seem."

"Are you saying my wife is alive?" Nick's voice cracked. "How? I saw —"

The man reached into the inner breast pocket of his Ralph Lauren jacket, pulled out a sealed letter, and slid it across the table to Nick.

Nick looked at the two-way mirror.

"Don't worry." The man smiled. "No one is watching."

"How do you know?"

"They're busy with the plane crash. Two hundred and twelve dead. This town, like your life, has been turned on its head."

Nick felt his world spinning, as if he were in that twilight between waking and sleep where the mind is peppered with incongruous images and thoughts that desperately try to coalesce into a coherent notion.

He looked down at the envelope and slid

his finger under the glue flap —

"Don't open that now." The man laid his hand upon Nick's.

"Why?"

"Wait until you're out of here." The man withdrew his hand as he leaned back in the chair.

"Out of here?"

"You've got twelve hours."

Nick looked at the clock on the wall: it was 9:51. "Twelve hours for what?"

The man pulled a gold pocket watch from within his jacket and flipped it open to reveal an old-fashioned clock face. "Time is not something to waste, a particularly true statement in your case." The man closed the watch and handed it to Nick. "Seeing you're short one timepiece, and the pressure you're under, you'd best hold on to that and keep an eye on the hour hand."

"Who are you?"

"Everything you need to know is in that letter. But as I said, don't open it until you're out of here."

Nick looked around the room, at the two-way glass, at the decrepit steel door. "How the hell am I supposed to get out of here?"

"You can't save her life if you're in here."

"What are you saying? I don't understand, where is she?"

29

The man looked at the clock on the wall as he stood up. "You better start thinking how you're getting out; you've only got nine minutes."

"Wait —"

"Good luck." The man tapped the door twice. "Keep an eye on that watch. You have twelve hours. In the thirteenth hour all will be lost, her fate, your fate will be sealed. And she'll have died a far worse death than you already think."

The door opened and the man slipped out, leaving Nick sitting alone. He stared at the envelope, tempted to open it. But he quickly tucked it, along with the gold watch, into the breast pocket of his jacket, knowing that if they were found he would never know what the man was talking about.

The man had offered no other information, no name, no explanation for how Julia could be alive.

Nick had seen her body, though he had not looked upon her face, as Marcus had held him back, protecting him from her image, her beauty stolen by the gunshot that ended her life. But he had held her leg, seen the clothes she'd worn when she left for work this morning.

There was no question it was Julia. She had called to him when she'd arrived home, but she didn't enter the library where he worked, knowing not to disturb him, knowing he was trying to finish a major acquisition analysis stemming from his week's travels and that if he didn't finish before they went out for dinner, he would be working the weekend.

He could still hear her voice; it was the last time she called his name. And the guilt rained down on him: He had ignored her not just because he was immersed in work but because he was still angry about having to go out for dinner.

Nick reached into his pocket and drew the letter halfway out, but the words of warning echoed in his head. He tucked it away and thought of the man's eyes, filled with such conviction, such honesty, such sense of purpose.

Where all hope had been wiped from the world, this man had reignited it. Nick couldn't imagine how Julia could be alive but . . . if there was even a glimmer of hope. If there was any chance of saving her . . .

. . . he would have to find a way out of this locked room and station.

Grief and confusion had been replaced with possibility and purpose. Escaping from an interrogation room, a police station, was an inconceivable, improbable, foolhardy task, but . . .

Not impossible.

Nick looked at the door, two inches thick, a heavy dead bolt as a lock. There were no windows or other doors. He looked at the white board, the clock on the wall ticking toward 10:00 P.M., and then his eyes fell on the ominous two-way mirror. He stared at his reflection sitting alone in the bleak, humid room in the uncomfortable metal chair, the deadly Colt Peacemaker in the center of the table, and he smiled . . .

The window was made of glass . . .

Detective Ethan Dance stepped back into the interrogation room. The thirty-eight-year-old detective's perpetually sleepy eyes stared at Nick as he threw a file on the table. His white JC Penney shirt was half untucked, while the bulge of his holstered pistol distorted his off-the-rack blue blazer.

"Before Shannon comes back into the room, you want to tell me what really happened? I mean" — Dance opened up the file with his latex-gloved hand and looked inside, staring at a photo, which he concealed from Nick's eye — "what drives someone to do this? Was it the money?"

"Money?" Nick asked in genuine confusion. "How dare you."

"Well, I'm glad to see you have a voice."

Nick glared at Dance, his eyes falling on the bulge in his jacket where he could just see the butt of Dance's gun poking out.

"I'm sorry." Dance paused in sympathy. "She was a beautiful woman. May I ask when you spoke last?"

"We had a fight this morning," Nick said, his eyes briefly looking at the clock.

"About?"

"Dinner with her friends."

"Mmm, I know how that goes. You sit there, she and her girlfriend are lost in conversation while you're left with the husband, who you have nothing in common with. My ex-girlfriend dragged me to the Jersey Shore for a weekend at her friend's house, rained the whole time, I was stuck in the house with an asshole while they went shopping, felt like arresting him for subjecting me to his boring life. I've hated the Jersey Shore ever since."

Dance was good, trying to win Nick over with sympathy and commonality, but Nick wasn't so stupid as to fall for it.

"Did you talk after that?" Dance continued.

"No, I was busy all day; conference calls and paperwork pretty much consumed me.

And I know she was up to her ears in issues."

"She was an attorney?"

"Why do you ask a question you already know the answer to?"

"Sorry, force of habit." Dance closed the manila folder and laid it ominously on the table, next to the Colt Peacemaker. "Was she in her office all day?"

"Not sure," Nick said abruptly.

"You didn't speak?"

"She called a few times but I ignored the calls."

Dance said nothing as he looked at Nick.

"Childish," Nick said. "I know, but Jesus — Why are we talking about this? Someone killed my wife, dammit, and it wasn't me!"

Nick's voice echoed in the room, seeming to linger for minutes as the conversation changed direction.

"So it says here," Dance tapped the manila folder, "you have a license for a nine-millimeter Sig-Sauer."

"Yeah."

"Where might that be?"

"In my safe, where it has been for the last six months. Julia hates guns." Nick hated the irony.

"So you do know how to shoot?"

"You don't buy a car unless you're licensed to drive."

"No need to be a smartass."

"No need to treat me like an idiot, like I killed my wife."

"I'm trying to help," Dance said.

"Listen, if you were trying to help me you'd be out looking for the real killer."

"Fair enough. If you didn't do it, you've got to talk to me, if we are to have any hope of catching who did do it."

"So you believe it wasn't me?" Nick said with a sense of hope.

"Well, the thing is this," Dance said, pulling over the gold- and brass-plated Colt Peacemaker, "this gun here is covered in fingerprints."

"But no one has taken my prints yet," Nick said, his voice thick with confusion as he threw his hands up.

"Actually, we got them off your wallet and cell phone, I did it myself." Dance paused. "And they were a spot-on match. So you're going to need to be real clear as to how your fingerprints and only your fingerprints are on this gun."

Nick sat there, his mind spinning. He had never seen this gun, let alone touched it. In fact, he hadn't picked up his own gun in six months, and that was with his friend Marcus Bennett at his buddy's shooting range.

35

He hated guns for the incredible power they placed in one man's hand, the power of life and death at the fingertip of anyone capable of pulling the trigger.

"I should also add," Dance continued, "ballistics isn't back yet, probably won't be for a few days with everyone working the plane crash, but your watch had explosive residue, gunpowder consistent with bullets. So if your story is factual, lay it on me, and if you're about to make something up, it's time to get real creative."

Shannon stepped into the room, locking the door behind him. "I would suggest real creative." His high-volume words laid bare the fact he had watched the whole exchange from beyond the two-way glass. "And feel free to look at the center of the mirror, right into the camera. It's always so much better at helping relate to the jury."

Nick was once again lost, the brief hope he had thought he saw in Dance obliterated by Shannon's entrance. He glanced up at the clock: 9:56.

With volatile force, Shannon slammed his billy club onto the table, shocking not only Nick but also Dance.

"Cold-blooded murder," Shannon said. "Plain and simple. You don't need to tell us a thing. We've got it all in that folder, everything we need for a quick and easy conviction —"

"Let's take a break," Dance interrupted, trying to calm Shannon. He leaned back on his chair, raising it up on two legs.

"No. A woman is dead," Shannon shouted. "She didn't get to take a break. I don't care if she was your wife or not. I want answers. Was she fucking someone else and you found out? Were you fucking someone else and she found out?"

Nick's eyes went wide with rage.

"Yeah, I see the anger rising up in you. Come on, do something," Shannon taunted him. "Use the same fury you struck out at your wife with. All this spit and polish, Italian clothes, foreign cars, minimansions in suburbia, it's all just window dressing for your dark heart. You're no different from the bum in an alley who guts a hooker."

Nick was doing everything he could to restrain himself, his muscles tensed, his blood racing.

"She was fucking some guy and you killed her." With a sudden crash, Shannon again smashed his billy club onto the table.

But this time the force startled Dance, to the point where he lost his balance on the two legs of his chair, falling backward while desperately trying to grab the table.

Shannon's outburst, the loud, shocking crash of the club against the table, pushed Nick over the edge. His wife was dead, he was being accused of her murder, and this Detective Shannon questioned his and her honor.

In the heat of confusion as Dance continued to fall backward, his sport coat flopped back, exposing his nine-millimeter in his shoulder holster, the butt of the gun protruding. Nick stepped past the point of no return and snatched the gun from Dance's holster with lightning speed.

Nick thumbed off the safety of the Glock as his finger wrapped the trigger; his muscle memory ran true and on reflex. That he hated guns didn't mean he'd forgotten how to use one. He spun the off-balance, tumbling Dance into a headlock and jammed the barrel against his head.

Dance's gloved hands flew up in panic, desperately grabbing hold of Nick's forearm.

And the moment spun out of control.

"Drop it," Shannon screamed, as he drew his gun, fell to a knee, and pointed it straight at Nick's head.

"You don't understand, neither of you understand, she's alive," Nick yelled, sounding like a madman, his eyes jumping back and forth between Shannon and the clock. "My wife is alive."

Shannon and Dance exchanged a quick look.

"Listen," Dance said calmly, despite the gun at his head. "Put down the gun. I know what you must be feeling —"

"Bullshit," Nick shouted over Dance. "You have no idea what I'm feeling."

"— losing her and all. Let us listen to your story. If someone else killed her, let us catch him. All this is going to do is send you to the morgue. There's no death penalty for killing your wife, but for killing a cop . . . it's a capital offense, they'll execute you for that."

"You don't understand, my wife is alive. I've been set up. I need to get out of here." Nick dragged Dance backward toward the two-way mirror.

"Put your gun down," Nick yelled at Shannon.

"Not a chance," Shannon shouted back.

Nick look at the clock: 9:58. He thumbed back the hammer of Dance's nine-millimeter Glock pistol, the click startling Dance.

"Bob," Dance yelled, looking at Shannon. "Do it."

"No way."

"Do it," Dance yelled. "You're not playing chicken with my life."

Shannon's eyes were defiant, but he complied.

And Nick instantly aimed the gun behind him at the glass and pulled the trigger, the gunshot sounding like a cannon as the two-way mirror shattered into a thousand pieces, revealing a small, dark room, a video camera in the center trained on them. Nick cocked his arm forward and tucked the gun back up against Dance's chin, scorching his skin with the hot barrel.

"Are you out of your mind?" Dance screamed.

And Shannon was back on a knee, his retrieved gun in his hand, aimed squarely at Nick.

"Look at me." Shannon's voice became eerily calm, his gun remaining fixed on Nick as he picked up the manila folder and poured a handful of eight-by-ten pictures out onto the Formica surface.

"Do you see these?" Shannon said through gritted teeth, picking them up one by one, shoving them toward Nick, inches from his face.

There were twenty in all, from various angles, in full color. The blood was thick, nothing like what Nick expected. It wasn't like TV or some movie, where the blood repulsed, but deep down your stomach stayed calm knowing it was just the trickery of Hollywood. These images were real, and they pulled Nick in. As much as he tried to avoid doing so, he looked at each and every picture: at the floor, at her clothes, at the black skirt she was wearing when last he saw her; at her ring finger, at the wedding band he had slipped on in St. Patrick's, and finally at her face, or what was left of it.

The left side was gone, the eye missing, the temple and forehead shattered, but the right side . . . It only took the sight of her blue eye, the hazel specks dancing there under her blond eyebrow, to convince him. The dead woman staring up at him was his wife.

And in that moment, the confusion rose. The scream in his head, the manifestation of his bleak reality. Julia was dead.

"I'm going to count to three," Shannon said. "I don't give a fuck if you shoot Dance, I'm going to kill you right here in front of the running videotape, fully justified in my actions."

Nick pressed the gun harder up into Dance's chin, the detective's grip about his forearm tightening in nervous response. And Nick realized Dance's right ring finger was missing, the vacant finger of the latex glove flopping about like an errant hair.

Nick looked up at the clock on the wall, the second hand ticking toward the top of the hour.

"One," Shannon whispered.

"This can't be," Nick said in desperation as he looked again at the pictures, wishing it was all a dream, wishing he was someone else so he could escape his now dead, hollowed heart. The pain in his soul was unbearable, as Julia's decimated image stared back at him. He tried to avert his eyes —

"Two," Shannon's voice was louder this time. There was no question of his threat.

"I need to get out of here," Nick said, an unnatural calm over taking him. "You don't understand, I can save her." But nothing made sense, not Julia's death, not this impossible situation. How could he save her if she was already dead? But the tone of the man's voice was still fresh in his ears, *"You have twelve hours."*

"Three."

And Nick watched as the hammer of Shannon's gun slowly drew back.

But before the hammer struck home on the back of the copper cased bullet, before

it exploded out of the barrel . . .
. . . the world fell into darkness.

CHAPTER 11

8:12 p.m.

The sixty-inch TV screen was filled with black scorched earth, the open field dotted with white debris, which upon closer viewing was revealed to be bedsheets covering the burned and shattered remains of 212 passengers. The AS 300 had left Westchester Airport at 11:50 A.M. and fallen out of the clear blue morning sky two minutes later, burying itself in a wide-open sports field in the upscale town of Byram Hills.

Aerial footage showed a quarter-mile debris field, as if the devil had reached out and scratched the earth. But for the intact white tail section sitting upright, the small pieces bore no resemblance to the modern aircraft that had been heading for Boston.

"No survivors," the overly blond newswoman said, her ebony eyes tinged with sorrow for having to condense such a tragic event into sound bites. "The National

Transportation Safety Board has been on the scene for several hours and has recovered the badly damaged black box of North East Air Flight 502. A news conference is scheduled for 9:00 P.M."

Images from earlier in the day began to cycle: hundreds of firefighters battling to control the intense flames that danced among the wreckage, shots of the continuing rescue effort, of luggage strewn about the ground, of weary firefighters with bowed heads and soot-covered faces. Heartbreaking video personalized the tragedy: laptops and iPods scattering the ground, a Yankees hat in perfect condition resting in a patch of undamaged grass; a child's shoe, backpacks, and briefcases, all devastating reminders of the fragility of life.

The flat-panel TV sat within the mahogany shelves of an Old World library. Books on everything from Shakespeare to auto repair, Dumas to antiques filled the bookcases. There was a majestic painting of a lion by Jean-Leon Gerome above the mantel. On the wall above the couch were two Norman Rockwells of soldiers arriving home from World War II to the embrace of their families. Large leather club chairs sat before an unlit fireplace, while the Persian rug with its blue-flecked earthen hues completed the effect of a 1940s gentleman's den.

Nick stood in the center of the room, his thoughts incoherent, his legs wobbly. A low, dull thumping whine echoed in his ears. He caught the arm of the button tuck sofa as he fell backward, directing himself into the maroon leather cushions.

He felt as if he had awakened from a nightmare. An odd taste filled his mouth, bitter and metallic. His lips were dry from panting as he tried to catch his breath. There was a golden hue to the moment, as if a bright light's echo had been burned into his eyes, a memento of some forgotten sun glare. As he looked about the room, desperately trying to get his bearings, he unconsciously flexed his hands as if pumping an unseen bellows. His mind overwhelmed with sensory overload, he had lost the moment, his bearings, but most of all, his track of time.

He looked again about the room, its appearance finally becoming familiar, slipping in from the periphery of his mind. He recognized the dull whine as the sound of a generator, which filled the house with electricity in this town without power.

And then the name leaped out at him: Marcus Bennett . . . his best friend, his neighbor. This was his house, his library.

Nick had been here an hour earlier, Marcus providing comfort, sympathy . . .

And then reality fell upon him like a two-ton stone.

Julia was dead.

As Nick closed his eyes, he saw her, her pure lips, her flawless skin, her natural beauty. Her voice was as clear in his ear as if she were speaking to him, the subtle odor of lavender fresh on her skin, fresh in his mind as it finally pulled him over the edge. The grief took him, carrying him into a darkness he had never known existed. It wrapped around his heart, squeezing it in its deadly grasp.

Nick finally looked up at the TV, at the wreckage of the jet, at the remains of the passengers strewn about like discarded keepsakes. He was surrounded by death. Life had gone from bliss to hell for many that day, but as tragic as the events before him were, he could only be greedy in his grief, selfish in his own tragedy and mourning.

He picked up the TV clicker. His thumb finding the off button, he took a final glance at the images of burning wreckage and caught sight of the ticker running along the bottom, pulling the eye with its crawling headline updates, sliding off the edge of the television only to start anew moments later. He stared at the opaque station logo in the bottom corner and finally saw the one sight that sent his mind into panic.

It was an image he had never once paid attention to. With the coverage of unthinkable death and destruction, with the too-much-information ticker crawl, with all of the confusion in his own mind, it had escaped him. It was displayed in the lower right-hand corner, in a highlighted white font, an impossible piece of information that sent his mind spinning. The clock was illuminated against its background, and he looked at it twice more as if his eyes were playing tricks on him, as if someone at the TV station had made a mistake. He read it again: 8:15 P.M.

Nick's eye snapped to his wrist, only to be greeted by pale skin where his watch was usually bound. And he remembered . . .

He reached into his pocket and pulled out the letter. The envelope was cream-colored, with a satin finish; in the left-hand corner was an elaborate blue crest, a lion's head above a slain dragon, its throat pierced by an ornate sword. Nick wasn't sure if it stood for a club, a prep school, or the crest of the stranger who'd given it to him.

He reached back into his pocket for the

watch the European man had handed him, withdrew it, and flipped it open like some Victorian dandy. The inside of the case was mirror-polished silver with a cursive Latin phrase engraved in the precious metal: *Fugit inreparabile tempus.*

Nick finally cast his eye at the watch face. The roman numerals were of an old English style and read exactly 8:15, a sight that released another wave of confusion.

His interrogation had started at 9:20; he distinctly remembered the clock on the wall of the police room as it marched toward 10:00, listening to the detectives' questions, looking at the ornate Colt pistol, the tension in the air growing, culminating in his stealing Dance's nine-millimeter and the entire moment hanging on the cusp of death.

And he remembered sitting in this room with Marcus for almost an hour, sipping scotch with the dull agony of Julia's loss tearing apart his heart. They'd sat in confusion and mourning. He remembered it all like a slow-winding film. Marcus had been sitting across from him, telling him everything would be all right, when the dark library door slowly swung open, and the two detectives stood in the doorway, grim looks on their faces, Shannon's hand resting atop his holstered pistol.

This was the room he had been arrested in, taken from in handcuffs at 9:00.

His memory seemed upside down, events falling in and out of order. Last he recalled, he was in the interrogation room. He remembered seeing the pictures of Julia, the ones Detective Shannon had shoved in his face, the ones that had brought him to the edge of sanity. He remembered grabbing the detective's gun, the Mexican standoff.

But he couldn't remember anything beyond the point of watching Shannon pull the trigger.

Nick shook his head as he closed the timepiece and tucked it back into his pocket.

He looked again at the envelope, praying that it would solve the multitude of questions running about in his mind. He tore it open, pulled out two sheets of off-white paper, and began to read.

Dear Nick,
I hope the fog is lifting from your mind though I'm sure it is now being replaced by an even greater confusion as to what is going on . . .

Nick read the two-page letter through three times. He folded it up and tucked it into his breast pocket, unsure what to make of it. He thought himself foolish for entertaining the idea, for allowing impossible hope to arise in his heart.

Somehow his mind was playing tricks on him.

The pictures of Julia's dead body that Detective Shannon had shoved in his face were so real, his mind and soul so wounded, Nick thought he was now surely succumbing to the loss of his sanity, to some fantasy, to wishful thinking. He felt trapped in a dream and willed himself to awaken.

He reached into his pocket and withdrew the watch that the letter spoke of, that the European man had given him in the interrogation room. Flipping it open, he stared at the Roman numerals.

Despite the doubt that coursed through his mind, despite the impossibility of it all, there was no question about where he stood at this moment, no question about the time on the watch face.

Nick had sat in this very room already, sipping scotch with Marcus, mourning Julia's death. It wasn't some figment of his imagination, some daydream. His tears were real, the pain in his heart was real, Marcus's comforting words still rang in his ears.

And the interrogation room at the Byram

Hills Police Station, sitting there enduring Dance's questioning, staring at the weapon that stole Julia away from him; the photos, the harsh reality shoved before his eyes by detective Robert Shannon at 9:58 P.M., it was all real. And there was no doubt about the time, the wire-caged clock on the wall having been his main focus for the nine minutes leading up to 10:00.

Yet here he stood, staring at the small black hands of the watch, a timepiece that looked to be over one hundred years old, that appeared in perfect working order, that read 8:15.

Nick picked up the remote from the antique captain's desk and pointed it at the TV, where the images of more death and devastation flashed up like a horror movie.

There was no question about the magnitude of the tragedy before his eyes, tragedy that all could relate to, a story that would transfix the country for days to come. And while he realized that much of the world was crying for the passengers of North East Air Flight 502, only he was crying for Julia.

So in a moment of illogical reasoning, entertaining the possibility of what the letter said, he thought, *What if?* He had nothing to lose and everything to gain. If he accepted the words of the letter as truth, if he accepted the time as being 8:15, then maybe . . .

No matter how impossible it all had sounded, no matter how insane his mind had gone, he realized that if there was truth to the letter, truth to the watch, he just might be able to save her.

The door suddenly opened. Marcus Bennett's large frame filled the doorway. Wearing gray pin-striped pants, a blue Hermès tie, the sleeves of his white shirt rolled up, he was the epitome of style worn upon a tough, lumberjack-thick build. He held a crystal glass in each of his large, pawlike hands as he walked into the room.

Neighbors for six years, he and Nick were more than the usual drive-by-and-wave friends. Sharing a love of hockey, they had become each other's excuse for catching 90 percent of the Rangers' home games. They were passionate in their fandom, both having played in high school but neither rising to the level their overconfident self-image thought they deserved. To compensate for their unrealized aspirations, to prolong the dream, to extend the revelry of youth, they played in a men's league every Wednesday night; Nick was goalie, Marcus his ever-present defenseman.

At thirty-nine, Marcus was seven years Nick's senior. An attorney by schooling, he had bypassed the law for the field of mergers and acquisitions. Highly successful, he had amassed a fortune by the age of thirty-two but had since seen it dwindle as the result of multiple divorces and never-ending alimony payments, though he still was one of the wealthiest men in town. His expert vision for vulnerable firms to be taken over and exploited was not matched by his selection of female companions. Nick wasn't sure if Marcus was blinded by lust or beauty, but there was no doubt that Marcus's insight into woman paled next to his business acumen: three marriages, three divorces, six years.

With each failure, Marcus buried himself in work, swearing off women, even drunkenly threatening to become a priest as his momentary hatred of the female sex blinded him to all logic. But blind hatred would inevitably dissolve and be replaced by a new blind love.

As a result of his failures of the heart, he was close not only to Nick but also to Julia. She was the voice of reason, of comfort. She was the sister that Marcus never had, helping him through his emotional journey. She watched as he rode the roller-coaster of emotions from sorrow, to anger, to utter confusion. With Marcus, the love he thought eternal always flamed out more quickly than his latest Bentley lease.

Currently, Marcus was on to his latest conquest. Sheila was a former spokesmodel, though no one could figure out who she spoke for or if she ever actually had a real modeling credit to her name. Stunningly beautiful, with thick black hair and deep chestnut eyes, she was the physical antithesis to redheaded Blythe, his third wife, the pale beauty who hung on to the brass ring for all of eighteen months and walked away a ten-million-dollar prize winner.

His premature gray hair having receded to nothingness, his off-kilter nose broken three times on the ice, Marcus was far from handsome. He had never been known for his looks, possessing one of those faces that was lost in a crowd, forgotten by most. But his wallet and warm sincere smile always led his charge into the battles of love, attracting many and helping him to overcome any insecurity caused by his prior nuptial failures.

Marcus remained silent as he handed Nick a glass. There were no words exchanged, the moment hanging heavy with grief as Marcus's brown eyes filled with anguish.

Nick stared silently at the glass, his mind briefly lost in the tawny color and smell of the scotch.

"I know you're not a drinker." Marcus's voice was deep and commanding. "But all rules are lost now."

Nick lifted the glass and took a long sip.

Marcus thrust his hand forward, opening his palm to reveal two Xanax. "They're Sheila's. She's got three bottles of them. If you prefer Valium, she has that, too."

Nick shook his head, avoiding the thought of taking an entire bottle to end this nightmare.

"The coroner's over there with two detectives. They're checking out everything. They said the whole place needs to be printed, evaluated, and photographed before they . . ." Marcus had trouble continuing. "Before they take her away."

Nick knew all of this, he knew exactly how the hour was about to unfold. He knew the black body bag would be wheeled out atop the gurney in five minutes, the white-haired coroner leading the way, he knew the detectives' names: Shannon and Dance, who would be coming through the door soon. And he knew all about Mitch Shuloff.

"You remember Mitch?" Marcus asked,

as if reading Nick's mind. "He came with us last year to watch the Red Wings crush the Rangers."

Nick remembered. He was the obnoxious one who never shut up, obsessed with always being right, and even worse, he usually was.

"He's the best. Plus I was about to call him anyway; he lost a thousand to me last night betting against the Yankees. Don't hold it against him, but he's a BoSox fan."

That was exactly what Marcus had said before, exactly how Nick remembered it.

"Despite all that, he's the best criminal attorney in New York," Marcus continued. "You need a personality like his to cut through the bullshit and beat back unfounded accusations."

Nick also remembered that Mitch hadn't shown up at the police station.

"His problem, though, I will tell you, he's not the most punctual. Let me get him over here, not that there's going to be an issue, but you should never talk to a bunch of cops whose education was a marginal GED and whose view of the world doesn't extend beyond Miller time and *American Idol*."

Marcus walked to his large leather-topped desk and picked up the phone.

As Nick watched him dial, he debated

what to say, wondering if he should let Marcus in on his little nervous breakdown.

"Before you make that call," Nick interrupted.

Marcus stopped, slowly putting down the phone.

"I don't know how to say this . . ." Nick paused, seeming to send a moment of unease through Marcus. "But I need to find out who did this."

Marcus walked around his desk and leaned back against it. "They will. And the bastard will be held accountable."

"No. I need to . . . I need to stop him."

"Stop him from what?" Marcus said, confusion surfacing.

"I've got to find him."

Marcus just stared, listening, pausing, searching for what to say. "Let the cops do that. Whoever did this is as dangerous as they come."

"She's not dead," Nick blurted out.

Marcus exhaled, gathering himself. "Words can't even express my sorrow for you. She was . . . perfection. Truly, if ever that word had a meaning, it was Julia."

Nick put the glass of scotch on the end table and ran his hands slowly down his face, trying to focus, trying to determine if he was about to step off into a psychotic abyss.

"I can save her," Nick said, jumping off into the illogical.

Marcus sat there patiently listening, watching as his best friend's mind fell in on itself.

"I can't explain it. I don't know how, but I can save her."

Marcus's eyes remained fixed on Nick, not angry, not condemning. His eyes were pain-filled, heartbroken. Though he tried, he couldn't imagine the depth of Nick and Julia's love for each other, and he knew that with love so deep, the pain must be even greater.

"What if I said I could tell you the future?"

"Like if the Yankees will win the Series this year?" Marcus asked, lost to where Nick was going.

Nick stared at the fireplace, thinking how to proceed.

"I'm sorry," Marcus said. "I . . . didn't mean to —"

"No, it's okay." Nick turned back and looked deeply at his friend. "This sounds crazy. But hear me out. In a little while, they'll arrest me, bring me in, try to get me to confess to something I didn't do, show me a gun I've never seen before."

59

Marcus's eyes grew nervous.

"I didn't kill her, Marcus. I love her more than life, she's the air that fills my lungs when I wake, she's the warmth I feel when I'm happy. I would give anything to trade places with her right now, to give my life for hers, to bring her back."

"I know you didn't do it," Marcus said with true compassion. "You're confused right now, it's all right."

The two sat there quietly.

Marcus finally turned around and picked up the phone. "I'm going to call Mitch, I think you should talk to him."

"He won't get here in time."

"Time for what?"

"They're going to arrest me in —" Nick reached into his pocket and pulled out the gold watch, flipping it open.

"Where did you get —"

"In thirteen minutes." Nick closed the watch and tucked it away.

"What? That makes no sense," Marcus said as he shook his head in doubt. "They're not going to arrest you."

"Shannon and Dance."

"What?"

"Detectives Shannon and Dance. The two detectives in my house right now will make the arrest."

Marcus had greeted the two detectives when they drove in the driveway, introducing himself, leading them to Julia's body. They told Marcus it would be best if he stayed over at his house until they were done. They asked about Nick and said they'd need to talk to him when they completed their preliminary investigation. They finally gave their names as Marcus headed out the front door: Detectives Shannon and Dance.

"You know them?" Marcus asked in confusion.

"I've never seen, or should I say, *saw them,* until they come over here to cuff me."

Marcus stared. "You're telling me you know what's going to happen?"

Nick nodded.

"Okay." Marcus fell silent. He put down the phone and took a seat in the leather wingback chair next to Nick. The sympathy in his eyes grew tenfold. "I don't suppose you can tell me what they're wearing?"

"Dance is in a blue, cheap blazer." Nick didn't miss a beat as he rattled off their attire. "White shirt, wrinkled tan pants. Shannon's an asshole with steroid arms bursting a girl-sized, too-small, black polo shirt and faded jeans."

Marcus tilted his head, taking a deep

breath as he digested what Nick had said. He got up from the chair, walked to the window, and looked through the slatted wood shutters toward Nick's house. He could see the vehicles, a perfect, clear view of Nick's driveway where the cops had emerged from their cars. Nick could easily have been watching their arrival, but Marcus didn't want to challenge his friend in his current state of mind.

"Listen to me," Nick said, his words growing impassioned. "I'm not crazy. The Yankees —"

"Why are we talking about the Yankees?" Marcus grew concerned.

"The game going on right now, they win in the bottom of the ninth, off . . ." Nick's voice trailed off as he realized how silly he sounded, his head bowing in defeat.

The two friends sat silently for a moment, frustrated.

But then Nick looked up in revelation. "His ring finger . . . Dance's ring finger on his right hand, it's missing below the second knuckle."

Marcus remained silent.

"You know there's no way I could see that from your window," Nick said, alluding to Marcus's doubt. "And ask him about the fun he had at the Jersey Shore."

■ ■ ■ ■

Marcus walked out the side door of his house into the late summer sun of the day. His heart was broken for his friends. Julia had been as close to him as anyone in his life. She knew his heart and had helped him heal time and time again; she knew his mind and how prone it was to jump to conclusions; she knew his mistakes and misgivings, his weaknesses and suffering, and had never once turned away.

Julia and Nick shared a bond, a love that he could only dream of. They were the touchstone which he judged each of his marriages, making him realize even before he said "I do" that the promise of love *till death do us part* would never come close to what they shared. They were like one, it was always Julia and Nick, Nick and Julia; rarely were they referred to in the singular. They spent their free time together and each always put the other first.

Seeing her dead on the floor, so heinously robbed of life, so violated, was an assault on all reason. Who could commit such an act, who could rob an innocent of life, who could rob a husband of his reason for living?

And while Julia was dead, it was as if the bullet had also struck Nick. His mind had collapsed, falling into denial, fantasizing about changing the past, about saving Julia. It was the fantasy of a wounded heart, of an insane mind.

Marcus had been in his garage looking through a file box in the trunk of his car when he'd heard the gunshot. It sent a chill down his spine, as it came from the Quinns' house. He ran as fast as he could, cutting through their open garage door, through the open mudroom door, to see Julia lying askew around the rear stairs. Half her face was gone, and it took every ounce of his energy to hold his stomach together as he became overwhelmed with grief and shock. And when he finally stepped over her body, he saw Nick sitting on the floor beside her, stroking her leg like a child uncomprehending of the reality of death.

Marcus crossed his expansive side lawn, approaching Nick's house, but this time there was no reason to run; nothing was going to bring Julia back.

The coroner's truck and two unmarked cop cars, a Taurus and a Mustang, sat in the driveway. Normally a murder in a town that hadn't seen a murder in twenty-five years would result in an overwhelming response by half the force, but the rest of the department, every policeman, desk clerk, secretary, and receptionist, was at the crash site. Every fireman, EMT, councilman, and doctor from the town had responded. There had never been a plane crash in Byram Hills, or the county, for that matter, but the well-off community responded as if it specialized in disasters. Every able body was out at the field working with the NTSB in whatever capacity they could. Whether it was helping the families of the deceased, searching for wreckage and body parts, or handling administrative details, the entire town of Byram Hills was out in force at the scene of the tragedy just three miles away. As a result, there were only two cops available to deal with Julia's death.

Nick and Julia's house sat on three acres, one of the few properties that hadn't been subdivided. Their house dated back to the 1890s, with additions in 1927, 1997, and 2007. The former main house of what was once expansive farmland was five thousand square feet and could truly be called a home. Every room was filled with pictures and mementos speaking to the character of their owners. Far from a museum showcase, as so many large houses had become, it was a home designed for family, a house that Marcus knew one day would be filled with children. But now, as he slipped under the yellow crime tape that wrapped the walk, as he opened the side kitchen door and stepped into the large white kitchen, Marcus knew not only would children's voices never be echoing the walls but Nick would probably never come home again.

As Marcus cut through the dining room, he could hear the detectives' voices in the front hall and stopped. He took a moment to backtrack, feeling himself pulled by some unseen force. And though he couldn't bear to look at Julia's body again, he craned his neck toward the mudroom where her body lay.

The white-haired coroner leaned over the black body bag, zipping it up, pulling out a dark marker and writing on the bag's label, an action as devoid of emotion as if he was filling out a grocery list. The man's black eyebrows stood in sharp contrast to his white hair, his hunched frame and weathered skin putting him no younger than seventy-five. Marcus imagined more than a few doctors, medical examiners, and coroners had been pulled from retirement today to deal with all of the death in Byram Hills.

Marcus could make out Julia's form under the black vinyl and morbidly wondered if there was any chance of a mortician's reconstruction to honor her, to allow her husband to look upon her one last time, to say his final good-byes.

The floor was still pooled with blood, the rear wall covered in fragments of flesh and bone, several tufts of hair drifting on an unseen breeze. With everything going on down at the crash site, no one would arrive up here to clean this tragic reminder of violence against the innocent for days to come. That wouldn't do. He would get on the phone and get someone up from the city, and while he was at it, he would begin the daunting task of arranging the funeral that Nick's fragile mind was incapable of planning.

"Hey!" The voice startled Marcus, shocking him back to the moment.

"What the hell are you doing?" Shannon said. "We told you to stay next door with her husband until we're done."

"I thought —" Marcus looked around. "I thought you were done."

"This is a crime scene, and it's just the two of us. We've got to do all the printing and investigation on our own. We're done when I say were done."

"I'm sorry." Marcus headed back to the kitchen door. "I'll be next door."

"Where's Quinn? I thought you were going to stay with him. Shit." Shannon paused, suddenly nervous. "Is he the type to run?"

"Run? Run from what? His wife is dead. He can barely stand."

"You know what?" the cop said, holding up his finger. "You're here. Let's have a conversation."

The cop turned and walked toward the living room as if he owned the place, indicating for Marcus to follow. "This won't take long."

Marcus nodded. "Whatever it takes to catch whoever did this." Marcus could feel the other cop come in behind him but chose not to turn around.

"You said previously that you were very close to both the deceased and her husband. How close would that be?"

"Best friends. Equally close to them both," Marcus said.

"Were either of them having an affair?"

"You're crossing the line." Marcus wanted to choke the cop for bringing up such a stupid question.

"We just need to ask," Dance said from behind him. "Where were you when Mrs. Quinn was shot?"

"I told you before, next door in my garage, about to head out to dinner. I heard the shot and came running."

"Anyone with you?"

"No, but I was on the phone with my girlfriend, who's in California for the weekend, which you can verify."

"What kind of relationship did Nicholas Quinn have with the deceased?" Shannon asked.

"Her name is Julia," Marcus said, abruptly, trying to keep his anger in check. "They were as close as could be, more in love now than the day they married."

"Were either of them emotional?"

"Not really. In fact, they're both pretty even-tempered." Marcus couldn't refer to her in the past, he couldn't get used to the fact he'd never hear her voice again.

"If that's the case, why would he kill her?"

Marcus didn't answer, as he thought he had misheard the question.

"Why would he do it?" Shannon continued to pressure Marcus. "Can you think of any reason, money, jealousy?"

"There is absolutely no way Nick killed her," Marcus said. "He would never raise a hand to her, let alone shoot her."

"Well, some things suggest otherwise," Dance said as he held up a large clear plastic bag. Inside was a large, impossibly elegant pistol, something that looked to be owned by a king or a sheik. There was a hammered-gold plate on other side of the stock. The handle was made of ivory, inlaid with jewels. "Any idea why he would be keeping such an expensive weapon in the trunk of his car?"

Marcus stared dumbfounded at the sight. He'd never known Nick to own such a gun. "That can't be his."

Without a word, Dance put the plastic-encased pistol in a box and turned back to Marcus.

"Despite your doubts," Shannon said, "I think he did it. If he has an attorney, I would suggest that you call him, because I'm going to interrogate this guy until he admits what he has done. And believe me, after a day like today, I have no time for lies."

Marcus stared at the cop and suddenly remembered why he had come over. He looked at the detective in his too-tight shirt and jeans and thought him an asshole. He looked at his right hand but saw five fingers, five complete fingers.

"It's Detective Dance, right?" Marcus said.

"No, I'm Robert Shannon, he's Dance,"

Shannon pointed to his partner as they all headed into the kitchen.

"Sorry." Marcus turned to Dance. "Did I see you at the Jersey Shore?"

"No." Dance glared at him and shook his head, suspiciously. "Why?"

"I thought maybe —"

"I hate the Jersey Shore," Dance snapped as he walked into the mud room.

Marcus watched as Dance walked to Julia's encased body. He pulled off his latex gloves, bent down, and helped Shannon and the white-haired coroner lift the black bag up onto the gurney.

Marcus looked once again at Shannon and Dance's clothes. They were exactly as Nick had described them, but Nick had probably seen them through the window, maybe forgetting that he had looked. In his fragile mental state who was to say that his mind wasn't retreating into its own reality?

Marcus felt an overwhelming confusion rush through him as he stared at the black bag containing Julia's body, still coming to grips with the fact she was dead. But what took Marcus's breath away, what compounded the effect of everything that had happened, was the moment when his eye was drawn back to Dance, now pushing the gurney out through the door, his eyes drawn to the detective's right hand . . .

. . . to his right ring finger

. . . where it was missing below the second knuckle.

Nick had not moved from the couch in Marcus's library. He had read the letter three times over, his thoughts bathed in a crippling confusion. All logic seemed absent from the European man's written words, but equally absent from Nick's own mind — how had he gotten here and how was it remotely possible? Nick wasn't a superstitious man; he wasn't prone to believe in the supernatural, myths, legends, UFOs. He didn't believe in lucky pennies, rabbit's feet, bad luck, or broken mirrors. But he would gladly embrace it all, preaching the merits of each, if it would bring Julia back.

He stood and walked about the library in a half-aware state looking at the pictures on the shelves. There was no consistency to Marcus's past, no stability. Several frames contained pictures of Sheila, several older shots were obviously cropped, excising a former spouse, and two frames were altogether empty. His eyes finally fell on a picture of himself and Julia arm in arm with Marcus prominently displayed on the center shelf. They were all smiling. Nick couldn't recall if it had been taken by Blythe or Dana of the discarded housewife crowd but he didn't care. It was of a joyous time, a time before murder and plane crashes, when happiness had seemed eternal.

Nick finally pulled himself away from the photo, in fear of being overcome with grief again, and looked out the window. His fear began to arise anew as he saw Detectives Shannon and Dance emerge from his house, helping the white-haired coroner push the gurney with the black bag containing Julia into the coroner's truck.

Marcus stood in the driveway, his head hung in sorrow as she was loaded in and the door was closed. The two detectives turned to Marcus and the three began a slow march across the large side yard.

Nick thought about running, but had no idea where he would run to, wondering if his fate was sealed no matter how fast or far he ran. He pulled the watch from his pocket and flipped it open, reading the time, 8:55, and became momentarily lost in the time-piece.

He pulled the letter from his pocket once again, rereading the impossible words, slowly, deliberately, digesting them as if he were reading the bible.

Dear Nick,

I hope the fog is lifting from your mind though I'm sure it is now being replaced by an even greater confusion as to what is going on as you have found yourself in the exact location where you were at eight o'clock this evening.

In life there are moments that are impossible to grasp, to come to terms with: the injustice at the death of the innocent, the inexplicable agony and confusion at the loss of those we love, the impossible cruelty of fate.

Nick couldn't help looking out the window toward the coroner's truck where Julia's body lay in a cold, black bag.

One simple selfish act can reverberate through time, through life, robbing a stranger of existence. A loved one could meet her death from the repercussions of a moment or an event she may never know or understand. Yet if this one moment didn't occur, if it could be found, could be taken back, the lives it touched could be changed, could be altered and that one life saved.

You are now standing in a room, in an instant that seems torn from your memory, a victim of magic, of some divine intervention, but I assure you it is neither.

You are in the very room you were in during the eight o'clock hour this evening, living that hour once again. But this time you are free to do as you wish, turn left where before you turned right, say yes where before you said no. No one will know the difference, nor will anyone else experience this phenomenon. You are on your own to choose direction as you see fit, to alter the future you have experienced.

You've been given a gift, Nick. A gift to live twelve hours of your life over again.

You must pay very close attention as time is short:

Every hour, as the minute hand of the gold watch sweeps to and arrives at twelve, you will slip back in time one hundred and twenty minutes to relive one hour of your life again.

One step forward, two steps back.

This will occur exactly twelve times, no more, no less, taking you back by the hour to ten o'clock this morning.

With your actions now, stepping back into each prior hour of the day, you have the chance to find and save your wife.

I will not bore you with explanations and

technicalities, suffice it to say that as the hour strikes you will be whisked back to the exact location where you were two hours earlier to live that hour anew.

But be aware, each choice, just as in normal life, has consequences that we may not realize in the moment of their choosing. You have the ability to save Julia, the ability to put your world back in balance but be warned, it is a precarious route you now venture on, and your choices must be well thought out so as not to unbalance the rest of your or anyone else's existence.

As to why you are being granted this gift, as to who I am, and how this all happens, those are not of import in this moment, but rest assured, all will be made known in time.

God speed, Tempus Fugit,

Z.

PS: Hold tight to this letter and the timepiece, and be warned, this watch you carry on your person can never leave you, for if it does, or if it is destroyed, you will be lost to the moment you are tied to, reintroduced to the forward-flowing existence of the rest of man, and saving Julia's life will be become a lost cause.

◆⏃⏛ℳⵁ⏃⏃⌂⏃ℯ⏚ℳⵁ⌐⏃⑀Ɏ ⌐⏌⏚⏃Ɏⵁℯ⌐ ▆⊒⌐⏌ ⌐⊔⊒▆

⊒⏌ⵁ⌐⊐⑀⊒⌐⑀ ⌐⊒▪⑀ⵁ⊰ℳ ⌐⏃Ɏⵁ ⌐ⵁ⌐ ⌐ℳ⊔⊁⊒⊒

⊒⏃Ɏⵁⵁ⊰ℯℳⵋ⊔⌐⊔Ɏⵁ⊒⌐▆⌐ℯℳⵁ⊒▆⌐⊱⊓⑀ℯℳ ‖

⊔⊒▪⊒⊒⌐ ⊑⌐⊪⊩⌊ ⵏⵁɎ ▪⊒⊒ ⊒⌐⊒Ɏℳℯ⊒

ℳ▪Ɏℯℳℳ⌐⏃⏛ℯ⏃ℯℳ⌐⊒⏛ℳⵋ⊔⌐⑀⌐⊒⏃Ɏⵁ⌐⊒⊒

Often when faced with impossible odds, when the future is darkest, a man discards logic and turns to faith, to prayer, to the mystical, convincing himself that a higher power will intervene in his favor. It happens in matters of a desperate heart, in business, even in war, when he is up against an enemy. A soldier will pray to God for victory, often not realizing that his adversary is also praying for deliverance, and in all likelihood to the same God. A man will wish on a star for love, throw a penny into a well with confidence that it will deliver the winning lottery ticket, or rub rabbits' feet so his favorite team will win the Super Bowl.

And so in that manner, Nick began to believe in the watch in his hand, in the written words of the stranger — though he was at a loss to know what language appeared at the bottom of the note. He believed that somehow, if he fought hard enough, he could stop Julia's killer, he could save her. If he could just hold out until 9:00, he would be able to confirm whether that hope was hollow, whether his faith was misplaced and he was doomed to relive his harrowing experience in the interrogation room all over again. As silly, as impossible as it sounded, it was all that he had to hold on to.

With a sudden focus, he raced out of the library and across the marble two story foyer to the front door. Throwing the dead bolt, he hurried to the French doors in the living and dining rooms that led to the rear slate terrace, locking them in succession. He locked the side and garage doors and hurried back into the library, closing the heavy mahogany door, locking it tight. He was thankful that Marcus had put a dead bolt on the library door, odd for an interior door, but not odd for a room that contained a Gerome and two Norman Rockwells.

Nick looked again at the watch: 8:58.

And he heard them arrive, pounding on the locked front door.

Nick went to the bay window and closed the slatted wood shutters, flipping them down, sealing any point of vision into the room.

He heard the front door being kicked open with an earthquake-like rumble, and Marcus's enraged voice suddenly filling the cavernous marble foyer, no doubt angered at the damage and the situation.

A knock sounded on the library door.

"Nick," Marcus's muffled voice came from the other side. "It's me. I put a call in to Mitch, he'll meet us down at the station. But these guys, they want you to go with them . . . and they say now."

Nick remained silent, staring at the room, staring at the watch in the palm of his hand: 8:59.

"Listen, I'll be right behind you," Marcus said, enormous compassion in his voice. "You've got my word, we'll get this all sorted out."

Nick remained focused on the watch.

"Nick," Marcus said through the door, "I don't know what's going on, but I believe you, I believe you —"

"Enough is enough," Shannon's voice interrupted. "Open this door now, Quinn."

Nick sat there, staring at the pocket watch, the second hand sweeping at a pace that seemed impossibly slow. Thirty seconds gone, thirty to go.

"Nick, please, I don't have my keys, and these assholes already destroyed my front door."

Nick continued to stare at the watch as if it would somehow deliver him from the moment, as if it were sacred and would reveal the truths of the hereafter.

"Get out of the way," Shannon yelled at Marcus. "You've got five seconds, Quinn."

And as Nick remained focused on the ticking watch, the door exploded open, splintered into toothpicks as Shannon's foot destroyed both lock and mahogany with an explosive kick. His gun was drawn and held before him as he burst into the room. Dance, also armed, came right behind him.

"On the ground," the overzealous detective screamed.

Nick tucked the watch into his pocket just as Shannon grabbed him by the shoulder and threw him to the Persian rug on the floor.

"Dammit all," Marcus shouted as he grabbed Shannon by the shoulder, pulling him off Nick. "Leave him alone."

Shannon spun about and snapped a punch, catching Marcus in the jaw. Without even flinching, Marcus poured his 220 pounds into his fist as it landed square on Shannon's nose, exploding it into a crimson mess.

But Nick had tuned them out, he tuned them all out. His mind was closed off, focused on the watch in his pocket as he counted down the seconds until 9:00 in his head.

And as the mayhem continued around him, as Marcus screamed and pile-drived Shannon, Nick continued counting.

Three . . .

Two . . .

One . . .

CHAPTER 10

Nick found his bearings much more quickly this time. He knew it was because he was accepting the impossibility of the phenomenon. The metallic taste was there but less pronounced; the bitter cold was still rising off his skin but all in all, he was in pretty good shape.

He sat on the front steps of Marcus's house. The front door was in one piece and hung wide open on the warm summer evening. Marcus stepped through it, walked across the slate front terrace, and sat down beside him. The color was drained from his face; his hands trembled in shock.

"The cops are coming, but with the plane wreck and all . . ." Marcus could hardly get the words out. "They can only spare two guys with everyone so involved with the crash site. They said to not touch anything and thought it best you stay with me."

Nick nodded. His eyes were fixed on his house, where Julia's body lay.

Nick reached into his pocket and withdrew the gold watch. He flipped it open, and while he expected what he saw, he was still shocked to see the time was 7:02, two hours earlier than the moments when he had counted down the seconds until 9:00. The cops were not at the house; they had not even arrived at the scene yet. Marcus had just seen Julia's body, his emotional core rocked with the sight of her gruesome death.

And Nick realized that while he remembered what just happened, that was all in the future. Marcus didn't know of Nick's eventual arrest, the names of the cops, or the damage that would be wrought upon his doors. All of which crystallized the rules of the game for Nick.

He was the only one with continuity throughout this ordeal. He was on his own and would have to achieve his goal every hour before being whisked back to where he had been two hours before, while losing the assistance of whoever was helping him in the present hour.

He was thankful it was a Friday, he always worked from home on Fridays and had remained at the house all day, working to complete an analysis related to his week's travels before the weekend arrived. He hadn't even ventured out for lunch, which was lucky as each time jump would bring him back home, allowing him the opportunity to stay focused during his investigation and the rescuing of his wife.

Nick closed the watch, shook himself out of his thoughts, and stood up.

"Where are you going?" Marcus asked.

Nick stared at his house. "I need to go in there."

"Back in there?" Marcus said in shock. "No, I think that is a bad idea."

"I agree," Nick said. "But I need to figure out what the hell is going on and I need to do it before the cops start poking around."

"They said not to touch anything —"

"My wife is dead, Marcus," Nick said, more to the situation than to Marcus. "I need answers, I need to know who did this. It's my house, I'm going back in."

"All right." Marcus reluctantly nodded. "But I'm coming with you."

Nick began walking, shaking his head. "I need to do this alone."

It had taken Nick the better part of the prior hour — future hour now that he thought of it — to convince Marcus of his situation, sending him to see Dance for proof of his clairvoyance. If Nick was going to get the help of Marcus, or of anyone, for that matter, he was going to have to find a way to convince him of the time slip in five minutes or less, otherwise too much time would be wasted, stolen from the limited twelve hours he had to save Julia.

Marcus remained seated on the front porch. "Please, whatever you do, don't look at her. It's not her anymore."

Marcus's voice faded as Nick walked across the wide expanse of lawn, battling his mixed emotions. He had been given a gift, a gift he didn't understand and was not going to waste time pondering. The internal debate on how it was happening, why it was happening, could last a lifetime, and he had less than twelve hours.

But despite the elation that he was being given a second chance, that Julia was being given a second chance, he still feared what he was about to walk into.

Now, despite what he knew he would see, as devastating to his mind as her image would be, he would have to willingly look upon her, if he was to have any hope of saving her, of figuring out who killed her. In order to stop that person, he would have to gather every bit of information, every clue, including exactly how she died.

Nick forced himself to push Julia's death

from his mind; his anxiety, his pain and grieving were selfish acts that would only impede him from getting to the truth. As difficult as the task ahead would be, he clung to the fact that it was all in an effort to save her from fate, to twist the past in order to save her future.

Nick walked across the driveway to the front of his white farmhouse and entered through the 110-year-old front door.

The foyer was dark. All the lights were out from the power failure caused by the plane crash. He opened the front hall closet and pulled out the oversized Maglite, switching on its blinding beam. Though the sun was still above the horizon, the light of late day was fading fast and would not provide the illumination he would need.

Nick had debated getting a generator like Marcus's but thought it to be a waste of twenty thousand dollars for that one annual moment when the lights didn't work for an hour. Now, as he walked around his house in search of a clue to why Julia had been murdered, he would gladly have paid double to make the light switches respond.

Married eight years this coming September, Nick and Julia had spent their time focused on only two things: their careers and each other. They had resolved to put away a healthy nest egg and own their house free and clear, unencumbered by a mortgage, by the time they elected to have children. Plans were made, schedules outlined, budgets created and adhered to, their life set on paper like a playbook for the Super Bowl. Their vacation expenses were kept to a minimum, forgoing Europe, Asia, and world travel until their later years. Wherever possible, trips were taken via car; camping, museum visits, and overnights at the shore were not only the simplest and cheapest getaways but the most fun. They both knew that a true vacation was not a destination of location, but rather a destination of the mind. So as long as they were together, their vacations were better than anything that could be provided by Paris, Monaco, or any exotic locale.

So their shelves and tables were littered with pictures of them fishing the lakes of Maine, surfing the shores of Huntington Beach, hiking down into the Grand Canyon, scaling the rocky peaks of Wyoming. They cherished the outdoors, the simple amenities that nature had to offer, and always returned home with refreshed, focused minds to tackle their flourishing careers.

While they had only been married eight years, they had been together for sixteen, having dated through high school and college. They had fallen in love at the age of fifteen, while their friends and parents laughed at the fact that they were so sure of their future together. But the laughter fell away when they said "I do" in St. Patrick's Church on that late May day. Neither ever said I told you so to the naysayers; they never needed affirmation or votes of confidence from their family and peers in something their hearts told them was right.

They had met at a swim meet. He was the star of the team, with a handful of school and county records by tenth grade in both long distance and sprint races. Julia had been a last-minute substitution for the 4 × 200 meter relay. As she had spent her brief swim career in the shorter sprint races, the two-hundred-meter leg she would be responsible to anchor was something she had never prepared for. To say she was nervous would have been an understatement. So the coach sent her to talk to Nick, who, as the school's youngest captain, possessed a quiet air of confidence that managed to infect all around him.

As Julia sat down, Nick smiled and told her not to worry, explaining the key was the pacing, conserving your energy, saving it for the final kick on the last few laps.

Of course, when Julia dove in, she took off like a bat out of hell and nearly choked up a lung by the time she got to the last lap. She never told Nick, she never told anyone that she never heard his advice, she never heard a single word he said, as she had gotten lost in his blue eyes, something she found far more intriguing than the strategies of swimming races.

And as she touched the wall, finishing last while seeing stars and heaving for breath, he was standing there with an outstretched hand to help her exhausted body out of the pool. He pulled her out with one hand and nary an effort, wrapped a towel around her, and led her over to the bleachers. As the evening turned to night, as they sat together on the three-hour bus ride home, they became lost in the most relaxing conversation either had ever experienced.

Nick never once asked why she didn't listen to his advice, instead steering the conversation to everything but swimming.

They both loved camping, Led Zeppelin, the New York Giants, and the Detroit Red Wings. They shared a love of spare ribs and fried chicken, Oreos and Coca-Cola. She was a dancer, something he found alien and fascinating. He had a passion for skiing and music, which she insisted on hearing more about.

Simply put, they fit. They fit perfectly. And as the years went on, as they each headed off in different directions — she to Princeton, he to Boston College — their love never waned. In fact, it continued to grow past college and in each and every year of marriage.

That was not to say they didn't have their disagreements. While few and far between, their fights were spectacular, as their passion for each other was equaled by their passion for being right. But the disagreements, always over the mundane things like white bread or wheat, roses or tulips, never lingered and were resolved by spectacular lovemaking.

Nick looked out the window of his high-ceilinged great room, at the evidence of last week's get-together with some friends: the deck chairs scattered around the pool, the tables and grill still a mess, three bags of garbage that he was supposed to have thrown out last Sunday. And amidst all the chaos, the pool was calm, the waters smooth and undisturbed, standing in sharp contrast to his current emotions.

The great room looked to be in its usual order: neat and clean but for the painting that had leaned against the far wall for the past six months, which he promised Julia he would hang, and the host of newspapers and magazines that lay on the ottoman, which he had yet to read. The dining room appeared as it usually did, the table perpetually set for a last-minute dinner party.

As Nick looked around his house, he couldn't imagine this to be a random murder. He thought maybe it was some opportunistic criminal who chose to profit in chaos. With everyone so focused on the plane crash, the town was collectively distracted, law enforcement stretched thin. But the randomness . . . something was surely missing, some unseen fact, a key to her death that would also be the key to her salvation.

Nick looked at his home with fresh eyes, searching for anything out of the ordinary, anything out of place or missing, anything that would provide a clue to why Julia was murdered.

He opened the pocket doors to his library and shined the Maglite around. Far smaller than Marcus's, more like a den, it was filled with the evidence of Nick and Julia's life together. If this single room were to survive a nuclear blast and were to be found intact five hundred years from now, an archeologist could draw an amazingly accurate picture of the lives of Nick and Julia Quinn. Their history was laid bare by the locked cabinet filled with trophies and medals from swimming, hockey, and lacrosse that they were too embarrassed to display but too nostalgic to part with; by the shelves of pictures and keepsakes, photos from their prom, graduation, and wedding, with dramatically different hairstyles but unchanged smiles; and by the dozens of pictures of their travels and family holidays. But mostly there were the goofy photos, the just-for-fun, what-the-hell pictures of snowball fights, carnival photo booth silliness, and ice-cream-covered faces that showed them unguarded and at their most natural.

Nick turned to his mahogany desk, moving aside the letters and files stacked to the side, and found his personal cell phone still in its charger. He picked it up and tucked it in his pocket. He had taken to carrying two phones: one personal and one for business, choosing to keep the two worlds separate. Having spent the day working from home, he'd left the personal cell in its charger and was thankful that he had done so as the police had taken his business phone along with his wallet and wristwatch when they brought him into the precinct on suspicion of Julia's murder.

Nick crouched and opened the cabinet behind his desk, shining his flashlight at the small green safe behind the stack of books. There was not a scratch on it, no evidence of a breach.

He headed out of the library and, with the bright beam leading the way, went down the stairs to the lower level. The unfinished basement was his favorite part of the house. A makeshift gym with a treadmill, an elliptical trainer, a stationary bike, and racks of free weights, this was the area that not only kept their bodies tuned but, likewise, their minds. A place to relieve stress, whether by hitting the heavy or speed bags or just by pumping iron, it was a room that was the ultimate detoxification sanctuary. Nick's flashlight bounced off the old dressing-room mirror that lay against the wall, refracting about the space, at the dance bar affixed to the wall, the mats on the floor. He could still smell the faint odor of Julia's perfume from her last workout.

The remainder of the cavernous, concrete space would one day become a playroom, maybe a home theater, but that was years from now. For the time being, it would exist as a storage room with boxes of Christmas decorations, forgotten wedding gifts, and unsorted junk lining the gray walls.

Making his way up the basement stairs, Nick continued to the second floor, quickly passing what would one day be the nursery, past the three unused bedrooms, and arrived at his and Julia's bedroom.

The cream-colored room with its tray ceiling had an enormous four-poster bed that faced an unlit fireplace teeming with cut flowers for the summer. Nick checked Julia's side table, its small drawers, but nothing was out of the ordinary, nothing was hurriedly ruffled or out of place. He checked her walk-in closet, checked his own and the cabinet hidden behind his tie rack, but again, nothing was disturbed. Both their bathrooms were as they'd left them in the morning, towels, toothbrushes, and toiletries in their respective spots. The unused sitting room still had a slight sheen of dust and pollen from the flowers in the fireplace, offering no evidence of an intruder. The French doors to the small terrace were locked, just as he'd left them this morning after Julia surprised him with breakfast.

As Nick walked from room to room looking for anything that might help point him in the direction of Julia's killer, he realized that they had built a perfect home, every room finished and paid for, the envy of

many, but it was missing the most important thing. They had dedicated themselves to work, to money, spending their time on acquiring life and things, but had left out the most important part. While they loved each other, never being selfish, they had no legacy, no children to fill the home they had created. With bedrooms lying in wait, it was always one more year and then we will have it all. Now, Nick was beginning to realize they were always counting on that one more year, but who was to say if it would ever come. All that planning, all that money, and now . . .

They had forgone what Nick knew to be the most important thing, and now it was too late, unless he could somehow find a clue to her death and stop it before it happened.

Nick took a last look at the bedroom, really the only area of the upstairs they used. It had not been ransacked; nothing was disturbed. If whoever killed Julia came for something, it wasn't up here.

Heading back downstairs, Nick opened and stepped through his front door. He walked past the open garage bay doors, glanced in at his eight-cylinder Audi, and continued into the driveway proper. Julia's Lexus SUV was right where she left it. Nick

quickly checked it, finding the doors open and the keys in the ignition, a sight that was a confirmation that this was no random act, no snatch-and-grab robbery. Her fifty-thousand-dollar car wouldn't be left behind by even the dimmest thief.

He walked to the end of his cobblestone driveway, stood between the two stone entrance pillars, and looked down at the skid marks where Julia's assailant had torn out of the driveway. Nick was smart, and thought he could piece her murder together in time to save her, but he wasn't an educated detective. The width of the rubber skid meant nothing to him, it didn't tell him anything about the type of car or about its driver, or give him some great aha moment as in some TV show.

He looked around their cul-de-sac and down the road, one of the wealthiest sections of Byram Hills, with streets filled with million dollar minimansions, perfect lawns and gardens, all tended by massive crews of gardeners, all except Nick and Julia's home. Nick cut his own grass, planted his own flowers, tilled his own gardens. He enjoyed riding the tractor, cutting the lawn, digging holes. Their house had been Julia's favorite since she was a child, riding by it on her bike. It had been her fantasy home, and

Nick had helped her realize that fantasy.

As he walked back up the drive, looking at their house, he thought of all of the upgrades that had been done by his own hand; the addition built with the help of his friends; the painting done on weekends by him and Julia. Some of his best memories were of the time spent together building their home, laughing at the mistakes and imperfections, the paint fights and hammered fingers. It was the simple things, as clichéd as it sounded, the peaceful times of being alone with no distractions, eating pizza on the floor, that he cherished most.

Nick walked through the garage and glanced at his dirty car. He was not one for car washes; he preferred his Audi to be a bit on the dirty side in the hope that as it sat on the streets of the city, it would not be noticed amongst the shiny BMWs and Mercedes, blending in and being avoided by the car thieves of the world. It was a practice he had adhered to, much to Julia's annoyance, but it had proven successful to date, so he wasn't about to change. With the accumulation of dust and pollen atop the dark blue metal surface, the handprint was clearly visible on the car's trunk lid, and there was no question it was not his, not Julia's. It was larger, meatier, and out of place.

Nick pulled his key fob from his pocket and hit the button, remotely releasing the hatch. As the trunk lid rose he could see the usual mess: his black duster purchased in Wyoming, the best raincoat he had ever had; jumper cables, a med kit, two coils of rope, all in the event of emergency. There were his hockey skates and pads from the adult league that he and Marcus played in, two boxes of golf balls, an umbrella, and the one object he had not placed there. He'd seen it back in the interrogation room at the Byram Hills police station. Dance had pulled it out, questioned him about it.

Nick was looking at the murder weapon, the exotically styled 134-year-old Peacemaker, the collector's weapon that had taken Julia's life.

There was no question now. He had known it before, but had had no confirmation: He was being set up.

As he looked at the gun he knew there was nothing he could do about it. He could hide it, but it would surely be found. He didn't want to pick it up. The cops had said his fingerprints were on the gun, though he thought it to be a detective's ruse to get him to confess, as there had not been time or personnel to examine the prints, but he would not give them the satisfaction of putting the prints there himself now.

He took a cloth and, wrapping his hand, closed the trunk. Whether the gun was found was irrelevant. If he found a way to save Julia, there would be no accusation, no murder investigation, it would be a moot point. And if he didn't save her, he didn't care what happened to himself.

Nick braced himself for the next five minutes. He knew that what he was about to do would haunt his dreams for all eternity. He was going to look at Julia's body willingly and dreaded what he would see.

Marcus sat on his front steps, his heart breaking, as he stared over at Nick's home. He watched his friend walk up and down his driveway after spending over a half hour in the house. Seeming to wander aimlessly, looking about the neighborhood as if he would happen upon Julia's killer, Nick looked to be chasing ghosts.

There had been an odd look to Nick's eyes when he had rejoined him on the front steps after calling the police. While they looked sad and troubled, they were not filled with the agony he had first seen when he found him sitting with her. There was such heart-rending grief in his face, such an inhuman cry of pain in his voice when he found Nick huddled with Julia's body. It was a sight that Marcus would never shake, a sight that would invade his thoughts till he passed from this earth.

But as Nick walked away from Marcus, heading toward his house, insisting on investigating a murder he could not possibly solve, Marcus's concern for his friend shifted.

There was something in Nick's eyes, something he couldn't identify, it almost appeared to be hope, an emotion completely contrary to a moment in which one's future had been lost, in which the woman one loved had been so violently snatched from among the living.

To Marcus there was only one explanation, only one thing that would cause all the agony to vanish from his eyes.

As he watched Nick step through his garage, on a course to see Julia's shattered body, he knew Nick was no longer in possession of his judgment.

Nick's mind had retreated to a false reality,

Nick's sanity had slipped away.

Nick walked through the door from the garage and entered the mudroom. Whitewashed wainscoting covered the walls, and the floor was of earth-toned Spanish terra-cotta tile. The room was designed with nooks for shoes, racks for coats, and storage closets, all in wait for their family yet to come. They had debated family size since the day they fell in love: Nick wanted two boys and girl, Julia preferred a Brady Bunch mix of three boys, three girls.

As part of their life-planning playbook, they had both gone to the doctor a year earlier to confirm there would be no unseen hurdles to Julia's getting pregnant when the time came. The doctor had actually laughed at the preciseness of their approach to life, telling them not to worry, that their reproductive systems wouldn't fail them. He assured them that when they were ready, if they knew what they were doing, and practiced enough, they would be pregnant in no time.

As Nick stepped around the corner, he saw Julia's Tory Burch shoe protruding at the bottom of the rear stairs. Slowly approaching, he ran his eyes up along her long, lithe leg, up past the black skirt she had worn to work that morning. As he moved closer, his eyes continued their slow travel up her body along the white shirt that was no longer white. The front was flecked with red, as if she had been caught in a rainstorm of blood, the shoulders were crimson, the silk blouse having wicked blood from the puddle of blood she was lying in. Nick stared at the red halo that circled Julia. He had never imagined there was that much blood in a body.

But his eyes halted at her shoulders, his vision mercifully obscured by the lowest step. Nick avoided her face; he couldn't bear to look at what was left of his wife, of the person that was his better half. As shallow as it sounded, he couldn't help thinking that when you destroyed the face you destroyed the person, robbing her of her identity, of her true self. He kept his head tilted down, averting his eyes as he scanned the ground looking for something, anything that would provide a clue to who committed this violation, this act of horror.

He was fighting his emotions, trying desperately to dissociate himself from the moment, trying to keep his mind from collapsing, trying to look at the room, at "the body," with an analytical eye.

Julia's purse lay wide open on the floor next to her, its contents strewn about the terra-cotta tile. It usually hung on a coat hook, the same place that Julia placed it every day when she came into the house. She had a habit of misplacing things, so, with a gentle persuasion, Nick had gotten her in the habit of putting it in the exact same spot every day, something she had done for over a year now, day in, day out without fail.

Nick pulled out his pen and used it to sort through her things: her eyeliner and honey rose lipstick, the menu from David Chen's Chinese restaurant, a birthday card from The Right Thing, her laminated ID from work. A set of keys and a security pass for one of her clients. But three obvious things were absent, things that should never be missing, the things she, like most people, accessed constantly: her wallet, her cell phone, and her personal data assistant, her PDA, made by Palm. A storage device not only for email, phone numbers, and appointments, but also for word, data, and picture files. It was, in point of fact, a small portable computer, an electronic lifeline to her office and personal life.

And then it happened. As much as he had tried to avoid it, he looked at her face, at what was left of the beauty that he often gazed upon while she slept, the eyes that he looked into when he held her, the same eyes that revealed her soul. Her face on the left side was gone, chewed up by the blast of the gun. His eyes rose up to the white rear wall where pieces of her skull were embedded with the bullet in the broken wainscoting, a cascade of blood flowing down like a waterfall.

The bile rose quickly in his throat, his head began to spin, he retched in agony, but it all paled next to the pain in his heart. He felt as if it was being torn from his chest. He couldn't breathe; he could no longer think straight.

And a cry emanated from his soul, rising up through his heart, roaring out through his broken mind. It filled the room, filled the house. It was primal, the world hearing his agony, a cry to heaven, a cry to God of rage and suffering and anger at the evil that had snatched his wife from this life.

He fought what he had do next. It was something no grieving man or woman should ever be called upon to endure. He reached into his pocket and pulled out his cell phone, hating himself for what he was about to do. He flicked it open and thumbed the camera button. And with tears rolling down his face, he held it up, both hands necessary to still his quavering nerves. He pointed it at Julia's lifeless body upon the floor, and snapped a picture.

He collapsed to his knees, overcome with grief, too weak to stand. He leaned back against the wall, his body shaking. It all came pouring out. The impossibility of the task before him, the ridiculous hope he placed in a stranger's written word and timepiece. Julia was dead, there was no question about that, she lay before him mangled and lifeless. There were no miracles, no gods to wave their hand and bring her back. There was simply the fact before him of her dead body, and he was sitting across from her having failed her, powerless, helpless, chasing the impossible.

He didn't know how long he had sat there, lost in pain, his head spinning, trying to right himself, to find a reason to live, when all at once Marcus stood above him. Nick looked up through distant eyes that seemed even more broken than Julia's, confused about where Marcus had come from. Marcus extended his oversized hand, helping Nick to his feet, and then . . .

It hit him harder than a shovel to the face. The world grew instantly black. What little air there was, was like an iceberg in his lungs. An empty silence filled his ears.

And suddenly, Nick was alone in the kitchen, standing before the fridge, a cold can of Coke in his hand.

He couldn't remember getting up or walk-

ing in, though he remembered Marcus leaning down, offering his hand with total sympathy.

Nick's breath was heavy, coming in great
gasps, his skin tingled, he was disoriented
from seeing Julia's shattered face, her body
dead upon the floor.

And just as suddenly, beyond all reason,
she stepped in the room.

She looked at Nick, her eyes confused at
his troubled state.

"Honey," Julia said, softly. "Are you okay?"

CHAPTER 9

Nick stood in the kitchen, unable to breathe, the words caught in his throat.

Julia came closer, not a strand of her blond hair out of place, her eyes bright, filled with life, love, and concern. Her body stood tall and confident, as if she had just stepped from an impossible dream, the coalescing of all the love and joy he had ever felt embodied in the woman before him.

"Nick?"

Without a word, he grabbed her, pulling her close, holding her as if she were about to slip away again, as if he were just being given a few moments to express his love for her before she would be ripped away for all eternity.

"Honey, what is it?" Julia asked, wrapping her arms about him in return.

He still couldn't form words.

And then she saw his tears. In all the years

they had been together, she had seen him cry only twice — at the age of fifteen when he failed to qualify for nationals and three years ago at the dual funeral for his parents.

"You're really scaring me." Tears of fear, of sympathy welled in her eyes. She hugged him, trying to calm him, to reassure him. "Please tell me."

But Nick didn't know what to say. He was overwhelmed by her presence, he had been granted an impossible wish. And he couldn't possibly tell her what had happened — he corrected himself — what would happen.

"I love you," he said as he took her face in his hands. "I love you with all of my heart and soul. I'm sorry about this morning, about what I said."

"This is all about that, about not wanting to go out for dinner with the Mullers?" She gasped in an uncontrollable sob that became intermingled with laughter. "You scared me so bad, I thought," she paused catching her breath, "I thought someone had died."

Nick pulled her close. He couldn't tell her what he was going through. He kissed her, deeply and lovingly, as if he were inhaling her. And she returned the affection, gently stroking his back.

And before they knew it, they were on the floor; their clothes couldn't come off fast enough. Their passion was driven by sorrow and forgiveness for their fight earlier, for taking each other for granted. Nick loved her with all of his being, with all of the emotion he could put forth, tenderly, forcefully, loving her in thanks as if she was a gift returned from the gods.

Julia laughed as she dressed in front of Nick, who sat with dangling legs on the kitchen counter, watching her every move. And as she stepped back in her black skirt she lost her balance, catching her foot in the zipper, tearing the seam. She grabbed the center island, recovering with a burst of laughter. "I love late-day passion."

"Sorry about that." Nick smiled back as he saw the tear in her dress.

"If you'd like, you could tear them all off again."

Nick laughed, but his humor quickly fell away as his mind resumed the fear he felt for her. He jumped down off the counter, reached into his pocket and pulled out the gold watch.

"Nice watch," Julia said as she buttoned her shirt, surprised at seeing the timepiece. "A gift from your girlfriend?"

"Believe me when I say this," he said as he flipped it open, looking at the time: 6:15.

"I have enough trouble handling just you."

"Do you think they'll get the power back on tonight? Not that I would ever complain."

Nick ignored her, hustling out of the room without explanation. He went to the dining room, locking the French doors that led to the rear slate terrace, drawing the curtains closed; he did the same in the living room. He checked the windows of every room, latching them before emerging into the foyer. Finally he confirmed the dead bolt on the front door.

"Okay, now what are you doing?" Julia asked.

Nick spun around to find her sitting on the third step of the maroon-carpeted main stairs.

"You're beginning to freak me out again."

"Just checking the doors," he said, but his lie was all too evident. After half a lifetime together, his face was easier to read than his sloppy handwriting.

"After what happened today," Julia said. "I think, karmawise, we're pretty safe."

Nick didn't know what she was talking about, but he wasn't about to correct her, to tell her how wrong she was.

He went into the powder room and latched the window that had been left cracked open since the exhaust fan had died.

"And our karma is in such good shape because . . ." he said as he came back into the foyer, taking a seat next to her.

Her face grew confused, "Are you kidding me? I'm still freaked over it."

Nick had no idea what she was talking about.

"I still can't get over that I'm alive," Julia said as if for the fifth time.

Nick's head spun around as if shot from a cannon. "What did you say?"

"I can't believe I'm alive."

Nick could only stare in confusion.

"The plane crash . . . ?" she said in a leading way, as if her point was obvious. "I was supposed to be on that plane."

"What?"

"I tried to reach you all day, I figured you were so buried in your work, didn't you get my message?" She looked into his eyes in a clinical sort of way.

"You were supposed to be on the flight that crashed . . . here? Today?"

"I thought that was what all the emotion was for, that somehow, by the grace of God, your wife cheated death."

"I'm sorry," Nick said honestly, his breathing quickening. "I'm confused."

"What happened today?" Julia laid her hand upon his leg, rubbing it gently as if he was injured. "You're not yourself."

"Tell me," Nick said. "About the plane."

"I was just running up to Boston for a last-minute meeting. An hour at most. Catching the shuttle back — I can't believe you didn't check your messages."

"Why weren't you on the plane?"

The phone rang, startling them both. The kitchen phone was old-fashioned, attached to the wall, the handset linked by a long, coiling wire. Unlike the electricity for the town, the phone lines still worked, drawing their power from a separate system.

Julia beat Nick to the phone, snatching it off the wall cradle in the kitchen. "Hello," Julia said as she answered it. "Oh, hi, I'm glad you called." She put her hand over the mouthpiece. "I'll only be two minutes."

Nick nodded and walked out through the mudroom, a chill coursing through his body as he examined the small space. He glanced up the back stairs, opened the back entrance to the basement, and quickly closed and locked the door. Finally he looked at her purse on the hook, took it down and checked inside, seeing her wallet, phone, and Palm Pilot. He again looked at the almost antiseptic space. There wasn't even a mote of dust in a corner, it was so clean. There was no blood on the floor, no mayhem, no body . . . yet.

He shook off the waking nightmare, hung the purse back up, and walked out into the garage. He reached into his pocket, withdrawing his keys, and thumbed the trunk release. As the lid rose, he looked inside, moved everything around, checked under his hockey bag, behind the med kit, but it wasn't there. The gun hadn't been planted here . . . yet.

He grabbed the handle of the lid and closed the trunk. He looked about the garage as he had one hour before — which was really one hour in the future.

It was so much to keep his mind wrapped around. Time was no longer linear, it was a series of surreal vignettes, each one forming a piece of a puzzle, and each piece he would have to pay strict attention to. Forward, backward, remembering the future as he headed into the past.

He was finding it hard to keep it all straight but fought his mind. He had to keep the pieces sorted without the distraction of his emotions if he was to stop Julia's killer.

And then the plane crash ran to the forefront of his thoughts. Did Julia avoid one death only to face another hours later?

Why wasn't she on that plane? He'd had no idea when she left for work this morning that she was going to Boston. Not that it was out of the ordinary. They both spent way too many hours in airports and in the air running from one meeting to another, all in pursuit of the American Dream. Nick hated flying. He knew it was an illogical fear when one looked at the statistics, but he was always filled with trepidation whenever either he or Julia flew.

He thought it the most horrible of deaths, helplessly falling from the sky, the screams of the desperate ill-fated passengers filling your ears until you all met a simultaneous death in a fiery crash. Nick had tempered his fear, learned to deal with it for work, but it always grew to new proportions when Julia flew, causing him sleepless nights and angst-filled days whenever she traveled by air. He had even once implored her not to fly, on the basis of a weather forecast and misinformed intuition. She had yet to let him live that one down.

But now, what stroke of luck had pulled her off? She didn't mention it to him, she didn't have time to explain before she got on the phone.

He walked out of the garage and looked again at Julia's car. He saw the keys in the ignition, something that bothered him no end. He thought it was like a free pass to steal the car, an invitation that said, "Please, I don't care, take me for a joy ride, sell me to the highest-bidding chop shop."

Nick thought of running, taking Julia as far away as he possibly could. But would that only delay the inevitable? Would whoever was trying to kill her get to her later, track her down tomorrow, maybe Sunday? Would she be killed at a time . . . at a time when he couldn't intervene, when he couldn't save her?

He pulled out the gold watch and checked the time: 6:35. The detective said she was shot before 7:00, and he had less than twenty-five minutes before he was pulled back again. He had to stop her killer, and he had to stop him now. He needed to know who it was so they couldn't reach out of the dark and snatch her away again.

As he looked back at his house, at everything they had sweated for, the cars, the garden, it meant nothing. Nick pulled out his cell phone and made the call he'd intended to from the moment he'd held Julia alive and well in his arms.

"Byram Hills Police, Desk Sergeant Manz speaking," the voice answered.

"Hi," Nick said. "This is Nick Quinn."

"How can I help you, Mr. Quinn?"

"I believe someone is going to try to kill my wife."

"What brings you to that conclusion?" the officer's voice was stern and without emotion.

Nick was suddenly at a loss for words. He had figured he would simply get the cops up here and have them apprehend the killers before they got close to Julia.

"Mr. Quinn?"

"We're at our house —"

"Is there someone else there?" Manz interrupted. "An intruder, someone outside?"

"No," Nick said as he looked around his property. "But I believe they are coming."

"I'm sorry to question you on the phone, but as you can imagine, we are very short-staffed as a result of the plane crash. Has someone made a threat against your wife?"

"No," Nick knew he couldn't take this too far without sounding crazy.

"Mr. Quinn," Manz exhaled. "I don't know how to tell you this, but everyone is at the crash site. I've got one car out on patrol. The best I can do is get them there in a half hour. We're on the verge of chaos with only two cops dealing with car accidents and various other emergencies. May I suggest you and your wife leave your house right now, go somewhere you may feel safe. In fact, why don't you come down here? Then you can give us a better idea of why someone may be trying to kill your wife so we can arrest them before anything happens."

Nick thought on the officer's words. The police were all down at the crash site. Sending a drive-by for what sounded like some guy's unfounded paranoia when a real disaster was at hand, when over two hundred bodies lay in pieces on Sullivan Field, was not going to happen. He was alone in this.

"That's a good idea," Nick lied to the officer.

"I'll try to send someone to do a drive-by as soon as I can tear them away from the crash scene. In the meantime why don't you head on down here."

"Thanks, I appreciate it." Nick closed his phone.

Nick was afraid whoever was after Julia would not stop until she was dead. Hiding in the police station would only put her killer off for the moment. There was no question in his mind that the killer would get to her later. Nick felt it, he knew it in his gut, and at that point in the future Nick would not have any watch in his pocket, no luck on his side.

He needed to catch the killer now, before he killed Julia. And if the police couldn't do it, he would have to do it himself.

Nick headed back up the driveway, back into the house. He was confident he could save Julia: He had the element of surprise, he knew they were coming, and they didn't know Nick would be there to stop them. But if he was going to save her he couldn't do it alone. He had struggled against it but if he was going to prevent Julia's death he needed help.

He needed her help.

He walked through the mudroom, being sure to lock the door behind him, and set the alarm. While the power was out, the alarm system had a twelve-hour battery backup to prevent those movie-type scenarios in which the thief cuts the power, shutting down security so he can steal $58 trillion.

As Nick stepped into the kitchen, he found Julia still on the phone.

"Julia," he whispered, interrupting her call.

She held up a finger, listening intently to whoever was on the other line, unconsciously tucking her blonde hair behind her ear as she continued listening.

"Yeah, sure," she said into the phone, and

finally looked at Nick. "I'm on hold, what's the matter?"

"Hang up, now."

"What, why? I'll only be two more minutes —"

Nick snatched the phone from her hand and hung it up.

"Dammit, Nick. What did you do that for? You don't understand how important that call was."

"Julia, look at me," he said, ignoring her, trying to get her to focus on him. "I don't have time to explain," he paused, not sure how to say it, and decided to just be direct. "Someone is going to try to kill you."

Julia looked at him as if he was crazy, the moment hanging heavy in the air, but seeing his intensity, her confusion quickly slid into fear. "What do you mean?"

"I don't know why, but they're almost here." He couldn't mask the dread in his voice.

"Who? How do you know?"

"I don't know who and I can't explain how I know. You just have to trust me."

Julia's head spun around, looking about the room as if someone would pounce on her at any second. "This is crazy."

A sudden knock on the door startled them both.

Nick crouched behind the center island, pulling Julia down alongside him onto the wide-pine-board floor. "Stay here."

"Is that them? My God, we have to call the police."

"I did. They're all out at the plane crash. We'll be lucky if someone gets here in a half hour."

"I think you're overreacting. This must be a misunderstanding," Julia said. "Why would someone want to kill me?"

"Julia," Nick said, his voice thick with anger. "Will you listen to me?"

Nick's voice and the fear in his eyes convinced her. If he was afraid for her life, then there was no doubt something danger-ous was happening, and she should pay at-tention.

"We should get out of here then, before they trap us in our own house," Julia said, suddenly desperate.

"Stay here." Nick said as he crawled around the island, leaving her on the floor of the kitchen, hunkered down behind the center island, next to the stove and out of sight of the windows. He grabbed a knife off the counter and headed for the front door. "Whatever you do, stay in the kitchen, stay down and away from the windows, and don't go near the garage door."

■ ■ ■ ■

Julia sat alone on the floor and pulled her knees up, wrapping her arms about her legs as if that would give her comfort. Nick was never paranoid, he never drew conclusions unless he had all the facts, and the one thing about him, the one thing that drove her crazy, was that he was seldom wrong. She had no idea what was going on; her mind was unable to focus. She had never felt true life-and-death danger. She had always thought of herself as good in a crisis. Now, there was a crippling fear such as she had never known coursing through her veins. Some unknown person was hunting her. Her usually rational mind began to fail her.

There was a sour feeling in her stomach. Her mind was locked up by fear, fear for her life, fear of being taken away from Nick.

She couldn't focus on the why or who. She reverted to the most primal of emotions, her survival instinct kicking in. All that mattered was staying alive, staying alive for Nick, for their future, which held such promise.

She had tried to reach Nick throughout the day to tell him of her brush with death, of how she had miraculously exited Flight

502 just before its departure. She would have raced home to tell him, but a situation with a client was dire and required her immediate attention. So she had made countless calls, all to no avail. With the power out, the house answering machine wasn't working, nor was the cordless phone in Nick's office. She had tried him several times on his cell phone and had left him a voicemail, but they had never gotten in touch. She knew he was working toward an imminent deadline, analyzing real estate and financial information, reading through dozens of annual reports he had gathered on his four-day whirlwind trip around the Southwest, hoping to finish so he wouldn't have to work over the weekend. She knew he was probably frantic without power, working by the daylight that poured through his window, forced to use his laptop until the battery died.

As the day went on and she never heard back from him, she had begun to grow angry, knowing he was ignoring her, avoiding her calls, still upset about tonight's dinner with the Mullers, but now . . . She never told him of her deception, of the deliberate lie. She had wanted to tell him the truth, had planned to tell him in private tonight. She had put it off all week and now regretted her delay.

The phone rang. Julia looked up. She knew who it was; he was probably pissed at being disconnected. But she put him out of her mind. Those fences were easily mended. She let it ring. As she looked around, the moment seemed to drag out forever.

Nick slipped into his library and peered out the window, ignoring the ringing phone, which seemed louder than he remembered. A car was parked at the end of the driveway, the distance making its identity — beyond the color, blue — hard to distinguish. He glanced toward the front door. The man was standing there, casually turning about. He was on the later side of his forties, maybe early fifties. While Nick had no experience with criminals, this man looked completely harmless. Gray hair, horn-rimmed glasses, probably 230 pounds on a five-foot-six body put him severely overweight. One hand rested easily in his pocket while the other hung at his side. There was no gun, no sense of threat to the man. But there was also no question someone was about to try to kill Julia, and he would take no chances.

Nick hunkered down on the floor and opened the cabinet behind his small desk. Pulling aside a stack of old books, he revealed his small safe. He'd installed it himself as a place to tuck away Julia's jewelry and their passports, deeds, and other important documents. He spun the dial right, left, and right, and with a click pulled it open. The nine-millimeter Sig-Sauer had been sitting there for over six months, oiled and wrapped in cheesecloth. He hated guns, but better safe than sorry had been drilled into him by his father on too many occasions. He was an excellent shot but hadn't fired the weapon since February. He unwrapped the pistol, letting it flop into his hand, grabbed a clip from the safe's internal drawer, and shoved it in the butt of the gun. He pulled back the slide, chambered a bullet, and went to the door.

As he exited the library into the living room, the phone stopped ringing, the sudden silence adding a sense of foreboding to the air. He stayed tight to the wall, held the gun against his chest, looked into the hallway, and realized he had forgotten all about the alarm. Angry at himself for not thinking of it earlier, he thought while it wouldn't bring the police running, it would put off whoever was trying to get in, and maybe it would give him the advantage he would need. Nick flipped off the safety of the gun, slipped into the foyer, and with an eye through the small windows that flanked the door, caught sight of the heavyset man still standing there. He quietly reached up and hit the panic button.

The alarm suddenly screamed in Julia's ears, sending her racing heart into double time. The phone began ringing again, adding to the cacophony of sonic distraction. She couldn't imagine who would be trying to kill her, but then, as her mind shed its panic, reordered itself, and returned to its logical state, the obvious fell into place, as if a thousand-piece jigsaw puzzle had spontaneously come together.

She realized why they were after her, and she knew they would never stop until she was dead. And as the seconds ticked on, her thoughts hyperfocused, she deduced who . . .

She couldn't answer the phone, as he was calling back, the man she had just spent five minutes on the line with. The man she had turned to with her problem was the man coming to kill her.

Julia quickly crawled to the mudroom and checked the door, making sure Nick had locked it. She reached up and grabbed her purse off the hook, pulling it down on the floor with her. She reached in and grabbed her cell phone, quickly dialing 911.

"Nine-one-one emergency?" the woman's voice answered.

"My name is Julia Quinn," she whispered, "5 Townsend Court, Byram Hills. You have to hurry, my husband and —" Julia's voice stuck in her throat.

A cold sweat rose on her skin and her breathing came in ragged fits and starts as the panic overwhelmed her.

Despite her confirmation that the door was locked, she heard it click.

And quietly watched as the mudroom door opened.

Nick tore open the front door and aimed the gun. But the fat man was gone. Nick stepped out onto the front porch, gripped the pistol in both hands, and spun left to right. And he finally caught sight of the fat man jogging in an awkward waddle to his car. He never looked back.

Nick breathed a sigh of relief as he lowered the pistol, thumbing the safety back on. The phone stopped ringing again, leaving the drone of the alarm as the only sound in the air. The world was calming down, a peaceful equilibrium was approaching.

But then his heart seized in his chest as

he watched the man open the door and slide into his car. Nick immediately choked the handle of the pistol in his hand, thumbing off the safety, and ran for the kitchen.

His mind went into a tailspin as he realized his fatal error. That he had been tricked, lured away from Julia for the briefest of moments, made him feel incredibly foolish. They did it so simply. He had never thought of there being more than one.

Nick just watched the heavy man get in the passenger side of the car.

There was someone else.

Julia stared up at the gun and the world slowed to a crawl, time flowing like molasses. She couldn't understand, would never understand how Nick knew this moment was coming. She regretted not heeding his words, not staying in the kitchen, for now she knew his prediction would come to pass.

She would never be able to point Nick in the right direction; no one would ever know the truth. Her murderer had kept her on the phone, had kept her in one spot as he drove up to their house, pinning her in place, distracting her with the phone call as he made his approach.

Julia saw the sudden flame within the barrel, wisps of smoke curling up from what looked to be a gun that bordered on exotic jewelry. And in that brief moment, she recognized the gun; she had seen its picture earlier in the day . . .

And as the bullet traveled out of the long barrel of the ornate Colt Peacemaker, time caught up. The projectile tore through the air and ended Julia's life.

Nick raced through the kitchen, the alarm screaming out. And as he rounded the corner he saw Julia hurtle backward, half of her head exploding on the wall.

Nick suppressed the nausea, the scream, and ran toward her. But he knew there was nothing he could do as she hit the floor. He knew exactly what she had looked at seconds earlier, the horror that she just experienced. He knew there was nothing he could do. He had already mourned her, he had already stood over her shattered body an hour earlier, in his warped time frame. Going through it again would only crush whatever was left of his soul and prevent him from identifying her killer to stop all of this madness.

He leaped over her body, tears of anguish already filling his eyes, and crashed through the half open mudroom door. He sprinted through the garage and exploded out the open bay door to see Julia's assailant running at a full tilt to his car at the end of the drive, where the open driver's-side door lay in wait for his escape. Without thought, his legs pumping as fast as they could, Nick rapid-fired his pistol. Bullets ricocheted off the ground, off the rear of the blue car, but the man kept running without hesitation, running for his life as the gunfire missed him by inches.

And faster than Nick could imagine, the man arrived at and dove into his car.

The tires screeched, smoke pouring off the ground as the rubber burned before finally catching and launching the blue sedan into the street.

On reflex, Nick pulled up and ran to Julia's Lexus, sitting in the turnaround. For once he was glad she left the keys in the ignition. He fired up the SUV, threw the car in gear, and tore out of the driveway in pursuit.

Number 5 Townsend Court was at the end of a cul-de-sac. Nick and Julia had chosen the house for its privacy and seclusion, far from town, far from any main road. The area was truly cut off, with the nearest access to the rest of the world over a mile and a half away.

Nick made the sharp right onto Sunset

Drive and caught sight of the fleeing blue car less than a quarter mile away. He punched the accelerator and was at sixty miles per hour in seconds, closing the gap. He watched Julia's killer try to make the left onto Elizabeth Place, tires locking up, squealing in protest as he missed the turn, running up onto the Tannens' front yard before finally emerging back onto Elizabeth.

Nick cut the distance to the fleeing car by half as he locked up the brakes, threw the car into a sidespin, and made the turn less than an eighth of a mile behind what he now identified as a blue Chevrolet Impala. He pinned the gas and raced up to within thirty yards of his prey, but Julia's killer wasn't about to give up so easily; he accelerated down the hill, his car going airborne several inches as he negotiated the sudden dips and descents of the hilly road.

Nick drove harder. They were less than half a mile from Route 128, a road filled with too many choices to count, too many ways out, too many chances for the killer to escape before Nick could identify him.

Ten yards away now, he saw the license plate — Z8JP9 — committing it to memory. Nick was thankful for the heavy-duty engine of the Lexus as it roared toward the Impala. Like most SUVs, it was designed to be pushed, to be driven off-road in more extreme conditions than a normal car, but usually they were only driven by housewives on trips to the market or soccer games. But despite its design, it was never meant for a high-speed chase like the one Nick was in now, where tipping over was a real possibility.

And all at once, Nick was upon them, the Impala just inches away, but he didn't stop, he rammed the back of the car at full speed, jolting himself forward. He braked for a second, easing off, and hit the accelerator again, this time pulling up alongside and ramming into the rear fender of the Chevy. Nick eased off a moment before his next charge.

A sharp turn was approaching. On its far side, less than a quarter mile away, was the access onto Route 128. He had only one more chance.

Nick turned into the oncoming lane — the inside of the sharp turn — praying to God no one was coming the other way or he would no doubt be killed and Julia's life would truly end on the floor of their mudroom.

Nick accelerated through the turn, the Impala right alongside him. He didn't look inside, he didn't risk losing focus on his driving. He threw the wheel hard right, slamming the assailant into the stone wall on the right side of the road. And the driver lost it, his car, traveling over sixty, began to fishtail, and both rear tires blew out, sending the Chevy into a spin. The car jumped the curb, crashing into a tree, its front end wrapping around the trunk.

Without thought, without care, Nick hit the gas and rammed the rear end of the car for good measure, his airbag exploding in his face, sending him hurling back against his seat.

He quickly pushed the deflating bag aside, ignoring the small burns on his face from its deployment, and rolled out of his car onto the ground, gun in hand, the safety off. He crawled toward the Impala, which was wedged at an angle into the tree and wall. Fuel was leaking, coolant hissed, steam poured from the hood.

From his vantage point on the ground, he peered up into the car. While he wanted to kill the driver, lay the pistol up against his head, exacting revenge as judge and jury, unloading his remaining bullets into this killer's brain, he remained focused on what he really needed to do. He needed to identify this man if he was to have any chance of stopping him in the past.

On his belly, Nick crawled up to the passenger side, next to the stone wall. Peering up, he saw the deployed airbags, the fat older man unconscious in the passenger seat. Nick slowly rose up on his knees, looking at the steering wheel, at the driver's-side airbag, but finding the driver's seat empty.

Gunfire exploded in his ear, ricocheting off the tree. Nick rolled down and scrambled to the destroyed front end of the car, where billowing steam rolled up into clouds, obscuring his position.

Gunfire whizzed by his ears, peppering the stone wall, shattering the bark of the tree, a shredding fusillade of bullets inching down toward his position. He was pinned tight. To his left was the eight-foot wall, behind him the tree. His only ways out were over the hood of the crashed car on his right, into the open, or back out the way he came. Either way led square into the killer's sights.

Nick lay flat on the ground, pressing his body into the torn dirt and grass, and looked underneath the vehicle. On the other side, by the rear left tire, he could clearly see the man's muddy loafers squared off in a shooting stance, and without hesitation, Nick aimed and fired three shots, hitting the man square in the shin.

The shooter tumbled to the ground, screaming in agony. Nick leaped up and raced out of his captive position, taking cover behind Julia's Lexus.

The killer fired haphazardly at him, six shots in rapid succession, until Nick heard the telltale click: out of ammo. He had him.

As Nick rounded the car, he saw a small, metal pick-gun lying in the mud by the driver's-side door, looking like a cross between a staple gun and a toothbrush, Nick realized how the man had opened the locked door into his mudroom without a key.

Beside it was the Colt Peacemaker, its six cylinders smoldering and spent. With Nick chasing him down, the killer had had no time to plant the weapon, to set Nick up.

The sight of the ornate weapon angered him. That this man would set him up for the murder of his own wife infuriated Nick no end, but as he thought on the moment, he knew the future was already changing, there would be no gun in Nick's car to tie him to the murder, and soon, there would be no murder at all.

Nick approached the man, finding him on his belly next to the wrecked Impala, his back rising in deep wounded breaths. The man's dark hair, caked in blood, poked out from underneath a New York Mets baseball cap, his left arm broken from the car crash, cantilevered out at an odd angle. He gripped his now-useless nine-millimeter pistol in his right hand, as his left leg extended out bullet-shattered and bloody.

Nick slowly knelt beside him. He reached out and grabbed him by the back collar of his shirt, catching a silver chain between his fingers, the holy medal of St. Christopher now dangling from his clenched fist.

Nick did everything he could to restrain himself from killing the man, breathing a sigh of relief with the first completed step toward saving Julia. And for the moment he felt hope rise up. Against all logic, he knew that he just might be able to bring Julia back.

Nick tilted the killer's head toward him, to finally lay eyes on the man who had just killed his wife . . .

But before his face came into view, before he could identify Julia's assassin . . .

Nick's world went black.

CHAPTER 8

5:00 P.M.

Nick stood in his library, heaving, out of breath, swirling his tongue about in his mouth to rid it of the metallic taste. He felt the chill, more pronounced this time due to his sweat-covered body. His pants and shirt were muddy and torn from the accident and from crawling around on the ground. His hands shook from the adrenaline still coursing through his system. With a white-knuckled grip, he still held tight to his pistol. And . . .

He still held tight to the St. Christopher medal. Like the other inanimate objects in his possession, the gold watch, his cell phone, his clothes, it had leaped back with him, still dangling from his clenched fist. He held it up, looking at its chipped surface, the engraved message on the back ironically seeming to call to him. *Miracles do happen.*

An overwhelming frustration rose up in

Nick as he realized how close he had been. He had literally held Julia's killer in his hand, but his hesitation had cost him. He had never seen his face, never learned his identity . . .

But as he looked again at the silver medal, he realized that he did have a piece of him, and more important, he did remember the license plate: Z8JP9.

Nick looked again at his condition, his clothes, his banged-up face, and bolted out of his library, through the living room, across the foyer, and up the stairs. He couldn't let Julia see him like this.

"Nick?" Julia called out from the kitchen. "Are you done with all your work?"

"Just going to take a quick shower," he called out as he continued his sprint to their bedroom, happy to hear her voice once again.

"Wait, I haven't seen you all day," she yelled.

Without a response, Nick went straight to his bathroom and shut the door, stripping out of his clothes and turning on the water, thankful that there was hot water in the tank before the power went out. He opened the shutters to let some light in and looked out the window. Against all logic, he saw Julia's Lexus, which he had taken out of the driveway and rammed into the blue Chevy, destroying the front end of the Japanese SUV. It sat in the driveway, its black waxed finish without even a scratch.

Unfortunately, he realized as he turned, looked into the mirror, and saw the damage, that wasn't the case for him.

He had two small burns above his left eyebrow from the airbag, along with a cut on his right cheek. The small scrapes, dirt, and grime made him appear as if he had just emerged from battle, which was how his body actually felt.

He hid his pistol underneath the stack of dark-blue towels and hopped into the shower. He was suddenly aware of his host of injuries as the hot water hit his raw skin. His body felt far worse than after a hockey game full of major checking and fights. As he chased Julia's killer, as he rolled from the car and became pinned by the gunfire, he had felt not a moment of fear for his safety. He had never been so determined, never fought harder in his life. Hope had focused him; his love for Julia had driven him.

He soaped up, rinsed quickly, and was out of the shower in less than two minutes. He realized that he literally had no time to waste, he had only eight hours left to figure out a way to stop Julia's killer, and the only way he was going to be able to do that was by finding out why he was after her in the first place.

"Care to explain?" Julia stood in the open doorway as she pointed at the muddy and bloody clothes on the floor.

Nick wrapped a thick white towel around his waist.

"My God, what happened?" she said as she saw the burns and the cut on his cheek.

"No big deal." Nick tried to slough it off.

"No big deal? It looks like someone made a big deal about your face."

"You should see the Mets fan in the baseball cap."

"What happened to you?"

"Car accident."

"Car accident? Whose car?"

He had no idea how to answer as he glanced out the window at her car in the driveway. Life was running backward, everything was resetting timewise, but as he felt the ache with his movement, he knew everything was resetting except him.

"I stopped to help someone who dumped their car in a ditch; I slipped a bit."

She looked deep into his eyes, not buying a word he said.

He quickly walked by her to his closet.

"Tell me again, why weren't you on the plane?"

"You're changing the subject."

Nick threw off his towel as he quickly put on a pair of briefs and Levi's 501 jeans. He was amazed to find his wallet on his dresser. It had been taken by the police at 9:00 P.M., but here it was now, four hours earlier, where it had been for most of the day before he grabbed it at 5:30 in order to get a credit card number. He shook off the warped déjà-vu moment and turned to Julia with the most serious of looks. "Julia, I need to know what pulled you off that plane."

Julia stared for a moment, though she finally relented, annoyance coloring her voice. "I got on the plane this morning; I had to run up to Boston for a short meeting. I had settled into my seat and gotten lost in a conversation with a lovely old lady." Julia paused with a sudden realization. Her angry tone vanished, replaced with the sound of sorrow. "Her name . . . her name was Katherine and she was going to see her husband, who was sick. She didn't say it, but I think he was dying. And despite her hardship, the pain she was in, she asked about me, my life, with such sincere interest, with such green, honest eyes."

Julia paused, tears welling up. Nick gently

laid his hand on her face, stroking it, pulling her into a reassuring hug as she began to sob.

"All those people. They all sat on that plane with such hope in their eyes," Julia said, her voice cracking. "Heading off to see friends and family; a business trip that they promised their kid they'd hurry back from; people going on vacation. None of them ever imagining they would all soon be . . ."

"Julia," Nick gently said, trying to bring her back to the moment. "Why did you get off the plane?"

"There was a robbery." She looked up at him.

"A robbery? What kind of robbery?"

Julia pulled away from Nick. She briefly went into his bathroom, returning with a tissue, dabbing her eyes, wiping away her grief.

"There's a large colonial home over on Maple Avenue called Washington House. It belongs to a man by the name of Shamus Hennicot. It's been in his family for three generations. He's at least ninety so, as you can imagine, it's rather old. The outside has that white clapboard New England look with the black shutters, wood shake roof —"

"I know the house, Julia," Nick said, try-

141

ing to hurry her along.

"Well, it's a bit more than some colonial remnant. They have kept the insides updated and reinforced with concrete and steel. While it is Hennicot's home, it also contains not only his office but a rather elaborate storage and display warehouse on the lower level."

"Warehouse for what?"

"The Hennicots have been clients of Aitkens, Lerner, & Isles since 1886. Shamus's grandfather, Ian Hennicot, was this wealthy Irish land baron and whiskey manufacturer. He was also a purveyor of antiques with an affinity for warfare. He had a collection of exotic weapons from around the world. Bejeweled daggers from Sri Lanka, diamond-encrusted sabers from Turkey, katanas from the feudal era of Japan, Chinese lances, English and Spanish swords from the age of knights. It was his true passion. He had a collection of pistols and rifles, with intricate engravings. The contradiction was bizarre: weapons of elegance and beauty whose only purpose was death.

"The tastes of Ian's son, Stephan Francis, were a bit more traditional. He collected fine art and statuary, jewelry and sculptures. And his son, Shamus, his passions are more benevolent. He would loan certain pieces of their collections out to museums around the world but always refused to sell them.

"I'm not sure if you remember, but a few years back, I was assigned as not only the junior attorney appointed to handle Hennicot's business affairs but also the emergency point person, which included being contacted any time the security system at the Maple Avenue building was breached."

"So, while you were waiting to take off, you were beeped?" Nick asked in confusion.

"It's quite a bit more than a beep." She smiled. "But yeah. A text message, actually."

"What did they take?"

"There was a velvet pouch with over two hundred diamonds, four gold swords and two silver rapiers, three sabers, five jewel-encrusted daggers, three gold-inlaid pistols along with their silver ammunition. All told, over $25 million."

Nick listened to her every word convinced that her future death was 100 percent related to what she had just told him. "What did you do when you got off the plane?"

"Headed over there, straight away. I wasn't sure yet if there had been a robbery; I thought it might have been a false alarm."

"What about the police?"

"The Hennicots weren't too trusting of the police. The procedure is we are contacted first, an automatic email and text message is sent for any unscheduled access to the lower-level vault, then, once we deem it necessary, we call the police. Hennicot's philosophy was the police were just one step above the criminals and who was to know if they didn't line their pockets during the investigation while pointing their fingers at the thieves?"

"A little cynical," Nick said. "Don't you think?"

"They call it eccentric."

"You mean high-class crazy?"

"If you ever met him, you'd think differently. He's probably the sanest, nicest man I've ever met. When I was first assigned to him, he sent me the kindest note. He has taken me to lunch dozens of times. He's so charming and wise. He's given me such great advice about my career, business, life . . ."

"Should I be worried?" Nick asked facetiously.

"Well, he's worth over $4 billion. And for a gentleman of ninety, he couldn't be more handsome. He doesn't get around too well, hasn't left his New England summer home in over a month. Everyone thinks he's this man of mystery, an anonymous donor to countless charities. When large donations are made and no one can track down the originator, many think it has to be Shamus trying to give away his fortune."

"Well, is it him?"

"Now it wouldn't be anonymous if I knew, would it?" Julia smiled.

"Does he know he's been robbed?"

"It was my first call after I saw what was stolen. I spoke to his assistant, who said she'd tell him, but they were crazy dealing with other matters."

Nick became lost in thought for a moment before getting angry. "You went inside this place? How did you know the thieves weren't still in there?"

"Well . . ." her face couldn't hide her answer.

"This isn't part of an attorney's job, you never told me this."

"He pays us a retainer of twenty five thousand a month in addition to what we bill them. I never thought this would happen. Besides, I'm fine."

"Yeah, but . . ." he didn't finish the statement, not knowing what to say.

"Look, I'm fine. And besides, you've seen that crazy eight-faced key in my purse and I know you've seen the security card. I told you what it was for."

"You said a client's home. You never

mentioned you were playing security guard."

"Client confidentiality," Julia said.

Nick brushed off her response. "If the key and the card are the means of access to a place of such wealth, why do you carry them around so nonchalantly?"

"The key is special. It's marked with eight letters, each corresponding to a specific date. Today happens to be a D-day. If you don't know the algorithm to get the date you've got a one in eight chance of its working, that coupled with the magna-card being passed before the reader three times plus you need to input your Social Security number . . . the key alone is pretty worthless."

"Julia, you said it was an extra key to someone's home. Not a place filled with weapons."

"Not this kind of weapons. You wouldn't use these to kill someone."

Nick didn't dare contradict her. "With all the great security, how'd they get in?"

"Not sure, but they knew what they were doing, they had definite inside knowledge, they knew the security system, destroyed the server, the whole magilla, but they forgot about one thing — we hired a separate firm to set up a remote backup."

"What?"

"Never put all your eggs in one basket for security or you're beholden to the integrity of one protector. Two separate firms for two separate aspects. The security server in Hennicot's building has a remote live backup to the computer in my office. Any time there's a security breach it sends the files to my computer for this exact reason."

"So everything, images of whoever broke in, is on the computer in your office?"

"Yeah, and here." Julia held up her Palm Pilot PDA. The handheld personal data assistant she carried in her purse stored far more than her contacts, calendar, and email, its large memory capacity far surpassing that of her BlackBerry and smart phone.

"What?"

"When a blackout hits, we have backup batteries that allow our computers to save and shut down so you don't lose the data you're working on. When the plane crashed, knocking out the lights, it initiated a backup and shutdown."

"And . . . ?"

"As a precaution, sensitive files are emailed to my PDA, so I'm not impeded in critical work. All of the security files for two hours prior to shutdown are on this."

"Can I see?"

"Why would you want to see?" Julia said,

confused. "The police will handle it after they deal with the plane crash."

"I just want to take a look."

"Even if we wanted to, I need a computer, and we have no power unless your notebook still has battery."

Nick shook his head.

"The file is unviewable on the Palm. It's a host of video and secure data files."

"I can't believe you put yourself at such risk." Nick couldn't hide his anger.

"When you think about it," Julia said, "that robbery saved my life."

Nick knew she was right, but it was only a temporary save: It actually cost her her life. He couldn't help thinking that no matter what he did, fate was going to take her away.

Nick pulled on a light-blue, button-up shirt. He reached out and took Julia's hand. "Listen to what I have to say, hear me out without interruption."

"You're freaking me out," Julia said.

"I don't mean to."

"Then reduce the drama factor," she said with a serious smile.

Nick took a breath. "There are no cops around, everyone is at the crash site."

"Yeah —" Julia shut her mouth as Nick held up his hand.

"Whoever pulled that robbery is trying to

erase their tracks." Nick paused.

Julia looked into Nick's concerned eyes before turning her attention to the Palm Pilot in her hand, her thoughts churning, until realization washed over her face.

Plumes of white smoke billowed up from the crash site two miles away; an all-day battle with no victors, no winners, but countless victims. And while the fight to contain the fire had neared its end, the mental battle would go on for days, weeks, years. Though the scar in the ground would heal, nature filling in the scorched earth with a green blanket of growth in mere weeks, the town would never be the same again.

As Nick drove his Audi A8 toward the village of Byram Hills, he glanced at Valhalla, their favorite restaurant, thinking how much the area had changed.

Byram Hills had once been a town right out of Mayberry: dirt roads and a single street light, a police station with three jail cells, a fruit and vegetable stand that sold fresh doughnuts and cider on the weekends. Houses were modest despite incomes, no one judged his neighbor on square footage. Children of firemen and janitors hung out with the children of CEOs and real estate tycoons, playing and fighting as kids do without the word lawsuit ever being uttered. High school coaches remained in place for the season, while parents had no illusion that their child was the next Michael Jordan. Marriages lasted longer, couples working together to make their commitments endure despite the hardships they faced. But over time, as with much of America, some of the town's character was sold off for higher returns, people became caught up in appearances, in perceptions, in keeping up with the Joneses.

Sadly, tragedy is the great equalizer, Nick thought. It knows no ZIP code, has no country club membership or two-room cold-water flat. It strikes without prejudice, reminding us of the fragility of life, of what truly is important when all *things* are stripped away. For sorrow and loss, pain and suffering are innate in our hearts, and while they may lie dormant they are quickly remembered when death fills the air.

And with an event of the magnitude of a plane crash, when 212 people are collectively ripped from this world, from your own backyard, life is reset, priorities falling back into their proper order.

Within moments of the crash, stores and businesses closed, summer camps were shuttered. Families came together. Churches and synagogues opened their doors for prayer. Volunteers arrived by the busful in the open fields less than a mile outside town where friends and strangers had departed this earth.

Julia rode in the seat beside Nick, her eyes fixed on the smoke on the horizon, unable to shake the thought of death and how it had passed her by today.

"You sure we can get a computer in your office to work?" Nick asked.

"Why do you need to see the security files? Let's just turn my PDA over to the police. This is none of our — and particularly none of your — business, Nick."

"When it concerns you, Julia, it is my business."

"Nobody is after me; you're being ridiculous."

"No, trust me, I'm not."

"You're not telling me something." Julia was getting upset.

Nick didn't respond.

"What aren't you telling me?" She grilled him as if she were in court.

"Julia," Nick said, losing patience. "Just answer the question."

"We don't have a generator," Julia snapped. "But we do have battery backups for the computers, they're good for a half hour."

"And we'll be able to view the files on your PDA?"

Julia nodded, suddenly distracted by the sight of the town as they drove down Main Street.

The village was eerily empty, stores closed, gas stations shuttered, a virtual ghost town. Not a soul on the sidewalks, not a car in the streets. Shop windows were dark without electricity to light their window displays. The pizza parlor, the barber shop, even the banks and post office, locked tight on a Friday afternoon in the middle of summer for the first time in their history.

The National Guard, the usual responders to disasters, were at a quarter capacity as a result of the war, so volunteers were needed. It didn't matter if you were a grandmother or an eighteen-year-old college student. You were put to work either directing traffic, filling out paperwork, or if you were a hardy soul, sifting through the crash site.

Julia's eyes returned to the smoky plume rising over the hill at the far side of town. Nick couldn't imagine what was going on inside her head, looking at a funeral pyre that she had escaped through a twist of fate.

But Nick had witnessed his own horror. He had watched Julia die, mourned her once, and he refused to do it for a second time. He would somehow find the man who pulled the trigger and would stop him. He felt the lump of the Sig-Sauer at the small of his back, fully aware that he would, in all likelihood, have to use it. No matter the consequence of his actions, even though he might lose his own life in the process, he would save his wife.

He made no mention of the gun he was carrying and was sure to keep the bulge of the weapon out of Julia's sight. She hated guns with a passion, an irony that was not lost on Nick. He rarely removed the gun from the safe and had never carried it. He was actually finding it awkward now as it rubbed against his skin under his hastily put on sport coat.

Aitkens, Lerner, & Isles was considered one of the top firms in the country, specializing in finance and tax law. The sixty-partner firm had the luxury of locating wherever they saw fit, which was naturally at the nexus of its three senior partners.

The firm had a three-building campus on North Castle Hill, its three hundred employees swelling the town of Byram Hills during the week, but that couldn't have been farther from the case today.

The four parking lots were entirely empty as Nick pulled his Audi up to the circular drive in front of the central building.

He and Julia hustled up the fire stairs two steps at a time to the darkened second floor, the emergency light's batteries already depleted. They raced to Julia's office in the rear. It was a typical senior associate suite, a large desk and a seating area with a couch and armchairs. But her usually fastidious work area had been destroyed: her desk tipped over, her computer missing, wires torn from the walls, the monitor shattered on the floor.

"My God! When I find the son of a bitch who did this . . ." Julia's temper was approaching its boiling point.

"Where's your server?" Nick said, without acknowledging her raging mood.

"You knew this was going to be like this, didn't you?" Julia said with a mix of anger and confusion.

"Where's the server?"

"End of the hall," Julia said, leading the way. "This is all about the robbery. What the hell?"

They arrived at a nondescript door that sat between the auxiliary kitchen and the office of the managing partner, Sherman Peabody. Julia punched the code into the keypad, tore open the door, and immediately saw what they both dreaded. The server towers within the computer room had been stripped of their hard drives; wires hung useless from the racks, looking like dead snakes.

"Midnight backups?" Nick asked

"Everyone's computer and all the servers back up on three separate nodes once a day at 2:00 A.M."

They both looked at the large computer room, now rendered useless, hundreds of thousands of dollars in damage inflicted, all in an effort to erase what had occurred earlier in the day at Shamus Hennicot's large white house on Maple Avenue.

"Now do you believe me?" Nick looked at the Palm Pilot in Julia's hand. "That's the only thing pointing at whoever ripped off your client."

"We've got to get this to the police —"

"There are no police to give it to."

"Let's just bring it to the crash site, give it to someone there."

Nick knew that would only serve to delay his finding Julia's killer, and the only way he was going to do that was to see the face on that PDA.

"How did you know this was going to happen, Nick?"

Nick took the Palm Pilot out of her hand.

"Answer me, dammit, what's going on?"

Nick pulled the pocket watch and looked at the time: 5:40.

"You've got to trust me, I'll explain later, but right now we don't have the luxury of time," Nick said as he stepped back into the hallway. "You said every computer here has a battery backup module."

Julia pointed them out under the assistants' desks in the corral area, a little larger than a bread box, configured like an enormous power strip.

"How long do they last?"

"Half hour, give or take a few minutes."

Nick headed back to Julia's assistant's desk. "Do you think Jo used it up?"

"She left right after the crash, I told her to go home."

Nick sat down at Jo Whalen's desk. She had been Julia's assistant for three years now, and if Julia was organized, Jo was supremely anal: pencils and paper clips perfectly aligned north to south in their respective holders, not a stitch of paper or a fleck of dust upon her work station. Nick fired up Jo's computer, the light wash of the monitor casting an eerie glow about the

156

darkened office. He turned to Julia as the screen asked for the password.

Julia leaned over him, typed it in, and the computer sang to life. The reserve battery began beeping, calling attention to its limited operating capacity.

"Let's go," Nick said, handing the PDA back to Julia.

Julia turned it on and placed the infrared link next to the computer station. She highlighted the files on the PDA and hit send.

Jo's computer began humming, and a video screen opened on the monitor as the file infiltrated her system. They both watched as six files appeared on the bottom of the screen just below the video viewing window.

Julia clicked on the first file. A detailed ledger appeared in an Excel spreadsheet.

"This isn't what we wanted," Julia said.

"What is it?"

"It's the inventory of Hennicot's collection." Julia pointed at the screen. "It can be sorted by age, type of weapon or antique, value, year acquired, and now," she clicked the screen, reordering the rows, "by what was stolen."

"We need to see the video," Nick said, hurrying her along.

Julia closed the file without a word and clicked the next file.

The screen filled with a video of alternating images of various security feeds, a time clock emblazoned in the bottom right-hand corner. There were static images of the parking lot, the front of the building, a well-appointed English-style office, pictures of display cases filled with elegant swords and knives, a fixed image of a safe, its size hard to estimate without something to scale it by, pictures of shipping crates, of doors and hallways, stairs and conference rooms.

Julia hit the fast-forward button with the mouse and the images cycled by at an extremely fast rate until all at once the monotony of images was interrupted. The exterior shot of the parking lot and front of the building became nothing but white snow.

Nick took the mouse and slowed the video.

The interior images remained on and unchanging, but suddenly, in one of them, a large brushed-steel door cracked open, and a flood of light cut through the room.

"What are you doing with that?" Julia suddenly shouted, pointing at the gun sticking out through the vent of Nick's jacket as if he was carrying another woman's panties in his back pocket.

"Please watch the screen," Nick said as all his focus remained on the open door.

"I told you how much I hate that thing." Julia's fury was growing. "You said it was only for the shooting range."

"Julia, please just watch the monitor."

"I hate guns, you know that." And just like that Julia's anger at the thieves, at those that had trashed her office, was turned upon Nick. "And how many times did you say you hate guns?"

Nick remained intent on the monitor, not wanting to explain how he had already used the gun to save his own life.

A man came into view on the monitor, his face filling the screen. Nick had never seen him before, but he had someone now to focus his anger on. The man looked to be in his early fifties, dark hair with a slight receding hairline. His eyes were obscured by glasses, but there was nothing hiding his gaunt face, his overly high cheekbones, and the prominence of his thick eyebrows.

"Promise me," Julia demanded, her eyes boring into Nick, "when this is all past, that you'll get rid of it like you promised me you already did."

"Who the hell is that?" Nick pointed at the screen. And as Julia finally returned her eyes to the monitor, the image turned to white snow, each room following in succession. The entire system seeming to fail.

"What the hell?" Julia said.

"Did you see him, an older guy, glasses?"

"No, I didn't see him." Julia's anger hit new heights. "Rewind it. If I —"

But Julia never got to finish her statement, as gunfire erupted around them, the cubicle exploding into hundreds of pieces.

Nick pulled Julia out of the hail of bullets onto the floor, reached up, and grabbed the PDA off the desk. The monitor with the useless images of snow exploded in a shower of sparks.

Nick snatched the gun from his waistband and fired off three shots in the direction of the unseen shooter. He took Julia's hand and, without a word, led her through the corral of cubicles, being sure to keep their heads below the shooter's line of sight. He kept his pistol aimed straight ahead to intercept anyone who might suddenly feel bold and show himself.

He tore open the fire stairs door, peeked inside, shoved Julia in, and turned back to scan the area. More gunfire answered his curiosity. Nick wanted to hunt the shooter down, kill him in his tracks, but he needed to get Julia out of harm's way.

He grabbed Julia and raced down the

stairs. He cautiously cracked open the lobby door and peered into the vacant marble vestibule. They slipped through the lobby on light, running feet and looked out the front door. With not a soul in sight, they charged out and ran to the Audi immediately in front of the building.

Nick fired up the car and hit the gas, the wheels spinning, throwing them both back into their seats. With a screech of tires he spun the car around and raced out of North Castle Hill.

Just as he emerged onto the main road, he caught sight in his peripheral vision of the blue Chevy Impala sitting at the rear of Julia's building.

"Now are you glad I didn't get rid of the gun?" Nick said, trying to contain his anger at the situation.

Julia said nothing. Fear flowed from her eyes as she buckled her seat belt, her hands shaking as she fumbled with the clasp.

Nick drove the Audi faster than he had ever driven before, pushing the speedometer over 110 miles per hour. As the car rocketed up Route 22, there wasn't another vehicle in sight. Like the town, the road was completely empty, it was as if they literally owned the road, as if they were the only ones alive. Nick glanced in the rearview mirror but saw nothing but open road behind them, no pursuers, no cars, no flying bullets.

He finally eased off the gas.

"What the hell," Julia said from the passenger seat, her right hand strangling the handle above the door. "And how did you know to bring a gun?"

Nick pulled a sliding left turn onto Route 128, ignoring the useless red light, and sped down through town.

"Listen to me, very carefully." There was an intensity to his voice. "When we get home, you get in your car. I want you to drive as far from here as you possibly can. Do not go to your cousin's, friend's, anyone's house. Check into a hotel and pay by cash."

"Stop!" Julia screamed. "What's going on?"

"Whoever burgled that building, whoever stole those guns and diamonds, is erasing everything leading to them." Nick paused as he looked at her. "Everything, including any possible witness."

Nick drove up Wago Avenue to Elizabeth Place, down Sunrise Drive and down Townsend Court into their driveway, and pulled into the garage.

"You've got your wallet? Cell phone?"

"Yeah." Julia nodded.

"Go now." Nick hopped out of the car. She followed suit and ran around to his side.

"What are you going to do?" She looked up at him. "I'm not leaving without you."

Nick looked at her, long and hard, memorizing her face as if he was looking at her with new eyes. "If you ever were going to start listening to me, please make it now."

He led her over to her Lexus and opened the driver's side door.

"Please don't leave me," Julia said, her tough exterior broken.

Nick pulled out the watch and quickly checked the time before stuffing it back into his pocket.

"I promise, I'll find you." He reached out and pulled her to him, the emotion of their embrace conveying far more than a kiss ever could. All of the fear and anxiety floating on the surface was briefly lost as they drew strength from each other, as they found a glimpse of hope that his words would prove true.

Despite the harsh language and anger, they both knew it was over the stress of the moment, over the fear each felt for the other.

"Julia, I love you." Nick directed her into the driver's seat. "You've got sixty seconds to get out of here."

He turned and walked to the house.

"Where are you going?" Julia called out as she rolled down the window.

Nick looked over his shoulder at her as he walked through the garage. "I think I know how to stop this madness." He didn't dare say that he was going to kill the son of a bitch who killed her.

He grabbed the door handle to the mud-room, pulled open the door —

— and found himself standing in his library. He shook off the cold, his body growing more accustomed to the jump. He didn't need to look at the watch to know what had happened. He felt for the gun at the small of his back, confirming its presence.

He walked out of the room through the foyer and into the kitchen.

"Can I make you something to eat?" Julia said as she looked into the darkened fridge, smiling, not knowing what lay ahead.

"I'll be back in a little while," Nick said, surprised to see her home.

"Don't forget about dinner."

As much as he didn't want to have dinner with the Mullers, and despite the fact that he had gotten so angry about it, he would gladly have dinner with the annoying Mullers for the next month if he could just get through this upside-down day and be assured that Julia would be dining at his side.

Everything revolved around the robbery that had occurred this morning. That's where the answers lay, that's where he would find and stop Julia's killer.

Nick quietly walked through the mudroom and reached into Julia's purse hanging on the wall. He grabbed her PDA, quickly searched for and found a security card and set of keys. He slipped them into his pocket and headed out the garage door.

CHAPTER 7

4:03 P.M.

The white colonial house on Maple Avenue was just one of several homes owned by Shamus Hennicot, who, for the past thirty years, had summered with his family at their home on Martha's Vineyard. The house had traditionally remained vacant during July and August but for Julia Quinn, who would stop by upon request to attend to any matters concerning Hennicot's art collection and charitable contributions.

Unofficially known as Washington House, Hennicot's home had been built at the beginning of the twentieth century, long after George Washington could ever have slept there. While it was considered a historic landmark of the town, a home from the hamlet's infancy, in actuality, it retained only two exterior walls from its original design.

At the time of its construction in 1901, at

just over ten thousand square feet, it was the largest house in all of the county. What was once the centerpiece of the quaint town of Byram Hills had, like the town surrounding it, become lost in a myriad of development over the last century. But unlike many of the neighboring homes and buildings that had been torn down for the sake of *progress,* Washington House had adapted with the times. With the advent of cars, garages were added. It had been the first home in town with hot and cold running water. The sixties brought air-conditioning and insulated, double-paned windows. The interior was in a constant flux, walls built, removed, expanded; rooms added, subtracted, combined; modern kitchens designed, starting with 1930s dishwashers and moving on to present-day Sub-Zero refrigerators and Viking stoves.

Wireless broadband, satellite television, energy-efficient heating, and multiroom entertainment systems were installed, all of which saw little use by the elderly Shamus Hennicot and his family.

But its greatest modification, one not known by the town planning board, or by the utility companies, or by any local contractor, was the elaborate renovation of the lower level, fondly referred to by the family as Dante's Vault — reinforced concrete walls, a half-inch steel ceiling and floor, all covered in a dark walnut sheathing of coffered ceilings, wainscoting, and ornamental trim. It was an elegant vault of enormous proportions, giving an aesthetically pleasing English Manor feel to a fortress that was thought to be impenetrable.

The securing of the basement was the brainchild of Shamus Hennicot. While he was considered the most benevolent and charitable of a long line of misers, making frequent anonymous gifts and loans from his father's art collection, it was he who had thought there were some things too tempting to modern man, things that needed to be hidden away for reasons that only he could explain.

Nick parked his Audi at the back of the house, grabbed his flashlight off the seat, and used Julia's keys and pass card to open the heavy steel fire door in the back. Once in the small vestibule, he used the magna-card to gain access to the magnetically sealed inner door. All the lights were out, the batteries on the emergency lights having died out hours ago, while the basics of the security system remained operational with a twenty-four-battery backup continuing to operate the pass system and locks.

Nick made the once-over of the first floor, the afternoon light more than sufficient to see by. It had all the trappings of a modern home: living room, dining room, kitchen, family room while in a separate wing was a library, billiard room, and music room.

Nick bypassed the upper level and, using the encrypted pass card, opened a large, heavy cellar door, its whitewashed wood veneer covering a three-inch steel core, that led to a dark set of stairs. Nick flipped on his flashlight, surprised to see the expensive green fleur-de-lis wallpaper and thickly carpeted stairs. Nick headed down the fifteen steps, arriving at another door. But this one was different, made of brushed steel and lacking doorknobs and hinges. He pulled out the oddly shaped key from Julia's purse. She had told him of the eight-sided key and explained the security system earlier — or later, depending on which time line he was riding on.

Octagonal in shape, the key could be inserted eight different ways, with only one providing access. Each face was labeled with a letter that corresponded to a rotating specific date of the year. If the key was inserted the wrong way twice you would be locked out for twenty-four hours. But even worse, the door behind you would seal shut, trapping you until someone arrived. The entire basement was truly worthy of being called a safe.

Nick punched in Julia's Social Security number on the keypad below the card reader, swiped the magna-card three times, and inserted the key with the D side up as Julia had mentioned. Finally, with a turn of the key, the door silently swung open.

Nick was greeted by a table-case display in the center of a large museum-like lobby, the beam of his flashlight refracting off its clear surface, its glass top conspicuously violated by a large perfect circle cut out of its center. The case, no doubt once the repository for some of the antique weapons Julia had described to him, was empty.

What struck him as odd was the picture of water lilies on the near wall. There was no question whose hand had rendered it. With its visible brush strokes and blurred images of flowers upon the water, the piece had a strong impressionist flavor. And while its beauty was beyond compare, it stood out like an albatross as it stared down upon the broken glass. For while the antique weapons snatched from this level were of staggering value, they no way near approached the value of one of Claude Monet's finest pieces, a work whose sister had recently sold for $80 million.

Going through the lower level, he found conference rooms, art restoration labs, humidity-controlled storage spaces filled with hundreds of crates with addresses to and from the world's finest museums: the Smithsonian, the Metropolitan Museum of Art, the Louvre, the Vatican. Crates of all shapes and sizes containing who knew what.

Shamus's elegantly appointed private office lacked the character and feeling of frequent use, as evidenced by the absence of a single picture or memento.

Nick stood at the desk and noted an odd six-inch-square box, a red half-moon dome on top. He'd seen similar ones on the wall by the Monet and in the hallway approaching the office and had thought them to be security-related, but he now realized they had been placed by the thieves and were the devices that had disabled the cameras.

Looking to gain some understanding of Shamus, Nick shined his light about the room, at the desktop, the wall shelves filled with encyclopedias, books on philosophy and religion, Dante's *Divine Comedy,* treatises on world hunger and poverty.

He turned and opened the drawers of the credenza and found an array of plaques and honoraria, medals and testimonials. But unlike the trophies Nick kept hidden away in his library, these were not for sports, but were of actual significance for deeds whose merit far outweighed hockey championships and swim races. The simple plaques were for actions whose value could not be assessed. UNICEF, the Wildlife Trust, Habitat for Humanity, Doctors Without Borders, and Environment Rescue had all seen fit to bestow their highest honors on Hennicot.

Without ever meeting the man, Nick gained more insight into his character with this one glance. This was a man embarrassed by his charity, who chose to hide away the recognition bestowed upon him.

Nick turned the flashlight on the windowless room and was about to exit when a slight crack in the wall was illuminated. He ran his hands down the darkly stained walnut and found the seam of the panel, something that shouldn't have been accepted in this finely crafted space. Nick laid his hand upon the wall and with a gentle push, it swung inward on whisper hinges. The narrow door, without handles or knobs, revealed a small room, eight feet square. There were no finishes here, no effort to mask the concrete construction. Three simple lights, which, like all the other lights, lacked power, hung from the ceiling. Another red-domed box was affixed to the wall. The two objects in the center of the room were as cold and plain as the room itself. Built in 1948, the two Harris safes had centered flywheels and brass bar handles. They were two blocks of steel four feet high and square looking to weigh over a thousand pounds each, but the weight wasn't the only deterrent to removing them, as they were bolted to the floor, probably sunk into the granite foundation. They were identical in appearance but for one distinction: The door of the one on the right hung conspicuously open. Its three-foot interior was covered in black felt so as not to damage whatever had once resided within. The safe lay empty, cleaned out, as the saying goes.

The antique weapons of gold and silver, their handles and bodies inlaid with jewels, were of considerable value, surely worth millions on the black market, but they were only the tip of an iceberg of wealth. An $80 million Monet hanging in plain sight, a storage room filled with artwork worthy of the finest museums — it was all passed over in favor of whatever lay in this empty Harris safe.

And while it may have been diamonds, Nick suspected it was something far greater, something that even Julia was unaware of, something that Shamus Hennicot chose to hide away in this lower-level, vaultlike museum, within this secret room behind secret walls within a four-foot steel safe.

"Hey," Marcus said as he opened his front door. He was dressed in his gray pin-striped suit, the pants perfectly creased, his shirt starched and unwrinkled, his blue Hermès tie straight and true.

"Coming to ask for a cup of sugar, or would you like some electricity?" The sound of a motor droned in the background. "I told you to install a generator."

"I need your help," Nick said as he walked through the door into the large marble foyer.

"Well, at least you're finally admitting it," Marcus said with a little smile.

"Do you have any contacts who can run a license plate?"

"Martin Scars over at DMV." Marcus grew serious, seeing Nick was not in a playful mood. "He was always good for helping me out. My legal department's pretty tight with him. What's up? You get another ticket?"

Nick shook his head no, not entertaining the joke.

Marcus led the way into his library, taking

a seat in one of the wingback chairs across from his desk. Nick sat in the matching one across from him.

A sadness washed over Marcus's face as he sat back.

"You look beat up; you okay?" Nick asked.

"I just got off the phone a little while ago with my office. You're not going to believe this. You know the guy I hired six months ago, Jason Cereta, he came to a Ranger game in March with us?" Marcus paused a moment, shaking his head. "He was on Flight 502."

"I'm sorry," Nick said.

"Young guy, two kids. Babies having babies. He was going up to Boston to check out another company to buy. Now he's dead. I feel like I sent him to his death."

"That's bullshit and you know it. You couldn't know what was going to happen."

"Yeah, is it? He was going to Boston to meet the owner of Halix Ski Company. I had mentioned to Jason that I've loved their skis since I was a kid and how much I would love to own them. Such a solid company would be a great investment, and it would be fun to test out their products — and their cute spokesmodels. He was a good kid, thought he was doing something that would make me happy while advancing his career."

Marcus paused. "May he rest in peace."

"My condolences. But don't be blaming yourself."

"If someone went on a journey to make you money and died in the act, how would you feel?" Marcus said, angry at himself.

"Julia was supposed to be on that flight," Nick said.

"You've got to be kidding me," Marcus said in shock, his tone shifting to compassion. "Why didn't she get on?"

"She did."

Marcus just stared.

"But she got off right before they left." Nick still couldn't get over the irony. "One of her clients was robbed. She got off to deal with it," Nick said.

"That's unbelievable."

"That's why I'm here." Nick paused. "She got off the plane only to be murdered."

Marcus sat up in shock.

"The robbery, the people who did it killed her."

Marcus ran his hands over his balding head, his eyes lost, filled with shock. "Oh, Nick," Marcus leaned forward in sympathy.

Nick held up his hand, stopping Marcus's emotions. "Do you trust me?"

"What?" Marcus said in confusion.

"Do you trust me?"

"Do you even need to ask? What the hell is going on?"

"If I was to tell you a fantastic story, one that no one else on this earth would believe, something that defies all reason, would you still believe me?"

"If you're trying to put one over on me —"

"If it was the key to saving Julia's life?" Marcus grew serious.

Nick reached into his pocket, pulled out the watch. He flipped opened the gold top, its silver interior refracting the light about the room, and handed it to Marcus.

"Fugit inreparabile tempus." Marcus read the inscription on the inside of the watch. "Irretrievable time is flying. From the Roman poet Virgil. It's where the phrase 'tempus fugit' comes from."

Nick pulled out the letter, opened it, and handed it to Marcus. Marcus laid the watch on his desk, leaned back in his chair, and began to read.

He read it through twice before looking up.

The moment held silent as they looked at each other.

"Julia will be killed at 6:42 this evening." Nick fought to hold back his emotions. "The only way I can save her is to find the man who did it and stop him."

Marcus sat there in total shock, watching his friend's nervous breakdown.

Nick pulled out his cell phone, opened it, and pulled up the picture of Julia dead on the floor. He had regretted taking it, thinking of it as a violation of her dignity, of her soul. It felt as if he was pulling the trigger of the murder weapon, but he also knew it would be the easiest way to convince Marcus. He averted his eyes as he passed the phone to his friend.

Marcus looked at the picture, unaware of what he was seeing . . .

And then realized exactly what he was looking at. "What the hell?"

Nick said nothing.

Marcus looked more closely at the picture, grief and nausea overcoming him in seconds. His breathing quickened, seeing what was left of Julia's face filling the screen of the cell phone.

"What have you done?" Marcus exploded at Nick.

Nick said nothing, his own eyes filled with heartache.

Without thought, Marcus charged out of the room, tore open the front door of his house, and ran across the open expanse of lawn as fast as he could toward Nick's house.

But he suddenly stopped in his tracks, coming to a standstill so abruptly he almost fell over.

"You always go for a run in a suit there, Marcus," Julia called out, her blond hair caught in a summer breeze.

She was standing in her driveway, the rear door of her black Lexus open, pulling out a canvas bag.

Marcus leaned forward, hands on his knees, panting hard as he caught his breath, not comprehending what he was seeing.

"Julia," he said through heaving breaths. "Are you okay?"

"I'm fine," Julia said with a laugh. She put down her bag and walked toward Marcus. "Are you okay? You look like you just saw a ghost."

"Nick said . . ."

"He's with you?" Julia looked toward Marcus's house. "He rushed out of here so quickly, is he scaring you?"

Marcus stood up as Julia arrived at his side. He looked at her as if he *were* seeing a ghost. The image on Nick's phone was so disturbing, so real, that as he looked upon her now, the memory of it chilled his spine despite the eighty-eight-degree temperature.

"You look like shit, Marcus." Julia said half in jest. "Can I get you anything?"

Marcus shook his head.

"Okay, then can you please explain why you were running over here so quickly?"

"It's . . ." Marcus was at a loss for words, unable to speak of what he had just seen on the cell phone screen two minutes earlier.

"You heard about my near death?"

Marcus was in shock, confused about what she was referring to.

"I still can't get over all of those people . . . dead. The plane just falling out of the sky." Melancholy filled her voice. "I'm so lucky to be alive. I'm tasting every breath, I'll never take life for granted again. It makes you believe in fate, Marcus. I almost died today."

Marcus stepped back into his library looking as if he had just been punched in the gut. He stood there a moment, trying to regain his composure.

"Is this some kind of sick joke?" Marcus said, his chest swelling in anger as he yelled. "Don't screw with me."

Nick sat in the leather chair staring at his friend and shook his head. "I would never joke around with something like this."

Marcus collapsed into the high-back wing

chair by his desk, emotionally exhausted. He looked around the room for two minutes; Nick could see his mind working. Marcus closed his eyes and put his head back.

"You're asking a lot. This an awfully big leap of faith, Nick."

"I know," Nick said quietly. His eyes pleaded with his friend. "I'm sorry to involve you, but you're the one person I trust, the one person I know who wouldn't think I was insane for telling this story."

"Do you see me in the future?"

"Yeah, a few hours from now." Nick nodded. "You're right by my side; you're my advocate when they try to say I'm the one who killed Julia."

"My God." Marcus placed his hands over his temples and squeezed as if he was keeping his head from exploding. "This is insane."

"I know." Nick nodded.

"How does it work?"

"I can't explain it," Nick said quietly. "And this could all be some nightmare, but I know she dies if I don't find her killer."

"And what will you do when you find him?"

"I don't care about the consequences."

"You didn't answer my question," Marcus said.

"You know exactly what I'm going to do."

"And if there is more than one?"

Nick stared at him. "I'll kill them all."

Marcus walked over to his brass-rail bar, grabbed two Tiffany crystal glasses off the shelf and poured two Johnny Walker Blue Label scotches. He walked back and handed one to Nick. "I don't know about you, but I need something to calm my mind, to keep me from slipping into confusion."

"Thanks," Nick said, tilting his glass in appreciation toward Marcus. "I need to find whoever pulls that trigger," Nick said.

"If you get her out of here, out of Byram Hills, she won't be home when the gunmen arrives."

"True, and I do send her away, an hour and a half from now, but that's not going to stop them from coming for her. Julia avoided death by not being on that plane, yet she was killed later in the day. Who's to say if I pull her away from that bullet they won't just kill her later? That's why I have to find the man who pulls the trigger now while I still have a way, while I still have time on my side."

"I can barely keep this straight in my head," Marcus said.

"Believe me, I've been dealing with this for hours and I still can't get my hands around it," Nick said. "Every move I make has repercussions, consequences on the events I already saw happen. By coming here, by telling you all of this, I'm changing the future in ways I can't foresee.

"Three hours from now, because I've told you what happens, you won't try to stop me from going into my own house to try to figure out who killed Julia; three and a half hours from now, you won't find me with her body; in four hours you won't lead me back here to your house, offer me scotch." Nick held up his glass, "and be a friend.

"We sat right in this very room. You called your buddy, Mitch Shuloff, said he was the best attorney but that he'd be late. Plus he owes you a grand for the Yankee win last night."

Marcus stared at Nick as if he had just performed a miracle. "I never told anyone that. That's totally nuts."

"Well, everything changes now."

"Nick," Marcus said, looking at his friend. "Some things don't change. I'll still do all that for you."

"No," Nick said.

"Yeah —"

"No, you won't, you won't be here, because I'm asking you to take Julia and get as far away from Byram Hills as you can.

Don't let her out of your sight."

"But I thought you already did that, that she leaves an hour and change from now?"

"I did, she drove off at 5:59, but if you go with her, if she leaves with you within this hour instead of an hour and a half from now, she'll have someone looking out for her, she'll be that much safer."

"You know I'd do anything for you guys."

"I know," Nick said, his head nod saying so much more.

"You know my buddy, Ben Taylor? I think we'll go hang out with him. She'll be in pretty good shape at the home of an ex-military guy."

"Great."

"How will I know when everything's safe?"

"I'll find you."

"What if I don't hear from you?"

"Then go to the police, because I'll be dead."

Nick quickly brought Marcus up to speed, telling him everything that had happened to him in each hour, and telling him what information he had gathered, from the St. Christopher medal, to the blue Impala, to the flying bullets at Julia's office, to what he had just seen in Hennicot's place.

"Let me ask you a question," Marcus said.

"On the bottom of the letter, there was that strange writing . . ."

Nick pulled out the letter and looked at the bottom:

[strange symbolic writing — four lines of unrecognizable characters]

"I'm not sure what it says," Nick said. "I've never seen that language before."

"Neither have I, but I don't have time to worry about it."

"What ultimately happens to you?" Marcus asked.

"They arrest me for her murder."

"My God, this is insane."

"That's what you say when they come to arrest me right here." Nick pointed at the library.

"You're arrested?" Marcus asked in disbelief. "Here?"

"You nearly knocked out the cops trying to stop them." Nick smiled. "I never thanked you for that."

"You're welcome," Marcus said with confusion. "I think — this is nuts."

"They kick in your door."

"What door?" Marcus asked through gritted teeth.

"Two doors, actually," Nick said apologetically. "Front and library."

"Dammit. They're both expensive."

"But you'll be happy to know the Yankees beat the Red Sox again."

"Ooh, that's another thousand Mitch owes me. I should give him a call now, offer him double or nothing."

"They win off a Jeter grand slam in the bottom of the ninth, six to five."

"Oh, I'm definitely calling him."

Nick smiled but it faded as he handed a sheet of paper to Marcus. "I've got the license plate of the car driven by her killer."

"Nick," Marcus said, trying to be a voice of reason in an illogical situation. "Give it to the police."

"For a murder that hasn't happened?"

"You can't screw around with this. Call them."

"I already did; they weren't very helpful." Nick took a deep breath. "Every cop in town is at the crash site. No one is going to deal with this before she is killed."

"You should show them the picture on your phone."

"They'd lock me up as crazy and then

she'd still die."

Nick picked the watch up off the desk and looked at the time: 4:30. "Please, help me find who owns the car? I don't have a lot of time."

Marcus looked at Nick with sympathetic eyes as he picked up and dialed his phone. "Helen?" he said, and continued without waiting for her response, "I need you to pull Nancy, Jim, Kevin, George, Jean, KC, Jackie, and Steve into the conference room now. Fire drill."

"Can I borrow your computer?" Nick whispered.

Marcus nodded as Nick sat down in front of the three screens, each filled with financial models, stock tickers, and news wires.

"Use the center one," Marcus said he walked out of the library, the phone pressed to his ear. "This is what I need . . ."

Nick placed the Palm Pilot in front of the computer and sent the files via infrared to Marcus's system. As before, six files popped up on the screen.

He quickly jumped to the second file, the multiple video images filling the screen. There was no audio, giving the footage a cheap, student-film feel. With a click of the mouse, Nick highlighted and enlarged an image, allowing him to focus entirely on the large, brushed-steel door. He fast-forwarded to the point of the door slowly opening to reveal the dark-haired man and froze the video.

He hit print and pulled the grainy but distinctive image from the printer. The man was painfully thin, dressed in a white oxford, his face gaunt, his eyes hidden behind sunglasses.

Nick looked hard at the printed image and back up to its original on the monitor, but couldn't see inside the collar of the man's shirt. Nick dug in his pocket and pulled out the St. Christopher medal, checking its length, realizing that it would hang below the man's shirt to at least the second button.

Nick clicked play and watched the video for a few more seconds before the image turned to white snow. He fast-forwarded through twenty more minutes of the white static before the file ended.

He went on to the third file, finding images of bedrooms and living rooms, fast-forwarding, finding no movement throughout the twenty-minute snippet. On the fourth and fifth files he saw images he recognized, images of the safe, the storage facility, views of hallways and conference rooms. The images cycled from the unbroken display case where a host of elegant swords, knives, and guns had rested before they were snatched away, to Hennicot's office, to the imposing steel safes where both doors were closed and secured. Then, starting at 11:15 on the time print, the images from both files turned to white snow.

Nick clicked on the sixth and final file, but instantly hit a roadblock. A window popped up stating File Not Recognized. He checked it again, reloading it from the Palm Pilot as Marcus came back into the room.

"It looks encrypted," Marcus said, looking over Nick's shoulder. "Probably an eyes-only file."

Nick pulled out and looked at the pocket watch. Only ten minutes left in the hour. He hadn't gleaned as much information from the files as he thought he would.

"What did you find?" Marcus asked.

"Not much." Nick handed the printed image of the man to Marcus. "It looks like the robbery started at 11:15 on the button."

"Okay," Marcus said as he studied the picture. "You've got a face. That's a pretty good start."

"If I had a month, yeah. I've only got a few more hours."

"You may have gotten a face but I got a bit more," Marcus said, reading from the fax printout in his hand. "Your Chevy is a rental."

"Shit." Nick shook his head.

"Relax," Marcus read through the fax as he handed Nick a picture of a square-faced man, his blond hair brushed back. Judging by the collar of his shirt and the width of his tie, it was obviously an old image, at least twenty years old. "His name is Paul Dreyfus."

Nick compared the two images. Nowhere near the same man.

"How the hell am I supposed to use that? He can be any schmo riding around."

"Give me a little more credit, will you? I had everyone in my office drop what they were doing and check this guy out." Marcus continued reading. "Pretty successful guy, lives on the Main Line in Haverford, Pennsylvania. Married, two kids, pretty boring life. Doesn't like to do much except fly his own plane."

"He came from Philly?" Nick said, surprised.

"Get this. My guys are so thorough," Marcus said with pride as he looked at Nick. "He flew up in his own plane today into Westchester Airport, but when we checked, there's no record of him departing out of any airport in Philly or Jersey."

"Maybe you missed an airport, does it really matter where he came in from?"

"We don't know yet, Sherlock," Marcus said with a smile. "Hertz has a contract with his firm. They delivered the vehicle to the private jet terminal at 8:35 this morning. Right to him as he exited his plane."

"Okay," Nick said, urging his friend on. "If he's going to commit a robbery then why leave an obvious paper trail by renting a car?"

"One piece at a time, okay?" Marcus said. "He works for DSG, he's known as the security guru to the wealthy. Next to Michael St. Pierre at Secure Systems, he's thought to be the best security system designer in the business. He's the CEO, the owner actually, along with his brother Sam. They're the top security company in the country. He *is* Dreyfus Security Group."

"It was an inside job," Nick said matter-of-factly.

"From what my people can find, he's got over fifty million in various assets around the globe. He's worth a hell of a lot. My bet is he probably made his money with sticky fingers or selling pass codes."

"No, wouldn't work," Nick said. "If word gets out that even one of his security systems failed — you said he's the chief designer

191

and the CEO — he'd be out of business and under investigation in a heartbeat."

"True, but the fact that he is here on the day of the robbery . . . ?"

"On the face of it, he's the inside guy, but there are others, and he is not the murderer."

"When my people initially looked for Dreyfus, the name came up as being on the 8:30 out of Philly."

"You said he got his car at 8:35. That doesn't make sense," Nick said.

"I know, but this is what makes things even odder. The Dreyfus on the plane was Sam Dreyfus, his brother. The flight got into Westchester at 10:10 this morning."

"Brothers working together."

"So one brother preps everything, picks up the other, they do the job and spend the next several hours erasing their tracks —"

"And killing Julia," Nick somberly added.

"I'll bet you the two thousand dollars that Mitch owes me that they were going to fly out of here tonight after killing her. But that's not going to happen. Is it?" Marcus said with a smile. " 'Cause Julia is going to be fine, she's going to live."

"Thanks," Nick said.

"Don't say thanks. It's a fact." Marcus nodded strongly. "You know, you've got the names of the Dreyfus brothers, you've got a picture of one of them, you've got a picture of one of the thieves who broke into Hennicot's place. If I were you, I'd go to the police with it. Tell them about the robbery, tell them you're sure they're after Julia, let them start an investigation while you look separately."

Nick smiled. "Do me a favor?"

"Another favor? Boy are you going to owe me."

"Write yourself a note."

"What, why?"

"Because I still need your help."

"I'm not going to stop helping you. I'm not going to give up on you."

"I know." Nick smiled, glad to have a friend in Marcus. "But when I see you again, it will be a few hours earlier, you won't remember any of this. And I can't go through the hell of convincing you again."

"This is nuts." Marcus quickly reached into his desk and pulled out a sheet of his personal stationery.

"Be sure to write things only you would know." Nick said. "If it's something I know about you, or something obvious, you won't be convinced."

"Dear Me," Marcus said with half a chuckle before growing serious. He wrote quickly, finishing in less than two minutes. He signed the letter, reached into his desk drawer, and pulled out a corporate seal. He slipped it over his signature, squeezing the handle and embossing the quickly written note.

"The raised seal on my signature is my personal seal," Marcus said. "No one has it. I only use it on corporate documents and only over my signature to verify its validity in transactions. There is only one such seal in existence."

Marcus folded the note, pulled out an envelope, and slipped it inside.

"Wait a minute," Marcus said as he spun around to his computer. He clicked on the Internet and pulled up the *Wall Street Journal* home page. The main headline was all about the crash of Flight 502, and next to it was the financial information on the daily closing numbers for the DOW, the S&P 500, the Russell Index, and the ten-year Treasury, while below were the latest financial headlines. He quickly hit print, grabbed the printout and stuffed it into the envelope.

"If I'm going to tell myself about the future, I might as well give some proof that has profit potential," Marcus said with a smile as he sealed the envelope and quickly addressed it to himself.

"I'm going to think both you and I are crazy when I read this," Marcus said as he handed the letter to Nick, who slipped it in the inside pocket of his sport coat.

"As long as it's convincing, I don't care what you think."

Nick looked at his watch: 4:59.

"I need you to get Julia out of here," Nick said. "Promise me, you'll take care of her."

"Hey, it's me," Marcus said, trying to reassure him.

"And if something should happen to me . . ."

"If anything happens to you, I'll raise an army to find the bastards and they'll regret every breath they ever took."

Nick smiled, his eyes filled with appreciation for his friend, and walked out of the library. He went across the foyer and quickly through the front door.

Marcus caught sight of Nick through the bay window walking across the long side yard to his house. He suddenly thought of something and ran out behind him, ripping open the front door. "Hey, what about . . . ?"

But the long side yard, the expansive field between their homes, was empty.

Nick was gone as if he had vanished into thin air.

CHAPTER 6

3:00 P.M.

Sullivan Field was a large stretch of land two miles outside the center of town. A mix of various sporting fields, it had been donated to the town by International Data Systems six years earlier in exchange for generous real estate tax incentives for their sprawling headquarters nearby. They not only provided the land but hired the architects, construction crews, and landscapers to build one of the best public sporting facilities in the state whose sole purpose was to provide a venue for the athletic endeavors, passions, and entertainment of school-age children.

There were baseball fields with dugouts and bleachers, soccer and lacrosse fields, tennis and basketball courts. There were football fields, a full track, an outdoor hockey rink that was open November through March. There was a central building with lockers, bathrooms, and a nursery for young children whose parents wanted to watch their older siblings kick, smack, or just throw a ball around.

The grass was as good as that of a golf course, with a full sprinkler system throughout, while landscaping crews saw to the upkeep of lush bushes and flowers that ran about the perimeter.

The fields lay just two miles northwest of the airport and provided a perfect vantage point from which to watch the planes coming and going on their daily journeys to and from Westchester Airport.

Finding a silver lining to a tragic event, an incident involving the deaths of 212 people, would seem an impossibility, except that it was a Friday in summer. School was out. The local camp was on the other side of town. The fields were mercifully vacant as eighty tons of jet slammed into the soccer fields, cratering a hole ten feet deep, the devastation of the tumbling and twisting aircraft dragging on for half a mile through the baseball diamonds and the football fields, finally stopping a quarter mile short of the locker facilities.

Intended for far more joyous purposes, that building had become the staging area for the recovery and cleanup effort of

Flight 502.

Fire trucks from all over the county formed a wagon train–like corral around the wreckage. Thousands of gallons of water steamed off the still-hot, smoldering ground. Firemen sat on the running boards of their trucks physically and emotionally exhausted from their efforts, devastated that all their actions couldn't save a single life.

A small contingent of National Guard stood watch over the site, never having imagined their stateside service would entail such tragedy.

The plane had been torn to shreds, as if some creature had sunk its teeth into a soda can and ripped it apart. The white tail section seemed to rise out of the ground at the edge of the woods, the North East Air logo unblemished by the flames, its registration number, N95301, still legible. It was the only piece that would give any indication that the objects in this debris field had once been part of a passenger jet.

The acrid smell of death hovered in the air, the odor of burned flesh, molten metal, and scorched earth enough to induce sickness if the images hadn't already taken one down that path. With a full load of highly flammable jet fuel, the aircraft was a fireball as it hit the ground, the heat of the initial blast scorching trees and plants a quarter mile away. The fireball rose in a great mushroom cloud visible for miles, while the black smoke darkened the sky, blotting out the sun for hours, only to be replaced by the steaming white smoke of the flames' watery defeat. Oddly, while much of the wreckage was burned beyond recognition, some had escaped untouched

Shards of aluminum skin lay twisted about the muddy earth, luggage was open and scattered. The sight of women's blouses and children's sneakers laid bare the magnitude and human devastation of what had happened.

And there were the bodies, over two hundred. Men, woman, and children. None recognizable, no one whole. Hundreds of white sheets, their edges muddy and wet, dotted the area, the grim reminder of the death that lay beneath them, the death that comes without warning.

Grieving family members were held back by townsfolk and family. Shrieks of agony, of loss echoed the air, the only sound besides the hissing, steaming ground. No one spoke. Eye contact was avoided.

Nothing was moved while the NTSB examined the wreckage and secured the black boxes, the recorders of life up until the moment of death.

Small yellow flags, bar coded and numbered, were placed next to every piece of debris, cataloguing the destruction so computer models could be formulated, enabling experts to analyze the cause of the incident. While the NTSB's combing of the debris, their meticulous reconstruction of the moments leading up to the point of the crash, was intended to solve a mystery, their directive, as always, was to prevent future occurrences, to help with the implementation of new guidelines so the particular yet-to-be-determined cause would not lead to another such event.

As Nick drove toward Sullivan Fields there was no way of avoiding the sight of the crash. The access road descended into the sunken, almost valleylike field, circling the perimeter and revealing the tragedy in all of its devastation. Over one hundred ambulances lay in wait, the EMTs' and paramedics' job now simply being the transportation of remains to the morgue.

Cars and trucks of volunteers lined the road, intermixed with army jeeps and several off-road vehicles. People walked by on their way out with hunched shoulders and tear-streaked faces.

Nick had rounded the bend of the final corner before the entrance to the field proper when he was abruptly stopped by a National Guardsman in full army greens, an M-16 rifle slung over his back. He circled his hand in the air, indicating Nick should turn around and leave, all of which Nick ignored as he rolled down his window.

"Sir," the Guardsman said as he approached. "Got to get out of here."

"I need to see the police," Nick said, talking over the younger man.

"What seems to be the problem? Maybe I could help."

Nick looked at the young blond reservist. He couldn't have been more than twenty-five, surely educated with the help of government loans that required years of service to your country in return.

"I need to see the police and I need them now."

"You're going to have to explain it to me," the young and eager soldier said, clearly enjoying his first taste of authority. "You're not allowed in there."

Nick stuck his finger out the window, curling it toward himself, bidding the solider to come close enough so he could read the name on the left side of his chest, and spoke in a soft, even tone, "Private McManus?"

"Yes, sir?"

"What's your first name?"

"Neil."

"I suppose you know how to use that weapon, Neil?"

"Top of my class in riflery."

"Well, good for you." Nick nodded. "Someone is trying to kill my wife, Neil, and I really need to see the police about it."

Seeing the sincerity in his eyes, McManus quickly waved Nick into the crash site. "They're stationed at the locker house."

If the prevailing impression out on the access road was one of death, then what greeted him as he inched into the main parking lot past the scores of emergency vehicles was nothing short of hell.

Stepping from the car and looking about, Nick momentarily forgot his own situation. He had never been to war, but he now knew what it looked like as he stared at the charred remains that scattered the once-pristine playing fields.

Hundreds of people swarmed the crash site, looking like ants on the blackened landscape. Some hovered over bodies, pulling back the white sheets to examine the charred remains, trying to figure out if they were looking at an adult or a child, male or female. Others marked debris, looking for clues, while still others photographed and videotaped the devastation.

Nick walked through the sea of people, past the news trucks and the temporary generators that provided power to the response team, past the flatbeds containing enormous halogen lights that would illuminate the shattered earth as the night fell, allowing the nonstop operation to maintain its twenty-four-hour vigilance.

Nick finally arrived at the command post set up under a series of tents that adjoined the brick locker house building. Card tables and metal chairs were set in an orderly fashion along the wall, temporary phones and computers had been hastily assembled, brought in from businesses and the local school to supplement the desktop and notebook units brought by the National Guard.

Nick found the table where a hastily scribbled sign read *Byram Hills Police.* A broad-shouldered older man sat behind the table, his gray hair desperately trying to hold on to its last bit of original black color. Nick recognized him at once as the man who interrupted his interrogation six hours from now.

"Captain Delia?" Nick asked.

"Yes." The captain looked up with weary eyes. "How can I help you?"

"I . . ." Nick paused, unsure how to start. "I know this a difficult day for you and everyone but I have a situation that requires immediate attention."

The captain gave a half nod for him to continue.

"There was a robbery this morning, a pretty substantial robbery. Over $25 million in antiques and jewels were stolen, from Washington House over on Maple."

"I heard nothing of this." Delia tilted his head in surprise.

"My wife is one of the owner's attorneys; she was notified of the robbery and has confirmed its occurrence."

"Of all days. Dammit!" The captain stood up, looking around, the weariness falling from his eyes, to be replaced with frustration. "I don't know who I can send over there. We're already stretched thin. Has the place been secured?"

"Yes," Nick said. "But that's not why I'm here."

"You here to confess?" He paused, wiping a sweaty strand of hair from his face, immediately regretting his statement. "Sorry, it's been a long day."

Nick looked away for a moment, debating crossing the point of no return before finally turning back. "Whoever committed this crime is after my wife."

"What do you mean 'after your wife'?" The captain grew suddenly serious.

"To kill her."

"And how do you know that?"

"They've already destroyed her office."

Delia took a moment. "Any idea who?"

Nick pulled out the printed picture. "This man is involved, but I'm not sure how, nor do I know who he is."

"What's this from?" the captain asked as he studied the picture.

"Security feed. The other faces didn't show up before video interference obscured everything. And I do believe the security company may be involved." Nick stopped, hoping the captain was convinced. "It's a start, right?"

The captain said nothing as he continued looking at the picture.

"There's a blue Chevy Impala that has circled our house," Nick lied about the car he had seen in the future, the car carrying the men who came to kill Julia. "Its license plate traces back to Hertz, and it was rented by a man named Paul Dreyfus. His firm handled part of the security for the building that was robbed."

"And you're a detective?" Captain Delia asked skeptically.

"No."

"Then how do you know all this so quickly?" There was suspicion in his voice.

"If someone was trying to kill *your* wife, you'd be amazed at how resourceful you'd become."

Delia digested Nick's words and nodded. "Where's your wife now?"

"She's with friends." Nick wasn't actually sure where she was in this hour, but he thought it best to not say too much until a trust had developed.

The captain picked up the walkie-talkie from the table and thumbed the button on the side. "Bob?"

"Yeah," the voice came back, overly loud and static-filled.

"Get your ass up here," the captain barked before laying the radio back on the table and turning back to Nick. "I'll tell you now, being as honest as I can be, we've got no men to spare. If a gun isn't being held to your wife's head, it's hard to assess whether the danger exists at all. I understand your concern, but whoever committed the crime — something we will investigate and solve — they're probably long gone and won't risk hanging around to be caught."

The captain sat back down, resumed filling out paperwork, and picked up the phone.

Nick turned and looked around. The door to the locker building swung open, the sound of grieving poured out. They had the building set up for the relatives of the deceased, a diverse collection of people from around the county who never imagined the day they would be facing as they woke up. Nick understood their pain, their agony, having endured the death of Julia, having stood over her violated body.

When faced with the sudden death of a loved one, the mind runs in all directions: rage, anger, self-pity, guilt, sorrow, finality, and even to the impossible: the what-ifs, the if-onlys. What if he got stuck in traffic and missed his plane? What if I just said she couldn't go and waited until Monday? What if I didn't make him change his flight to today so I could go to the shore next week?

. . . what if she was suddenly called off the plane for a business matter?

Nick knew himself lucky, blessed. He could be standing alone in that building, sharing his grief with strangers with no chance of Julia ever coming back. She had been on the very jet that lay twisted in the distant field, checked in, her carry-on stowed, her seat belt buckled, on the aircraft whose destination was death.

But Julia was saved, plucked from destiny, pulled off to survive . . .

. . . for all of seven hours. Seven hours of life given back by a twist of fate, by a crime of greed that she never would have the opportunity to understand. Shot down in the end by the very people whose actions saved her life.

As Nick heard the sobbing of children whose fathers wouldn't be coming home as they promised, of wives left to face the world alone, he thought of the watch in his pocket and wondered why he was in the middle of this twisted daydream trying to pull Julia from her grave. Was it all a fantasy, a dream of hope that he couldn't escape? He had watched as the hours flowed backward, as the unexplainable embraced him. He had seen Julia dead on the floor only to see her alive in the kitchen moments later — moments that existed in his time of reference, in his current flow of living, running contrary to that of everyone else around him.

As the door to the locker facility slowly closed, trapping the sounds of mourning within, he brought himself back to his current reality. He would shut out all of the il-logic, all of the pain he had experienced. Against the laws of physics so elegantly stated by Einstein, he would bridge the gap of time with his heart. He would pull Julia from the jaws of fate for the second time this day. He would make the *what if* happen.

With full resolve, Nick turned to find the captain talking to a tall, muscled man in a tight-fitting black shirt, his badge and gun worn on the belt of his blue jeans. His hands were darkened by soot, streaked with sweat. His tousled black hair told the story of his day.

"Mr. Quinn," the captain called him over.

Nick approached the detective, hoping he finally had an ally who would listen and help him stop Julia's killer.

"Mr. Quinn, this is Bob Shannon."

Nick turned around and looked straight into Shannon's slate-blue eyes, and a wave of panic fell upon him as he realized who he was looking at.

"Bob Shannon." The detective held out his hand in greeting.

Nick's world spun. For standing before him was the man who had arrested him in the future, who had treated him as something less than a rodent. The man who in the interrogation room had wielded a billy

209

club; who had screamed and accused Nick of murdering Julia; who had held a gun to his head with every intention of pulling the trigger.

The look in Shannon's eyes was one shared by most of the volunteers Nick had seen today: exhaustion, devastation, and hopelessness.

"What's up?" Shannon asked.

Nick's eyes fell to Shannon's neck, his tight-fitting black shirt unbuttoned in the heat, exposing his well-muscled chest. There was no St. Christopher medal there, which eased his mind a little about trusting the police.

Nick didn't know where to start, finding it hard to shake the fear that the man would somehow recognize him and shoot him for his escaping the interrogation room. Reminding himself that that was yet to happen, he said, "Someone is after my wife."

"What do you mean 'after'?" There was a weariness in Shannon's voice.

"Trying to kill her."

"Shit," Shannon said with surprising concern. "Okay, what's your name?"

"Nick Quinn."

"And your wife's?"

"Julia."

Shannon led him over to a corner of the

tent, pulled up two folding chairs, and took a seat, indicating Nick to follow suit. "Can I get you a drink: water, soda, or something?"

Nick shook his head as he sat down.

"Why don't you tell me what's going on?" Shannon said.

Nick told him of the robbery, of Julia's computer's being swiped from her office. He explained how the thieves were erasing their tracks, each word out of his mouth carefully chosen so as not to indicate anything from the future.

"May I ask where she is now?"

"She's . . ." Nick paused. Though Shannon didn't appear like the animal he had been in the interrogation room, he had yet to earn Nick's trust, so he thought it best to hold back some truths. Though he didn't know exactly where she was, he lied. "She's with friends."

"Alone?"

"She's with some coworkers at one of their homes in Bedford."

"Why didn't she come with you?"

"She's scared, she didn't want to leave. And she said she couldn't bear coming down here."

"I understand that," Shannon said, looking out at the mayhem.

"Yeah, she was supposed to be on that plane."

"Whoa." Shannon's eyes went wide with surprise "Okay, you failed to mention that."

"She got off because she got a text message about the robbery in progress."

Shannon sat there, his face registering the irony. "Fate is so unpredictable. She must be a mess, thinking she lived only to be in the gun sight of some maniac."

Nick began to see sympathy in Shannon. There was more to him than the single-note man who arrested him. "Are you married?"

"I was. My wife couldn't handle being married to a cop. She didn't think the pay matched the risk."

"Sorry."

"Her loss," Shannon said quickly. "She just doesn't get it. Life's not about money, its not about getting paid for risking one's life for others. You do it because it's the right thing to do."

Nick began to see the world a bit from Shannon's point of view. When Shannon had interrogated him, he had thought he was interrogating a killer, a husband who murdered his wife. While his intensity had been intimidating, it was part of his process, part of getting to the truth of a murder, and when Nick grabbed the other detective's gun . . . Well, Shannon reacted as anyone would have.

"Listen, I know you think your wife is in danger," Shannon said. "And I believe you. If I was in your shoes, I'd come right to us. It's the right thing, the best thing to do.

"Even with the information you mentioned on the people who own the security company, you're asking for us to track down these individuals on a day where minds can't possibly think straight, and electrical power is haphazard at best. Now, I'll tell you, I'm good, we're good, but not that good. From the security you described, these people knew exactly what they were doing, they're well informed and intelligent, and if they're that good, the evidence they left behind is minimal. Not to say there isn't any, but it's going to take manpower, something we're sorely lacking in."

Nick knew Shannon's words to be true; he had drawn the same conclusion in his mind. The chances of finding Julia's killer were slim, but then again, what were the chances of being called off a plane just before it crashed? The last six hours he had experienced were impossible, beyond the imagination, yet they had happened — it was a day where odds could be beaten and he was not about to give up so easily.

"I printed this out from the security tapes," Nick said as he handed Shannon the picture of the dark-haired thief from the video feed.

"I'd like to see the rest of this tape." Shannon studied the man's face before finally looking up. "Let me ask you a question. You said the security system at Washington House was disabled and that the backup in your wife's office was stolen. If that's the case, you're not telling me something."

Nick silently berated himself for his foolishness. He had wanted to keep the information on Julia's PDA private, as he knew that was her killer's ultimate goal. "She had the info backed up from her computer," Nick admitted, knowing that if he appeared secretive suspicions would rise.

"Well, I definitely need to see that. Where is it?"

"In my car," Nick said. It was actually in his pocket but the walk to his car would give him a few minutes to decide whether he was making the right move.

"There's also a blue Chevy that drove by my home. A rental car leased by Paul Dreyfus. His company did the security for the building where the robbery took place."

"Okay, well, between the security video backup you have, the car, and this guy

Dreyfus, we've got some pieces to work with. I'll tell you what, let's take a ride over to Washington House, you never know, we may just get lucky." Shannon rose from his chair.

"There's nothing to find," Nick said.

"There's always something to find," Shannon said confidently as the captain came over, hearing the end of the conversation.

"Why don't you take Dance with you as backup?" Delia said, more as a statement than a question.

"I'll be fine," Shannon said, more than a little annoyed.

"I don't recall giving you the option. I'll have him meet you down by your car."

"This is just the worst nightmare I've ever been in. Nothing prepares you for this," Shannon said as they walked down the road that wound about the fields where the wreckage scattered the grounds. "We all have those morbid thoughts of how we'll die. They're few and far between but I can guarantee 90 percent of the world fears death in an airplane above all else. Helpless, trapped inside a metal tube, your heart in your throat as you're tossed about, catching glimpses of the ground rushing toward you out the porthole windows. Don't let your wife come down here — seeing this will send her over the edge."

Nick couldn't pull his eyes from the blackened ground, from the white sheet-covered bodies that seemed to lie everywhere. "No one should ever have to see something like this."

"Makes you wish you could stop it," Shannon said. "Ease all of this suffering."

"Over forty thousand people are killed in the United States in car accidents every year. That's like 120 a day. Yet we don't react to that. But something like this happens, it haunts us for the rest of our lives." Nick shook his head. "Do they know the cause?"

"Does it matter?" Shannon said. "I've heard rumors, but it's not going to change a thing, it's not going to bring these people back."

They walked silently for the remaining half mile past the host of emergency vehicles, red lights uselessly spinning and flashing. Fourteen news cameras focused on fourteen slick, talking-head reporters conveying death with collagened lips and perfect hair, each hoping to top the other in the evening's ratings.

"Shit," Nick said, seeing his car boxed in by two fire trucks and an ambulance treating an overcome, hysterical relative of one of the victims. He wasn't about to press anyone to unblock him.

"Don't worry about it." Shannon said. "I'll drive. Why don't you get the backup security file out of your car. I'm the black Mustang up there." Shannon pointed at the slick muscle car fifty yards up the crowded road.

Nick nodded as he opened his car and feigned grabbing something from his glove compartment, pretending to place it in his breast pocket where Julia's PDA already rested. He hoped he wasn't creating a greater jeopardy than Julia was already in but knew if Shannon was to help him, he would need to see and know *almost* everything.

"You can't handle this on your own?" a man in a cheap blazer and bad tie said on approach.

"Nick Quinn?" Shannon said. "Say hi to Detective Ethan Dance."

Nick extended his hand but Dance didn't even bother to look his way.

"We've got 212 victims here, I'm sifting through wreckage and death, and I have to come and hold your hand?" Dance said as he stormed right by them. "I'm in no mood to go to some compromised crime scene.

I'm going to the station to change. If you want my help that's the only place you're getting it."

Nick thought this was not the "good cop" that had arrested him, that had interrogated him with charm and a smile. Sweat was gathered at his temples, running down his cheeks, as he huffed and puffed from carrying his worn-out body up the road. Aggravation burned in his drooping, bloodshot eyes, his cheap loafers covered in mud, his gray pants caked halfway up his calves.

"Listen." Shannon pulled Nick aside as Dance kept walking. "Dance is an asshole but he's a really good detective. Go with him to the station. Let him take a look at your video file. This guy can spot water in the Sahara, plus he can get more info on this Dreyfus guy. I'll go by Washington House and your wife's law firm. See what I can find."

Nick nodded and jogged up to Dance, who took off his JC Penney jacket and threw it in the backseat of his green Ford Taurus. The underarms of his white shirt bloomed with large perspiration stains. Nick opened the passenger door, silently getting in next to Dance, who slammed the driver's-side door in anger.

Without a word Dance started up his car

and spun out of his mud-filled parking spot. He cut off two exiting cars and drove out of the disaster response staging area.

Streams of volunteers, municipal workers, and National Guardsmen flowed in and out of the area, marching silently up and down the access road that had, up until this morning, only known minivans and SUVs filled with kids and soccer moms en route to fun.

As they drove out, the parked cars thinning out, Nick couldn't believe his eyes as they drove past the blue Chevy Impala. He caught sight of the license plate and confirmed it was Dreyfus's rental.

"Stop," Nick said.

Dance ignored him.

"Stop. That's the car I was telling Shannon and your captain about. The son of a bitch is here."

Dance said nothing to Nick as he picked up the walkie-talkie on his seat and thumbed the talk button. "Captain?"

"You got to be kidding me, Dance," Captain Delia shot back. "You're gone all of three minutes and there's an issue?"

"Send a Guardsman out to the side road where all of the local volunteers parked. Blue Chevy. License plate —" he turned to Nick to finish his sentence.

"— Z8JP9."

219

"Tell him to unobtrusively watch the vehicle. Make sure he knows what that word means. When the guy shows up to leave, have him detained until we get back."

"Gotcha," Delia said.

"Relax." Dance finally spoke to Nick. "If that guy is here he won't get out."

"Why would he come here?"

"That'll be the first question you can ask him when we get back." Dance said as he wiped his sweaty brow with the sleeve of his white shirt and pushed his moist brown hair back off his face.

They drove out through the slow-moving traffic, Dance didn't bother to throw on his siren or lights; it wouldn't move anyone along any faster.

"Sorry about being so short with you," Dance said. "Shannon's kind of an asshole, he's got a tendency to piss me off, and this is the fourth time today."

"It's okay, this is a bad day for everyone," Nick said.

"Your wife's okay though, right?"

Nick nodded.

Dance loosened his tie, taking it off and throwing it in the back. He unbuttoned the top two buttons of his shirt and directed the a/c vent at himself, sighing as the cool air hit his body.

"The captain told me everything you and your wife have been going through today. When something like this happens, we get blinded to the rest of the world, forgetting it's still moving despite the tragedies we face."

As Nick listened to Dance's short speech, he couldn't help looking at the detective's exposed neck, looking for the St. Christopher medal, before admonishing himself for his paranoia.

They finally emerged from the long access road back onto Route 22, finding it eerily empty, in sharp contrast to the chaos behind them.

"So, they said you have a copy of the security video?"

"Yeah." Nick nodded, patting the breast pocket of his blazer.

"Did you look at it?"

"Just parts, but I saw one face. I've got a printout, if you want to take a look. But there's a lot of snow, they seemed to have disabled the cameras at some point."

"All right. We'll check it out at the station. You don't mind if I shower first, do you?"

Nick shook his head, instantly regretting it, knowing that the clock was ticking. His time with Dance was limited. He needed to glean as much info as he could before the hour was up.

"I feel like I'm covered in death."

"What time do you have?" Nick didn't want to pull out the watch.

The car approached a green-railed bridge, a quarter-mile span that rose fifty feet above the Kensico Reservoir, one of the most peaceful sites in all of Byram Hills.

"Three-forty-five," Dance said.

"I hate to ask this, but . . . do you think, maybe, we could . . . it's just, my wife — who knows where . . ."

Dance looked at him, his face unreadable, before he finally nodded. "Sure, I didn't mean to be insensitive. We're only a minute from the station. We're on a generator, we'll dive right in."

"Thanks." Nick smiled, regretting not turning to the police earlier. He could have been much farther along in finding Julia's killer.

"Do you me a favor?" Dance tilted his head toward the rear of the car. "On the backseat is my gym bag, can you grab it?"

"Of course," Nick unbuckled his seat belt, turned around, and awkwardly twisted around to grab the small canvas bag that was just beyond his fingertips' reach.

Without warning, Dance slammed on the brakes, the wheels locking up, the antilock system working overtime to avoid a skid as the car ground to a halt in the center of the bridge. Nick was hurled back into the dash, half his body thrown to the floor. A nine-millimeter Glock came to rest on his forehead.

"Hands on the dash," Dance yelled.

"What's the matter?" Nick said as he climbed up from the floor back onto the seat and complied, his hands shaking from the sudden change of events and the cold barrel pressing into his flesh.

Dance held the gun in his right hand as he used his left to pull out his cuffs and snap them over Nick's wrists, binding them together.

"What the — ?"

Dance pushed Nick forward and snatched Nick's Sig-Sauer from the waistband under the rear of his jacket, throwing it in the back of his car.

"Why are you carrying a concealed weapon?" Dance yelled.

"Relax —"

"Open your door, slowly. Step from the vehicle. And don't be an idiot."

"Relax." Nick gave a relieved smile. "I have a license for it. God, you scared me."

"Out now!" Dance flipped on his police lights, the overly bright red strobes disorienting as they flashed.

"Come on, I have a license for it," Nick said as he awkwardly opened the door with his bound hands and stepped from the car. Dance slid out right behind him.

"Hands on the bridge rail," Dance yelled as he walked to the rear of his car, popping open the trunk.

"Dance, please. What's the matter? I was carrying it for my wife's protection."

Nick couldn't see what Dance was doing but suddenly felt something wrap his lower legs as two large plastic ties were secured around his ankles.

"Come on, don't you think you're over-reacting?" Nick said as he looked at his now-secured legs.

Dance spun him around, reached into his jacket pocket, and pulled out Julia's PDA.

"Dance, now you're pissing me off. What the fuck are you doing?" Nick tilted his body to the left and looked into the open trunk and everything made sense.

The trunk was filled with duffel bags, one of them half open, and protruding from it, gleaming in the afternoon sun, was the gold pommel of a sword.

"You've got to be kidding me? You?"

Dance opened the rear door of his car, grabbed Nick's gun off the seat, took him by his collar, and shoved him in. Slamming the door, leaving Nick alone, locked inside.

Nick sat there staring over the seat at the ticking clock on the dashboard, the LED reading 3:50.

Everything began to make sense. Why he had been arrested, why Dance was running the investigation: He was controlling it all, involved in the robbery, Julia's murder, the cover up, his frame-up.

As bad as the situation had just gotten, Nick now knew the man responsible for Julia's death. He knew now who he had to stop.

For the next few minutes, it was all about staying alive. He needed to survive until the top of the hour.

The clock read 3:52. Nick had never felt time move so fast and so slowly at once.

Dance opened the rear door and, with his gun, motioned Nick to get out.

"You stay the hell away from my wife or so help me God —"

Nick fell instantly silent as Dance rested the barrel of the loaded gun against his lips to quiet him.

"Great thing, those PDAs, found your home phone number along with everyone she works with, friends, neighbors. Thought I'd give her a call, tell her to come on down to the station. Maybe tell her you've been injured —" Dance drew back his fist and punched Nick square in the mouth, drawing blood, sending his head snapping back. "That'll make her hurry. Of course, now we'll have to figure out who else knows, what friends you've involved."

Dance hoisted a large metal plate out of the trunk of his car, a heavy bicycle cable threaded through its center. With great difficulty he waddled forwarded, carrying it to the edge of the center span of the bridge, and dropped it with an enormous clang on the roadway.

"We were going to wait until this evening," Dance continued talking, "kill her at home, blame it on you, but seeing you've chosen to stick your nose in things, we'll just have to go kill her now."

Nick's heart fell. He hadn't saved Julia, his incompetence had actually moved up her murder. "Shannon's going to figure out what you've done."

"Screw Shannon, he couldn't think his way out of a paper bag."

Dance slid the hundred-pound plate underneath the green guardrail. He reached over and grabbed hold of the bicycle cable, holding it tightly in his left hand. Standing up, he pressed the gun to the back of Nick's head, urged him forward and, with his left hand, clipped the cable to the center chain of Nick's handcuffs.

"Did you ever have that feeling of déjà vu? Like you've done something before, been somewhere before? Like time is all upside-down?" Dance asked.

Nick couldn't believe what he was asking.

Dance pushed the plate with his foot, guiding it toward the edge, half of its iron weight hanging out over the reservoir.

And that's when Nick saw his chest. Dance's shirt hung wide open to his waist, the exertion of carrying the weight having popped open the three lower buttons. As dark as this man was, as much as he talked about killing Julia, he was not the man he had chased down and tackled. His neck was empty, there was no St. Christopher medal hanging against his chest.

Nick stood there, his belly pressed up against the green rail, looking out over the enormous lake, peaceful and still, in contrast to the horrific goings-on just a mile away, in contrast to the happenings on the bridge above. Dance was part of the robbery, he in fact may have been the one calling the shots, working directly with Paul Dreyfus, but he wasn't the trigger man, he wasn't the man who had killed Julia.

Nick turned and looked at Dance with hate-filled eyes. He might not have pulled the trigger that killed her, but he was an accomplice, someone who wanted her dead. And as Nick continued to glare, if he could have reached out, he would have ripped the man's throat out right on the spot.

"Good-bye," Dance said with a smile as he tapped the plate with his foot, the edge of the bridge acting like a fulcrum as it teetered a moment before slowly rising up and tipping into space.

It fell for all of two feet before it was jolted to a stop. The cuffs dug into Nick's wrists. He tried to grab hold of the cable to alleviate the pain but found it to be too thin. It was one hundred pounds, a weight that was difficult for Dance but less than average in Nick's workout routines. Though the pain throbbed into his constricted wrists, he easily lifted the plate upward using his shoulders and back, finally leaning back to try to pull it up and over the rail . . .

When all at once Dance grabbed him by the plastic ties about his ankles and lifted his legs in the air. Nick's stomach fell upon the metal bar. Like the edge of the bridge, the green rail acted as a fulcrum. He wasn't happy that he paid such close attention in Mr. Stout's physics class, the disproportionate weight of the iron plate making it easy for Dance to lift Nick up and over the bridge.

And in the blink of an eye Nick tumbled over into midair, the iron plate leading the way to a watery grave.

Fifty feet, headfirst. Nick hit the water as if hitting a concrete pavement, the water exploding out around him. The weight pulled him instantly under, his body descending into the darkness. The lake's depth varied from twenty to three hundred feet, but at this point under the bridge it was sounded at only twenty-five. Not that the depth would have any bearing on his chances for survival.

Lungs burning, the pressure in his ears growing with every foot of his descent, Nick was pulled toward his death.

And the weight hit bottom. Nick floated upside-down like a sunken buoy. Stars danced in the periphery of his watery vision. Shafts of light glistened and broke the surface above, refracting about the depths, lighting the rocky, silt-covered lakebed.

Being a swimmer, Nick could hold his breath for far longer than most, but he had no idea of the time, nor how long his lungs could truly hold out.

But it wasn't his pain he dwelled upon,

not the suddenness of his inevitable death. It was Julia. Everything that was good in his life, everything worth living for, had been taken. He felt a crushing shame that he couldn't save her from her fate. He had been so easily deceived, so gullibly accepting in the help of strangers, only to be thrown to his death by those who were paid to protect.

Nick was upside-down, steadily exhaling a very small amount of air to keep his nostrils from filling up and drowning him prematurely. With the glow of the surface light above, he finally caught his bearings when something bumped up against his upward-facing legs. Nick jerked his body around and stared into the vacant eyes of the dead.

There was a body, floating upright, bobbing about, his wrists cuffed together, his legs tied, with the plastic ties wrapped about a similar iron plate. And there was another body ten feet behind it. Nick couldn't see it well, but there was no mistaking the uniform on the skinny, redheaded man. It was a police officer. And through the white shafts of light that cut down through the water, he saw the shadows of a third, dressed in a blue shirt, his long dark hair wafting in the shifting currents. He was in a graveyard, an assassin's underwater dumping ground.

Seeing the corpses, Nick instantly understood why Dance had mentioned déjà vu.

The man immediately next to him was freshly dead, his half-mast eyes revealing rolled-back pupils, his right eye was swollen, black and blue, his mouth slack-jawed, the left side of his lower lip distended as if someone had danced on his face before killing him. He had gray hair that drifted about his face like wind-whipped grass.

Nick's lungs began to burn, his air running low. He knew it had been a minute. Another forty-five . . . maybe sixty seconds and he would pass out.

He grabbed the bicycle chain that tethered him to his death anchor and pulled himself slightly deeper. He grabbed hold of the belt of the man adjacent to him, reached into his pocket with his cuffed right hand, and pulled out his wallet, holding it tight as if it would somehow save him.

But it was a useless final act. His lungs were on fire, his head throbbing with the final pulsing of his oxygen-deprived heart. It had been over two minutes, there was no doubt he would die, surrendering to the seductive call of death.

And as the last bit of oxygen fed Nick's thoughts, he dwelled on Julia, her beauty, her kindness, and how the world would be robbed of her presence because . . . Because he had failed her.

CHAPTER 5

Julia sat in her SUV in the driveway of a modest split-level colonial in the town of Pound Ridge. Like so many of the people in Byram Hills, once Julia learned of the crash, she had rushed to the site to help. But when her eyes fell on what remained of Flight 502, and she realized it was the flight she was supposed have been on, she couldn't stop picturing the faces of the passengers she had been sitting next to and how close she had come to sharing their fate.

Instead of working at the scene, she agreed to go pick up a doctor who had been called out of retirement to help with the emergency effort. She had driven up to Bedford a half hour earlier to get gas and now waited outside the doctor's home while he gathered his things.

As she sat alone, her mind a whirlwind of thoughts, the full impact of what she had escaped finally fell upon her: She was not the only one who had escaped death; Julia placed her hand on her belly, knowing that two lives had been saved today.

The irony was she was on the plane heading up to Boston not for a meeting as she had told people but rather to see her doctor.

She and Nick had lived in Winthrop, Massachusetts, a year after being married. He had been transferred up there and she followed him, finding a job with a small firm in Boston. A colleague had recommended a doctor by the name of Colverhome, a man who not only maintained an impeccable reputation, but had a manner that was both gentle and humorous.

After moving back to Byram Hills, she never changed doctors, finding it easy enough to schedule her annual exam to coincide with a business trip.

She had called him earlier in the week to tell him of her suspicion, and he had arranged for a local doctor to give her a pregnancy test. The test was positive — six weeks pregnant. It filled her with an elation she had never known. She was bursting to tell Nick but had wanted to make it special. So she had arranged with Colverhome to fly up for a prenatal exam and a sonogram of the small beginnings of their child that she could frame and surprise Nick with over a romantic dinner this evening at La Cremaillere. It was the restaurant where he had asked her to marry him, it was the beginning of their life together, a monumental occasion, and she wanted the same gravitas for this most blessed — and surprising — of events. Their morning argument, the one that sent Nick into such a foul mood, had been over a dinner that would never happen. Their plan with the Mullers was a ruse to throw Nick off what would be one of the most profound moments in their sixteen-year relationship.

While they had planned on children, she didn't intend to get pregnant until next year. Their lives were so structured, with their careers, with building a nest egg to allow them to comfortably raise children, that the actual thought of pregnancy had been far from her mind. She realized now that they had spent so much time planning, working to achieve a level of success before having kids, that the thought of actually carrying a child had become foreign.

The news of her pregnancy had taken her by surprise, and she knew it would absolutely floor Nick.

She had been so absorbed in her career as

an attorney hoping to make partner that she had lost countless friends who had journeyed into motherhood leaving their aspirations behind. But the moment the pregnancy was confirmed her focus changed entirely. She knew it wasn't hormones, it wasn't some false sense created by the fantasy of not working. It was simply love.

She and Nick had been together for half of their lives now. They had more money then they needed, they had bought and renovated their dream home, traveled and enjoyed life. And yet, there was a void. A void that was acutely felt at the holidays. She longed for the return of Santa Claus and the Easter Bunny, the Tooth Fairy and Halloween candy.

As Julia thought of the plane crash, of all the lives lost, of the kind, older woman whom she had been sitting next to, tears filled her eyes. She had been called off the jet by an automatic text message that stated that Shamus Hennicot's Washington House had been breached. It was that call that had allowed her to live another day. But not just one life had been saved. Two lives had been rescued from death's grip.

She took it as sign that this child was meant to be. As far as she was concerned it was a miracle.

Initially annoyed, thinking it to be a false alarm, she had exited the plane, hopped right into her car, and gone to Washington House. She walked the perimeter, checking all the doors, all the windows, finding them all secured.

But upon entering, she knew something was amiss. She had been inside for all of thirty seconds when a rumble shook the house. The china in the cupboards rattled, the glasses in the bar clinked as if an earthquake had hit the area. While there was a deep fault under the New York granite mantle, earthquakes were as few and far between as snowball fights in Bermuda. The lights flickered, fighting to stay on, and went out. The emergency lights quickly flashed on, illuminating the stairwells and exit doors. Intermittent beeps sounded from the computer battery backups signaling the power failure and shutdown protocol. She looked at her watch: 11:54. She should have been on her way to Boston instead of walking about in a power-deprived vacant house that shook from the slippage of some fissure deep beneath the county.

She headed to the kitchen, ran her security pass card over the reader, knowing it had a twenty-four-battery backup, and opened the heavy fire door to the basement. The overly bright halogen emergency light guided her down the stairs, its glow abusing the expensive fleur-de-lis wallpaper that Hennicot had had shipped from Paris. She punched her Social Security number in on the keypad and waved her magna-card over the card reader three times. She pulled out the octagonal security key, inserting it, with the letter D on top, into the large brushed-steel vault door.

With a forceful turn, she opened the door and was greeted by darkness. Pulling a chair over, she propped the door open, allowing the bright wash of light to pour forth.

Her eyes immediately fell on the broken display cases in the center of the room, the out-of-place red-domed box on the wall. An anger instantly rose in her, as if she herself had been violated. She walked about opening doors, poking her head in. An emergency light was lit in the climate-controlled storage room; it didn't appear any of the crates had been disturbed. She walked back through the main room, through the shaft of halogen light pouring out of the stairwell, and opened the door to Shamus's office. She stepped right to the hidden wall panel door, seeing it cracked open, and pushed it in.

The room was almost completely dark. Slight reflections of the outer room's light danced about, but not enough for any clear vision.

She knew there were only two items in the room. In the center. She took two cautious steps forward, her eyes desperately trying to adjust, and came upon the safes. She ran her hand over the first, finding it closed, but the second . . . she didn't bother with any tactile investigation. She could just make out the shadow of the thick open door.

And all at once, she felt fear wash over her.

She had entered the house and come down here instantly to confirm the robbery, her anger blinding her to the danger as she ran about in the darkness, foolishly tempting fate. Julia had never been stricken with claustrophobia, but now she felt the darkness closing in on her. She didn't know if anyone was in here, if someone was hidden behind a doorway, feeling trapped like a wild animal, prepared to kill her in order to make his escape.

This was not a good day to die.

She charged out of the room and up the stairs. She pulled out the octagonal key and opened the hidden security room behind the false wall in the pantry. Her eyes fell immediately on the broken computer servers, the hard drives torn out and missing. Whoever pulled this off knew exactly what to do, knew exactly how to erase their tracks.

Julia was thankful for the redundant backup in her office, resident not only on her computer but also on the company server. Whoever pulled this job would never think of looking there.

Stepping from the security closet into the pantry, Julia's fear abated. Whoever had pulled this theft was gone. This inside job had probably been pulled off in a matter of minutes, without leaving a trace.

She grabbed a flashlight off the pantry shelf and a digital camera from her car and re-entered the basement. She took an inventory of what was missing, snapping pictures of the broken case, the open safe. There was a specificity to the robbery, the storage room surprisingly untouched, despite the crates containing tens of millions in paintings. The thieves' only focus had been the armory items and the simple safe.

While Julia had possession of the inventory on all the art, antiques, and gems that Shamus updated a few times a year, she did not have the specifics on the safe. Other than the fact that he stored several pouches of diamonds and some personal effects, the contents of the two safes remained a mystery.

Once back upstairs, she called Shamus Hennicot at his summer home in Massachusetts to give him the bad news. She didn't hesitate as she dialed the number — she had learned early in life that bad news couldn't wait.

When his assistant, Talia, told her Shamus was unavailable, handling some family emergency, Julia simply asked Talia to have him call her as soon as possible and to tell him there had been an incident at Washington House. Julia followed his directions concerning *incidents* to the letter. He didn't want the police involved on any matter until he knew the facts and could decide the best course of action. That was his decision and she would respect his wisdom as she had done for the last three years.

Shamus had been sick for the last few weeks, but for a sick man of ninety-two, he still had more energy than she could muster at the age of thirty-one. They had spoken two weeks earlier regarding a loan of some of his Monet collection to the Metropolitan Museum of Art in New York, but as was so often the case, their conversation had veered to matters of family and life. She had such respect for Shamus and his accomplishments, she so trusted his advice and counsel, that she often found herself confiding in him, seeking his perspective on matters far beyond business.

Though he had no children of his own, Shamus always spoke of what was truly important in life: love and family, the true legacy of success, the true key to happiness. As anxious as Julia had been to tell Nick her news, she was equally looking forward to telling Shamus, knowing the genuine joy he would feel for her. Julia's parents were older when they had her and had passed away several years earlier. In an odd way, Shamus Hennicot had filled that empty space in her heart, becoming like a surrogate grandparent, praising her achievements, sharing wisdom, imparting guidance with a warm smile and cheer in his voice.

She was genuinely touched by the man's selfless spirit, his charity and nobility. He was a gentleman in a world where that word had become forgotten. He was a man who still cherished the written word, sending her letters in his impeccable cursive handwriting, avoiding the impersonal world of email.

It troubled her to have to tell him of the burglary, of the theft of his family's valuables that had been passed down through the years. While she knew he would simply say,

"Not to worry dear, pieces of metal and rock and canvas are not the true valuables in my life," she wondered if he would be troubled by the incident, if there was something more to the collection he possessed that was not in the inventory.

As Julia exited the house, her PDA began humming with an incoming email from her office. Surprisingly, it was the Hennicot files and security data. She realized it was the download protocol when a power failure hit: Her offices were obviously under the same blackout that had hit this part of town.

As she drove out of the driveway, police and fire trucks flew by. The traffic lights were out, and people milled in the streets, all looking south. And as she finally turned her head, she saw the giant plume of black, acrid smoke.

Now, sitting in her Lexus, fifteen miles north of the crash site, Julia could see the dissipating smoke hovering on the southern horizon. She looked at the clock on the dash of her SUV. It was just after two and she had yet to speak to Nick. She had picked up her cell phone to try him again when the passenger door opened and an old man climbed in.

"Thank you for the ride," the man said as he fastened his seat belt. "I'm Dr. O'Reilly."

"Julia Quinn," Julia said as she extended her hand.

As they shook hands, Julia looked more closely at the old man. Though his hair had gone to white, his eyebrows were as black as night and seemed to imbue him with a touch of youth. Tilting her head in curiosity, she asked, "Have we met before?"

"I don't think so." O'Reilly shook his head. "Unless you had business with the medical examiner's office more than five years ago. Sadly, my retirement has been ended by today's tragedy."

The doctor looked out the window, ending the conversation, becoming lost in what could only be horrible thoughts about what he was heading off to see.

Without another word, Julia started the Lexus, drove out of the driveway, and headed back to Byram Hills.

Nick sat in his leather office chair behind the desk in his library. He was soaked, heaving for breath, his mind a jumble in its disorientation. He had thought himself dead as his mind went blank on the bottom of the lake, his last thought that he had failed Julia.

Calming himself, he looked at the wallet clutched in his hand. It was calfskin leather, black, Gucci. He had taken it from the pocket of the dead man on the bottom of the Kensico Reservoir. He opened it, finding it filled with hundred-dollar bills. There was a black American Express Card and a Gold Visa, but he bypassed it all, finding the driver's license, the object of his search, right on top.

But identifying the dead man was not a eureka moment; it instead created more questions than Nick had had an hour earlier. He reread the license once more: 10 Merion Drive, Haverford, Pennsylvania. Born May 28, 1952. Five feet ten inches tall, brown eyes, the organ donation box checked. Paul Dreyfus, the owner of the security company that did the installation on Shamus Hennicot's building, was dead, drowned, his body at the bottom of the Kensico Reservoir.

Nick ran upstairs and tore off his wet clothes, quickly throwing on another pair of jeans and a white shirt. He grabbed another dark blazer from the closet and emptied out the pockets of his drenched pants and jacket. He found Marcus's letter to Marcus, along with the letter from the gray-haired man he'd received in the interrogation room, the ink on the exterior envelopes only slightly running. He picked up the watch and flicked open the watch cover. The timepiece was well crafted and watertight, seemingly unaffected by its submersion, as the second hand swept past twelve to read 2:05. His phone was another matter, shorted out. He was actually glad it was ruined, as that had erased Julia's death image from the world. He grabbed his wallet and keys, the St. Christopher medal, Dreyfus's wallet, and the letters and tucked it all in his pockets.

He ran downstairs, back to the library, and opened the safe. He let out a wide grin as he found his gun sitting there along with a supply of cartridges. This wasn't some kind of magic. It hadn't leaped here through time from Dance's car. As it was now 2:05, it simply had not yet left the safe.

Nick grabbed it, along with several cartridges, and tucked it in his waistband, at the small of his back. He moved the stack of papers on his desk aside and found his personal cell phone sitting there dry as a bone, ready for use. He momentarily laughed, but the humor quickly faded as he became angry with himself. He had almost died, and in so doing, he would have taken Julia along with him. He had been foolish and arrogant, thinking he could simply ride backward in time and easily save Julia.

He had not used anything he knew of the

future to change the past. This was like a game, a game he was playing very poorly, running around relying on chance-met strangers for help. He had to effect change and he had to effect it now. Time was ticking down; the time to save Julia was running out.

He picked up the wet wallet he had plucked off the corpse and slipped it in the pocket of his blazer.

He would no longer passively let things play out by chance. He had a plan now.

He was going to see Paul Dreyfus.

Nick parked his car just outside the roadblock at the crash site, right behind the blue Chevy Impala, the car that would carry Julia's killer, the car he would chase down hours from now, forcing it off the road and into a tree.

He walked briskly toward Private McManus, the same National Guardsman who had stopped him from entering when he came and met Shannon.

"May I help you?" the young man said.

"I'm bringing evidence concerning the plane crash to Captain Delia." Nick held up the wet wallet without stopping.

The young guard didn't question Nick's authoritative tone or manner and nodded as he passed.

Nick stood looking at the crash site. Firemen were rolling up their hoses, not yet able to sit on the running boards of their trucks for a rest. Family members were being bused to the locker building to be close to the remains of their loved ones, to hear any updates on the cause of the crash or even, possibly, word of a miracle survivor.

The devastation was like nothing Nick had ever experienced. Though he had seen it an hour earlier in his time, he had not grown accustomed to the sight. The tragedy was on a grand scale. But for the tail of the plane, he couldn't see any piece of debris larger than a door. He looked at the hundreds of volunteers assisting the emergency crews, helping the grieving families. It was humanity at its best and life at its worst.

And somewhere in here, among the sea of people, was Paul Dreyfus.

Nick pulled out Dreyfus's still-wet wallet, found one of his business cards, and dialed the cell phone number on it.

"Hello," a deep voice answered.

"Mr. Dreyfus?" Nick asked, looking around at the sea of volunteers.

"Yes."

Nick looked among the crowd by the

locker, by the situation tents. "My name is Nick Quinn."

"Yes," Dreyfus said, with no emotion, no formality.

Nick scanned the field, surrounded by miles of police tape, and finally saw him, cell phone to his ear, standing in the open field of death. Nick hung up and headed straight for the man, never taking his eye off him.

Dreyfus was heavier than Nick had thought, a man who had once been built like a rock. His weight had shifted about but he still appeared strong. His gray hair was neatly parted, unlike the mussed, drifting locks Nick had seen on his corpse at the bottom of the Kensico Reservoir.

The man wore rubber surgical gloves, his shirtsleeves rolled up as he lifted sheet after sheet, examining the bodies underneath.

"Mr. Dreyfus?" Nick said on approach.

Dreyfus didn't stop looking under the white sheets, as if Nick was a nuisance.

"My name is Nick Quinn," he said as he extended his hand.

Dreyfus ignored it. Nick was unsure if it was because of the gloves or out of rudeness.

"You flew up here today?" Nick asked.

"I'm supposed to know you?"

"I don't know how to tell you this —"
Nick paused, unsure how to proceed.

"I don't have time for mind games; get to
the point."

"They're going to kill you," Nick blurted
out.

"Who?" Dreyfus didn't look up from his
task, as if he didn't hear or didn't care.

"Your partners."

"Partners?" Dreyfus asked, finally looking
up. "You have no idea what you're talking
about."

Nick grabbed the man by the shoulders,
spinning him around to get his attention.
"Then they are going to kill my wife."

The man's face softened for an instant.
"Then I suggest you go protect her instead
of harassing me."

"Do you know Ethan Dance?" Nick
pressed him.

"Are you a cop?"

"He's going to drill you in the eye and the
mouth. He's got a mean right hook." Nick
rubbed his lip. "Then he's going to tie a
heavy iron plate to your ankles and drop
you into a lake."

"Are you trying to scare me?"

"Yeah, I am," Nick said in earnest.

"After seeing all this," Dreyfus waved his
gloved hand around, "you'll excuse me if I

ignore you. I've got bigger issues to deal with."

Dreyfus glared at Nick before walking off. Nick stood there a moment, not sure how to crack the man, how to get him to talk.

Nick caught up to Dreyfus, walking beside him along the charred ground, every step avoiding pieces of what had once been an AS 300 jetliner. Dreyfus would pause before a white sheet, bowing his head as if in reverence, and then slowly lifting it by its corner.

Hastily brought in from Northern Westchester Hospital, the sheets were serving a purpose they were never designed for. While Nick knew they covered bodies, he hadn't realized what was actually under the sea of white cloth that dotted the hellish landscape. There were no people lying in elegant repose. The bodies were broken, dismembered, burned beyond recognition. Some sheets covered torsos, others limbs, visions Nick had never borne witness to, sights that turned his stomach and wrenched his heart. How Dreyfus could search, how he could look at each face was something Nick couldn't understand.

"What are you doing here?" Nick asked.

"I was an army medic, Vietnam. I thought I'd never see anything like this again."

"You think coming here," Nick said,

"volunteering will clear your soul?"

"You have no idea what you are talking about. I'm going to tell you once, get away from me before I call the cops over."

"Trust me, you don't want to do that." Nick paused. "What are you hoping for, redemption?"

Dreyfus stopped, turning to Nick with a mix of anger and pain in his eyes. "I'm hoping to find my brother."

Nick stared at the man, so sure of a darker side, only to be floored by the fact that Dreyfus's brother had been on the plane.

"I'm sorry," Nick said. "I didn't realize."

"Now, will you let me be?"

"There was a robbery this morning of Washington House, the Hennicots' place. You did the security." Nick reluctantly pressed on. "They stole a bunch of diamonds and swords, some daggers and guns. They're covering their tracks and I know for a fact they are coming for you. You need to get out of here. I'll help you do that, but you've got to tell me who was involved in the theft. I need to know every name to save my wife."

Dreyfus finally looked at Nick with different eyes, sympathetic eyes. "I'm sorry about your wife." And his sympathy slipped away. "But she's still alive. That's more than I can say for my brother. Now, if you'll excuse me."

Dreyfus leaned down and lifted another sheet.

"Mr. Dreyfus?" a voice called from behind them.

"Great, now who are you?"

"I'm Detective Ethan Dance."

Nick turned to see four uniformed police standing beside Dance.

"You need to come with us." Dance took him by an arm as one of the uniformed cops took the other. Nick quickly looked at the patrolmen, checking whether any of them were the police officer he had seen bound, floating dead in the bottom of the Kensico Reservoir, but none had red hair and all four were far from skinny.

Nick felt the gun at the small of his back but knew if he drew it he'd be either dead or in handcuffs.

"Let him go," Nick called out, not knowing why.

"Who the hell are you?" Dance said.

"My God, don't you have any compassion?" Nick said. "The guy's looking for his brother."

"That's not all he's looking for out here," Dance said as he turned and led Dreyfus away.

■ ■ ■ ■

Nick stared out at the white-draped bodies, all of the men, women, and children, his mind puzzling over why the innocent had to die. What purpose did it serve? How many loved ones were left behind to grieve? He knew what it felt like to lose the one you love most in this world.

He wished he could stop it, take it all away. He wished he had more than five hours. If it took twelve hours to save Julia, to solve a crime, how long would it take to save 212? Could he ride time backward and tell each one not to get on the plane, could he find and stop the cause of the accident? His heart broke when he knew he couldn't end all the suffering.

But Dreyfus had not shed any new light on the robbery before he was whisked away by Dance to what would inevitably be his death. He was searching for his brother's body. Nick never realized, never thought there was the possibility of something other than the robbery that Dreyfus was dealing with.

And what did Dance mean, he was not just searching for his brother's body, *he was searching for something else?*

Nick was actually surprised. Though Dreyfus was filled with grief, Nick felt he could actually like the man. He had served his country, he was medically trained, he'd built a huge business.

And Nick realized he didn't have to die. He might not be able to save the passengers, but he might be able to save Paul Dreyfus, and by so doing maybe he would get some answers.

Nick knew where they were going; there was still time.

Paul Dreyfus was thrown in the back of a green Taurus while Dance spoke to and dismissed his underling cops.

Dance slid into the backseat beside him, drew his gun, and pressed it into Paul's stomach. "How's it feel to be the brother of the murderer of over two hundred people?"

Dreyfus stared at Dance but remained silent.

"He double-crossed us. Was that your plan all along? I want to know where the box is." Dance paused, his agitation and anger growing. "And I want to know now!"

Dreyfus wasn't about to answer his questions. No one would get him to talk, especially not this corrupt cop.

On the Laos border in '72, while treating

what was left of Lieutenant Reese's platoon, Paul Dreyfus had been captured by the Vietcong. He was thrown into a pit, a makeshift holding cell, and they had questioned him for five days. No food, just water. They beat him over the back with tree switches and rifle butts, but he never said a word, not even name, rank, and serial number. On the sixth day, a team of Navy SEALs liberated him but not before he had snatched a rifle off a dead Vietcong solider and shot his interrogators' heads off.

Dreyfus hadn't answered questions then and he wasn't about to answer questions now.

Arriving back in the United States in '75, Paul Dreyfus started his security company — a small shop at first. Door and window alarms for friends' homes gave way to video surveillance for local mom and pop stores, which gave way to sophisticated corporate security designs. With a combination of luck, sweat, sleepless nights, and stressful days, Dreyfus built his company into one of the finest in the country.

Samuel Dreyfus ran a far different path than his older brother. Where Paul went to college to pursue a career in medicine, Sam dropped out of high school to pursue girls. Where Paul enlisted, Sam protested. Where

Paul flew off to Vietnam, Sam ran off to Canada.

Paul, an athlete since childhood, had built his body through exercise and diet into a machine that tackled quarterbacks as a Georgia Bulldog and carried the wounded off the battlefield in Southeast Asia. Sam, on the other hand, preferred to pour chemicals in his body to find *enlightenment* and *truth*.

Forgoing a career in medicine after seeing too many battlefield wounds and too much blood, Paul Dreyfus followed a path he could never have imagined. Success provided him a Georgian colonial mansion outside Philadelphia, Ivy League educations for his two daughters, a life of luxury for Susan, his wife of thirty-five years, even his own modest boat and plane, both of which he preferred to four-wheeled vehicles. He loved flying, embracing his father's passion at the age of fourteen. Twice a month their dad took him and Sam on little excursions around the Lehigh Valley, letting them each handle the controls, planting the seeds of a lifelong passion, imparting that feeling of flight that was unlike anything he had ever experienced.

People viewed everything in his life with envy. Everything except his brother. Back in the United States after President Carter's amnesty for draft dodgers, Sam returned to the States thinking the world owed him a living. Or if not the world, at least his brother, Paul.

Sam might have been many things, but he was still Paul's brother, he was still family. Draft dodging and drugs were the extent of his crimes, and they were all in his youth. Being obnoxious, rude, and self-centered were not felonious acts. If they were, Sam would have been in jail long ago.

Paul had employed his brother off and on for the last twenty years, paying him a salary that grew to over a million dollars a year for doing absolutely nothing. He actually gave him a small piece of the firm out of sympathy, so there would be something to leave his kids. He'd hoped it would spur some pride, some drive, but like so many efforts before, it proved useless. Sam made few contributions, brought in not a single contract, and seemed uninterested in the business. It had gotten to the point that Paul was seriously considering giving up on his brother altogether.

But during the last year, Paul had seen a change. Sam was at his office by 8:00 every morning, working full days. He gradually began showing up at the main office with ideas, treating employees with respect. It took Sam Dreyfus forty-nine years, but he had finally grown up. With increasing responsibility Sam grew into the family name, trust was restored, their families reconnected. Paul proudly introduced him at presentations. He landed three major multimillion-dollar contracts in six months. Sam wasn't just working, he was earning his keep.

But then the world spun on its head.

Paul had entered his office at 6:45 this morning to find a receipt for one of his patented octagonal keys lying on the floor. He picked it up quietly, cursing the fool who dropped it, and saw the signature on the bottom. He suddenly realized what Sam had done.

Paul was apoplectic when he found their own security system breached, the Hennicot files and plans gone. Pass codes stolen, combinations to safes and locks accessed, security cards initiated and authorized.

He tapped into Sam's computer. Though his brother had renewed his faith and trust with his exemplary performance over the last year, Paul kept a back-door access to his files in case his brother ever had a relapse to his former self. Paul felt horrible for his lack of confidence in him, but the guilt was washed away by what he found as he opened his brother's personal files. His heart broke as he printed out and read through Sam's notes, as he came to terms with the extent of the betrayal.

Without a word even to his wife, Paul grabbed his emergency briefcase, filled with pass-code resets, five hundred thousand in cash, and his Smith and Wesson. He tucked the three pages he had printed off his brother's computer inside and raced to the small airfield where he kept his Cessna 400. He paid Tony Richter, the air traffic controller he had known for twenty years, ten thousand dollars to forget he ever saw his plane take off at 7:15, asking him to say that his plane was still tucked in its garage. He didn't want anyone to know he had left, didn't want anyone to know he was coming, didn't want Sam to find out what he was about to do.

Dance's fist caught Paul square in the right eye, shocking him out of his thoughts, pulling him back to the present moment.

"Where's the box?"

Paul stared at the man, laughing at his punch. "He said you were going to do that," Paul taunted Dance.

"Who?"

"He said he knew all about the robbery," Paul added, reveling in the destabilizing effect it had on Dance. "Said you were going to throw me into a lake, I should have listened to him."

"Who?"

"I don't know, but he looked pretty pissed." Dreyfus paused. "Murderously pissed."

"The guy you were with?"

Paul just smiled back.

And without warning Dance drilled him right in the mouth. "Did he say I was going to do that?"

And then he punched him in the stomach. "Or how about that?"

Without another word, Dance jumped out of the car and into the front seat, turned on the engine, and turned into the constricted road.

"Let's see if you know how to swim."

Nick ran at a full clip, faster than he had ever run before. He cut down the field, past the locker house, out across the lacrosse fields, and into the woods. The access road wrapped around the entire complex. If he ran fast enough, with the slow-moving traffic and the far shorter distance by foot, he could intercept them.

Cutting into the small forest on his right, he drove his legs harder, lactic acid pouring through them as if he was in the final kick of a marathon.

Through the woods, he pressed on under the low green canopy of leaves, thinking only of Julia as he leaped logs and bushes. Hurtling out of the brush and trees, his legs pistoning even faster, he emerged into the high grasses that abutted the access road.

Without breaking stride, he reached behind his back and drew his pistol, thumbing off the safety as Dance's car came into view.

It was traveling slowly, a quarter mile up the road, on approach to the place where Private McManus was standing guard to prevent anyone from trying to enter, never thinking he would have to prevent someone from leaving.

"McManus! Private McManus," Nick shouted through heaving breaths as he ran toward the National Guardsman.

McManus turned toward him, the confusion in his eyes evident even from this distance.

Nick pointed at Dance's approaching car.

"Stop him," Nick shouted at the young Guardsman.

"What?" McManus shouted back as he turned and saw the approaching green Ford Taurus.

"They stole from the wreckage," Nick

screamed, knowing that would get his attention.

"How do you know?" McManus shouted back.

"You were top of your class in riflery, prove it."

"How the hell did you know that?" the private yelled as he looked toward the approaching car.

"Raise your rifle, don't let them by." Nick was less than one hundred feet from the Guardsman.

And suddenly the Taurus accelerated, the large police engine roaring as it sped up.

Blocked by barriers, the open lane was only wide enough for a single car. McManus stood in the gap and raised his M-16, playing chicken with the three-thousand-pound vehicle.

Nick came running up alongside him, his gun drawn, aiming at the driver.

One hundred yards off, still accelerating.

"You can hit the tire, just focus," Nick said.

"Are you sure about this?" McManus held his gun high, aiming . . .

"You can do it, just like the range."

Fifty yards.

"Take the shot," Nick said.

McManus flexed his finger, focused, and

fired off one round from his rifle.

The rear tire of the Taurus exploded in a shredding hail of black rubber, the spinning aluminum wheel falling on the roadway, sending up a shower of sparks.

Nick aimed at Dance. McManus held his ground beside him, his finger beginning to depress for another shot, when the brakes locked up, the car spinning into a sideways skid, grinding to a halt as the tires and bare wheel screamed in protest.

Nick and McManus both focused their guns on Dance, who reached for his weapon but thought better of it.

"What the hell is going on?" McManus asked through gritted teeth, his focus never leaving Dance.

"Look at the guy in the backseat, look at the blood."

McManus glanced over, and upon seeing Dreyfus's condition, aimed his rifle with even more purpose at Dance's head. "Out of the car, now."

"Son," Dance said as he opened his door, raising his hands to half height. "You are making a life-changing mistake."

Nick reached into the car, thumbed the door locks, and let Dreyfus out of the vehicle.

"Don't listen to him. Wait till you see

what's in his trunk. This so-called cop here just stole two bags of antiques from the wreckage. Antique swords and daggers and diamonds. These were someone's belongings, someone who just died." Nick knew the lie would be much more convincing, much more vile than the truth.

"He's lying," Dance shouted as he glared at Nick.

Nick answered by flicking the trunk latch. "You'll also find some iron plates and bicycle cables he was going to tie to Mr. Dreyfus when he dropped him into the Kensico Reservoir."

Dance's head snap-turned to Nick in surprise.

The trunk lid rose slowly to expose the two duffel bags and the iron plates. Nick reached in and unzipped a bag to reveal an explosion of golden color — Daggers, swords, three gold-inlaid pistols. Nick pulled out the coup de grace: a black velvet pouch, which he opened, the diamonds rolling about in a brilliance of color.

"Son of a bitch," McManus said as he jammed his rifle into Dance's head. "Up against the car."

Dance reluctantly complied.

With McManus holding his rifle head-high, Nick took Dance's gun, handcuffs, and keys and patted him down, finding a small revolver in an ankle holster. He cuffed Dance's hands in front of him.

Nick walked over to his Audi, opened the door, and threw the detective's guns on the seat. Dance's gaze remained fixed on his every move.

"You have no idea what you've done," Dance said to Nick, his eyes on fire as he stared. "We will find you, and understand this, I'm coming for you, I'll cut the beating heart right out of your chest —"

The butt of the rifle slammed into Dance's stomach, doubling him over. "Shut the hell up." McManus raised his gun again, but instead just pushed him in the car. "And get in there. You talk a lot of smack for someone going to jail."

Dance rolled about in pain in the back of his own car.

"Do you have keys for those?" McManus asked Nick, pointing at Dance's handcuffs.

Nick passed them to the private, who stuffed them in his pocket.

"This wasn't in the National Guard brochure when I signed up."

"What do you do in your real life?"

"I just got my MBA, but with this economy, it doesn't seem to matter much. I'm still flipping burgers."

Nick nodded, rushing the conversation along. "Look, I've got to get him to a doctor," Nick lied to the private as he pointed to Dreyfus. "You're a good man, I appreciate your help. If you ever need anything . . ."

"Yeah," McManus said with a dismissive smile sensing a hollow promise.

"I'm serious," Nick said, seeing the doubt in the private's eyes. "Give me your cell phone number."

"It's 914-285-7448."

Nick punched it into his own cell as he listened. "You have my word, I'll hook you up."

McManus smiled, beginning to believe Nick's offer.

"You need to get some people from your unit over here," Dreyfus said, wiping the blood from his mouth. "Don't call his police buddies in on this. They'll pull a blue code on you, saying he's innocent."

"I'll radio Colonel Wells, my CO. Let him deal with this." He looked more closely at the blood on Dreyfus's face. "You all right?"

Dreyfus looked at Nick and nodded. "Yeah."

Nick drove his Audi up Route 22 with Dreyfus in the seat beside him, his briefcase in his lap, having grabbed it from the trunk of the blue rental car, still parked on the access road.

"Thank you," Paul Dreyfus said. "I owe you my life, I think."

"You're welcome." Nick nodded as he cracked the ice pack he had pulled from the car's emergency kit and handed it to Dreyfus. "Again, my condolences on the loss of your brother."

"You knew almost exactly what that guy Dance was going to do to me."

"It's kind of his MO." Nick thumbed his swollen lip, hoping to avoid further questions about his foreknowledge.

"Listen, I don't have much time, but I really need to know what's going on," Nick went on. "I need to know if you know anything about this robbery."

Dreyfus looked out the window at the vacant town of Byram Hills.

"They're going to kill my wife." Nick's tone was pleading, heartfelt.

Dreyfus pressed the ice pack to his eye and nodded. "My brother was responsible for the theft. He pulled all the info from my private files. He was the brains, for lack of a better term, of everything that happened. I only found out this morning what he planned. He took a flight up, got here at 10:15. Dance picked him up at the airport and they went to Hennicot's place to rob it. I flew up here hoping I could stop him before he made the worst mistake of his life."

"I'm sorry." Nick couldn't imagine how Dreyfus was feeling about this betrayal by his own flesh and blood.

"There were five of them, including my brother, who led them down into the candy store. They got in fine, got what they were each there for, but then the whole thing dissolved into disaster. Dance and his crew thought my brother was trying to screw them, my brother accused them of being ungrateful. A textbook meltdown of power and greed."

"There's hundreds of millions down there," Nick said.

"Yeah, and nobody was really aware of that except for Hennicot, his attorneys, myself and, eventually and unfortunately, my brother. The people who helped him, that guy Dance and the others, wouldn't know value if it smacked them in the face."

"Why would your brother involve anyone else if he had the keys to the place?"

"You always have a backup security protocol. Sadly, my brother was a fool. Thinking some alarm might ring at the police station, he figured he needed them on the inside if he was going to pull this off, so he got Dance to put together a team. They planned it out, watched the place for activity, stood guard, and hauled the stuff out. My brother promised them, lured them really, with shiny gold and diamonds. He never told them what he was going for, thought it was none of their business. He let Dance and his men take the daggers and swords while he went for the safe."

"They couldn't just take the Monet on the wall?"

"Nice to see someone knows their art. The idiots he hired probably thought it was a finger painting. My brother, on the other hand, knew exactly what it was but he wanted something more."

"What do you mean, more?" Nick asked.

"There was something else besides diamonds in the safe." Dreyfus paused.

"What?"

Dreyfus was slow in answering. "He wanted Hennicot's mahogany lock box."

"What box?"

"My brother didn't even know what was in it. He had only heard rumors but thought it worth the risk."

"He wanted that more than the Monet, all the gold and diamonds?" Nick said with confusion. "What was in the box?"

"Did you ever hear of the concept of the perception of value?"

"No," Nick shook his head.

"If I were to hold a box in my hand that I would desperately not part with, you would be curious about its contents. If I wouldn't sell it to you for a million dollars you would have confirmation of its value. But that value may be only personal. Maybe it's my father's ashes in the box. Mere dust that would float away on the wind. Worth nothing to you. But to me . . . its all that I have left of my father. It's priceless."

Dreyfus turned away from Nick. He reached into his pocket, fumbled around, jingling his change for something, and then turned back.

He held out his two hands, one clinched in a fist, the other, palm up, with a quarter resting in its center.

"Look at my hands," Dreyfus said. "Choose one but only one."

Nick looked at the quarter, then at Dreyfus's closed hand, and quickly touched it.

"That is what nine out of ten people do. They choose the mystery. Why?" he asked rhetorically. "For a host of reasons. To learn what is there, always thinking the unknown is more valuable than the known.

"How many people live in the moment? A

few? How many people live for tomorrow at the sacrifice of today?" Dreyfus opened his fist to reveal it to be empty. ". . . When tomorrow is never a guarantee."

Dreyfus's words hit Nick hard as he thought of Julia, as he realized they were always looking toward the future at the expense of the moment.

"That is the box. That is why my brother is dead, that is why they will kill me if I don't help them find it. Your wife will be killed to cover their tracks. And they don't even know yet what it contains."

"Dance had a trunk full of gold and yet would trade it for this box, and he has no idea what's in it?"

"The whole thing went bad. Dance and his men were going for the antiques and the diamonds, which would have made them very happy. Then they saw the box. Not knowing what it was, and seeing my brother wanting it so badly, they thought its worth far exceeded what they were taking and thought they were being ripped off. Paid cheap for their help."

"All over a box?"

"We all have a special box, something we hold dear. Something we dare not part with for any price. Yours is your wife, mine is my children. Shamus Hennicot's was in a box;

272

it weighed twenty-five pounds and was passed down from father to son to son. It was said to contain their philosophy, their family secrets." Dreyfus took a deep breath. "We cling to our hearts, to what warms them, to what gives us hope, to things we can look upon and know the world will someday be okay again."

"What could weigh twenty-five pounds and be held most dear?" Nick asked.

"Curiosity is infectious, isn't it? You haven't even seen the box and you want to know what's in it."

"Do you know what's in the box?" Nick asked.

Dreyfus smiled a knowing smile. "You didn't think this whole thing was about a handful of diamonds and some old swords, did you?"

The rear door of the Taurus was open, Dance sat in the backseat, his hands cuffed, barely able to contain his anger.

The young National Guardsman stood outside the car, his M-16 in one hand, his cell phone in the other pressed to his ear, waiting for his superior officer to answer.

Dance's mind was working on overtime, looking about, weighing his options before a contingent of weekend warriors came to haul him away. He hadn't come this far to fail.

Dance looked at his missing ring finger: They called it a down payment on his life.

No one knew it, but he had until midnight tonight or he would be dead. And that just didn't fit into his schedule.

Dance had moonlighted on many jobs that were contrary to his profession. The sixty-thousand-dollar salary of a detective wasn't enough to live on, not in Westchester, among the wealthy who looked to the police for protection but treated them as second-class citizens.

Little jobs supplemented his income — the thefts here and there, the shakedown and blackmailing of the young drug dealers, the kids whose millionaire parents would disown them if they knew what Biff and Muffy were selling to fourteen-year-olds.

Dance had robbed, stolen, committed arson for hire, and on two occasions, killed. Ten thousand a head, drug-related hits down county. He wrapped the bodies in nylon reinforced feed bags, wrapped them tightly in chains, and with hundred-pound iron weights strapped to the corpses, tossed them into the East River beside Manhattan. Secured tightly, they wouldn't be found for years, if at all.

No one was wise to his dealings except for Shannon, who knew better than to talk, and Horace Randall, his mentor, who was three months from retirement. Goods were quickly fenced, evidence never found, and if legal suspicions arose, he would use his police knowledge to direct investigations in another direction.

But not all jobs went smoothly.

Fourteen months ago, he had been running a small crew of punks, teens he had arrested and blackmailed into working for him in order to avoid jail.

Two of them had hijacked a panel trunk filled with computers on East Tremont in the Bronx and had driven it to a warehouse in Yonkers where Dance was waiting. The buyer of the stolen notebooks and high-end desktop models paid him forty thousand in cash, five of which he gave to the two teens, ensuring their silence and loyalty until the next job.

A week later the two punks were found dead in an alley, shot through the head, execution style.

The following day, two wide-shouldered enforcers grabbed Dance as he exited his car in the driveway of his two-family house and drove him to a machine shop in Flatbush where they tied him to a heavy wooden chair.

He sat there in the darkened shop for three hours under the silent gaze of the two enforcers before he heard someone enter.

"You stole my truck." The heavily accented voice came from behind him.

Dance sat still, staring straight ahead. He didn't need to see the man, he knew his voice.

"You of all people should know better." The short, black haired man circled Dance's chair, finally stopping in front of him and leaning down into his face. "Now children are dead."

The Albanian had a dead left eye and a horrific scar running down his cheek, an appearance that struck fear into his victims, particularly at night. Ghestov Rukaj was one of the new wave of Eastern European crime lords who preferred using the tactics of terror to control his territories and victims, and did not understand honor or the old Cosa Nostra ways of criminals.

"Wasn't your truck." Dance glared into Rukaj's one good eye.

"I had scoped it out, it was in my territory, my two associates here were just about to grab it when your *children* beat us to the punch."

"Do you have any idea the line you have crossed or what will happen to you? I'm a police officer."

"Do you have an idea what will happen to you, Mr. Police Officer? I didn't realize the law was in the business of stealing and fencing goods."

At a nod from Rukaj, the two granitelike men stepped forward and stood on either side of Dance. Each took hold of a shoulder, and they pressed him down into the seat. Each grabbed a wrist and pressed it to the wooden armrests.

Rukaj sat on the table in front of Dance, reached into his pocket, and withdrew a large switchblade, flicking it open.

"There is a price for the life we have chosen to lead." Rukaj ran his finger down his left eye and trailed it along the thick scar on his cheek. "Our egos, our invincibility, sometimes need a reality check."

Rukaj laid the blade against the second knuckle of Dance's right ring finger.

"Do you have one million dollars, Mr. Policeman?"

Dance remained silent, his face impossible to read, though sweat had begun to appear on his brow.

"You cost me fifty thousand dollars and I would like it back, plus damages. You have access to drug money, to drugs, stolen merchandise," Rukaj said with his slithering accent. "This is not a question."

Dance's eyes were on fire as he stared defiantly at Rukaj.

Without another word or a dramatic pause, Rukaj pressed all his weight onto the blade, severing Dance's finger with a single slice.

Dance's head snapped back in agony and he roared in pain.

"It's okay to scream, there is no shame. I promise to tell no one."

Rukaj wiped the blood-soaked blade on Dance's pants, folded it back up, and tucked it into his pocket.

"You are a valuable man, Ethan Dance, so I will trade you one million dollars for your life. Now before you get all nervous, I'll give you one year. That will give you time to find the right situation to take advantage of. Pay in installments or in one lump sum, whichever you prefer.

"Consider this" — Rukaj held up his severed finger — "a down payment."

It had been fourteen months. Dance heard from Rukaj daily now, reminding him that there would be no more extensions, no more leeway. "Time is up. Time to pay or time to die," Rukaj said every morning.

Now, as Dance sat as a prisoner in his own car, with its trunk full of antiques and diamonds — a fraction of which would pay for his life — he was filled with an anger and rage such as he had never known. He had been betrayed by Sam Dreyfus, who had run off with a box of untold value, he had been arrested by a nine-to-five soldier, and someone else was looking forward to removing the rest of his body parts.

Dance glared at the young private who was playing policeman, who would go back to his real job come Monday and talk about how he arrested a dirty cop and recovered —

"Hello, Colonel?" McManus said into his cell phone, turning his back to Dance as his superior finally came on the line.

Dance leaped out of the open door of the Taurus, threw his hands over the unsuspecting McManus, and violently pulled his cuffed wrists back, crushing McManus's trachea.

McManus dropped his cell phone and released his hold on his M-16, his hands going straight to his throat. He had been trained in combat, trained with a rifle, but as a National Guardsman, he had never seen or tasted anything close to war. The young private had never even been in a bar fight.

Dance leaned back with all of his two-hundred-pound weight, grinding the hand-cuff chain into McManus's broken throat, driving the broken cartilage of his trachea into the soft inner flesh of his windpipe while cutting off the flow of blood to his brain. He fell back into the Taurus, pulling McManus off his feet and into the car with him, the young man's arms desperately tugging at the chain about his neck, legs flailing, seeking purchase, as a wet gurgling sound of death escaped his now-blue lips.

McManus's struggle finally abated, his arms falling limp. A spastic twitch began in his right leg.

And he died.

On the side of the road that led to a disaster, Private Neil McManus became the 213th death at Sullivan Field.

Dance reached into the dead private's pocket, pulled out the cuff keys, and freed himself.

He threw the dead body into his backseat so as not to draw attention, pulled the jack and spare from his trunk, and changed his tire as if he were on pit-crew time. Two minutes later he picked up McManus's M-16 and his cell phone and threw them into the car. He hopped in the front of his unmarked police car, started up the engine, and peeled out, leaving the jack and the wheel in the middle of the road. He'd dump McManus's body in the reservoir when he had time, but for the moment, there were more pressing matters.

Before he hit sixty miles per hour, he flipped down the keyboard on his police computer and punched in the license plate he had memorized. The owner of the Blue Audi A8 popped up. Nicholas Quinn, 5 Townsend Court, Byram Hills. The picture was a spot-on match to the man who had just run out of the woods to stop him, who had cuffed him and left him to be hauled off to jail. The man who somehow knew the exact contents of his trunk.

He looked down at the address on the Post-it stuck to his dash, the address for Hennicot's attorney, whose offices contained the security video, who had probably viewed it.

Dance had already spoken to her. He had already gained the trust of Nicholas Quinn's wife.

Nick drove down Route 22. As he headed onto the overpass of Interstate 684, he saw the uninterrupted flow of traffic below. It was like another world, cars filling the roads, people chatting within their vehicles, unaware of the disaster just a mile off the highway. It was as if Byram Hills were a dead town, under quarantine, the disaster already pushed from the minds of the world beyond.

Nick continued into the vacant town and pulled into the empty parking lot of Valhalla, his friend's restaurant.

"You sure you don't want to go to the hospital?" Nick asked, as put the car in park.

"I'm fine," Dreyfus said. "I've gotten more banged up from hits in a flag football game."

"Well, where do you want me to take you?" Nick asked as he looked at his car's clock. "I have to be somewhere at three."

"I can't go back to the airfield, yet." Dreyfus said.

"Tell you what," Nick said. "You drop me at my house, take my car."

"I can't do that." Dreyfus shook his head.

"Yeah, you can. It's not like you're going to keep it. Just call me when you're done with it. With the loss of your brother and everything else going on, you need it more than me."

Dreyfus nodded in thanks.

"Besides, I'll have another car just like this one at my house in ten minutes," Nick said, with an irony no one could ever understand.

"I appreciate it."

"But you need to help me in return." Nick looked at Dreyfus. "One of Dance's men is going to try to kill my wife, I just don't know who."

"You know, I didn't realize . . . I didn't make the connection between you and your wife, Julia. I met her, Nick, on more than one occasion. She's terrific. Hennicot really cares for her, thinks the world of her, and in my book, nobody is a better judge of character than that old man."

"Yeah, well, if I don't start getting some help," Nick said, "she's not going to live through the day."

Dreyfus pulled his briefcase up on his lap, opened it, and pulled out three sheets of paper.

"I only figured out what my brother was doing this morning. I tore through his files and found this." Dreyfus handed the paper to Nick.

Nick read quickly. It was a haphazard checklist and hastily typed notes on the planned robbery.

"It's not much, just his notes, but it gives the names."

Nick skimmed the details of the mechanics of the break-in but paid close attention to the bullet-note bios Sam had compiled:

DROP DEAD — 7/28
Dance — Ethan Dance. 38. Detective.
  Dirty. Two-faced.
  His three:
  Randall — Cop. 58. Fat
  Brinehart — Cop. New guy. Kid.
Punk.
  Arilio — Cop. 30s.

Fence — Confirmed — Chinese national, five million cash for weapons.
  diamond price t/b/d upon inspection.
Rukaj — Not a cop. Who is this? Called
  Dance at lunch, unnerved him, scared
  him. Dance in debt? Owes him?

"If someone's after your wife," Dreyfus
said, pointing at the names. "It's got to be
one of these."

"Drop dead?" Nick said, looking at the
top note.

"That's today's date."

"Who's this Rukaj?"

"Not completely sure, but I believe it may
be Ghestov Rukaj, an Albanian who has
been staking claim to organized crime in
New York. But I'll tell you this, if he scared
Dance, he can't be all bad."

"Or maybe," Nick said ominously, "he's
far worse."

"I'd keep my focus on Dance," Dreyfus said.

"As insane as he is," Nick said, "I don't think it was him."

"Did you say, *was* . . . ?" Dreyfus asked in confusion.

"Is." Nick quickly corrected himself. As much as he agreed with Dreyfus, he held the evidence in his pocket. Without doubt, the St. Christopher medal hung on the neck of Julia's killer, and Nick had seen Dance's neck, his exposed chest: There was nothing hanging there. Randall, the fifty-eight-year-old fat cop on Sam's list, wasn't the trigger man, Nick was sure of this, as he had seen him getting in the blue Chevy Impala at the moment Julia was shot. It had to be one of the other three who pulled the trigger: Brinehart, Arilio, or Rukaj.

"After the robbery this morning, Dance came after my brother. If he hadn't died in the plane crash, they were going to kill him. Dance was relentless looking for this box, thinking it was worth a fortune. I'm sure he is just as relentless in making sure that he covers his tracks, that he never gets caught," Dreyfus said, confirming the danger to Julia.

"How do you know so much about what happened during the robbery?" Suspicion leaked into Nick's voice.

Dreyfus paused as if he were about to reveal a death.

"After the robbery, I tracked down my brother, I saw the box he took from Hennicot's safe. I tried to convince him to let me help him, that the box didn't contain what he thought, that it couldn't fill whatever hole he had in his life. He said it was too late, that Dance was after him and would kill him on sight."

"Where did you see him last?" Nick asked.

"At the airport."

"My God, I'm sorry."

Dreyfus looked at Nick. There was a look in his eye, something he was not saying.

"Nick, my brother died in that plane crash, but he wasn't on Flight 502."

"What do you mean?"

"He showed up at the airport in a stolen police car, the wooden box under his arm. I tried to tell him . . ."

"Tell him what?"

"I tried to stop him." Dreyfus's voice filled with a painful regret.

"I had no idea," Nick said.

"He stole my plane," Dreyfus continued, looking out the window, unable to meet Nick's eye. "He held a gun to my head, took the keys, and stole my plane. If I had any idea, I would have stopped him, I would have killed him to prevent what happened."

Nick stared at Dreyfus as he struggled to speak, confused about where the conversation was going.

"I watched him fly my plane right into that jet, into Flight 502. I watched them fall from the sky to their deaths."

Nick sat there in stunned silence, never having imagined that the two horrible events in Byram Hills were related.

"I'm sorry," Nick finally said. He realized the look in Dreyfus's eyes was not a feeling of betrayal but one of anguish and sorrow, of overwhelming guilt, for his brother was responsible for the deaths of 212 innocent people.

Not another word was spoken as Nick pulled out of the parking lot and drove the mile and half home.

Nick pulled in front of his house. He and Dreyfus got out of the car and solemnly shook hands. "I appreciate the loan of the car.

"And Nick," Dreyfus continued with a serious look. "If they think your wife can identify them, if she has a video of the robbery, they won't stop until they silence her. If I were you, I would get her away from this town now. If you've got friends you can trust, I'd find them. Because I wouldn't trust anyone in that police department if I were you."

"I agree," Nick said.

Dreyfus nodded in appreciation as he climbed in the driver's seat of Nick's Audi, closed the door, and rolled down the window. "Good luck, Nick."

Nick watched Dreyfus pull out of the driveway and disappear around the corner. He pulled the watch from his pocket and checked the time: 2:57. Julia's Lexus wasn't in the driveway. He didn't know where she was at this moment but this moment would soon be over.

He pulled out his cell phone and dialed McManus, glad that he had taken the young private's phone number. He looked at the sheet of paper from Dreyfus with the names of the other cops on it.

"Hey, Private McManus." Nick said as the call went through. "It's Nick Quinn."

"Yes?"

"There are three other cops involved with Dance: Randall, Arilio, and Brinehart. Tell your commanding officer to pick them up. Again, the names are Randall, Arilio, and Brinehart."

"Mr. Quinn, to be honest with you, Mr. McManus is no longer of this world." Nick recognized Dance's voice.

"Where are you? Are you home?" Dance paused. "Understand something, I'm coming for you, I will find you, and when I do, I'm going to snap your neck."

"You listen to me —" Nick began, but was quickly interrupted.

"No!" Dance exploded. "You listen to me. Your wife? Julia? Can you picture her dead? Can you do that?"

Nick froze in shock. He tried not to conjure up the image that he knew so well but couldn't avoid it.

"A bullet to the head," Dance continued, "or how about a knife, drawn across her belly so she can watch her insides spill out?

"My men are already looking for her, and when they find her — well, why don't you just let your imagination run wild on that?"

CHAPTER 4

Nick ran across the side yard straight to Marcus's house. He barged through the unlocked front door without bothering to knock, raced through the foyer, and tore open the pocket doors to the library where he knew Marcus was working.

"Well, good afternoon to you," Marcus said, unfazed by Nick's abrupt entrance. He sat behind his large desk, his three computers humming.

Nick pulled the envelope from his pocket and laid it before Marcus.

"What's this?" Marcus stared down at the water streaked letter, curious, finally recognizing his own handwriting.

"Before you open it, I need to ask for your help."

"Why do you always say that? Just sit down and ask."

Nick reluctantly sat in the wingback chair

290

across from Marcus.

"I've got three minutes to convince you of the impossible. What's in that letter is absolutely true; you wrote it at my insistence."

"What are you —"

Nick held up his hand. "Before you say anything, know that I would never deceive or manipulate you. Know that I'm totally sane."

Marcus stared at him in all seriousness before finally picking up the letter and tearing it open. "You're an idiot," he said, half in jest.

"Dear Me," Marcus read. The words were water blotched but legible, and most important, recognizable as his own. *"I know this sounds crazy.* Oh, that is rich. When did I write this?" he looked up at Nick, his eyes slowly squinting with confusion.

"Just read it," Nick said quickly.

Marcus's reading fell off into silence.

Dear Me,

 I know this sounds crazy but I'm writing to myself. You (meaning me) know this is my handwriting as no one could possibly duplicate our chicken scratch except Uncle Emmett, but seeing he's dead . . .

 As hard as this is to believe, Nick is

standing before you asking for your help, asking you to help save Julia.

Marcus briefly looked up at Nick, before casting his eyes back at the letter.

Somehow Nick knows the future without question. Now before you start thinking he's crazy or you're crazy for writing this, I will prove to you the validity of my-our words.

You don't know this yet, but Jason Cereta is dead. You won't know this until after three o'clock when his wife calls the office in tears. Jason hopped on the flight out of Westchester this morning and was killed in the crash. He was going to Boston to speak with Reiner Hertz about opening discussions for the purchase of his Halix Ski Company. Remember that you never mentioned your desire to purchase Reiner's company to anyone but Jason, never told anyone including Nick about how you loved their skis and particularly the Swiss spokesmodels they hired each year. I loved their black and orange design since I was little when Dad bought me a pair for Christmas against Mom's wishes and taught me at Hunter Mountain on that blizzard of a day, it was December 27, and

Mom was especially pissed because we didn't get home until after midnight. Anyway, Jason was a good kid, thought he was doing something that would make you-us-me happy while advancing his career. May he rest in peace.

Nick is standing before you now asking for your help to save Julia. Suffice it to say, I have seen the future and what Nick had to do to convince me of the truth was the most shocking, horrible thing I have ever seen. They are coming to kill Julia and if you don't help him, she will die.

You already feel guilty about losing Dad without ever reconciling with him. Know this, the future is coming and if you don't help Nick, Julia will be dead before the sun sets and the fault and guilt will lie squarely on your shoulders if you don't do what he asks.

With sincerest imploring,
Me — which is you, Marcus Bennett

Marcus stared at his signature, at the raised corporate seal that he hadn't removed from his desk in weeks. He reached back into the envelope and pulled out the online *Wall Street Journal* headline page and quickly scanned it.

A whole minute went by before he looked

up at Nick.

Without a word he picked up his phone and dialed.

"Helen? It's me. I need to speak to Jason right away."

Marcus listened.

"What do you mean he's not in," Marcus yelled into the phone. "Don't tell me that. Give me his assistant."

There was a five-second pause.

"Christine, it's Marcus, where's Jason?"

Racing down Sunrise Drive in Marcus's Bentley Continental GTC convertible, Nick was glad not to be driving for once today. Glad to have an ally he could trust implicitly. Nick had called and found Julia at the gas station just north of town in the village of Bedford. With all of the stations and pumps in town closed, she had driven the five miles to fill her nearly empty tank before heading to pick up a doctor who was needed to help with the recovery effort.

With a quiver in her voice, Julia had told him of getting off Flight 502 before it left. He told her not to move, to get into her car and wait for him there.

"I can't believe Jason is dead." Marcus shook his head. "I had no idea he was going up to Boston."

"I'm sorry," Nick said.

They fell silent.

"I'm pretty convincing." Marcus finally broke the moment, alluding to his letter as he cut through the ghost town of Byram Hills.

"Thank God." Nick nodded, looking at Washington House as they drove past.

"This whole thing is too incredible. But you've got to tell me what's going on."

It took Nick five minutes to bring Marcus up to speed, about his near scrapes with death, about Dance and Dreyfus and Julia and the mahogany box.

Nick pulled out the gold pocket watch and opened it, holding it out for Marcus to see.

"Put it away," Marcus said.

"You don't want to see it?"

"Sometimes in life there are some things we shouldn't see, some things we shouldn't know."

As they headed up Route 22 past Sullivan Field, they both fell into silence. Flames licked the sky as heavy black smoke filled the air, blotting out the sun. It was 1:15, fire departments from Banksville, Bedford, Mount Kisco, Pleasantville, and five other jurisdictions supplemented the Byram Hills volunteers who had been fighting the raging conflagration for over an hour now, in a battle that would have no winners.

"Don't take this the wrong way, because what you are doing is the right thing to do and I would do the same, but have you thought about how your actions are changing the future? Have you thought about the impact every step or interaction will have?"

A red Toyota four-runner flew past Marcus, cutting him off as it raced off to who knows where.

"Our actions have far-reaching implications that we never see." Marcus pointed to the Toyota as it disappeared down the road. "The simple act of a reckless driver can initiate a domino sequence of events affecting hundreds of lives, each of which in turn affects every life it touches.

"A man races down a highway, causing an accident, which delays countless people from making it home on time. And among those delayed is a doctor whose small child ingests a rubber ball, clogging his airways, his panicked babysitter has no idea what to do, and the three-year-old dies. Now, if the child's father was to make it home when he was scheduled to, he would have Heimliched the kid, clearing the ball, and they all would have sat down to a normal dinner. And then that child would grow up to cure cancer, as he was so inspired by his father."

"Makes you want to kill the asshole on the highway doesn't it?" Nick said.

"But who knows what fate holds? What if that child grew up and cured cancer?"

"He cures cancer, you said that," Nick said.

"But . . ."

"There's always another but —"

"But in so doing he created something far worse that killed millions. If we were to know all that, then that maniac driver just saved millions of lives. Who's to say what the consequences of our actions, whether noble or selfish, will be for the future?"

"For the want of a nail," Nick said, referring to the old poem.

"For the want of a nail." Marcus nodded in agreement.

As Marcus continued up the highway, the bright midday sun painted a glare on the world. He slipped on his mirrored sunglasses and reached into the side pocket of his door, pulled out some sunscreen, and rubbed it on his bald head.

"My God, though." Marcus laughed. "Think of what could happen with the power you hold in your hand."

"I'd be a hit at the horse races." Nick laughed in return.

"Horse races? How about the stock market? Business deals? Knowing your opponents' moves before they make them?" Marcus pulled the envelope addressed to himself from his pocket, pulled it out, and looked at the *Wall Street Journal* page. "Do you realize just with this almost-four-hour advance information, I could make millions?"

"Okay, glad to see the capitalist in you is still alive."

"Seriously, think about international relations, peace negotiations. You could change the course of history, prevent disasters and . . ." Marcus paused. "Plane crashes."

Nick listened to Marcus. His thoughts having been so singularly focused on Julia, he hadn't pondered the value of what he held in his hand.

"It could change the outcome of murder trials, the capture of criminals . . ." Marcus's tone returned to bitter truth. "The outcome of wars. In the wrong hands — and that's just about everyone's — that thing is as dangerous as can be. The power of knowing the future could corrupt even the most noble heart."

Nick had not given much thought to the dark purposes of what he held and the consequences it could produce.

"Promise me you'll destroy it once you're

sure Julia is safe."

"You have my word," Nick said.

Marcus looked again at the *Wall Street Journal* page, stuffed it back into the envelope and handed it to Nick. "I can't tell you how tempting that is. With one phone call . . ."

Nick tucked the envelope into his pocket. "Glad to see not all men are so easily corruptible."

"Nick." Marcus turned to him. "Does Julia know about her death?"

Nick shook his head. "She experienced it, it happens, but that's hours from now. As far as she knows, right now, she feels lucky to be alive, having gotten off that plane."

"I'll never get used to this concept." Marcus shook his head. "You talk about the future as if it's the past."

"It's how life has been running for me for eight hours now."

"With no continuity, with no one else remembering what happened, how do you keep it straight? I couldn't keep my mind focused."

"I just think of Julia. I don't care about time, I don't care about anything right now but finding and stopping her killer. She gives me all the focus I need."

Flames climbed sixty feet into the sky, the intense heat like a force field preventing the fire crews from getting within fifty yards. The roar of the fire sounded like an inhuman beast as it singed the air, searing the metal of the fuselage.

White cloudlike foam had been shot across the debris field to aid in dousing the gas fire. Eight water cannons and countless hoses arced streams across the sky, fighting the spreading flames as they nipped at the surrounding woods.

The tanks in the wings were mercifully half full for the short flight to Boston; no need to endure the cost of the additional weight with the price of gasoline these days. But that small piece of good luck was lost on the firemen who fought desperately to contain the three thousand gallons of impossibly flammable liquid.

Men in fire suits searched the grounds in hopes of a miracle but found nothing but shattered bodies, and mere splinters of metal. National Guardsmen arrived by the truckload to supplement the effort. Crowds of the curious, morbid, and shocked looked on before being escorted away or led to assist.

Dance walked about the perimeter of the flaming wreckage, ignoring the wayward water spouts dousing the flames as they sprinkled on his blue blazer. With all of the death before him, all of the senseless loss and suffering, Dance didn't feel a moment of pity; he couldn't muster a tear of sympathy for the dead. Somewhere in there was the body of Sam Dreyfus, somewhere in there was the box he wouldn't part with, a box whose value was inconceivable. If a millionaire like Sam Dreyfus wanted it instead of all of that gold, all of those diamonds, its worth had to be in the hundreds of millions.

He couldn't help smiling, knowing that Dreyfus had gotten what he deserved. He hoped he had been fully aware of his imminent death as the plane fell out of the sky.

There was no fear in Dance of someone's getting near the box — if it had survived the crash — before he did. The crash site was a crime scene, and anyone caught stealing from here would be facing multiple felonies in addition to public scorn. If the heavy wooden box had managed to survive, nobody would know what it was, and Dance, as a detective in the crash's jurisdiction, would procure access to the debris holding area and steal it before anyone was the wiser.

With Sam Dreyfus's betrayal and death, it was up to Dance and his men to clean up the evidence, to find and erase the security tapes, to track down anyone who might have seen them.

When Sam Dreyfus had contacted him a month ago, Dance had thought it was an internal affairs setup. He thought the police-police had finally caught up to him and were luring him with promises of gold and diamonds.

But with the research tools of a detective at his disposal, he found Dreyfus to be the impotent younger brother of DSG's chairman and founder, the designer and installer of the security system for Shamus Hennicot's Washington House. And while DSG's chairman, Paul Dreyfus, was hailed as a brilliant, hardworking innovator, Sam Dreyfus was his absolute antithesis, a consummate failure, always looking for more, never appreciating his ridiculous income and the lifestyle he led.

Sam Dreyfus was the perfect partner in crime: a man of weak character, an individual he knew he could control. He was also a miracle, sent by the devil himself, one that would help ensure Dance's survival and keep Ghestov Rukaj at bay for good.

Dance had looked at drug dealers to rob, evidence rooms to rip off, criminals to blackmail, but none of the prospects would net him anywhere near the million-dollar bounty he was to pay for his own life.

As much as Rukaj's ultimatum enraged him, he knew there was nowhere to turn, nowhere to run. The Albanian had connections everywhere, listening, watching, following whomever he chose. There would be no sympathy for a crooked detective, someone who would be hated by cop and criminal alike. And Rukaj's reputation was based on history, not rumor. The executions he had personally participated in were legendary for their slow, unending torture, his victims pleading for death hours before it mercifully embraced them. There was no question Rukaj had Dance by the balls, and the only way out was one million dollars.

Dance had met Sam Dreyfus four times at Shun Lee Palace in Manhattan, going through the job, the plans, the security, and how they would fence their ill-gotten gains. Sam explained that there had to be a secondary backup for the security's video feeds and that if it wasn't in the police station then it had to be in Hennicot's locally based attorney's office.

Sam confirmed that Hennicot's lawyer was Julia Quinn at Aitkens, Lerner, & Isles and that the feed ran directly to her computer with a redundant backup on her company's server. Dreyfus was to visit her right after they completed the robbery to review what had happened under the auspices of his company's concern for the break-in. He was then to deposit a virus in her computer system, thereby wiping that piece of the evidence from existence before it was backed up at 2:00 A.M. to a confidential off-site firm.

But now, as Sam had gone off and died, it fell to Dance to deal with Julia Quinn.

He and his men didn't know from viruses or internal security protocols. They didn't know the law firm's procedures entailed in reviewing security evidence, but Dance had other means of making evidence disappear.

Now, after breaking into Shamus Hennicot's amazing collection of gold and jewels, with Dreyfus dead, with time quickly elapsing, he couldn't risk anything tying the crime to him.

What was supposed to be a by-the-book heist had fallen into disaster. But as quickly as best-laid plans fell to pieces, planes fell from the skies, offices and homes went dark, and death pulled everyone into distraction.

The plane crash was a fortuitous event in a morning filled with complications and betrayals. The disaster was already serving as the perfect diversion: power was out across the town, families had run to their homes in shock, leaving Byram Hills deserted. Confusion and chaos were the order of the day, providing the perfect smoke-screen for cleaning up the mess made by Sam Dreyfus.

Dance's men would shortly enter the law firm of Aitken, Lerner, & Isles to remove any video files pointing in their direction, even if it meant burning the place to the ground. And with regard to the matter of Shamus's personal attorney . . .

Dance pulled the cell phone from his pocket. It was Sam's, foolishly left behind in his panic as he escaped to the plane with his precious mahogany box. Dance flipped it open and thumbed through the phone book, finding Julia Quinn's office and cell conveniently programmed. But Sam wouldn't be calling her as planned, wouldn't be meeting her at her office to discuss the robbery.

Dance chose the cell phone number and hit send. It was so convenient that the caller ID would read Sam Dreyfus, the first seed planted in his deception.

"Ms. Quinn?"

"Yes?"

"This is Sam Dreyfus at DSG," Dance lied.

"Oh, Paul's brother. We haven't had the pleasure."

"You obviously know why I'm calling."

"Yeah," she said. "I can't figure how they got in."

"Have you seen the video yet?" Dance asked, trying not to sound anxious.

"No, they destroyed the primary server at Hennicot's place, and with the plane crash and blackout, I never got back to my office."

"The blackout makes it hard to see those files," Dance said, glad that they could get to the computers before she had a chance to see anything.

"Not to worry. I have a backup on my PDA. It's pretty large. But once I have access to a computer . . ."

"Well, that's fortunate," Dance lied again, working hard to mask his anger.

"I have a call in to Shamus. I feel terrible having to break the news to him."

"As we all do." Dance had completely fallen into the role. "Have you contacted the police?"

"We don't involve the police until he gives the go ahead. He said he doesn't trust them."

"That's wise," Dance said with a smile. "Are you in town?"

There was a long pause. "I was supposed to be on that flight this morning."

"Really?" Dance feigned sympathy, wishing she actually was dead in the field right now. It would have wrapped everything up so nicely. "The whole thing is just so tragic.

"Could we perhaps meet?" Dance continued. "Maybe we can try to reach Shamus together?"

"I'm running all over the place right now. I'll be home later, though."

"Perhaps we can speak this afternoon?"

"Try my cell or my home number, which is —"

"Let me get a pencil," Dance said, faking the need, still playing the role. "Shoot."

"It's 914-273-9296."

"That's 9296. Got it. And listen, if you become available sooner, call me at this number."

Dance hung up Sam's cell phone, glad that he had it. But that being said, he hated technology, preferring spoken words to email, address books and calendars to computers. And PDAs . . . he particularly

307

hated PDAs right now. How the hell had technology gotten so advanced as to be able to carry surveillance video in a hand-held device?

Dance pulled out his radio and punched in a code. "Listen up," Dance spoke on a secure channel. "Drop what you're doing. You need to locate a Julia Quinn, attorney at Aitkens, Lerner, & Isles, lives in Byram Hills. Run a DMV check on her for her car, she's out there somewhere. Do periodic drive-by of her house. I don't care what you do, but we need to find her or our freedom may be coming to a swift end."

"What's up with the box?" a static-filled voice came over the radio.

"Don't worry about that, that's my problem. You just do what you're told. Again, Julia Quinn, once you locate her don't take your eyes off her and call me. If she runs, feel free to take her down."

Julia hung up her cell phone, glad that someone else was involved now with the robbery. She had been on a roller coaster of emotions: elation at having escaped death, sheer agony at the tremendous loss of life, the pain she felt for the theft at Shamus's offices and her inability to reach him. But her emotions were dominated by survivor's guilt. All of it weighed heavy now, as she sat in the parking area of the gas station in Bedford.

She turned as Marcus's Bentley drove up, Nick leaped from the car and ran to her, hugging her in his strong embrace.

Julia wrapped her arms around Nick as if she hadn't seen him in a month, and the moment her head hit his shoulder the tears poured out, all of her confusion, all of her joy at being alive, all of her sorrow for the tragedy she had barely avoided, which had taken the lives of all the passengers she had sat amongst.

"Listen," Nick said. "I don't have a lot of time to explain but we have to go."

Julia lifted her head and looked into his eyes. "I love you," she said.

Nick's smile grew wide as he placed his hand behind her head and pulled her into a gentle, heartfelt kiss that communicated his feelings far better than words ever could.

"Mmmm," Marcus cleared his throat, standing by his car, calling their attention. He tapped his watch as he hung up his cell phone.

Nick took Julia by the hand and led her to the Bentley.

"Hi, Marcus," Julia said. "I didn't realize you guys were together."

"It's good to see you, Julia."

Julia turned back to Nick. "I'm supposed to pick up a doctor in Pound Ridge and bring him back to the crash site."

"Let someone else deal with that," Nick said abruptly.

"What about my car?"

"Don't worry about it. We've got to get you out of here." Nick held the car door open as she climbed into the backseat.

"What's with all the drama?"

Nick sat in the front passenger seat, closed the door, and turned around to face her. "It's about the robbery at Washington House."

"How'd you know about the robbery?" Julia asked in surprise.

"Let's just say word is getting around."

"That makes no sense." Julia went into cross-examination mode. "How did you know?"

Nick's mind was working overtime. He didn't want Julia to know what was truly going on, he didn't want her to know anything about the watch in his pocket or what he was trying to prevent from happening eight hours from now. He had already given her a glimpse of things, telling her someone was after her twice — once in their kitchen at 6:30 just before she died and again at 5:30 just before facing gunfire in her office. Neither revelation had proved to be of any help in achieving her salvation.

"I spoke to Paul Dreyfus."

"How do you know Paul?" Julia asked in surprise, continuing in her lawyer mode.

"I don't, he called the house." Nick was afraid his lie would go too far. "We were making small chat, when I introduced myself. He told me about the robbery." It was the longest and deepest lie Nick had ever told Julia.

"That's odd. I just spoke to Sam Dreyfus, his brother, a couple minutes ago. He wanted to meet, see the videos from the robbery that are stored on my PDA." Julia held up her Palm Pilot.

"What?" Nick said in shock, knowing that Sam was dead, killed in the crash.

Hearing her words, Marcus started the car and pulled out. Marcus drove through the winding section of Route 22, past the lakes and forests and the occasional house, his car hugging the road as he kept the speedometer at seventy.

"Julia," Nick said, turning to face his wife, who rode in the backseat. "Listen to me very carefully —"

"I hate when you do that, Nick," Julia scolded him. "You scare me. Just tell me

311

what's gong on."

"Whoever pulled the robbery is after you and your PDA," Nick said. "And I'm not taking any risks."

"Hey, don't you think your imagination is a little overdeveloped today? I'm fine. Look at the muscles." Julia flexed her arm, like a prize fighter.

"This is no joke," Nick snapped at her. "They are trying to kill you."

"Lower your voice," Julia shot back. "Who? If you know who, let's call the police."

"Absolutely not," Nick cut her off. "You know Shamus was right when he said not to involve the police unless he signed off on it."

"How did you know that?" Julia stared at Nick, the moment growing silent, a pause hanging in the air. "I never told you that."

"Yeah, you did," Nick's lie was filled with self-righteousness.

"Nick," Julia corrected him, "Shamus did say that, it was his policy, but I never told you, I never told anyone. The only people who knew that were the Dreyfuses. Sam and I just talked about that not fifteen minutes ago."

"Julia," Nick said solemnly, looking over the leather seat into Julia's eyes. "Sam Dreyfus was killed in the plane crash. I don't know who you spoke to but it wasn't Sam."

Julia fell to silence.

The Byram Hills train station was like something out of the early twentieth century: an English-style, fieldstone ticket booth and waiting room capped with a patinated copper roof, its green color blending with the leaves of enormous oak trees that shaded the small commuter parking lot. An old-fashioned platform of thick cedar planks ran for seventy-five yards, echoing with the steps of its passengers, who lined up by the hundreds at rush hour.

Now, though, the small station was empty except for the elderly ticket agent.

Marcus drove into the parking lot and pulled up right in front of the ticket booth.

"What the hell is this?" Nick asked from the passenger seat.

"You turned to me for help and I turned to my friends for help."

Nick looked around, not seeing a soul in sight but the clerk in the ticket window.

"The express train to New York comes through in three minutes. First stop Grand Central. Ben and his men will be waiting on the platform for her. Of everyone we know, who better to trust her life with? Ben could protect her from an invading army, let alone a bad cop or two."

Ben Taylor had been a close friend of Marcus's for too many years to count. He had retired after twenty years in the service — five as a Navy SEAL, five as a Delta Force team leader, and ten that no one ever spoke about. He had left the military and set up his consulting business with seed capital provided by Marcus, the first and only friend he had stayed in touch with from basic training. His small business was successful, procuring contracts both stateside and abroad on situations Marcus preferred not to know too much about. Marcus had maintained a small interest in the operation, partly for the bragging rights and cool factor but mainly for the quarterly executive committee meeting when they knocked the ball around at Winged Foot and shared stories of their female conquests.

"I don't know," Nick said with hesitation.

"Who taught you to shoot?" Marcus challenged. "Who got you your gun and permit so easily? Who would you trust with your life without question? This was Ben's suggestion; he couldn't get anyone up here in less than an hour — your time frame, remember? He said once she's on the train, it's a clear shot to the city."

Marcus jumped out of the car, stepped up to the ticket booth, and bought a one-way off-peak ticket to Grand Central.

He walked back and handed the ticket to Julia. "Listen, he'll be waiting on the platform, you can't miss him: six feet four, red hair, flirts like a son of a bitch. You've met him at my weddings."

Julia smiled, nodding, as she got out of the car. She silently gave Marcus a hug, which he returned.

"You'll be fine. There's no one I would trust more," Marcus said.

"I was just about to say that about you. You'll take care of him? Make sure he doesn't do anything stupid?" Julia said, alluding to Nick.

"You know that's never easy."

"What are you doing?" Nick asked.

"I'm going with you." Marcus looked at him as if it were obvious. "You think I'm letting you do this on your own?"

"I'm not putting you in the middle of this."

"What are you talking about? You already did."

Nick couldn't deny the truth. "But I need you to go with her —"

"I'll be fine," Julia said. "It's a train ride —"

315

Nick held up his hand for her to stop talking.

"Why do you think I have Ben taking care of Julia?" Marcus said. "In the whole scheme of things she's now safe, out of danger, so you can focus . . . so we can focus."

The roar of the train could be heard approaching from the north.

Julia took both of Nick's hands in hers, looked up into his eyes, and spoke to his heart. "I love you. I love you more than life."

Nick stared at her with fear in his eyes, worried that she was traveling alone.

"I'll be fine," Julia said, squeezing his hands with reassurance the way her mother used to do to her when she was a child. "You be careful."

"I will, I just want you away from here till I get things sorted out."

"You come and get me, because we've got things to talk about, lives to get on with."

"I'll see you this evening, no later than 10:00 P.M., I promise. But I don't think we'll be seeing the Mullers for dinner."

"You planned it this way, didn't you?" Julia smiled. "I have something to tell you when you pick me up, so don't be late."

The train came around the bend, heading into the station.

"I won't be late," Nick said as he walked her up onto the platform.

"You should probably have this," Julia said as she pulled her PDA from her purse and passed it to him.

"Thanks," Nick said, tucking it into his pocket.

"Remember what you promised," she shouted back at Marcus. "Nothing stupid."

The train pulled in, its brakes squealing as it came to a stop. The door whisked open with a release of air right where they were standing.

"Ten o'clock," Julia said.

Nick pulled her into a long, hard kiss, a lifetime of passion passing between them in seconds. He finally released her as the door buzzed in preparation for closing. "Ten o'clock. No later," Nick said in agreement.

Julia stepped into the train, the doors coming together, closing between them.

"I love you," Julia mouthed from the other side of the door.

And the train pulled from the station.

"Protect the goalie," Marcus said as he walked up behind him. "That's my job."

"You're an idiot."

"Ah, maybe," Marcus said as he straightened his tie and tucked in his white shirt. "But right now, I'm your idiot."

■ ■ ■ ■

Horace Randall was six months from retiring. Twenty-five years on the force. He had put in an extra five hoping to put away enough money to retire. But life being what it was, he had already spent his retirement fund and would be leaving the department in December without a dime in the bank.

He had come in at the age of twenty-eight filled with piss and vinegar and an altruistic view of justice. But the years of exposure to a system that had no true black-and-white demarcation of right and wrong but instead was filled with gray areas of political expediency had broken his spirit. He had spent the last ten years going through the motions, pushing paper, and drinking beer.

He had never fired his gun on duty, never chased a suspect down, never lived the life of a romanticized cop. And that suited him just fine.

He had mentored Ethan Dance when he joined the force ten years ago, taking him under his wing, showing him the ropes, watching as he quickly rose to detective. He knew full well of Dance's extracurricular activities but as long as they didn't affect Randall, they didn't bother him and besides, though he wasn't a model cop, he was true blue and would never turn on his fellow officers.

Randall weighed in at 240 pounds. He'd averaged ten pounds of additional weight a year for the last eight years, his thirty-two-inch waist a distant memory. His horn-rimmed glasses were considered retro cool by some of the young patrolmen but truth be told he'd worn the exact same frames since he was fifteen.

Dance knew Randall's situation and had offered him a retirement solution, a healthy bank account that would provide for him for the rest of his life.

It had fallen to Horace Randall to find Julia Quinn. While they planned to get her at home this evening, the timetable had been moved up by Dance for God knew what reason. Things would have been so much simpler if they'd stuck with their original plan.

While Randall was known as lazy, most people didn't realize that laziness bred ingenuity; if necessity was the mother of invention, then laziness was the father. Randall wasn't about to drive all over looking for Julia Quinn when just a few strokes of the keyboard could accomplish so much more.

While life had come to a standstill in Byram Hills, people still needed to shop, to eat, to get gas. As sad as it was, life went on despite tragedy. Randall sent out Julia's image as a missing person in connection with the North East Air crash, emailing and faxing it to the bordering police jurisdictions, the rail stations, and the neighboring towns' restaurants, gas stations, and businesses.

She was a beautiful woman; her DMV photo couldn't diminish that in the least. There was no doubt she would catch the eye of everyone he reached out to, he just didn't expect to get a call so quickly. But it was good to know that in this day and age, the citizens of this county could really pull together when a life was on the line.

The express train was practically empty. As it was midday there wasn't much travel to and from the city, unlike rush hour, when nary a seat could be found. There were only two others in the train car: an older woman, dressed in Chanel on her way to some Friday evening function, her face buried in a tawdry novel, and a young man, dressed in doctor's scrubs, who struggled to stay upright and awake as he read his newspaper.

Julia rarely took the train, finding it inconvenient and confining, preferring to drive her car in and out of the city with the option of listening to the radio or talking on her cell phone at her leisure.

As she finally settled back in her seat, she couldn't believe she had been on Flight 502, buckled in, prepped to go. And now she sat in this train, on the run. Her feeling of being saved, of being plucked from death had been short-lived.

She could never understand what ran through the minds of those who inflicted pain and suffering on others, how they could willingly bring people to harm. She had never feared for her life before, never contemplated her own death, but now in a space of less than two hours she had found herself looking at death from a variety of angles, all of which made her appreciate the value of life, the value of the moment and how precious it truly is.

Both Marcus and Nick had told her not to worry, which only made her worry more. She had no idea why Nick was so fearful, but in the sixteen years they had been together, other than lightning and flying, he wasn't afraid of anything. She quelled her own fears, placing her trust in her husband. He wasn't foolish — far from it. He had a combination of street smarts and intelligence that manifested not only in a successful career but in a successful life. If anyone could save her, if anyone could make matters right, it was Nick.

Julia ran her hand along her belly. Though it was still flat, she could sense the life within her womb, growing, developing, a completion of her union with Nick, truly a child of their love that would bind them together for all eternity, a combination of the best parts of both of them. She wondered how the genetic slot machine of life would play out. Would he or she look like Nick or Julia, or would the child be a combination? Blonde hair, brown hair, maybe red hair, as it did run on both sides of their families. Green eyes or blue? There was no question the child would be predisposed to athletics, following in its parents' footsteps . . . or maybe not. What if the child hated sports? Whatever the newborn was, she would be happy, as the child would be theirs, a new focus in their lives that would change all priorities.

She had planned to tell Nick as soon as she saw him — her grand plans of sonogram pictures and paternal surprise having been dashed — but then Marcus had shown up with Nick. Her good news would have to wait for a more solitary moment.

As she pondered what was going on, the

train slowed and came to a stop. Julia looked out the window, her heart suddenly thundering in her ears. They were in the middle of nowhere, in a no-man's-land between stations. This was supposed to be an express train, next stop Grand Central Station, smack dab in the middle of Manhattan.

Julia poked her head into the aisle, looking up and down the narrow walkway, through the glass doors that separated the train cars, but saw nothing. Praying this was strictly train business and not her business, hoping it was just a coincidence, she sat back in her seat. There was no announcement from the conductor, no information offered on their status, the ticket taker didn't show his face, and no one seemed to care, except for Julia.

And with a gasp, the doors slid open. The other two passengers looked up from their reading but quickly went back to their own thoughts, burying their heads in books and newspapers, unconcerned with what was going on.

This was not a coincidence. Julia crouched in her seat and pulled out her cell phone. Panic such as she had never known flowed through her. She wanted to run — she could outrun almost anyone — but had no idea in what direction to flee.

She speed-dialed Nick, her words, her plea for help ready to explode from her lips. His cell phone rang. And rang again and again before finally going to voicemail.

And then he was there, standing over her, an older man with a bad haircut, horn-rimmed glasses, heavyset, and breathing hard. He held a photo in his meaty hand, glanced at it, and then back to her.

"Hello, Julia Quinn."

Nick turned on and read from Julia's PDA. While he couldn't open the video files, the documents were properly formatted for viewing. He read the inventory of what Hennicot had stored away in numerous crates at Washington House: Monets, Picassos, Renoirs, and Gordon Greens. Some of the finest works of art the world had known from all periods, distant past to the present. The antiques and sculptures were many and varied.

Nick read through the inventory three times, each time astounded by the collection, which rivaled those of the finest museums. But as he read it through, there was no mention of any mahogany box. He sorted the file by year, by type, by location in the lower level, but time and again found no mention of it.

"What weighs twenty-five pounds, can be contained in a two-foot-by-two-foot mahogany box, and bears a value of untold millions?"

Marcus shook his head as he drove through the back roads of Byram Hills, heading toward town. "A few gold bars weigh that but don't come close in value. Twenty-five pounds of diamonds, now that has to be in the hundreds of millions."

"I suppose."

"What are you looking for?"

"It's what Sam Dreyfus took; it's why everything in their little robbery went bad."

"Nothing is worth dying over. Except maybe love. If you felt strongly enough about someone."

"I don't think anyone ever really intends to die for what they want, for their cause. Somewhere in their mind they think they'll survive."

"Well, if it was in that plane, it's probably nothing but vapor now. Who cares?" Marcus pressed on. "How are we going to get this guy Dance?"

"With bait," Nick said as he held up the PDA.

"And what do we do with him once he's trapped, how do you know the whole police department isn't bad?"

"I think I know someone I can trust." Nick opened his cell phone and dialed.

The two cars faced each other, the green Taurus and the blue Bentley. They were parked in the middle of the Byram Hills High School parking lot, a wide-open expanse with a single half-mile driveway acting as the only entrance and exit. With no school in session and the plane crash a mile down the road, the school was deserted like the rest of the town.

"Who are you?" Dance said as he stepped from the green Ford.

Nick stared at him, holding back his anger and rage at the soul within this man, a man who would try to kill him in the future, who would kill Private McManus and Paul Dreyfus, who would be the catalyst for Julia's death.

"Are you alone?" Nick asked.

"Yeah, even though you're not," Dance said as he looked at Marcus standing against his Bentley.

Nick held up the PDA. "You know what this is?"

Dance said nothing.

"It's a copy, one of several that contains footage of you and your friends breaking into Washington House." Nick had actually not seen any footage of Dance or anyone other than someone he had yet to identify, but Dance didn't know that. "Sam really screwed up."

"Who?" Dance feigned ignorance.

"You remember, Sam, the one who brought *you* in to help, who you pretty much turned on? The same Sam Dreyfus who is dead along with two hundred others in Sullivan Field."

"If that's a PDA," Dance said, "then it probably belongs to Julia Quinn."

Nick hated poker, as he tried to mask the hate from his face.

"Maybe I have something to trade for it." Dance smiled. "Maybe I have her."

Nick was relieved, knowing Julia was on the train to New York, knowing that he had the upper hand.

"Or maybe you committed the robbery?" Dance pressed on.

"What?"

"Do you know it's a felony to bribe a police officer?"

"Nice try."

With his back to the access road, Dance didn't see the green jeep coming down the road behind him. The army vehicle drove past Dance and came to a stop. Private

McManus stepped out of the driver's seat followed by three young, green-fatigue-dressed Guardsmen with pistols at their sides and rifles slung over their shoulders.

Nick was glad to see the young private alive and hoped that maybe now he would stay that way. "I'm Nick Quinn, the one who called."

"I don't know what we can do for you, Mr. Quinn. This isn't part of our mandate, we are supposed to be working the crash site."

"This won't take long."

"How do you know me?" McManus asked. "I don't recall meeting."

"Colonel Wells gave me your cell phone number," Nick said, knowing soldiers rarely ask questions when their CO's name is invoked. Nick wasn't about to mention that the young private would give him his number in the future, a future that was currently dim for McManus, a future that would include his death before the afternoon was over. But with what Nick was doing now, he hoped to save lives, he hoped to give McManus back his future. "Top of your class in riflery, just got your MBA, you hate flipping burgers."

McManus looked surprised that a stranger would know such things about him.

"Why don't you just get back in your little jeep and go play army at the crash site?" Dance said through gritted teeth.

"Why don't you watch what you say?" McManus shot back.

"You have no jurisdiction here," Dance snarled.

"The governor would beg to differ with you on that, as would the Constitution. In times of emergency, at the discretion of the governor, we can be mobilized with primary authority granted by the governor's decree."

"I don't need this weekend warrior bullshit," Dance said, placing his hand on his gun.

McManus instantly raised and cocked his rifle, the three other Guardsmen following suit, their rifles pointed, held in the hands of men no older than twenty-two who had never been in a *situation* before.

"If you wish to challenge my authority," McManus barked at the older policeman, "I suggest you do it by calling your commanding officer, because I can promise you, with the course you are choosing by drawing that gun, you'll never get to hear the answer, which is, I overrule you."

"You're interfering with my investigation," Dance said, as he stared at the four rifle barrels aimed at him.

"We'll sort all that out when you remove your hand from your gun."

"We'll see," Dance said as he looked over the shoulder of McManus. "Maybe we'll sort it out by different means."

Two police cars flew down the road, engines growling, lights flashing, sirens silent. They pulled up with a skid, disgorging four uniformed police, who drew their guns, taking up positions behind their open car doors.

The three Guardsmen instantly crouched behind their jeep and turned their weapons on the police.

"Drop your weapons," a young red-haired patrolman screamed. "Now."

McManus kept his gun and eyes aimed at Dance. "My name is Private McManus of the National Guard, we are here under the authority of the governor of the state of New York, we have jurisdiction in this town at this time that supersedes yours. Pick up your radio and confirm it."

"Lower your weapons," the patrolman shouted again, his skinny frame trembling.

The situation continued to escalate, no one relenting, as the air filled with testosterone-driven aggression. The police and Guardsmen peered over and from behind their vehicles, guns sweeping back and forth; McManus's gun sight remained trained on Dance's forehead for the kill shot; Dance's quavering hand floated just above his pistol, ready to draw.

And Nick and Marcus were caught in the middle.

"Make the call," McManus shouted, "before someone makes a mistake."

The moment hung in the air. Time ticking . . .

And the red-haired patrolman disappeared into his car. The three other cops maintained their positions, their guns held high, as did the National Guardsmen, no one flinching.

Nick and Marcus exchanged glances, never having imagined that they would be on the edge like this.

The patrolman stepped from his vehicle and calmly walked around to the front of his car, his hands at his side, his weapon holstered. He turned to his fellow police and nodded for them to stow their guns.

"You have no idea what you have just done, Brinehart," Dance said to the young patrolman.

"Detective," Brinehart said to Dance, "this man is correct. I suggest you remove your hand from your piece."

With hate-filled eyes, Dance complied.

"Now," Officer Brinehart said, "will someone tell me what is going on?"

"There was a robbery of Washington
House this morning," Nick said. "Detective
Dance was part of the team that pulled it
off."

Brinehart turned to Dance.

"Do you really think that?" Dance said in
response. "These two men were the perpe-
trators of the crime. They were trying to
bribe me."

McManus and Brinehart turned their attention to Nick.

"That's ridiculous." Nick pointed at the
green Taurus, knowing what was there.
"Check his trunk."

"Why don't you check their car?" Dance
yelled, sweat beading at his temples. "They
offered me diamonds, a million dollars'
worth, to keep my mouth shut."

Private McManus and Officer Brinehart
looked to each other, the two young civil
servants thinking, wondering what to do.

"Why don't you both give us your keys?"
McManus finally said.

Brinehart walked to Dance. "Sorry, sir,
but I need them."

Dance pulled out his keys, his eyes boring
into Nick as he slammed them into Brinehart's hand.

Marcus reached into his pocket, waited for Brinehart to turn his way, and tossed them to him.

Without a word, with the eyes of both police and Guardsmen upon him, Brinehart walked to the Taurus and opened the trunk, the lid obscuring everyone's view as he peered inside. He paused a moment, reaching in, before quickly closing it. Without a word, he walked to the Bentley convertible. He opened the trunk, again staring inside, but quickly closed it. He stood there a moment looking at Nick, Dance, and Marcus. He walked to the passenger side, opened the door, and sat in the plush leather seat. He stuck the key in and opened the glove compartment. Again, the vehicle obscured everyone's view as he reached into its small confines.

Brinehart stepped from the opulent luxury car, closed the door, and pulled out his handcuffs.

He walked to Dance and with a troubled voice said, "I'm sorry about all this."

He then quickly turned to Nick. "Hands behind your back, please."

"What?" Nick looked at McManus.

"Officer, what did you find?" McManus asked.

"Please don't make this situation any

harder than it is," Brinehart said to Nick, forcibly turning him around and slamming the cuffs over his wrists.

"Officer, what did you find?" McManus said.

Brinehart handed him the keys.

McManus walked to Dance's car and opened the trunk of the vehicle. He peered inside to find a spare tire, some iron plates, a medical kit, an AED, some plastic zip-tie restraints, a box of bike chains, and three flares.

McManus turned to Marcus's car, reached over the passenger door, opening the glove compartment, and pulled out a small bag. He loosened the draw string on the small black velvet pouch and peered in at a handful of glistening diamonds.

"You son of a bitch, you planted those," Marcus yelled at Brinehart. He turned to Dance. "How many work for you? All of them?

"How much did you sell your integrity for, officer?" Marcus turned back and yelled at Brinehart.

Marcus turned to Dance, walking into his space. "You won't get away with this."

"Turn around," Dance ordered Marcus.

"In your dreams, you bastard."

Dance grabbed Marcus by the arm, but

that was a huge mistake. Despite his size, despite the fact that he was in his late thirties, Marcus was bottled lightning. He snap-grabbed Dance's hand from his shoulder and in one motion, pulled him toward him while throwing a bone-crushing punch, the combined momentum exploding into Dance's jaw, knocking him to the ground.

Marcus had cocked his fist again and reached down for Dance when the butt of McManus's rifle crunched the back of his head, sending him unconscious to the ground next to the detective.

McManus turned to his men, nodding them to get back into the jeep. "Sorry about this," McManus said to Dance.

Dance glared at the young weekend soldier. "Maybe you and your men should get back to the crash site and leave us to do our job."

"My apologies, sir," McManus said.

The soldier offered his hand to Dance, but the detective ignored both the offer of assistance and the apology as he slowly got to his feet, rubbing his bruised jaw.

Without another word the young private jumped into the driver's seat and drove off.

"Brinehart, you help take them in." Dance turned to the three other police officers. "We've got it from here. Get back to the crash site and help those poor people who lost their loved ones."

The three cops got into the patrol car and left.

Dance turned and leaned into Nick's face.

"Does he know?" Nick said.

Dance continued glaring at Nick but remained silent.

"Know what?" Brinehart said as he knelt over the unconscious body of Marcus, pulling his hands behind his back to cuff him.

Nick looked down on the young red-headed cop in his crisp, blue police uniform. It had taken Nick a few minutes, but he had finally recognized him. "That detective Ethan Dance here is going to tie one of those weights in the trunk of his car to your ankles and throw you to your death in the Kensico Reservoir and —"

Dance's gun smashed into the side of Nick's head, driving him to the ground.

"Maybe I'll just toss *you* in the reservoir," Dance said as he gave Nick's dazed, writhing body a swift kick in the gut.

"Where the hell were you?" Dance yelled as he got out of his Taurus.

"It's not easy getting away with everything going on," Brinehart said as he closed the twenty-foot loading bay door behind him.

He stepped to the rear of his car. "Did you see the crash site? It's inhuman."

Brinehart opened his trunk, lifted the two duffel bags out of his car, and put them in the open trunk of Dance's Taurus.

"I could have been killed." Dance continued berating the young officer.

"Relax, I saved your ass," Brinehart waved his hand.

"Where are the diamonds?"

Brinehart pulled the black velvet pouch from his pocket and handed it to Dance.

"So help me God, if a single stone is missing —"

"You talk a tough game for someone who just had to be saved from walking into a trap."

"Watch yourself." Dance jabbed his finger into Brinehart's face. "I was smart enough to pull the bags from my car. Smart enough to have you gather some backup to save me. So in fact, I saved myself."

"Yeah, of course. And if the two guys in the warehouse behind me know you're involved in the robbery, how many others know?" Brinehart stepped closer to Dance, moving into his space. "And what the hell does he mean, that you are going to drop me in the reservoir? Are you thinking of killing me, Dance? Are you thinking of killing all of us? Because I don't think you know me very well."

"Listen to me, very carefully." Dance leaned even closer to Brinehart. "Watch your step or you will not get a dime."

"Hey, Dance," Brinehart said. "Remember, they came for you, not me."

"You think I would take a bullet for you, Brinehart? You don't know *me* very well. Careful — if things get too crazy, I just may drop you in a lake."

Brinehart's face crumbled. He was outmatched. He quietly pulled a pistol from his waistband, handing it to Dance. "I pulled it off the one with hair."

"Good job, Brinehart. Now both our prints are on it."

Nick and Marcus sat ten feet apart, facing each other in a dimly lit room, the sole light coming from the wash under the steel bay door. Their hands were cuffed behind their backs, their feet secured to the legs of the chair.

"You all right?" Nick said.

"No, dammit. I'm pissed and my back hurts. And I'm going to break the jaw of that bastard who hit me," Marcus shouted as he turned his head back and forth, trying to work out the kinks. "Do you have any idea where we are?"

Nick looked around the room, at the large open space. There were crates along the wall, a single desk in the corner. The power was out, as it was everywhere else in Byram Hills.

"In a dark room," Nick said, trying to calm his friend.

"Smartass."

"It's a warehouse."

"No shit?" Marcus said facetiously. "Where the hell is everybody?"

"Everyone is over at the plane crash or home."

"You know how much money I give to the police retirement fund each year?" Marcus looked down at his wrinkled shirt, his torn pants. "That's over. They ruined a perfectly good shirt and pants."

Nick looked at the clock on the wall. 1:50.

"Stop looking at that clock," Marcus said. "Time's not going to slow down."

Nick had less than ten minutes to get himself and Marcus out of here before he slipped back in time again, leaving Marcus alone and at the mercy of Dance.

Nick fought to keep the guilt out, the feeling of what he was putting his best friend through. He had set out to save Julia, but had inadvertently put his friend in mortal danger. Nick refused to have Marcus's blood on his hands, and as soon as he had the chance he would free them, but he had to think quickly, as there was little likelihood they would survive if left in their current state.

Dance walked through a side door, slamming it behind him with a loud, jarring crash. He quietly walked into the room, circling his two captives. Finally stopping in front of Nick, he leaned into his face and whispered in his ear, "Where's your wife, Nicholas?"

Nick stared at him, rage boiling in his eyes.

"Why do I bother asking you?" Dance turned to Marcus. "Where is she? Who else knows about the robbery?"

Marcus smiled a taunting smile, a Cheshire Cat smile, one he used often in toying with his business adversaries during negotiations.

"Listen to me, did you hear me?" Dance yelled, suddenly riled up. "Where is she? Who else knows about the robbery?"

Dance drew back his fist and unloaded it into Marcus's nose, breaking it for the fourth time in his life. The blood ran down his lip, dripping on his white shirt and blue Hermès tie.

"Now," Marcus said in a whisper, unaffected by the sucker punch. "You listen to me, you coward. Free my hands and hit me, let's see how tough you really are."

Dance pile-drived the side of Marcus's face in answer.

"Tell me where she is," Dance yelled at Nick as he pulled a gun, aiming at him, the moment hanging in the air. "Recognize your gun?"

And Dance spun around, smashing the pistol against Marcus's head before jamming the barrel up under his chin.

"Tell me where your wife is, or he dies," Dance said to Nick. This wasn't just a threat, Nick could see Dance's eyes confirming the truth in his words.

Nick stared at Marcus, his heart breaking as he was forced to choose one life over another.

Marcus looked at Nick, subtly shaking his head, and smiled. It was a warm half-smile, the kind he gave him after Nick had let the puck slip by into the goal, after he had missed a match-winning putt. It was the everything-will-be-okay-because-we're-friends smile, the one they shared every time one of Marcus's wives left him.

"You do it, so help me God, I'll kill you," Nick said with hate.

"That will be a pretty neat trick," Dance

said. "Seeing I'm going to kill you next."

"You mother f—" Nick struggled violently in his chair, the veins on his neck distended, his shoulders and arms uselessly shaking.

"Nick," Marcus said softly.

"You listen to me, you piece of shit," Nick yelled at Dance, ignoring his friend.

"Julia is safe," Marcus said, continuing his words in a softly spoken plea.

"I'll rip your heart out!" Nick screamed at Dance, violently shaking his chair in frustration.

"Nick," Marcus whispered, finally getting his attention, calming his friend, his soft words contrary to his character. "Julia is safe. Know that, take comfort in that. Don't worry about me."

And the door slowly opened. A heavyset man, a man Nick recognized, stood in the doorway. It was the accomplice to Julia's murder, the gray-haired man who had stood at his front door ringing the bell, distracting him from protecting Julia as she was killed.

"Perfect," Dance said, relief in his voice.

And he pulled the trigger. The sound of the gun shattered the moment. Marcus's head exploded backward in a rain of blood before falling forward against his chest.

Nick couldn't pull his eyes from his dead friend, the sound of the bullet's report echoing in his ear, only to be replaced by a bloodcurdling scream coming from the doorway.

And as Nick turned his head, all hope was lost, everything he had tried to do was for naught. His best friend was dead, he was powerless, and Dance would get away with it all.

For standing in the doorway, screaming in fear, with terror-filled eyes, was the last person he thought he'd see.

And his heart broke as he saw Julia helplessly standing there.

And his world went black.

CHAPTER 3

Noon

Nick fell to the floor of his library, howling in agony at his best friend's death, at leaving Julia behind to die once again.

It was no longer just about saving her from her death at 6:40 P.M. It was about saving her at 1:00 from the future he had just created for her, in which he left her alone to perish at the hands of Dance. It was about changing the future he had created for Marcus, his best friend who helped him without question, who believed him when he spoke of impossible scenarios and gold watches, who gave his life to save Julia's, a sacrifice that had proved in vain.

Nick had been playing God and was now reaping the consequences.

Lives are set, actions irrevocable, yet Nick was playing chess, running about, moving the pieces on the board of a game already lost. He couldn't reach forward and save his

344

friends, constantly tossed backward as if he was a character in a Greek myth with Zeus and Athena playing with his life. Only this time Zeus wore a double-breasted blue blazer and gave out mysterious watches that Einstein had never heard of.

Every ripple, every misstep of the last nine hours had led to consequences that compounded his initial situation. His life had been torn apart bit by bit.

Who can predict the paths our lives will take, what fateful detours will steer us either into or away from disaster, what unselfish deed will provoke a war.

Nick had to stop it all from happening, if he was to have any chance of putting things right, but with each step he took, each change he made, he was creating a future that was far worse than the one he had originally been faced with.

Marcus was right, he realized. The unintended consequences of our actions change not just our own future but the future of all of those around us, all those we care for.

Nick raced down Sunrise Drive, pushing the Audi as hard as he could. He had grabbed his personal cell phone from his desk, having left it in Marcus's car in the future. He did likewise with his car keys, finding them in the red rooster key box in the mudroom. He had pulled the pistol from his safe and now felt its cold steel at the small of his back. He was amazed when he spun the dial left, right, left and opened the safe to see it sitting there. He had once again left it behind in the future only to find it here in the past. He tried to wrap his mind about the paradox. He thought of the consequences of pulling it from his safe so many times, each removal eliminating it from the possibility of its being there in the future. But as far as he was concerned there was no future if Julia wasn't alive.

As Nick hit town, he drove right into the center of mayhem. The sidewalks were packed, the streets were filled, traffic was jammed in gridlock, drivers standing beside their idling cars. All eyes were cast skyward at the thick black plumes of smoke, the fiery explosions that lit the dark underbelly of the jet-fuel-created clouds, their ground-shaking rumbles pouring in three seconds later.

It was as if war were being waged in Byram Hills, or as if there was a giant creature on the horizon that would reach out and swallow them whole. Panic filled the air as shopkeepers locked their doors, as parking lots emptied.

Men and women frantically dialed cell phones with shaking hands, forgetting what flights their loved ones might be on. Kids looked up in wide-eyed wonder, unaware of what they gazed upon.

Death had come to Byram Hills.

There were shouts, and screams, and gasps of awe, all directed at Sullivan Field. People raced down the sidewalk, pedestrians jumped into cars. The scream of fire engines en route filled the distance. Police cruisers raced through side streets, their chirping, intermittent wails clearing a path. All were converging on disaster.

Prayers were said, mundane problems forgotten, all concern directed toward the victims and the families left behind.

Nick inched his car forward, caught within the panicked masses. His eye was drawn to the clock on the dashboard, the sight of which made the watch in his pocket feel like a piece of lead: 12:05.

Less than three hours before time ran out.

As the traffic finally abated, Nick turned onto Maple Avenue, heading for Washington House. He flipped on his blinker but quickly flipped it off and hit the accelerator.

He had forgotten about time.

Julia's Lexus sat parked in the side lot of the building owned by Shamus Hennicot.

Julia was alive somewhere inside, coming to grips with the fact that her client had been robbed, entirely unaware of the consequences the burglary would have on the future that awaited her.

He thought of running in, wrapping his arms about her, and holding on forever, but the robbery had already happened. Paranoia was already setting in on Dance and his team. Their search for witnesses, security video, and ultimately Julia had already begun.

He thought of re-enlisting Marcus in his quest, but he had already led him to death once. He thought of whisking Julia away but knew that somehow she would be found, her death inevitable, as he had seen twice already. McManus had yet to arrive on the scene and he had no idea where Paul Dreyfus was.

Nick pulled out and looked at the St. Christopher medal, pulled from the neck of Julia's killer. He had initially thought it would be the talisman that would lead them to Julia's murderer, but it had been just another piece of metal weighing down his pocket, a clue that proved useless. He had been so convinced it was Dance's, but Dance wore nothing about his neck.

He had seen Shannon in his sweat-covered

tank top, but again there was nothing there. Brinehart had been killed by Dance before Julia was shot, Randall was the overweight accomplice who had distracted him at his front door. That left Arilio, whom he had yet to see, and Rukaj. It could be either of them, or even someone who had yet to be revealed to Nick. He would remain diligent but had abandoned hope in the necklace's power of identification.

Nick realized that the St. Christopher medal, the mahogany box, the gold swords and daggers, every hour, every death all pointed back to a single point of origin. All things converged on the robbery of Shamus Hennicot.

Everything, saving Julia, saving Marcus, it would all come down to preventing that singular incident, to seeing that Dance never pulled a job that he would have to cover up. But to do that, he could not impede it now, not after it happened. He would have to wait until 11:00, before they went into the building. Which would give him forty-five minutes to put the pieces together, forty-five minutes to formulate a plan for taking on a team of armed men, a team lead by Detective Ethan Dance, a man who took lives as easily as he took a breath.

■ ■ ■ ■

The Byram Hills police officer sat in his unmarked car, his eyes fixed on the white building fifty yards ahead as he nervously drummed his fingers on the wheel. His dark-brimmed hat sat on the seat beside him. He hated that hat, how it flattened his red hair, how ridiculous it looked, wondering why the pillbox, patent-leather-brim style was still in use seventy-five years after its design when the rest of fashion lived in the present.

Nolan Brinehart had longed to be a detective since he was a child, dreaming of being one of those brilliant TV heroes who rights the wrongs, who figures out the impossible crimes from vague, inadequate clues. But he had trouble with figuring out quadratic equations and algebra, not to mention that he could barely do jigsaw puzzles as a kid.

He had gone to Byram Hills High School and had a fair amount of experience with the police as a youth. Of course it was from the other side of the law. Never charged with or convicted of anything, he was your typical delinquent, drunk and disorderly, causing fights, but nothing beyond the wildness of male youth.

Hoping for the fast track so he could begin to earn a decent wage and leave the ridiculous hat and blue uniform behind, he had cozied up to Detective Dance. He knew Dance had helped Detective Shannon along, had taken an interest in the fellow Brooklynite several years earlier, helping him to achieve his promotion in one-third the usual time.

And now, as with all masters and apprentices, Brinehart had found his opening. He was a willing pupil and Dance was a teacher in need of a new student.

Dance told him the romanticized world of detectives, the one that everyone knew so well from movies and television, did not exist. Crimes were usually easily solved or impossible to figure out, and the pay was underwhelming. But if Brinehart was willing to walk a slightly different path, he could not only achieve detective status in a year's time but have a bank account that would allow him a lifestyle impossible to attain on a detective's abysmal salary.

So Brinehart became a last-minute addition to Dance's crew, acting as a lookout, as a gofer, as whatever Dance needed to pull off the job.

He was looking forward to his share — a million dollars promised, money to be spent gradually, money that would allow him to be everything his wife wanted him to be. It was money Dance convinced him he deserved, taken from a man who would not even miss it, whose wealth he could never conceive.

He was counting on Dance's talent and experience to make their crime impossible to solve. He had been told it would be an easy job, with inside information. All he had to do was keep an eye out for anything suspicious, any problems or people that might approach the house while they were inside.

He had watched as Sam Dreyfus led Dance, Randall, and Arilio into Washington House, remaining outside on lookout. He watched as Randall and Arilio carried the two duffel bags out and put them in the back of Dance's Taurus before heading back inside.

Sam emerged two minutes later carrying a brown wooden box under his arm. The middle-aged man spoke to him briefly about the success of the operation and the easy money they just made before he hopped into Randall's Chrysler and drove off.

Moments later, Dance exploded out the door like a wild animal, diving into his car and tearing off after Sam.

Brinehart had never realized that the problem to watch for would come from within the house, from within their group of five. He was the last-minute guy; he thought they were all connected, friends, partners. He had never thought that their inside man had issues, issues that could throw their entire scheme into disarray, sending it skidding into disaster.

Dance called from his car ripping into Brinehart for letting Sam get away, for being so stupid as to let him get into Randall's car and drive off without even challenging him. Dance went on to tell him to remain and watch the house for anything suspicious and to report anything he saw. And to not continue on the path of stupidity.

Brinehart watched the woman in the black Lexus drive in at 11:50. Her car had been sitting in wait for twenty-five minutes now. He had run the plates. Julia Quinn, a name they had thought might arise, the attorney for Shamus Hennicot.

He had ignored the all-hands call to the plane crash, sitting in his unmarked patrol car under the hedges of Wampus Park, watching as his police brethren, along with every fire truck and volunteer fireman, raced to the scene. He heard the cries over his radio of a disaster like nothing that had ever been witnessed. His curiosity constantly baited him to leave his post, but he had been posted here by Dance, told to watch any activity and to keep an eye out for anything out of the ordinary.

The Audi had circled three times now, which would not normally be too suspicious for someone who was lost, but with black smoke and flame filling the air, the streets clearing, and emergency vehicles racing off, no one who is lost circles about three times.

He ran the plates, finding the car belonged to Nicholas Quinn, who resided at the same address as Julia Quinn. His heart beat a bit faster as his suspicion rose; it was almost as if Quinn didn't want his wife to know he was there.

Brinehart watched Julia Quinn emerge from Washington House and look up into the sky. She pulled her cell phone from her purse and dialed as she got into her Lexus, quickly pulling from the driveway and heading off.

And as she disappeared down the road, the Audi returned, slowing as it approached Washington House, finally pulling into the driveway.

That was all the confirmation Brinehart needed. He started his car, drove across the street and blocked the driveway.

■ ■ ■ ■

Nick had driven around the mile-square block, circling back to Washington House three times now. On each round, the mayhem grew. A panic was overtaking people, as they were unsure what was going on. Crawling through the traffic, he could hear the murmur of the crowd, feeling the anxiety of the people, the shouting about a plane crash, a pipeline, a terrorist attack.

And there was Larry Powers standing in front of his wife's gift shop. People circled him, surrounded him as if he was the town crier who had all the answers.

Nick heard people talking in amazement.

". . . I saw it. I was looking up, it was horrible. It was two planes —"

"— Two planes?" someone yelled. "What kind?"

"One slammed right into the other, like two birds crashing into one another, both falling dead out of the sky . . ."

Caught in the flow of traffic, horns blaring behind him, Nick drove on as Paul Dreyfus's words floated up in his mind. It was his plane, his brother at the controls. The fateful robbery of Shamus Hennicot did not just result in Julia's death, it also caused the crash of North East Air Flight 502, killing 212 passengers. So many innocents killed by greed.

Nick's focus throughout this upside-down day had been so trained on Julia that he hadn't thought of what was truly behind the crash, what had caused the AS 300 to drop from the sky on a cloudless summer morning.

Nick thought of calling what he knew in to the NTSB so efforts could be focused on things other than the cause of the crash, but they would learn the truth soon enough.

And then Nick realized that, if he was truly successful in stopping the robbery, if he was to halt Sam Dreyfus and Ethan Dance from carrying out their plan, not only would Julia be saved . . .

As Nick made the turn onto Maple Avenue, he saw Julia's Lexus in the distance, driving away toward Route 22. He slowed and scanned the area again. On each pass he looked about for Dance, but he was nowhere to be seen, the roads filled with cars exiting town, everyone escaping as if another plane or a house would drop out of the sky landing atop their heads. Byram Hills was awash in the survival instinct of fight or flee; while many were heading home, just as many were heading across Route 22 onto the access road to Sullivan Field. Some went out of morbid curiosity, most went to help, some drove, others ran, and it all grew to a steady stream of townsfolk rushing to the rescue.

And he realized it was true: Mankind is at its best when things are at their worst.

He wished there was something he could do, that he could join the effort, but if Julia was to live, he needed every second of every minute devoted to figuring out how to stop the robbery. Only fifty minutes left in the hour. Fifty minutes until he was thrust back to the time when the robbery of Washington House would occur, when all the wheels would be set in motion and all paths would lead to Julia's death, Marcus's death, the loss of everything and everyone he cared about.

Nick turned into the driveway of Hennicot's Washington House. A tinge of excitement entered him as he felt the hope growing inside his heart. His plan was coming together; what he had once thought to be the fantasy of a broken man, of resurrecting his wife from the dead, was coming to fruition.

Then, as he pulled into the driveway, stepping from the Audi, the unmarked police car pulled in behind him.

■ ■ ■ ■

Brinehart stepped from his vehicle, putting on his police hat, his hand resting on his holstered pistol, and approached the Audi.

Nick stared at him, knowing full well this was not a traffic stop. He had seen Brinehart play the innocent, had seen him lie to everyone, planting the diamonds in Marcus's Bentley, which resulted in their arrest and Marcus's death.

He had actually seen Brinehart before that meeting in the high school parking lot but . . . Brinehart hadn't seen him, he was already dead at the bottom of the reservoir.

Of course, to Brinehart, this would be their first meeting.

"Is there a problem?" Nick asked.

"May I ask what you are doing?" Brinehart asked.

Two fires trucks raced by, their sirens blaring, drowning out the moment.

Nick grew suddenly conscious of the weight of his own gun pressing at the small of his back. He could reach around and grab it in seconds but thought better of it. One mistake on his part and Julia was dead.

"Sir, may I ask you to turn around and

place your hands on the roof of your vehicle?"

"Why? I haven't done anything."

"Please, sir, turn around and put your hands on the car."

Nick slowly turned, cursing himself for being so foolish as to have lulled himself into a false sense of security, thinking Dance's people weren't watching the place after the robbery.

"Before you frisk me," Nick said, looking over his shoulder, "I have a Sig-Sauer in the waistband of my pants. It's legal and licensed."

"May I ask why you're armed?" Brinehart asked as he raised Nick's jacket and removed the pistol.

"I carry it for protection."

"In Byram Hills?"

"The city," Nick said. He hated how comfortable he had gotten with lying. "I have some real estate in some rough areas."

"Mmm." Brinehart checked the safety, slipped the gun in his own waistband, and frisked Nick, running his hands from his ankles up to his arms.

"Do you mind emptying your pockets? Slowly, please."

Nick reached in and pulled out Dreyfus's wallet along with his own, placing them on

the trunk of his car. He pulled out his cell
phone and some spare change; he removed
the two envelopes from Marcus and the
European from his coat pocket, cursing
himself for still carrying them.

"Is that everything?" Brinehart said, seeing a small lump in his left front pocket.

Nick reluctantly stuck his hand in his
pocket and pulled out the gold watch and
the St. Christopher medal, watching Brinehart's eyes closely for any sign of recognition.

"Nice watch." Brinehart's focus was on
the antique. "Don't see too many of those."

Brinehart's eyes drifted over the two wal-
lets, picking them both up. "Any reason you
carry two?"

Nick remained silent as Brinehart opened
the first, seeing Nick's ID and credit cards.
He put it down and opened Dreyfus's.
There was a subtle widening of Brinehart's
eyes. He quickly turned to Nick. "Please
place your hands behind your back."

"You've got to be kidding me. What's the
problem?"

"I won't ask again." Brinehart laid his
hand back on his holster for emphasis.

Nick shook his head as he threw his hands
back, the cuffs instantly slamming about his
wrists, feeling like a death sentence.

Brinehart stepped to Nick's car, removed the keys from the ignition, and pulled the two-way radio from his belt.

"Dance?"

"Yeah," the detective's unmistakable voice answered back.

"Where are you?"

"Still at the airport, what the hell do you want?"

"We may have a problem. I found a Nicholas Quinn, snooping around Washington House."

"Quinn? As in Julia Quinn?"

"Yeah, she was here separately but left."

"Was he just watching her back?"

"He has Paul Dreyfus's wallet."

"How would he get that?"

"You want me to interrogate him?" There was glee in Brinehart's voice.

"No." Dance shot him down. "Take him to the station. Hand him off to Shannon. I want him questioned by someone with some experience."

Nick looked around the room, at the sparse metal table he sat at. The chipped metal door with the porthole glass, the dark mirrored window along the wall. The power was on, unlike everywhere else in town. He had been here over nine hours ago as the gold watch read, at 9:30 P.M., in the future. He had met Dance then. He was kindly, caring, and, as he learned later, entirely full of shit.

It had all started here in the interrogation room of the Byram Hills Police Department when he was brought in on suspicion of murdering his wife. All a setup, as he came to see, by the very man who had interrogated him.

Brinehart had taken everything from his pockets: Paul Dreyfus's wallet, his own wallet, his keys, his gun, Marcus's envelope with his letter and the *Wall Street Journal* page, the letter from the European, the St. Christopher medal, and the thing that struck terror in him, the one thing he had been told not to let out of his possession if he was to succeed, if he was to save Julia: the watch.

He had taken it for granted. Where he had at first been a skeptic, laughing at the insanity, the impossibility, now, after nine jumps, he trusted it implicitly, without doubt. He trusted it like he trusted the sun to rise every morning, no longer holding it in awe, looking at it with reverence or wonder. He hadn't pulled it from his pocket in hours to watch it tick down, believing in its sweeping hand, trusting its inner workings to pull him back through time.

It was his bridge, it was the light that would lead him to save Julia.

And now it was gone.

He looked at the clock on the wall: 12:30.

Detective Bob Shannon came into the room carrying a small, shallow, wicker basket filled with Nick's personal effects and two cups of coffee.

Shannon's dark hair was pushed back, well groomed, his hands clean, no sweat or grime on his body. He looked fit and well rested, far different from when Nick had met him at the crash site several hours from now, when the horror of death could be seen in his eyes, when the stress of the crash had nearly broken his spirit.

"Sorry to keep you waiting," Shannon said, a greeting far different from that of nine hours ago when they sat in this very room, when Shannon verbally assaulted him, accused him of killing his wife. He put a cup of coffee in front of Nick and sat down across from him.

"So you're playing the good cop?" Nick said

"Believe it or not, there's no one else here. Just you and me. I'm both good and bad," Shannon said with a smile, which quickly faded as he became distracted. He ran his hand over his dark hair as he leaned back in the metal chair. "That damn crash is something awful. Every able body is out at the site. I've got the station all by myself, just me and the desk sergeant who's handling phones for the moment. So no, I'm not pulling some cliché cop thing, it's just a good cup of coffee on a really bad day."

"I'd like to know what's going on," Nick said.

"You haven't been charged with anything, Mr. Quinn. I just need to ask you some questions. Officer Brinehart's a little green. With everything going on, we are beyond short-staffed. Detective Dance called, asked me to ask you a few questions before he got here."

"Then ask your questions," Nick said, looking at the clock on the wall, watching time slip away.

"Dance wants to know why you have this guy's wallet."

"You think I stole it?"

"No, Mr. Quinn. I've already checked you out. I know who you are, that you grew up in this town. I'm sure half the people in it would vouch for you. I know you're licensed to carry that pistol — it's locked away for the moment. So, no, despite what Dance may think, I don't think you stole it. Dance said he is looking for its owner, Paul Drey-fus, in connection with some preliminary investigation he's running."

"I found it," Nick blurted out the lie, hoping to get this over with.

"Where?"

"Outside Washington House, on the sidewalk."

"May I ask what you were doing there?"

"My wife's client is Shamus Hennicot, it's his house. She thought his place might have been burglarized; I drove by for her."

"Burglarized? What do you mean? We heard nothing of that." Nick couldn't tell if Shannon was screwing with him, whether he was one of Dance's inside guys, but the surprise on his face appeared genuine.

"She says they may have been burglarized." Nick threw his hand up in frustration. "Look, she was supposed to be on that flight today; she's really freaked out right now. I would like to go find her."

"Okay," Shannon nodded. "I just have one other question."

Nick watched Shannon reach into the basket. He saw his hand drift over Marcus's letter, over the European's letter, toward the watch, but then detour for the St. Christopher medal, lifting it out by its silver chain. He laid it on the table, the necklace dribbling down like water, and pushed it across the counter surface in front of Nick.

"Where did you get this?"

Nick picked it up, turning it over in his hand reading the fateful inscription. "I don't know who it belongs to."

"That's not what I asked." Shannon reached into his own pocket and drew out his hand, he laid it upon the table, looking at it, and finally pulled his hand back to reveal the same medal.

Nick's heart pounded, trying to explode from his chest. He looked up at Shannon, the detective who had interrogated him, had beaten on him, had actually been poised to kill him here in this very room nine hours from now, accusing him of killing his wife when he was the one who actually pulled the trigger. As much as he hated Dance, this was the man who had killed Julia.

The man he had chased from his home, through the streets, forcing him off the road into a tree. The unseen man he had a gun battle with and almost caught. The man who he had ripped this very medal off in the future, whose medal now existed in two separate times. Nick's eyes suddenly burned with hate.

"Whoa, did I hit a nerve? What's with the stare of death?" Shannon asked. "It's just a

366

religious medal."

Nick sat there wanting to reach out and kill the man who sat before him, the one person in this department he had thought he could trust.

"All other things aside," Shannon continued, "I really need to know where you got it."

"Why?" Nick whispered, as he stared at the two medals.

"Because I know who owns that, and I didn't realize it was missing."

Nick's world, for the umpteenth time, turned upside-down.

"What do you mean you know who owns it?" Nick asked. It hadn't occurred to him that there could be more than one medal.

"The inscription on the back," Shannon said as he took the medal out of Nick's hand, turned it over, and did likewise to the one on the table. And Nick saw the difference: There was no engraving on Shannon's.

"He always takes it off, along with all of his rings and his bracelet and watch, when he gets to work in the morning, tucks it in his shoe inside his locker, then puts it all back on at the end of the day before he leaves.

"Thing is, I saw him take it off at seven this morning and there is no way you could get into the locker room. This place is locked up tighter than a steel drum, and until the plane crash, it was swarming with cops."

"Whose is it?" Nick said, his voice anxious.

"Ironically, it's Detective Dance's," Shannon said.

"Are you sure it's his?" Nick asked slowly.

"Positive." Shannon leaned forward. "Look at the edge, see the chip? It happened when he was moonlighting on some job down county. And the note on the back, his mom had that done, *Miracles do happen.* She was a great lady, very religious, believed in God's influence, that it was his hand controlling fate, that we'd all be held to a higher judgment at our demise. Dance was her only child, her miracle."

And everything fell together. Dance was Julia's killer, as he was Paul Dreyfus's, McManus's, and Marcus's. He was as evil and depraved a man as Nick had ever known. Nick's mind took on a sudden focus. He needed to stop the robbery, but most of all he needed to stop Dance from ever initiating the robbery at 11:15. For if the robbery didn't occur, there would be no reason for Julia to be killed, for Marcus, for anyone to die.

But Nick took comfort in the fact that

even if he couldn't stop the robbery from happening, at least his search for Julia's killer was over; he knew who he had to kill.

Nick looked up at Shannon, his opinion of him changing for the third time today. "Why do you guys wear the same medal?"

"Dance can be a real ass, but he's family, he got me this job a few years back, we went to the same high school in Brooklyn. He's my cousin."

"He's your cousin?" Nick said in shock.

"Believe me, there's no love lost. Anyway, we went to St. Christopher's Catholic High School in Brooklyn. They gave these out at graduation."

"I hate to interrupt, but my wife . . . she has no idea where I am." Nick knew he needed to get out of here as quickly as possible in order to be in place to stop Dance and stop the robbery from ever happening.

"Right, right," Shannon said. Standing up, he gathered up the two medals, putting his in his pocket and Dance's in the basket, and opened the interrogation room door. "I just need to process you out, get you to sign for all your stuff. I promise we'll be quick."

Nick stood and followed him out of the room, happy to be free, happy to be on his way to finally setting things right, to saving

Julia, to ensuring a long future ahead of them.

Shannon laid the basket on a small desk in the hall and quickly set to filling out a triplicate legal-release form. "Your pistol is in our gun safe, I'll get it as soon as we get you signed out."

Nick picked up Marcus's envelope along with the letter he had received from the European, glad that Shannon hadn't peered at either, and tucked them back in his coat pocket.

"Shannon, what the hell are you doing?" Dance called from the corral area of the police station. He was dressed in his blue blazer, white JC Penney shirt, and blue-striped tie, and the rigors of the day were not yet reflected in his appearance.

"Where the hell have you been all morning?" Shannon shouted back. "I can't find you for hours and then you drop a silly Q&A in my lap."

Dance stormed down the corridor, walked right past Shannon, and took Nick by the arm, leading him down the hall.

"Hey," Shannon yelled as he chased after him. "What the hell are you doing?"

Dance continued down the hall, pulling Nick along with him. He opened a large metal door, revealing a large room containing five jail cells.

"Dance, let him go. He's done nothing wrong."

"Shannon here gets all touchy-feely," Dance said to Nick.

Dance pulled the door of the first jail cell fully open, shoved Nick inside, and, with a crash, slammed the iron-barred door closed behind him. The cell was ten by ten feet, surrounded by typical vertical bars with metal cross-hatches. There were two folding chairs in the center of the room and a wooden bench anchored into the wall.

"What the hell you putting the guy in there for?" Shannon asked as he came into the room. "Cut him a break. His wife just narrowly missed getting on that plane. And besides, you actually owe him, he found your St. Christopher medal that you lost."

"What?" Dance tilted his head. "I didn't lose my medal."

Silence filled the air as confusion reigned.

Shannon and Dance stepped out of the room, closing the door behind them.

"What the hell is going on?" Shannon pressed him.

"Do you mind telling me what you were doing letting him go?" Dance said.

"What are we holding him on? The only thing he did was be in the wrong place at the wrong time —" Shannon stopped. "And you never answered my question. Where the hell have you been?"

Shannon was several inches taller and carried twenty more pounds of muscle, but that didn't stop Dance from rushing into his face, staring up at him like a junkyard dog.

"You listen to me," Dance said. "Since when did you become my keeper? You work here by my grace and my grace alone, not the captain's, not anyone but me. I got you the job and I can take it away. And mind you, if I take it away it'll be by blowing the whistle to Internal Affairs."

"Give me a break," Shannon shot back. "Neither you nor they have anything on me. I'm lily-white."

"Really? How about that five grand you took off the drug bust last year?"

"Bullshit. You gave me that money, shoved it in my pocket." Shannon jabbed his finger at Dance. "And I gave it right back to you. I never want anything to do with your scheming bullshit."

"Funny, that's not how I remember it," Dance said mockingly.

"You'd make up a story to have your own flesh and blood thrown in jail?"

"Cousins doesn't make us flesh and blood. Our parents couldn't have been more different, thank God."

"You've done something," Shannon said. "I see it in your eyes. And it didn't go well, did it? If it did you'd be smiling ear to ear even with two hundred people dead in a plane crash. What the hell did you do? And what does this Quinn guy have to do with it?"

Dance opened the door to the jailroom, stepped in, and turned back to Shannon. "You go to the crash site and think long and hard about the future you want." Dance paused. "And remember who controls it."

Dance slipped the jail key in the slot, opened the heavy barred door, and stepped inside the cell, pulling it closed behind him as he stuffed the key in his pocket. He carried the small wicker basket of Nick's belongings and stared down at him as he sat in the middle of the confined space in a metal folding chair staring at the beaten-up clock on the wall.

He waved the basket before Nick's eyes. There was Paul Dreyfus's wallet, his own wallet, his cell phone, his keys, all of which he ignored, choosing to stare at the wall, but then his eyes were inexorably pulled toward the gold watch lying there, its appearance belying its power. And it was all he cared about, not the jail key in Dance's pocket that could free him from these confines, not his keys, so he could drive away. All that mattered right now was getting the watch back into his possession.

And Dance pulled the basket away, a taunting reminder that Dance controlled the moment.

"Some nice watch you have," Dance said as he pulled it from the basket. He rolled it about in his hands, running his thumb over the golden case, about the winding stem on top. He thumbed it open, staring at the old English face. "An antique. Was it your dad's, maybe your grandfather's? Big sentimental value to it? *Fugit inreparabile tempus,*" he said, reading the inscription. "I bet it would probably crush you if you lost it, huh?" Dance deposited it in his right jacket pocket.

The two envelopes in Nick's jacket pocket felt as if they were on fire. If Dance was to find them, to see the *Wall Street Journal* page, to read the letter explaining the watch . . . Marcus's words ran in his ear, ". . . in the wrong hands . . ." Nick knew there were no worse hands then Ethan Dance's.

Dance reached back into the basket and lifted up the silver St. Christopher medal. "I know if someone stole something of mine, something I held dear, something that was given to me by mother . . . well, I would be angry, to say the least."

Dance slipped the small wicker basket through the bars, laying it on the floor. He turned around and stood over Nick.

"Where did you get this?" Dance said as he dangled the St. Christopher medal in Nick's face, swinging it back and forth like a pendulum. "Were you in my locker? Was it Dreyfus? How the hell did you get in there?"

Nick remained silent as he watched Dance's eyes lose focus.

"I got this for graduation," Dance said as he turned it over and read the worn engraving. "*Miracles do happen.* My mom had that engraved because my father said it would be a miracle if I graduated, it would be a miracle if I amounted to anything. She always called me her miracle kid."

For the briefest of moments, Nick thought he saw a twinkle of humanity in Dance's eyes as he slipped the chain over his neck, the medal falling against his chest, lying oddly upon his shirt and tie, as if it was an award bestowed by royalty for service above and beyond the call of duty.

"I take it off at work because I never want to lose it. It's just about the only thing I hold dear in this world. I'm not sentimental about much, but its meaning to me is something you couldn't understand. You know, I should kill you for stealing it."

Dance reached into his pocket and pulled something out, clutching it tightly in his hand. "You're going to tell me what the hell is going on. Where did you get that medal?"

Nick didn't answer.

Dance looked at his right fist, the one clutching whatever it was he had pulled from his pocket, and without a second thought, drew it back and unloaded it into Nick's face, knocking him out of his chair.

"You better start talking," he said as he stood over Nick.

Nick rolled about the floor in pain, his right brow split open, blood boiling up, but he shut his senses down, his eyes fixed on the clock on the wall: 12:56.

"How did you do it? What kind of trick are you trying to play with me?"

And with that, Dance hit him again. The blow glanced off the side of Nick's head; Dance's aim was off from his anger.

Nick watched Dance pace around the small cell. He stopped and looked out through the bars before turning back.

Dance crouched over Nick and held his fist before Nick's face. The seconds ticked by as the two stared at each other, and then Dance opened his fist, palm-side down, and let the chain fall out of his hand, holding the dangling medal between his fingers, the medal swinging and spinning about in the air.

The St. Christopher medal hung there, a medal identical to the one that hung about Dance's neck, identical in every way. Not in the sense that it was identical to the one Shannon had, that he had also gotten when he graduated St. Christopher in Brooklyn. This medal was a carbon copy of the religious piece draped upon Dance's shirt and tie. Every nick, every scratch, the slight indentations from life. Everything was a spot-on match, and as it hung before Nick's eyes, it spun about and Nick could plainly see the engraving, *Miracles do happen.*

"How the hell did you do this? Is this some kind of sick joke to mess with my head? It's something you and Dreyfus cooked up, isn't it?" Paranoia laced his every word. "You thought that you could play me, with some twisted kind of magic?

"Well, Nicholas Quinn, Shannon was going to let you go, but I know who you really are and what you have been doing."

Nick glared at Dance.

"You're working with the Dreyfus brothers, aren't you? Helping them to screw me." Dance paused, a grin forming on his lips. "You should know, your buddy, Sam Dreyfus, is dead. He's dead because he knew I was going to kill him and he ran off like a coward clutching the prize he stole from us. I couldn't have dreamed up a better death for that twisted fuck. His brother, Paul? No doubt he was involved in trying to double-cross us, too. I'll take care of him right after I deal with you. And your wife." Dance paused. "I know who your wife is. I know she's Hennicot's attorney and she's got the security video of the robbery in her office. Maybe I'll kill her in front of you; I'd take pleasure in that."

And with those words, Nick snapped. Everything that had happened — seeing Julia dead, her face torn apart by the gun blast; her living in peril; Marcus's death; his own frustration at chasing shadows, living in a microcosm of time separate from the world, knowing the future and struggling to figure out how to change it; and now this son of a bitch pulling him from his destiny as Julia had been pulled from the plane crash — all seemed a cruel mockery, letting him get so close, but killing him before he could save her from what fate had in store for her.

Nick grabbed Dance's leg, pulling him off-balance. He leaped to his feet and with a bone-crushing right hook drilled Dance in the nose, stunning him. All Nick's anger, all his rage filled his fist as he drew it back and hammered it into Dance's jaw. He continued with a rain of blows, a release of his pain and frustration. All his emotions poured out of his clenched fists as he hit the man who would end Julia's life, who would shoot her in cold blood, a devil playing God as he ripped her from this earth. Nick would kill him right here, right now, with his bare hands. Dance might have been strong, he might have been tough, but there is a point of desperation all men reach when everything they hold dear is taken from them, when what they love most is stolen away. Nick had endured Julia's death, her danger, her fear, he had left her behind in the future to die with Dance, a man who through the twisting of time, seemed to haunt his every living second.

He hit him again and again.

But Dance was tough. He blocked Nick's next punch and countered with a hard right that sent Nick staggering back. Dance jumped on him, holding him by the collar, as he rained blow after blow upon Nick's body, doubling him over, knocking the wind out of him. Nick could feel a rib crack, the pain excruciating as he struggled to breathe as Dance's attack raged on.

Nick's awareness was slipping, consciousness drifting in and out, but a single image filled his mind. The golden timepiece. Without the watch, he would be trapped in this time line, continuing forward with his and Julia's fate set on a course of death, a death he knew for himself was only moments away. And Julia would be dying all the sooner, alone, with nothing but questions swirling in her mind.

Nick could barely see through the blood that ran down into his eyes, he could barely make out the clock on the wall, but his vision was just clear enough to see the time: 12:59, the second hand sweeping up toward the top of the hour.

And then Nick thought of Julia, of everything she meant to him. He thought of her gentle touch, her lips as she woke him this morning, of her hope-filled eyes and her blonde hair as it fell upon him as they made love. He thought of her heart and her passion. He thought of her as she swam too fast at the age of fifteen, gasping as he pulled her from the pool but never complaining. She was his life, everything he cared about, everything he lived for.

With a last bit of strength, reaching into what was left of him, Nick hit Dance in the nose, continuing his momentum, driving the detective up against the bars of the jail cell, his adrenaline-infused muscles pinning him there.

And in a final moment of clarity, as the clock struck one, Nick reached into Dance's jacket and pulled the watch from his pocket.

CHAPTER 2

Julia Quinn pulled into the short-term parking at Westchester Airport. She grabbed her purse off the seat and raced for the terminal. Held up by an unexpected conference call that had lasted over forty-five minutes, she was behind schedule and afraid she'd miss her flight.

She had made the appointment with Dr. Colverhome on Monday and cleared her Friday afternoon schedule to indulge in a little bit of future mommyhood excitement.

She left the three frames on the seat of her car. They were of different sizes and designs. She had grabbed them from The Right Thing in Byram Hills on her way to the airport this morning, as she was unsure exactly how big a sonogram picture actually was. She was excited about giving it to Nick tonight, surprising him with the news. She had teddy bear wrapping paper and a copy of Dr. Seuss's *Fox in Sox,* her favorite from childhood, something she'd loved to hear her dad read, a tradition she was looking forward to Nick's continuing with their child.

Though the scientific, in utero image of their child would be tiny, it would be the first picture to define them as a true family, a picture they would place on a bookshelf in the library among all their crazy vacation pictures from around the country.

She checked her watch: 11:01. With the flight scheduled to hit the air at 11:16, she just might make it. As this was a small regional airport, ticket lines were short and security checks were rarely congested.

With her boarding pass validated, she flew through security and was relieved to see that boarding had just started. She felt an overwhelming excitement. She was bursting to call Nick, to tell him what she was doing, to tell him about the baby, but her patience won out. She wanted to see the surprise on his face, she wanted to feel his arms wrap her with the same joy she had felt when she learned of the life within her.

Nick was unaware of her schedule, unaware of her flying today, which made her feel a bit guilty. He had no love of air travel, always insisting on knowing her flight plans when she flew and that she call him upon landing. But she was afraid it would lead to too many questions, her answers being transparent lies to a man who could read her face like a clock.

They had parted on a sour note just a few hours ago. He was angry about having to dine out with friends he didn't much care for, and while she returned his anger, she was laughing on the inside, knowing it was all a ploy, knowing that it would make the surprise all the sweeter.

Her heart still skipped a beat when she thought of Nick. That feeling still arose in her stomach, as it had the moment she first saw him standing poolside in his bathing suit sixteen years ago. And while Nick had no idea where she was, she knew his routine as if it was her own. He was working from home, he'd probably be sitting in his leather chair in the library toiling away for the next eight hours, forgetting to eat or even look up, losing all track of time.

Nick sat in his Audi, the Sig-Sauer in his hand, checking the safety and slamming in the clip before tucking it in his waistband at the small of his back. He had driven through the bustling town of Byram Hills, in the midst of its late-morning summer routine

— mothers with strollers heading for an early lunch at the Country Kitchen; day laborers getting the first pie of the day from Broadway Pizza; landscapers filling their trucks with foliage at Mariani's Garden Market; real estate brokers sipping coffee outside their offices while chatting about their latest listings as fathers ran into the local bank to grab cash for the long weekend at the shore.

Intersecting lives, hand waves and kisses, smiles and hugs, a town linked by its commonality of existence — lives that would be changed forever in less than one hour.

Nick turned into the Byram Hills Police Department. After all of his ideas, all of his brainstorming, he went back to the simplest of solutions. Nick wasn't some superhero, he had never been in the military, and he had no illusions that he was some skilled crime fighter. He couldn't arrive on the scene, guns blazing, killing everyone involved in the theft and think he could succeed, let alone live — and who knew the consequences? He was simply a man trying to save his wife.

And he realized there was one person he could not only trust but who had the skill and authority, he had seen his allegiance to the law when the man stood up to his corrupt cousin, his character in the face of disaster at the crash site, he had seen his sense of right and wrong. Nick felt it in his gut that he could trust this man to do the right thing.

Sam Dreyfus extended the small tripod legs and placed the six-inch microlaser firmly in the ground, aiming it straight at the lens of the east camera, which overlooked the parking lot, its beam filling the camera's image with spectral noise. While it wouldn't break the camera, it would interfere with its imaging capability, disabling it for fifteen minutes, at which point an alarm would sound, indicating a disturbance in the system that required investigation.

He repeated the process on both the west and north cameras, throwing a virtual blanket over any occurrence in the parking lot for the next quarter hour. He pulled the radio from his pocket and thumbed the talk button three times.

Sam Dreyfus was painfully thin but for a small beer gut that hung over his crocodile belt. He was dressed in a pair of tan chinos and a white oxford shirt, the sleeves rolled halfway up his forearms. His matching Crocs loafers completed an ensemble not worn by most thieves. His brown hair was parted to the side and had yet to see the onset of gray, while his eyes were bloodshot and tired, a fact currently hidden behind a pair of dark Ray-Ban sunglasses.

At forty-nine, Sam felt at once young and yet painfully old. Living life without a care, running off and doing as he pleased had been his habit, had been his reputation since he was a teenager, but it was a reputation in conflict with how he felt.

The shadow cast by his brother, Paul, was enormous. Most people forgot Sam's name, referring to him only as Paul's brother. He would grow particularly angry when people said, "Oh, I didn't know the Dreyfuses had two sons."

From a young age, Sam didn't measure up — in their parents' eyes or in those of the public — so he chose to run in the opposite direction of his brother.

Sam slipped in with a bad crowd and found drugs and alcohol, fighting and mischief to be more his speed. He enjoyed the high, the rebellious pleasure of the moment.

At the age of seventeen, Sam ran off to Canada, not so much because he was afraid of going to war but because he knew it would piss off his father. He became the proverbial black sheep, something that, at last, gave him his own identity.

Over the years, he dabbled in various business ventures — real estate, finance, marketing — always looking to be the man at the top but never lasting more than a year at the bottom. He knew he was smart, he was just never given a chance.

But despite his failings, Paul had always looked out for him. He gave him a job when he needed it. Kept him on the payroll in perpetuity. Even gave him a piece of the company so he had something to leave his kids. Paul never spoke a word about his mistakes. Despite the vitriol and disappointment from his father, Paul had never passed judgment on him.

And then, about a year ago, Sam had faced reality. Sam's house, Sam's life existed by the sheer grace of his brother. He finally admitted to himself what he had known all along: He was nothing more than a charity case. Paul had felt sorry for him and had looked out for him as a result of pity.

And it angered Sam, it enraged him, it focused him.

He called Paul, told him he wanted to work, truly work, and took a real job at his brother's company. He showed up every day, worked a full eight hours, pulled in business, and for once actually accomplished something. He found himself tired, more tired than he had ever been, but it came with a sense of accomplishment.

And his drive continued for over six months, at which point Paul rewarded him. And this time, it was not out of pity but out of gratitude, out of pride for his accomplishments. Sam became more integrated in the company, his brother looking at him as a full partner, providing him with full access to the security company's jobs, technologies, and strategies.

It was on a Wednesday evening in January, in the dark days of winter. Alone in his office after seven, he was educating himself, reading through the secure files, when he came upon the name of Shamus Hennicot, a name renowned for its wealth and generosity, a man whose worth was well into the billions of dollars.

Paul handled the account personally and not just on a relationship, transactional basis. He actually did the installation, designing the high-tech security system himself, something he usually left to underlings. And that piqued Sam's curiosity. He dug deeper into Paul's files, learning of the unique access systems, alarms, and surveillance designs that had created a vaultlike environment for Hennicot's prized art collection.

With an even more focused eye, Sam uncovered the inventory of Hennicot's mini-museum. Antique weapons, jewels, paintings, sculptures, with appraised values noted for each item, from the hundreds of thousands to the tens of millions. Paul had designed display cases for the antique weapons, humidity-controlled rooms for the artwork, pressure-sensitive stands for the sculptures, and a special octagonal key for the main vault door.

But what stopped Sam cold was the special box built personally by Paul in his home. Unlike every other security item in the secure sanctuary, this one had no plans, no specs. It simply said Mahogany Box. Size: two feet square, one foot high. Contents: personal & confidential. There was a special safe purchased for it, a special hidden room constructed for it, all without any indication of its contents.

Sam's curiosity went through the roof. He searched every file, every cabinet, every drawer of his brother's office until he finally came upon the handwritten note in Paul's private shop. It was a crumpled-up five-by-seven piece of lined paper in his tool box. It wasn't detailed. It seemed cryptic if one didn't know what one was looking at.

And as Sam read the handwritten note, he found something that could change his life, that would give him the wealth, the power, but most of all, the respect he so desired to emerge from Paul's shadow.

The case was designed to guard the family secrets, the knowledge that had been passed down from father to son to grandson.

Sam finally smiled, for he knew what was in the box.

Over the next four months, Sam secured copies of the floor plans and the camera positions. He found the special codes needed for obtaining keys and pass cards. He procured combinations and access codes, most of which were in Paul's personal file, a file that Paul gave him access to, a file whose access he said was only worthy of a brother, of a partner.

After scoping out the property, Sam found the perfect inside man at the Byram Hills Police Department. Greedy and already corrupted, he would provide the manpower and knowledge to keep his law enforcement brethren at bay. The pieces had come together nicely. It was and would be his greatest accomplishment.

Sam actually thought of the undertaking as a victimless crime. The loss would be less than half a percent of the Hennicot family fortune, something earned back in just a few weeks of simple interest if not recouped from the insurance claim.

And the contents of the box . . . well, Sam thought, there was no way to put a price on it. Ideas weren't insurable, secrets weren't insurable. Without an heir, Shamus had no one to leave the box to, so why not let it reside with someone else for the future, why not let it reside with another family, with someone whose aspirations were greater than family trusts and security companies?

Sam would finally achieve success on his own terms. He would finally emerge from the shadow that had hung over him his entire life.

Within ten seconds of Sam's thumbing the walkie-talkie, a green Taurus drove in and parked in the back lot of Washington House, followed by a white Chrysler Sebring. Dance stepped from the driver's seat of the Taurus while Randall and Johnny Arilio emerged from the Chrysler.

Arilio was a ten-year veteran, outgoing, with a big smile. He thought himself to be the most popular person in the police department, never realizing he just came off as obnoxious. At thirty-two, his long dark hair made him look like someone who couldn't let go of his childhood. He fancied himself a ladies' man, though he had actually hoped to find someone to settle down with. Unfortunately, with his champagne tastes and beer wallet, he never had the income to support the women he was attracted to.

Arilio tucked his blue shirt into his tan khakis as he and Randall walked about the rear of the house, looking as if they were on official police business. Brinehart drove his unmarked cruiser in, pulling up right next to Dance and getting out with an excited smile on his face.

Dance pulled two half-full duffel bags from his trunk and placed them next to the rear door.

Sam jogged down from the small berm where he had placed the last laser, pulling out a key and security card on his approach. "We've got fourteen minutes."

Julia walked down the aisle of the AS 300, happy to be carrying nothing but her purse. Used to traveling with a briefcase and a too-heavy carry-on, she kept on thinking she had forgotten something.

She found her seat in business class, the wide-body leather chair enveloping her as she sat. She'd made it with time to spare. An elegant older woman, her silver hair swept up in a bun, sat in the seat beside her, her eyes focused on the airline magazine from the seat pouch.

Passengers continued boarding, the Friday mix of travelers always different from that of the rest of the week. While the flight was usually populated with businessmen and women, a number of families took the morning flight to get up to their vacation homes for the weekend. Julia looked at the young noisy children in an entirely new light. Two sisters, no more than five, played a singsong hand-slapping game that reduced them to fits of giggles every time they uttered the words "Miss Mary Mack, Mack, Mack."

What used to test her patience as she tried to concentrate on work now brought a smile as she saw the wonder and excitement in the young faces. She was viewing the world from a different perspective, through different eyes.

"Nothing better," the young blond businessman across the aisle said.

"I had forgotten all about the honesty of a child's laugh," Julia said with a nod.

"My kids are bit younger but they giggle just like that."

"Going home to see them?" Julia asked.

"Day trip to Boston. Hopefully, I'll be on

the early evening flight back and get home in time to kiss them good night."

"Last-minute business?" Julia said, having taken too many of those quick trips.

"Looking at a new deal." The guy patted the spreadsheet in his lap. "My name's Jason Cereta."

"Julia," she said with a smile.

"How many kids do you have?"

"In nine months, at least one." Julia patted her belly, her first public admission of being pregnant.

"That's so exciting." The elderly woman in the window seat looked up from her magazine at Julia.

"And are you traveling on business or pleasure?" the old woman asked.

"Actually, I'm going to get a sonogram."

"Now, that's pleasure," the woman said as she took off her jacket, folding it in her lap. "But a long way to go for a picture."

"I know, but I love my doctor, and I wanted to surprise my husband with the first photo of his child."

"He doesn't know?"

"No, and it's killing me."

"My name is Katherine," the old woman said. Her green eyes sparkled with life, her attitude and smile making it hard to tell her true age.

"Julia," she said in return. No need for last names, just enough to allow for cordial conversation to pass the flight time before they disappeared from each other's lives forever.

"We never had children," Katherine continued. "But my husband and I love kids, always have. I've got plenty of grandnieces and grandnephews. Kids give us perspective, they remind us of what's important in life. Am I right?" Katherine said as she leaned forward, looking at Jason.

"They are the reason I do what I do." Jason said with a smile. "Believe me, I would never work this hard for myself."

"And where are you heading?" Julia asked Katherine.

"Back to Chilmark. I was visiting my sister in Larchmont. My husband has been taken ill."

"I'm sorry to hear that."

"No worries, you know how men are with a sniffle or fever. He'll be fine." But her eyes didn't reflect the confidence of her words. "We each go through a spell of bad health a few times a year. It's his turn this time."

A buzzing came from Julia's purse. "Excuse me," she said as she reached into her bag and drew out her cell phone.

Julia paged through to the text message

and began reading the short and to-the-point note.

Have a safe flight and a great weekend,

Jo

Julia loved her secretary, an organized yin to her frenetic yang.

She thought of calling Nick to tell him of her plans, but figured he was in the midst of business and didn't want to disturb him.

And so she settled back in her seat, pulled out a magazine, and indulged herself with a little me-time while waiting for takeoff.

Detective Bob Shannon pulled into the driveway of Washington House in his black Mustang Cobra, his single indulgence in life. He didn't play golf, didn't fish, wasn't much for cards, but he'd loved muscle cars since he was a kid, and with no wife to talk him out of it, he bought the '99 used Shelby Cobra for $38,800, keeping its black finish factory new with a weekly buff and polish.

Dance, Brinehart, Randall, Arilio, and Sam turned in surprise as he got out of the car.

"Guys," Shannon said with a nod as he walked toward them.

"Hey, Shannon," Brinehart said, acting as

if they were best friends.

Shannon ignored him, keeping his full attention on Dance.

"I thought you were at the station," Dance said, "following up on the arrest of those kids from the Bronx who got caught jacking cars over on Wampus Lake Drive."

"Yeah, well. I got a call."

Everyone turned to watch as Nick stepped out of the passenger seat, staring back at everyone.

"You guys responded, too, huh?" Shannon continued.

Dance just stared at him.

"The robbery . . . ?" Shannon said, pointing out the reason for his visit.

"Yeah," Brinehart blurted out, to the consternation of Dance.

"This guy," Shannon thumbed his finger back at Nick as he cast his eyes on the young Brinehart. "He called you, too?"

Brinehart knew better than to make the same mistake twice.

". . . Because the robbery wasn't mentioned over the radio."

The air grew thick. All eyes focused on Dance, who just stood there without a hint of emotion on his face.

"I want to know what the hell is going on," Shannon said, an edge growing in his voice, the tendons in his neck distending as he fought to hold back his anger.

"Who's this guy?" Brinehart said, alluding to Nick.

"Never mind that," Shannon snapped at Brinehart as his eyes bored into Dance. "Answer my question, Ethan, what are you doing here?"

Dance looked at Brinehart and Randall, who remained calm, while Sam adjusted his sunglasses, taking a step back against the building, trying to disappear.

"Who are you?" Shannon said, glaring at Sam.

"I'm —" Sam stuttered, his hands shaking.

Brinehart walked around Nick, standing directly behind him. "And who are *you?*"

Brinehart's arm shot out, snatching the pistol from the back of Nick's waistband. "What the hell is this? You a cop?"

Shannon looked at the gun and back to Nick. "You didn't tell me you were armed."

"Considering the day I've had," Nick said, "I thought it was a good idea."

"Dance," Shannon turned back to his partner. "This guy said you're here to steal, let me see if I remember this: four gold swords, two rapiers, three sabers, five daggers, three guns, a bag of diamonds, and," he paused, "some kind of box."

Everyone remained silent.

"Look," Shannon softened his tone. "You haven't done anything yet, why don't you get in your cars, get out of here, and we'll forget about this?"

"You the type that would rat on a fellow officer?" Brinehart interrupted.

"You've been a cop for what, a year? Please. Don't give me this blue code of silence shit." He turned back to Dance. "Ethan, what the hell are you doing?"

Dance stared for a moment, all ears waiting on him.

"You might forget, but he won't," Dance said, pointing a finger at Nick.

Dance suddenly pulled his pistol and shoved it into Shannon's gut.

"Are you fucking kidding me?" Shannon exploded, not bothering to look at the gun. "Put that thing away before I shove it down your throat, dammit. I'm your cousin."

And without breaking eye contact, Dance pulled the trigger.

The bullet ripped into Shannon's stomach, knocking him back.

But Shannon didn't go down. He took three steps forward and grabbed Dance by the neck, slamming him against the building, choking the life out of him.

And Dance shot him again in the gut.

This time Shannon teetered on wobbly legs, stumbling backward, finally collapsing.

Dance's cohorts swung their heads, looking for witnesses.

Nick stood there in shock, watching the life bleed out of Shannon.

"That's great," Brinehart's voice cracked. "You just killed a cop. In front of a witness, no less."

"Cuff him," Dance said, pointing his gun at Nick.

"You going to kill him, too?" Sam finally said, his voice panicked.

Dance walked over to Nick and pulled out his wallet, reading his license. "So, Mr. Quinn, how'd you know what was going on here?"

"Quinn?" Sam said. "That's the name of Hennicot's lady attorney. Are you going to kill him?"

"Why would I kill a suspect? We've got someone connected to this place to pin this on now. Killing a cop's a capital offense," Dance said as he looked at Nick, patting his cheek in a taunting fashion. "Sucks for you."

Julia watched as the stewardess pulled the cabin door closed and turned the crank, sealing them in.

"Ladies and gentlemen, we have now closed the cabin door and ask that all cell phones and pagers be turned off for the duration of our flight. You must also turn off all electronic devices until such time as we are airborne and give the direction that you may resume using them."

Julia quickly dialed Nick's phone. Finding it going directly to voicemail she quickly spoke. "Hi, honey. I love you. I'm sorry about our fight over having dinner with the Mullers. Not to worry, if you really feel strongly, I'll cancel them. I've got something better planned. Just us. I'm running up to Boston for a quick meeting. Sorry I didn't tell you that —"

"— I'm sorry, ma'am," the stewardess interrupted as she leaned down. "The cabin doors are closed, all cell phones must be turned off."

"Sorry," Julia mouthed. "Honey, I have to go, I love you. I'll call you when we land."

Julia ended the call. "Sorry about that."

"I never fly without squeezing one last call to my husband either," the stewardess said. She smiled and headed to the galley.

Julia couldn't wait to see the surprise on Nick's face when she told him about the baby.

And she turned off her cell phone, tucking it back into her purse. She put her head back against the soft leather seat, her thoughts still on her husband as she closed her eyes for a quick nap.

"Put them both in the back of my car," Dance said. Brinehart and Arilio opened the door of Dance's Taurus and hoisted the body of Robert Shannon into the backseat. Brinehart turned to Nick, his hands cuffed behind his back, and took him by the arm.

"Better yet, Brinehart, you stay out here, keep an eye out." Dance took Nick by the arm. "Why don't you just come with us and smile for the cameras."

Sam turned to the door and slipped his key in the lock. "We're four minutes behind schedule."

"And we'll be five minutes behind if you don't quit jabbering. I really don't give a shit, everyone will have to work twice as fast."

They all pulled on surgical gloves.

"Don't forget our new partner," Dance said, handing Nick off to Sam.

"Yeah, right." Sam said, pushing Nick up next to the door. "For all the world to see."

Sam hoisted the two duffel bags onto his shoulder, ran his security pass over the scanner, turned the key, and opened the door.

He pulled a small box from his bag, a clear red half dome atop it. He flicked a switch on its side and affixed it to the wall. He moved quickly through the house to the whitewashed wood veneer door. He affixed another box to the kitchen counter, flipped the switch, and gave out a low whistle.

Everyone came in behind him.

Again, Sam passed his security card by the side of the door where the scanner was concealed, releasing the magna lock. He pulled back what he knew was a three-inch steel core barrier that led to a brightly lit set of carpeted stairs, the walls covered in a pale green fleur-de-lis wallpaper.

Sam took Nick by the arm, leading him along, ensuring his face was prominently displayed to the hidden camera in the stairwell wall, while shielding himself.

"Wait until I have the door opened and the cameras disabled," Sam said to Dance, Randall, and Arilio, holding them up at the top of the stairs.

Sam and Nick arrived at the basement door, made of brushed steel and lacking doorknobs or hinges. Nick knew it well, having passed through it several hours ago his time but several hours in the future for everyone else.

Sam pulled the octagonal key from his

pocket and triple-checked that the letter D was on top.

"Make sure the letter D is on top or we may not only get locked out but locked in," Nick said with a smile.

"How the hell did you know that?" Sam shouted at Nick. You could hear the fear in his voice.

"Lucky guess," Nick said. "But before your friend Dance catches up, you may want to know that he's going to kill you. I know he's going to dump Brinehart and Arilio in the reservoir."

"You think I trust Dance? You think I haven't already taken steps to protect myself?"

"And how will you protect yourself from your brother, Paul? He knows what's going on."

"That's how you know everything. You work for him, don't you?" Sam was getting angry. "Don't you?"

"Actually, he hasn't met me yet. Wouldn't know my name or face if he was standing in front of me."

"What the hell are the two of you talking about?" Dance shouted from the top of the stairs. "Time's ticking. We've only got ten minutes."

Sam slipped the key into the octagonal

lock, the letter D on top, as Nick had said. He entered his brother's Social Security number in the keypad on the wall, ran the security pass three times by the card reader, turned the key, and pushed open the two-ton door.

Sam knew there was a breach alarm on the steel vault door for unscheduled openings; he knew that it didn't go to the police as most alarms did, but rather, signaled Dreyfus Security and Hennicot's attorney. But by the time they were notified and reacted, he would already be gone.

Sam had actually read all of the schematics on the breach alarm and knew how to disable it. It was, in fact, quite simple to take out of service. But the breach alarm was not just for notification, it was also the trigger for the secondary protocols. Not only were the video feeds routed to Hennicot's attorney's office, but the secondary cameras not on any grid or plan were activated, their images sent to an encrypted file — cameras whose location he knew and would avoid but that would now capture Dance and his men as they came down the stairs.

It was his insurance policy, the leverage he would use when Dance turned on him. He knew there was no honor among thieves, and the warning, uttered by Quinn, that Dance would kill everyone, was no surprise to him. It merely confirmed a fear he had lived with for the last month and a betrayal that he had prepared for. But it was fear he could live with, a risk he was willing to take in order to get the box in Hennicot's safe.

"Okay, Dance," Sam said.

And the detective, Randall, and Arilio came down the stairs to stand in the small vestibule next to Nick.

As the steel vault door swung open, Nick saw the large glass table prominently displayed, its glass top pure, unmarred — not violated, as it had been when he saw it five hours from now. Within the case he saw the swords and daggers, the rapiers and sabers, and most specifically, the gold-inlaid Colt Peacemaker that would be used to kill Julia.

With his surgical-gloved hand, Sam pulled four more small boxes from his duffel bags, half-moon, red glass domes on each. He spun Nick around. "Hold this," he said as he placed one of the boxes in Nick's restrained hands. "Fingerprints can be so telling."

"Nice touch," Dance said with a smile.

"Wait here," Sam continued, as if Nick were capable of doing otherwise in his handcuffed state, with three armed men standing around him.

Sam took the box back from Nick, flipped the switches on the sides of the boxes, and ran into the room, affixing a box on the wall opposite the door before running off through the basement area.

Thirty seconds later he was back. "Let's go, all cameras jammed."

Dance and his men grabbed Nick and pulled him into the room with them.

Sam dumped his two bags on the floor and extracted a large metal bar with an attached suction cup, which he affixed to the large center case where the weapons were displayed. He affixed a matchbox-sized square box to the right inner leg of the display. The small device generated electromagnetic interference, impeding the case's alarm system.

Dance and his men surrounded the case, watching as Sam set to work, etching a circle in the glass, moving the diamond-tipped bar in a wide arc.

Nick couldn't help laughing as he stared at the $80 million Monet on the wall behind Dance. The single picture of water lilies, even on the black market, could provide them with more wealth than they could imagine, far more than the items in this single case.

Sam continued cutting the glass. Holding the suction cup, he tapped along the etched area and lifted out the large clear circle.

"Dance, you and your men fill those two duffel bags. Use the towels to wrap the items so they don't scratch each other."

"What, no pressure switches under them?" Dance asked.

"Don't be an idiot." Sam looked at him as if he was a child. "What do you think the box I just stuck on the leg does? Its small pulse disables the magnetic pressure switches." He grabbed Nick by the arm and headed down the hall.

"Where are you going?" Dance called out.

"Diamonds," Sam replied.

Sam raced into Shamus's office as if he had been there a thousand times, even though this was his first. He pushed Nick into the corner as he affixed a red-domed box to the center of the desk and switched on the desk lamp. He picked up the Tiffany-style lamp in his gloved hand, spun Nick around, and placed it against his hands, cuffed behind his back. He put it back in place on the leather desk top and spun Nick back around to face him.

"Just in case they need some extra physical evidence at your trial."

"Thanks," Nick said. "Too bad you won't live to see it."

Ignoring Nick's jab, Sam turned, faced the dark walnut wall, and ran the security card over the left corner of the desk. There was a barely perceptible click. He walked up to the wall, placed his hand against it, and gave a gentle push, and the hidden door swung inward on whisper hinges.

"Wait here," Sam said with a laugh, picking up the last domed box. "Not that you'd get past Dance and his men."

"Let me know if you need help with the safe," Nick said, leaning against the desk.

Sam ignored him and stepped over the threshold, affixing the last box to the wall. The small, unfinished room was made of concrete. The three lights hanging from the ceiling lit the two Harris safes.

Sam looked at his watch. They had less than five minutes before the disabled cameras in the parking lot set off an alarm.

He removed his Ray-Bans, tucked them into his pocket, and crouched before the four-foot safe on the right. He grasped the brass flywheel and spun it right, three times around, to clear the pins. On the fourth spin he slowed and stopped at 64, spinning it back around to the left a full turn before halting at 88, then back around right to 0 and finally left to 90.

As if he had done it hundreds of times, Sam grasped the brass handle, turned it with confidence, and pulled open the large steel door.

And as the light poured into the confines of the safe, he saw it sitting there in all of its simple glory. Constructed of Shamus Hennicot's favorite wood, the dark African mahogany was like arboreal gold in its shining luster. The box was two feet by two feet by one foot high, the lid, two inches thick at the almost-imperceptible seam. The interior hinges at the rear were to prevent compromise while each of the three other sides contained a single keyhole. They were not key locks in the traditional sense, but rather three octagonal steel holes, similar to the steel door lock he just breached two minutes earlier.

Sam pulled the octagonal key from his pocket, quickly trying it, but it was too large. He stuffed the key back into his pocket; he'd worry about breaching the wooden case later.

He opened the small drawer on the top left side of the safe and pulled out a large velvet pouch. He quickly untied the pull string, verifying the contents, seeing the explosion of rainbows as the light played off the faceted surfaces of hundreds of large diamonds. He pulled the string tight and stuffed the pouch into his pocket.

And that's when he saw the note, affixed to the interior of the safe door. He couldn't understand how he'd missed it. The five-by-seven sheet of plain white stationery might as well have been a time bomb.

Sam couldn't figure out how it got there, how he had known. He thought he'd felt a presence when he'd come in but had shrugged it off to his raw nerves.

Sam took hold of the box, lifting it out of the safe, surprised at its weight, at least twenty-five pounds. He snatched the note from the safe door and read the single sentence one more time — *Please consider what you're doing, you know where I'll be waiting* — and crumpled it up in anger.

Dance lifted out each sword, each dagger, each rapier and saber, inspecting each piece before passing it to Arilio, who wrapped them in separate towels before placing them in the duffel bag. Made of pure gold, the hilt of each sword was a jewel-encrusted masterpiece of sapphires, rubies, and emeralds.

The buyer for the haul was a man of

Chinese and Japanese descent, an avid collector who was said to be worth billions. His agent would take delivery at nine o'clock this evening, paying $20 million for the collection, an amount four times more than Dance had told his partners, including Sam Dreyfus. Each thought he'd get one million in cash and all were happy about it — though only Randall and Sam Dreyfus would actually live to collect. And with the diamonds that Dreyfus was getting, Dance's take would be over $20 million: one million for Rukaj and nineteen to enable him to slip out of Byram Hills forever.

He pulled out the three pistols: an 1840 Smith & Wesson, an 1872 Colt Peacemaker, and a 1789 Belatoro. All were custom-made, fully functional, with gold and silver stylings along the stock, engravings around the handle, and religious text and scripture imbued upon the barrel. Dance grabbed a handful of silver-etched bullets, bullets whose owners had ordered them etched with curses, blasphemous imprecations against the victims and their gods, each personalized with the name of the intended target, the enemy it would shoot through the heart.

As Dance handed the last pistol to Arilio, he realized that Shannon's description of what he had just put into the bag was spot-on. The exact count of swords, daggers, guns. Shannon had even mentioned the diamonds. It was as if he had found a shopping list and recited it from memory.

Sam and Nick emerged from the hallway into the open area by the now empty case. With Nick's hands behind his back, Sam pushed him along while carrying an awkward box under his other arm.

"Put the bags in the trunk of my car and hurry back," Dance said to Arilio and Randall.

He stared at Sam and the mahogany box under his arm, thought a moment . . . "And you know what?" Dance turned and looked at Nick. "Take this guy, lock him in the back of my car with Shannon, tell Brinehart to keep an eye on him."

Arilio threw the two bags over his shoulder while Randall took Nick by the arm and disappeared out the brushed-steel doorway.

Finally alone, Dance stepped closer to Sam. "What's in the box?"

"Here you go," Sam said, handing him the large pouch of diamonds.

Dance pulled open the black velvet satchel and looked at the pile of diamonds, more than he had ever seen in all of his years. He poured a small pile into the palm of his hand, flicking them about with his forefinger. They were even larger than he had expected, two, three, four, and five carat. Perfect clarity. He and Sam had underestimated the haul from the safe. With what looked to be over two hundred such stones, he was thinking they more than doubled their estimate of $22 million.

"I think we'll be making a bit more than you had thought," Dance marveled.

"I didn't realize there would be that many," Sam said.

"You never mentioned anything about a box either," Dance said with a smile as he looked up at Sam, though his eyes said something different. "Now that I think about, Shannon did mention something about a box."

"It's mine," Sam said.

"What is it?" Dance asked as he poured the diamonds back into the pouch that he held tightly in his left hand. "You're not trying to take an uneven share, are you, Sam?"

Sam stared at him with nervous eyes.

"Sam . . . ?"

"It's Hennicot's —"

"— this is all Hennicot's." Dance interrupted as he waved his hand around at the room.

"It was in the safe. It's trade secrets,

papers, and things."

"Do you mind?" Dance pointed at the box.

Sam couldn't help being intimidated by Dance. He had been from the start, but was even more so now after seeing him gun down his own partner in cold blood. He reluctantly handed Dance the box.

"Heavy," Dance said in surprise, needing two hands to hold it. "Too heavy for a couple pieces of paper. What is it really? Gold, more diamonds?"

"No, nothing of the sort."

"Well, I want half of whatever is in here." Dance lifted the box. "We won't split it with the others, but I want my half."

"We've got to go," Sam said, looking at his watch. "We've only got four minutes."

"When you tell me what's in the box," Dance said, positioning himself between Sam and the exit.

Sam remained silent, figuratively boxed into a corner. His eyes darted about, his brow growing moist. "Look, I'll give you my share of everything, the diamonds, the antiques."

And it was the worst thing Sam could have said, his words confirming the value of what he held.

"You're choosing box number one over

everything we just took?" Dance said in shock.

Sam nodded.

"I don't want your share," Dance said. "You earned it. I just want to make sure no one is trying to screw me out of a few extra dollars."

"I'm not trying to screw you."

"Are you working with your brother?"

"What?" Sam said in shock.

"Is he picking you up, you going to try and run out on me?"

"Yeah right, I would steal all the info on everything down here *from him* and then call him for a ride."

"Let me see your cell phone." Dance held out his hand.

"You know, you're getting paranoid," Sam said as he took his phone out of his pocket and handed it to him.

"Not paranoid, just cautious. I don't want you calling him to pick you up somewhere."

"You're being ridiculous."

"Why don't you open the box and show me what's inside? Then we can see how ridiculous I am."

"I can't."

"Why?"

"I don't have the keys here. Look," Sam said, pleading, "It's worthless."

"To everyone but you and Hennicot." Dance laid the box on a side table, turning it about, looking at the three keyholes. "An awful lot of odd locks for something of so little value."

Sam stood there playing mental chess with Dance.

"Why don't you just tell me the truth?" Dance said as he pulled out his gun, holding it at his side.

"If I'm dead, you'll never get this box open. And understand something," Sam said with growing confidence. "If I'm dead, you won't know how to erase the backup security system that recorded your face."

Dance raised his pistol. "What the hell did you do?"

"Let me show you something." Sam led Dance to the steel vault door and motioned him to step into the small area at the base of the stairs.

"Look up," Sam said as Dance stepped into the small foyer.

Dance looked at the wall, at the fleur-de-lis wallpaper on it. He tilted his head up at the crown molding in the corner of the ceiling and, with a jump in his heart, he saw it. It was small, looking like a seam in the wallpaper where it met the molding, but there was no mistaking the minuscule lens.

"The camera is pointed right at the top of the stairs. It's not on any plan. It goes to a security file in Hennicot's attorneys' office, but this lone camera, its digital video file is encrypted. The code to view it or destroy it is only known by Hennicot, my brother, and myself. A pretty good idea, a safeguard against an inside job. All Hennicot's attorney has to do is forward it to Hennicot, Paul, or me and we can open it for all the world's viewing pleasure. They'll see your face and Arilio's and Randall's."

"And yours," Dance said concealing his emotions as he pointed his gun at Sam.

"Actually, just Quinn's. I knew the camera was there, so I just kept my face out of range when it kicked on."

Dance glared through the doorway at Sam.

"Remember this," Sam said. "I'm the only one who can get close to those files and ensure that no one sees them. But if we have a problem . . ."

Dance walked back into the fortified basement.

"Enjoy your proceeds from this job," Sam said. "Enjoy my proceeds, but the box is mine."

Randall and Arilio came back down the stairs and into the room.

"What's up with the gun?" Randall asked. Dance and Sam ignored the question.

"Grab the glass cutter and take the piece of glass with us," Dance said to them, pointing at the tools on the ground. "And don't take off your gloves until we have disposed of it."

"We're running late, we've got less than two minutes before the system alarm for the nonfunctioning cameras goes off," Sam said. He looked at Dance. "And I've still got to take care of the primary video server."

"Fine, let's go," Dance said. "But you know what? You lead the way out."

Arilio and Randall looked between the two, not comprehending what was going on.

"If your face was covered by Quinn on the way in, it won't be on the way out," Dance said, pointing his gun at Sam. "And don't forget our box."

Sam looked at the gun. With shaky hands, he picked up the box and walked out the door. Randall and Arilio fell in line behind him.

"You two, hold up," Dance said. "Let him go first."

Sam stepped through the brushed-steel doorway.

"Sam, I hope you realize that I don't care

about your threats, I don't care if my face is on some security video, I'd just as soon shoot you in the back for the hell of it and leave you here to take the blame as the mastermind behind this crime. A crime I caught you in the middle of." Dance waved his gun, motioning Sam to head up.

Sam walked up the fifteen steps and stopped at the top.

"Now, Sam," Dance said, pointing his gun straight at him. "Please turn around and smile."

And Sam did, looking right at the spot where the small hidden camera was. "What a team we make, huh?" Dance said.

Sam smiled back at Dance.

It took a moment for Dance to realize that Sam's smile wasn't forced, it was genuine. But before Dance could get two steps up the stairs Sam stepped through the door at the top of the stairs and slammed the three-inch metal door closed with a floor-shaking thud, the magna lock instantly catching, sealing them in.

Sam ran to the pantry of the kitchen, ripped open the door, slipped the octagonal key in the slot, and pushed open the hidden door panel to reveal the air-conditioned computer room.

The rack mount server contained four individual hard drives. Each pop-and-lock unit had five hundred gigabytes of memory, enough space to record five days' worth of video.

He inserted a cable into the PC port. With his knife he stripped the other end and jammed the bare wires directly into a wall socket. Designed with a surge protector to guard against electrical spikes and breakers to guard against lightning, the fail-safes all guarded the primary power source and communication cables into the system. There was nothing to stop the destructive force of the 110 volts as they poured through the PC cable directly into the circuits.

Within seconds, the mainframe began sparking, smoke rolling out of the media bays. With the system fried, he unplugged the cable from the wall before a fire started. He might have stooped to stealing, but he could justify his actions in the end. On the other hand, murder and arson weren't part of his vocabulary.

Using his knife, he popped out the four cooked hard drives, placed them atop the mahogany box, and picked it up. He closed the hidden panel in the pantry, closed the door, and raced out through the kitchen, bursting out the back door into the parking lot.

"We done?" Brinehart asked.

"Success," Sam said, hiding his nerves as he looked at the young cop.

"Wow." Brinehart broke out in a big smile. "That was easy."

Sam walked straight for Shannon's Mustang, finding the driver's-side door still open and the keys still in the ignition as he'd hoped. He threw the box and hard drives in the passenger seat.

"Hey," Brinehart called out. "Dance decide where you're going to put Shannon's Mustang?"

Sam turned to see Brinehart leaning against Dance's beat-up Taurus, Nick's face staring at him through the rear window.

"You've got to admit, Shannon had good taste in cars," Brinehart said as he walked toward Sam.

"Yeah," Sam replied as he climbed into the driver's seat, glad that Brinehart hadn't taken the keys. Sam checked under the seat, in the door pouches, and finally found what he was searching for in the glove compartment. He knew Dance carried two guns and was glad his partner, Shannon, had chosen to follow the same path by sticking a backup nine-millimeter in the glove compartment.

"So we're done?" Brinehart asked, continuing his approach.

Sam turned the key. The three-fifty engine growled to life as if awakened from a long sleep. He gripped the pistol tightly and felt a warm feeling of safety course through him as he tucked the gun in his waistband. He hit the gas, threw the car into first, and popped the clutch. The wheels spun wildly as the Shelby engine roared, launching the car out of the parking lot.

"Oh, yeah, we're done," Sam said to himself.

Dance charged up the stairs, ramming his shoulder into the three-inch steel fire door. Not only did it not budge, but it made no sound as his two-hundred-pound body bounced off its thick surface.

"Son of a bitch," Dance said, aiming his gun at the door.

"Whoa, whoa," Randall shouted, "the ricochet will kill you."

Dance began shaking violently in frustration and charged down the stairs. He ran through the vault door and from room to room, frantically looking for a way out, through the storage room, the conference room, and to Hennicot's elegant office looking for an alternative exit for emergencies, such as the one they were in right now.

As he was about to exit the office, he saw the white crumpled-up piece of paper on the floor, a piece of debris in one of the cleanest spaces he had ever seen. He picked it up, quickly read it, stuffed it into his pocket, and ran back out front.

"What if we set off the sprinkler system," Arilio said as he pulled out his lighter. "I bet you it releases the door. I can guarantee, Hennicot wouldn't want one of his employees to get accidentally cooked down here."

"Put that away," Dance said. He pointed to the flat metal disks interspersed throughout the ceiling. "It's a Halon system to protect the valuables. They don't want water getting on anything. You set it off in here, we'll choke and pass out. Besides, it calls the Fire Department, you fool. Any other bright ideas?"

"Well," Randall said, "the door's magnetically sealed, on a battery backup. I'm sure cutting the power won't work."

"Thanks for pointing out the obvious, moron," Dance said.

"Ahhh," Randall said in an all-knowing tone.

"What?" Dance asked, seeing hope bloom in Randall's eyes.

"We just need to turn off the magnet, interrupt the flow of electricity," he said, walking over to the display case and snatching the small box off the leg. He ran straight for the stairs and headed up, Dance and Arilio two steps behind.

He affixed the box to the top of the door upon the magnetic plate and without fanfare, without a sound, the door slipped open.

The AS 300 sat on the tarmac waiting for takeoff, already fifteen minutes behind schedule. There had been no update since the announcement that they would be briefly delayed. Rumors circulated that they wouldn't be leaving due to a mechanical problem and would need to change planes. A murmur of disappointment grew among those heading off for vacation, those heading home, those who would be missing business meetings and doctor appointments. But that scenario seemed unlikely as there were three planes ahead of them awaiting clearance to depart and a growing number behind them entering the queue.

Julia thought about quietly checking her phone for messages but didn't want to break FAA rules and end up having to explain herself.

"Ladies and Gentlemen, good morning. My name is Kip Ulrich, I'll be your captain on our short flight to Boston. As you have probably realized, we are a little backed up this morning, but I assure you it's not mechanical difficulties or weather holding us back. Today our delay is a rather cute, four-legged animal. If you are on the left side of the plane, you can see him. Maybe give him a little wave."

Julia and Katherine looked outside to see a yellow Labrador running wildly about the tarmac, four ground-crew members frantically chasing him.

"I can pretty much assure you, ladies and gentlemen, that the chase is nearing its end, as I've just been told a mechanic is en route with a nice juicy steak. We'll be under way shortly."

Julia smiled at Katherine. They both took one more look at the running Lab before closing their eyes to await takeoff.

Nick sat in the backseat of Dance's car next to Shannon's body, his blood-soaked corpse propped against the window, strapped in by a seat belt as if it was some sick joke. Nick struggled against his cuffs, but with each subtle movement, Brinehart banged against the window in a threatening manner, thinking he was a tough guy on the cusp of wealth and success; he had no idea he'd be dead in three hours, tossed from a bridge by his mentor.

Nick couldn't believe the cold detachment in Dance's eyes as he shot his own cousin without a moment's hesitation. He knew without ever having seen it that it was the same cold stare he'd fixed on Julia as he killed her.

Just then, Dance burst from the building, howling like a madman. He raced across the parking lot as Randall and Arilio came out behind him. Dance grabbed Brinehart by the collar, slammed him against the car, and threw him aside. There was an animal-like rage in him as he tore open the door and jumped into the driver's seat.

He started the car, gunned the engine, and raced out of the driveway of Washington House, turning onto Maple Avenue. Nick found himself pressed up against Shannon's body as the car fishtailed out of the turn, only to be thrown to the other side as Dance made the left onto Route 22.

Nick watched a bead of sweat rise on Dance's temple as he snatched up his police radio.

"Hey, Lena?" Dance said, with a false mirth in his voice, a false smile on his face

428

to match his deception.

"Hey, Dance," the static-filled voice answered back.

"Shannon's radio is on the fritz and I can't raise him on his cell. We were supposed to meet this morning but I don't have the address."

"Hold on." Lena laughed. "He's on 684."

"Love that GPS stuff."

"It's for finding you guys when you're in trouble so we can send backup, not for when you forget to write things down."

"What direction is he going?"

"South — no, wait, he just got off at the airport. You two flying away for a romantic weekend?"

"Ooo, you caught us." The lies flowed so easily from Dance. "Want to come along?"

"Yeah," she said facetiously. "He's heading over to the private air terminal. Now some of us have real work to do. And Dance, next time write it down."

"Thanks, Lena."

Nick was tossed about on the backseat as Dance pushed the Taurus to the limit, hopping onto U.S. 684, bobbing and weaving through traffic, over 110 miles per hour, lights flashing, sirens blaring as he raced two miles down the interstate and exited at the airport. He turned left and swerved in and out of oncoming traffic, as if the world would part for his approach.

Dance's phone rang. He flipped it open and answered. "Yeah."

"Detective," the thick Albanian accent filled the car through Dance's speakerphone. The voice made Nick's skin crawl.

"How many times a day are you going to call?" Dance yelled, but Nick could sense the detective's anger-filled voice was mixed with fear, an emotion he had not yet seen in Dance. And it wasn't just subtle fear, it was panic, a dread bordering on terror.

"I'm a generous man," the foreign voice said. "You should consider it a favor that you're still alive. Two extensions you've received, there will not be any more. Perhaps you'd like to start paying me in more body parts."

"I said you would have it by Friday."

The entrance to the airport loomed ahead.

"Yes, I know," the Albanian said. "It is Friday."

Dance slammed the phone closed and stuffed it back into his pocket. Blinded by anger, he punched the accelerator and tore off toward the private air terminal.

Sam Dreyfus drove into the open tarmac field where thirty different planes were parked, Pipers, Lear Jets, Cessnas, Hondas — A parking lot for the literal jet set.

He drove directly to the white Cessna 400 where his brother Paul was standing, skidded to a stop, and leaped from the car.

"What the hell is going on?" Sam yelled.

"Took the words right out of my mouth," Paul said, shaking his head. "After everything I've done for you, after everything you said this past year. I really thought you had become human, gained a heart."

"From the lips of God," Sam said. And though his words were sarcastic, there was pain in his voice.

"You're always looking for a fight."

"Do you realize the wealth contained in here?" Sam pulled the mahogany box from the front seat of the car. "Do you realize what we could do with this?"

"Why do you say *we?* That word has never existed in your vocabulary. You always wanted the easy way, the lazy way, getting angry at the world when it didn't provide for you."

"You left me a fucking note, *Please consider what you're doing, you know where I'll be waiting.* Was it to fuck with me or do you want a piece of this now?" Sam held out the box.

"I wanted you to think how easy it is to

catch you."

"You knew exactly what I was doing. You could have called the cops —"

"Seems you already did that."

"Why would you leave the box if you knew I'd take it? You thought a little note could change my mind?"

"Sam." Paul stared at his brother with disappointment. "You've never done anything like this. Give me the box. Let me try to make things right."

"What, are you crazy?" Sam exploded. "You're not taking this from me."

"No one ever needs to know you were involved, there's still time."

"Time for what?" Sam railed against his brother. "You think you can make this all go away? You think you can just erase the robbery? Make the others give all those golden knives, swords, and guns back? I don't think they'd be too keen on returning the diamonds." Sam laughed. "You truly are a golden boy, aren't you? All your life thinking only in absolutes, black and white. Well, Paul, the world's a messy place. And you know, you're right, I spent my life thinking the world owed me something, that I should be provided for but you taught me the truth. We have to take what we want, snatch it before someone else does."

Out of nowhere, bullets erupted around them, tearing up the ground, ricocheting off the planes and cars. They turned to see Dance running at them, his police-issue nine-millimeter Glock pointing straight at Sam.

Sam and Paul dove out of the line of fire, taking refuge behind a large Cessna Caravan, the low underbelly and thick fuselage of the converted freight carrier providing perfect cover.

"Give me the keys to your plane," Sam yelled as he knelt on the ground.

"What? You haven't flown in twenty years. It's not mechanical gauges and meters anymore, it's a glass cockpit. This thing is more complicated than any puddle jumper or computer you ever touched."

"Up, down, left, right." Sam pulled Shannon's extra gun from his waistband and aimed it at his brother. "Keys, please."

"You're going to kill yourself," Paul said, ignoring the pistol.

"Maybe." Sam peered around the nose of the plane. Dance was sixty yards away and fast approaching. "But I'm not going allow anyone else to have that pleasure."

Sam jammed the gun against his brother's heart. There was no fear in Paul's eyes, no tremble of panic or alarm, there was just a profound sadness, a disappointment that the brother he had thought he could reason with, the brother whom he had never stopped loving, could even consider taking his life.

"You really want to leave Susan a widow?" Sam barked. "What about your daughters, would you trade a pair of keys so they could have you in their life for twenty more years?"

Against his better judgment, Paul reached into his pocket, pulled out his keys, and handed them to his brother.

Sam tucked the box under his arm, checked the clip in his gun, and ran. The Cessna was only thirty yards away, pointed out at the access road, ready to fly. He sprinted as fast as a forty-nine-year-old could, his lungs huffing from a lifetime of cigarettes.

Dance had cut the distance by half and the bullets began to ring out in one-second intervals like clockwork.

Sam pushed with everything he had; he would make it. He would escape this town and this murderous cop, and once airborne, he was home free. The three locks on the mahogany box would take time, maybe months, but he had the basic plans from Paul's files. There was no doubt in his mind that he would breach the case, and once he did . . .

He was just five yards from the plane when the bullet hit him in the side, a tearing, searing pain that knocked him from his feet, sending him headfirst toward the ground. And as his forehead hit the black tarmac, the box tumbled from his hands, bouncing end over end under the Cessna 400.

Seeing Sam Dreyfus across the field with his brother Paul, standing next to a bevy of planes, the mahogany box tucked under his arm, Dance lost himself in his rage and stormed from his car, pulling his gun from his holster and raising it to take down the man who had betrayed him.

But in his rage he had left Nick alone in the back of the Taurus.

With his hands cuffed behind his back, Nick quickly tucked his knees to his chest and pulled his cuffed wrists down and under his rear, pulling his legs through his arms, thankful that swimming and workouts had kept him limber. He reached over with his bound hands to Shannon's body. The blood was thick and caked within his shirt, no longer flowing out, as his heart had stopped almost a half hour earlier. Nick fumbled in Shannon's pockets and found the cuff key.

Pulling it out and inserting it in his restraints, he freed himself.

He grabbed Shannon's pistol, the Austrian-made nine-millimeter Glock, checked the butt of the gun, and found the magazine clip missing. He pulled back the chamber and found it empty. He tipped Shannon's body over, looking for more clips on his belt, but they were gone. Brinehart wasn't that stupid. He hadn't put Nick in the car with a dead man and a loaded weapon.

Nick took the gun anyway and smashed the butt against the window, shattering it. Sweeping the pieces of safety glass away, he climbed through the window, opened the front door of the car, and popped the trunk.

He ran around to the back of the car and tore open the duffel bags. He pulled the towels out, dumping the exotic weapons on the trunk floor — swords and daggers, rapiers and . . . guns.

He picked up the elaborately engraved, gold-inlaid Colt Peacemaker, the one that would be stashed in his garage. He didn't need to test it, he knew it worked, it was the one that Dance would use in the future to kill Julia if he weren't stopped now. He spun the cylinder and popped it open. He dug through the bag and saw the silver-etched bullets scattering the bottom. He grabbed a handful, filled the six chambers, tucking the rest in his pocket, slammed the cylinder closed, and took off in an all-out sprint.

Running as fast he could, Nick finally caught sight of Dance standing over the prone, bleeding body of Sam Dreyfus. He pushed himself even harder as he watched Dance lay his gun to the back of the thief's head execution-style. Without hesitation, Nick raised the gun and fired three shots in quick succession, sending Dance running for cover among the planes and cars.

Nick worked his way closer to Dance, peering around corners and under the planes' bellies. He was careful to check his back, to check the sides so as not to be caught in an ambush.

He came upon Shannon's Mustang. Nick slowly looked under the vehicle and saw the feet of the man crouched there in wait, unaware of his position. Nick slowly crept around the car, silently working his way around the back. Then he felt the barrel of a gun at the back of his head.

"Drop the gun," a voice said. "Hands on top of your head."

And as Nick complied, dropping the gun, he realized his foolish error. He had never been under fire before and had rushed his conclusion. It wasn't Dance's feet he had seen; it hadn't been Dance he was so cleverly sneaking up on. It was Paul Dreyfus, who had now disappeared to a new location.

Nick slowly turned and looked into Dance's eyes.

"I can't tell you how much I wish I had killed you already, but that regret won't happen again." Dance's finger contracted against the trigger, slowly pulling it back when . . .

Nick's left hand shot out in a blur, snatching and twisting the gun from Dance's hand. In a fluid motion, he threw the gun to the side as his right fist came up and exploded into Dance's jaw. He leaped at him, pummeling him with blow after blow to the face, to the ribs, knocking him to the dusty ground, unloading upon him all of his anger, all of his desire for revenge for everything that Dance had done, for everything that he would do in the coming hours: Julia's death, Marcus's death, Paul Dreyfus, Private McManus, his own cousin, Shannon, Dance's flesh and blood, who had come to Nick's aid.

Nick would stop it all from happening, he would stop Dance in this moment, it all would end here. He would remove Dance from the future no matter the consequences to himself.

Suddenly, out of nowhere, a cloud of dirt hit his eyes, blinding him, disorienting him. And his head snapped to the side as Dance's punch caught him in the ear. Again and again, Dance hit with adrenaline-stoked rage. Like a cornered animal he fought back, finally beating Nick onto the ground.

Nick lay there, his head spinning, struggling to move. And before he knew it the gun was once again where it had started: against his head.

"No time for soliloquies," Dance said, wiping the blood from his face as he wrapped his finger about the trigger.

And the gunfire exploded, the .45-caliber parabellum round hurtling out of the barrel, through the air, and through the side of his skull. Dance stood there momentarily, stunned, nothing but confusion in his head — and the silver bullet.

And Dance fell to the ground dead.

Nick rolled over to see Paul Dreyfus in a crouch, a two-fisted grip on the exotic Colt Peacemaker.

"I was in Nam. A medic," Dreyfus said with a deep breath. "But I was a hell of a shot."

With a giant roar, an AS 300 passenger jet hurtled down the south runway behind Nick and Paul, startling them from the moment, its screaming engines hurling it at over 150 miles per hour, finally lifting it gently into the blue, late-morning sky.

Nick and Dreyfus turned to see Sam hoisting the mahogany box up onto the seat of the Cessna 400. He reached in, hit the primer, then the ignition switch, and the Teledyne Continental engine coughed to life.

Bleeding from his side, Sam turned to face his brother and held up the gun, waving it back and forth between Nick and Paul as he climbed into the small, two-seat Cessna.

"Sam, please," Dreyfus shouted over the noise of the propeller. Though he still held the large Colt, it dangled unthreatening at his side. "You haven't flown in years."

"Don't you dare tell me what I can and can't do," Sam shouted back. "My whole life, that's all you've done, control everything. My job, my paycheck. Life comes so easy for you, Paul —"

"We can work this out," Dreyfus pleaded at the top of his lungs.

"What the hell are you talking about? I don't need you anymore," Sam said as he patted the box.

"You'll never get it open! It's a three-inch titanium-core box, that's what makes it so heavy, the mahogany is just for show. The three locks only work with three specific keys, which must be turned simultaneously."

"Again, you assume I'm stupid." Sam took a painful breath, the crimson stain on his shirt growing wider as his face grew ashen. "I'll figure it out."

Nick finally stood, realizing what was about to happen.

"You have to stop him," Nick shouted at Paul as he came to his side.

"Stay out of this," Paul yelled at Nick without taking his eyes off Sam. "I know what I'm doing."

"You don't understand," Nick pleaded. "If he takes off —"

"He's my brother, dammit, I don't know who you are, but I just saved your life, so stay out of this before you get yourself shot."

Without warning, Sam shot at the tarmac. "I suggest you listen to my brother; he's never wrong."

Paul looked at Sam, at the growing wound in his side. He squeezed the exotic gun in his hand out of sheer frustration.

"If you're going to shoot me, if you want to kill me, now's the time," Sam challenged.

Paul Dreyfus dropped the Peacemaker where he stood and took several steps forward.

The two brothers stared at each other, the moment hanging . . .

"Sam," Paul said. "Please . . . ?"

Without another word, Sam slammed the door closed, revved the engine of the Cessna, and pulled away from the small field, the plane picking up speed along the small access road.

Nick grabbed the Colt off the ground. He spun out the cylinder, grabbed four bullets from his pocket, and refilled the chambers. He took off down the tarmac after the plane and without hesitation, began firing. With his shots going wide, he stopped and took a knee, steadied his aim with two hands, and continued his barrage at the fleeing Cessna.

But after only two more shots, the pistol was twisted from his grasp. Dreyfus stood over him as he threw the pistol into the distant bushes.

"You don't understand," Nick shouted at Dreyfus as he raged up into his face. "So many will die."

"What?" Dreyfus said, dismissing Nick's

statement. "I don't care what you may think. But he's still my brother; I'm not going to let someone kill him in cold blood."

Nick watched the escaping Cessna 400 bounce down the taxiway, swerving onto the runway without clearance, its speed increasing as the tarmac began to run out. Nick had never been a pilot, never professed an understanding of the physical dynamics of lift and how it applied to the wing of a plane, but he knew if Sam's velocity didn't increase he would never make it over the fence at the end of the runway.

The Cessna's nose began to lift as the engine strained, the wheels bouncing up and down. And as horrible a thought as it was, Nick hoped he wouldn't make it, that he would crash into the fence, that somehow, maybe, one of his bullets had caught the engine. He was not hoping for Sam's death but rather an interruption of his destiny, an interruption that would save 212 lives.

But then, with a final surge, the Cessna leaped into the sky, clearing the fence by inches. Nick watched it climb at an odd angle, the inexperienced pilot wounded and panicked, desperately trying to control the aircraft, hoping to escape.

And then Nick saw it: The AS 300 was

circling back after takeoff, adjusting its heading toward Boston.

Julia took one last look out the window as they flew over the Kensico Reservoir and closed her eyes, hoping to get a quick nap in so she would be rested for what was sure to be one of the most memorable evenings of her and Nick's sixteen-year relationship.

Without warning the jet tipped hard to the left. Drinks spilled, luggage came crashing out and down from the overhead storage bins, people shrieked in terror, as a collective fear consumed the passengers.

The jet engines screamed, their pitch climbing as they strained, pushing the jet into an unnatural angle of over sixty degrees.

Julia pushed herself back in the seat, her arms pressed tight against the armrests, her fingers clutching the edge in a death grip, holding herself in place as the jet continued to bank hard left.

And she thought of the life within her, unsure whether it was a boy or a girl. All that mattered was it was hers and Nick's. She wanted to protect it at all costs, knowing that if she was facing imminent death she would offer up her life so the child might live.

Out the window, Julia could see the

ground, only a few thousand feet below. She couldn't breathe; her heart had surely stopped in panic. She turned and saw Jason across the aisle. His face was calm as he pulled out his phone, turning it on, no doubt calling his wife to say good-bye, to tell her that he loved her one more time.

All around her were cries for help, passengers pleading for some divine intervention, begging for somebody to do something, as if the pilot wasn't doing everything he could to not only save them but save himself.

And then she felt the hand upon hers, it was Katherine's, a reassuring gesture like the one her mother used to give her when she was frightened. Julia turned and looked into her elderly, wise eyes and saw a peace that contrasted with the terror surrounding them.

"Don't worry, child," Katherine said.

And everything slowed — the whine of the jet engines, the screams of the people all fell away as the warmth of Katherine's loving hand held her.

And Julia glanced out the window once more. She saw the reason for the jet's evasive actions, the reason everyone was on the brink of a nervous breakdown: A small Cessna was heading right at them. She could clearly see the man flying it, slumped forward. She could see the panic in him as he desperately steered right.

All eyes were fixed on the skies, the AS 300 banking so hard to the left it appeared to be on the verge of tipping over. The wings of the Cessna wobbled as Sam tried to swerve, but the looming disaster seemed inevitable. Nick could see Paul's face, his breath held, hoping, praying for a miracle, but Nick knew there would be no miracle.

And though Dance lay dead on the tarmac before him, this was all his fault. He was the one who had sent Sam into a panic, trying to kill him, causing him to run for his life. There was no telling how gravely Sam had been injured, how much blood he was losing, but whether or not the one-inch projectile had lodged in a vital organ or severed a crucial artery, the wound would prove fatal.

Nick had altered fate. Dance had been eliminated from the world, and with the head of the serpent removed, the collective body of his group of corrupt cops would fall. But Nick now realized as he watched the two planes heading for each other that he hadn't changed fate enough.

Nick watched the tiny Cessna on its

intersecting pattern with the enormous AS 300 and knew all hope for the passengers was lost.

And they crashed, the Cessna driving nose-first into the jet. From this distance — the planes a mile up and a mile away — it was like a dragonfly attacking a bird, becoming entangled, but the damage the small craft inflicted on its giant victim was lethal. The jet's banking left turn uselessly continued, Flight 502 was now inverted from the impact. A small ball of fire erupted as the two aircraft began to tumble down out of the sky like an omen from God. All eyes were fixed on the falling planes.

"Oh, my God," Dreyfus whispered, crossing himself. He glanced at Nick, realizing what his brother had just done.

Nick could not imagine the panic within the jet. The crash surely did not end the lives of most of the passengers. They were no doubt all alive, trapped in the falling wreckage, knowing they were about to die a death everyone who ever flew feared.

And the twisted metal continued its fall, now tumbling end over end, specks of debris falling out of the back of the plane, specks that Nick knew were live passengers, all of it accelerating toward the ground like a stone at thirty-two feet per second.

A sense of helplessness permeated Nick and Dreyfus. They wished there was something they could do, wished they could reach up and stop it.

And the falling jet, what Nick thought of as a tomb, filled with chaos, filled with the damned, disappeared behind the trees. A fireball erupted, rolling up into the sky hundreds of feet, the volatile jet fuel igniting instantly upon impact. Seconds later, the explosion reverberated, the ground shaking as in an earthquake, like a mortar shell striking the town. Black smoke billowed upward, a beacon for rescuers who would find no one alive.

Nick couldn't imagine what he would have done if Julia were on that plane. He was oddly thankful, in the face of the loss of so many lives, that she had narrowly escaped death, being called off the jet at the last second as a result of the robbery. Fate was something he couldn't understand, and though he had briefly touched it, manipulated it, it was something that no one could foresee or control.

The moment hung silently in the air, silent prayers said for the dead.

"How did you . . . ?" Dreyfus looked at Nick but abandoned his question. He finally exhaled, pulling out his cell phone.

Nick followed suit. He needed to hear Julia's voice. Despite the death of Dance, he needed to tell her that he loved her, that everything was right in the world.

He dialed and found the call going directly to voicemail. He thought about where she could be and remembered she was at Washington House, just now seeing evidence of the robbery.

"Hi, honey, it's me." Nick said into the phone. "I just needed to tell you that I love you. I love you with all my heart and soul, with every ounce of my being. I'm sorry we fought this morning, I'm sorry if I upset you, but I was wondering, I know you're busy with work and all but I'd just love to stop by and see you. I hate that I left you on a sour note, thinking I was mad. Call me when you get this."

Nick hung up his phone and saw it light up with a message and one missed call. Nicked dialed his voicemail, knowing it was from Julia. She had probably called him as he called her.

Nick listened to her message, their words of love so similar. The warmth of her voice comforted his sorrow-filled mind. He stood there, the phone pressed to his ear as if it was a talisman, a magical link to her. He was so glad she left him the message. But then he heard the stewardess interrupt, telling her that she had to turn off her phone, that the doors were already closed.

And with a gut-wrenching realization, Nick knew what he had done.

Somehow, his actions had interfered with Julia getting off the plane, his delaying the robbery by five minutes had delayed the text message to her. She never heard about the break-in, she never knew to get off the plane.

Nick fell backward against Shannon's Mustang, his breath gone, his heart burning. Everything he had done, everything that he had gone through to save her was for naught. He had played about in time, he had toyed with fate as if it would bend to his will. But it was a force for which there was no match. No magical watch, no violation of the laws of physics could alter it. For fate was the most powerful force in nature.

And in that moment, Nick knew 213 passengers had perished. Julia was dead, lying in the midst of the charred wreckage of Flight 502.

Nick pulled the watch from his pocket: 11:55.

Julia was dead. She was dead over and over again. He thought he was trapped in a time-warped hell, having to endure Julia's death in every hour in a new way.

And this time it wasn't at the hand of Dance. It was his fault and his fault alone, pulling her out of harm's way only to push her onto that flight. He had taken the scythe out of Dance's hands and killed her himself in his misguided arrogance.

All he strived for, everything he had done, everything he thought he was tasked to do, was wrong. The singular action that was to alter fate now was not killing her assassin, it was not killing Dance. It was the plane, everything tied back there now.

Nick grabbed the Colt Peacemaker from the bushes. He ran to the body of Ethan Dance and tore through his pockets; he found the dead cop's cell phone, flipped it open, and memorized the phone number of his last call. He stood, threw down the phone, and broke into an all-out sprint, racing for Dance's car. Racing to the body of Shannon.

He still had time.

CHAPTER 1

10:00 A.M.

All was right in the world, at least for the moment. The lights were on, planes weren't falling from the sky, robberies hadn't occurred, and Julia was safe and alive. Smiles were still worn on the faces of the shoppers, people went about their routines in anticipation of another fun-filled summer weekend.

No one was aware of what was coming, no one knew the terrible turn life would take in an hour and fifty minutes except Nick. He had glimpsed the world of Byram Hills and knew how time would unfold from now until nightfall. But he had an ability that the men of fiction and history did not possess. Fate lay in his hands, he could change the future, by his actions he could change the course of time.

Julia stood in the back of The Right Thing, staring at frames. She had no idea how big a sonogram picture was and had no idea what size frame to buy. She grabbed a set of three, each a different size, and figured she'd just make it work. She raced to the book section, grabbed her favorite Dr. Seuss book, *Fox in Sox,* and on her way to the checkout counter, grabbed a roll of teddy bear wrapping paper.

She was bursting with anticipation as her friend, Angela, checked her out. It was an excitement like that she felt as a little girl on Christmas, a feeling that Santa would make her dreams come true. But the excitement she was feeling now was not in receiving but in giving, the giving and sharing of life, providing Nick with the ultimate expression of their love, the gift of a child.

She got back into her car and turned out of the parking lot heading for the airport. Though check-in and security were brief at Westchester Airport, she wanted to give herself plenty of time for once, instead of having to rush, instead of having to make a mad dash for the gate.

As she entered Route 684, her cell phone rang.

"Hey, Jo," Julia said as she saw the caller ID and hit the speakerphone.

"I'm so sorry about this," Julia's secretary, Jo Whalen, said. "Mr. Isles and Mr. Lerner are in court and, of course, there's another *crisis* on the Collier deal. They say the merger can't and won't happen if the Collier children's trusts do not reflect the appropriate caveats in the event of the children's divorce."

Julia laughed. "The kids are five and seven."

"Maybe their parents can look into the future, I don't know. Mr. Lerner wants you to handle the conference call in their absence."

"You're kidding? When?"

"Now. Mr. Lerner prefaced his call by saying the $12 million in billables on the Collier account should be worth taking a later flight for."

"Let me turn around," Julia said, crestfallen, feeling as if Christmas had been canceled.

"I don't think so," Jo snapped at her. "I've got the call set up, I can patch you in. You'll straighten out this lucky sperm club trust in plenty of time and make your flight."

Julia smiled. No one was better than Jo. "I'm going to pull over so I don't lose signal. Why don't you patch them all in?"

"Have a safe flight, honey."

"Thanks, you're the best."

"Okay, everyone," Jo said. "I have Julia

Quinn for you."

"Good morning," Julia said as she pulled to the side of the road. Jo was so good, she had saved her and kept her life orderly for the tenth time today.

With the unexpected delay, she'd just have to do her usual run for the gate, but she'd still make her flight. She looked at the teddy bear wrapping paper sticking out of the bag and smiled, Nick was going to be so surprised.

"So, I understand there is some concern on the matter of the children's trusts," Julia said out loud as she leaned back in her car seat. "Well, let's see what we can do to protect their future."

Bob Shannon walked out of the bagel store, his bottle of Gatorade already half gone. He ate his bagel as fast as he could, trying to finish it before he got into the Mustang. He hated crumbs, and the poppy seed bagel had a tendency to make its presence felt weeks after it had been eaten, as the seeds permeated every nook and cranny.

With his last bite, he arrived at his car. Brushing himself off, he hopped in just as his cell phone vibrated with an incoming text message. He looked at his phone, not recognizing

the number. Another message came in, and
then another, and another. He paged
through his phone and found the incoming
messages to actually be five pictures. He
clicked on the first one but was interrupted
by an incoming call from the same number.

"Detective Shannon," he said as he answered.

"Did you look at the pictures yet?" the
caller asked.

"Who is this?"

"I'm at the private air terminal at
Westchester Airport. I'm driving a blue
Audi. And detective, trust no one, especially
your partner."

The line went dead.

Shannon stared at his phone as if it was
somehow pulling a prank on him. He looked
again at the number but didn't recognize it,
so he pulled up the first picture.

It was a shot of a green Taurus. Dance's
piece of junk. Shannon at first hadn't
understood why he drove it. Though it had
the souped-up 350 V-8 police engine, it still
looked like a banged-up vehicle that someone had left at the side of the road. But as
Shannon learned, Dance spent a good deal
of time down county and in the Bronx,
moonlighting in less-than-legal side jobs,
and had chosen a car that would never be

noticed, that would never call attention to itself, as a black Shelby Cobra Mustang would.

Shannon thumbed through to the next picture. It was from the rear of Dance's car, the trunk sitting wide open. Shannon chuckled, he was being goofed on. The pictures looked like those various-angle photos you saw of used cars in the back of magazines, but he could never imagine who would buy Dance's car.

But as he clicked on the third picture, he realized this was no game. It was a much closer shot of Dance's trunk, and it was filled with what looked like treasure. Swords of gold, bejeweled daggers, several ornate guns, and sitting among it all was a black velvet bag, its mouth wide open, the diamonds inside sparkling in the sunlight.

Shannon grew suddenly serious. If this was a joke, someone had gone too far. But as he clicked to the next picture on his phone he knew that the situation went much farther.

The rear door on the right side hung open. The passenger was belted in, sitting in a pool of blood that seemed to cover his entire torso. Shannon looked closer but could not make out the face. But no matter, he knew he was looking at a corpse, he was looking at a murder scene.

He finally clicked to the final shot, a shot that sent his mind spinning, a shot that nearly seized his heart. It was a much closer image, this time through the left rear passenger door of the Taurus. The face could be seen plain as day. It was pale, almost blue from bleeding out. The mouth hung open, slack-jawed. The eyes were lifeless, dry, and without any sign of a soul.

Shannon looked up, suddenly feeling a rush of paranoia such as he had never known. He looked back down at his cell phone, thinking he might have been seeing things.

But there was no doubt, Bob Shannon was looking at himself.

Nick sat in his car at the private air terminal waiting for Shannon. He couldn't afford to waste time explaining things again, so he had formulated the perfect device to get the detective's attention.

He had run back to the Taurus before his last time shift, opened the door on Shannon's side, reached in, and grabbed the cell phone from the detective's waist. He read Shannon's number, entered it into his own phone, and threw Shannon's back in the car. He quickly circled Dance's car, taking the five pictures he'd just sent, building them in intensity as he went, creating an invitation that Shannon would never refuse.

On the seat beside him was the Colt Peacemaker he had plucked from the bushes, its chambers emptied of the spent silver bullets. It was the same gun he had stared at nearly twelve hours ago in the interrogation room, the pistol that Dance had shot Julia with and had planted in the trunk of his car to frame him for her murder. It had become a symbol of death and greed. But now, the etchings upon its barrel and stock became prophetically personal, reflecting Nick's own quest for justice: *The gate that leads to damnation is wide — To hell you shall be gathered together — Yet ye bring wrath — Darkness which may be felt — Whoever offers violence to you, offer you the like violence to him.*

The whining roar of an American Air jet shook Nick's car like sustained thunder as it leaped off the tarmac into the crystalline blue sky. Planes and jets took off and landed with regular frequency, without incident, as the aviation business went about its morning routine.

Nick stared out through his windshield across the large expanse of tarmac at the central hub of Westchester Airport's main terminal where six medium-sized passenger jets took on travelers to whisk them out to all parts of the country. On the outermost bay was a white AS 300, its red and blue circular logo prominently displayed. The North East Air jet sat quietly being fueled and prepped for flight: food and drink carts were replenished, aisles were vacuumed, fresh pillows and blankets brought on in preparation for the boarding that would commence in an hour's time. It received the temporary designation of Flight 502 with a one-hour flight time to Logan International Airport in Boston. It was the plane that would carry Julia aloft, carry so many unsuspecting passengers only two miles before it fell from the sky, plunging them all to their death in a tangled heap of flame.

Nick had fought so hard to stop the robbery, to save Julia, he'd neglected to think about the 212 on the plane who died. But now, as impossible at it seemed, Julia was among them.

It took ten hours to save Julia from her imminent death, to remove her killer from the world. Yet despite all of his effort, he had delivered her right back to the first death she had avoided, the first death she was saved from. Through his missteps he had placed her on the plane with no excuse to get off, through his poorly executed moves she had been left to experience the most horrible of deaths, a death he had feared all his life. He couldn't imagine what had gone through her head as they crashed in midair and tumbled out of the sky.

Nick realized all moments, every tick of the watch led to now. Led to stopping the plane crash to save not only Julia but the 212 others who had needlessly died.

And though he had initially thought it was simple to stop the tumbling domino of the robbery in order for Julia to live, he knew now that the impact of his actions could have far worse results.

He wasn't about to rely on simply taking the key for Dreyfus's plane, or on just leaving a message for Julia to not get on Flight 502. He couldn't call the airline or the FAA, explaining he had a premonition. He had considered an anonymous bomb threat but dismissed the idea, knowing he had to do more than prevent the plane crash in order to keep Julia alive. He also had to keep the robbery from ever happening.

He knew that every action he took had repercussions, no matter the nobleness of the intention. He had seen it with Marcus's death, with McManus's death, with Shannon's, and with Julia ending up on the doomed airliner. As each moment was modified it would ripple through time, having hundreds, even thousands of effects.

If Nick made the wrong move, the wrong decision, it would reverberate through the future, and instead of stopping the plane crash, his misstep might compound the tragedy of the crash of Flight 502, perhaps sending it tumbling onto the populated town of Byram Hills or, even worse, the children's day camp instead of the wide-open, vacant sports field.

Who was to say that fate was even reversible? Was Julia destined to die this day no matter what, whether by gunshot, plane crash, or some other means? Were the 212 passengers aboard Flight 502 meant to go down in a horrific aviation disaster despite every effort to halt the Cessna 400 from taking off?

Nick suddenly shook off the pessimistic thoughts, returning to hope, the greatest of emotions, something that could wipe away fear, could eliminate doubt, could inspire faith in even the most impossible of situations. He was here now, he had inexplicably marched back through the day, to this last of hours, to this final chance to save Julia's life.

So with hope in his heart, Nick focused,

searching for that singular action, that one deed that would change the future for everyone. Julia, Marcus, Shannon, Dreyfus, McManus, himself. He didn't know what it was, but he knew that he would find it before the hour was up.

Nick picked up his phone again and tried Julia; for the second time he went right to voicemail.

"Julia," Nick said. "It's me. Do me a favor, do not get on that flight to Boston. I don't care why you're going, I don't care if you get fired, do not get on that flight. I have a terrible feeling, I can't explain it. Just do what I say. Call me when you get this."

Nick turned his attention to the Cessna 400. Parked within a long line of small jets and planes, the white aircraft looked like a Corvette of the sky, its sleek lines, its swept-back window giving the impression of a man-made bird of prey.

The blue Chevy Impala sat just behind the small plane, its trunk open, as Paul Dreyfus removed his briefcase and a small duffel, laying them upon the ground. He was neatly dressed in gray slacks and a blue tie, his sport coat hung on the open door of the Impala, his gray hair combed as if he were off to Sunday mass.

Nick had watched him for several minutes

moving around his plane, talking on his cell phone, when up the single-lane drive came a dark green, waxed and polished BMW. The car drove across the nearly vacant lot and parked on the other side, right next to where Dreyfus was waiting.

A man in a crisp blue shirt and pleated pants emerged from the car and warmly greeted Dreyfus with a two-fisted handshake. There was a polished, regal air about the man. He looked to be in his late fifties, his strong shoulders and narrow waist evidence that he was more than fit, his dark perfect hair flecked with gray that dominated his temples.

The two engaged in an animated conversation full of hand gestures and head nods, until finally, the regal man popped his trunk. Dreyfus crouched and unzipped the black duffel. With a great deal of effort he withdrew an object, carried it over to the BMW, and placed it inside the trunk, closing the lid.

Nick's heart ran cold as he instantly recognized the mahogany box. There was no mistaking the two-by-two foot dark wood case, its three silver keyholes glistening in the midmorning sun.

And then the man in the blue shirt turned, the sun hitting his profile, and the last twelve hours of Nick's life were turned inside out, sending his mind reeling, for he realized who he was looking at.

It was the European, the man who had showed up in the interrogation room, who had given him the watch, who had set him on this journey to save his wife. Yet here he was taking delivery of the mahogany box Sam Dreyfus was supposed to steal one hour from now, the box that created the impetus for so much violence and death, for Julia's torturous demise on two separate occasions, the box whose theft and possession would ultimately precipitate the crash of Flight 502.

Nick's mind filled with confusion at the alliance of Paul Dreyfus and the European. He had never formed a connection, never thought he had been sent on his journey for anything but Julia. He thought of the box as simply the goal of thieves, the prize sought by Sam Dreyfus. He'd never truly pondered its contents or worth, dismissing it as the precious secrets of an old man. But now . . .

It was inextricably linked to Julia's death, to the crash of Flight 502, a wooden box whose contents were sought by too many.

He had never expected to see the mahogany box here already, thinking it still in the safe in Hennicot's basement, which, in his mind, meant only one thing: The true thieves were standing before him on the other side of the parking lot.

Nick leaped from his car and broke into an all-out sprint across the blacktop lot. The European caught sight of Nick's frantic approach, quickly got into his car, and pulled out. Nick sprinted across the fifty-yard-wide lot, past Dreyfus, running alongside the moving car as it headed for the exit, pounding the driver's-side window. The man briefly looked at Nick before hitting the gas and leaving him in a cloud of dust where he finally slowed to a halt to watch the man's escape.

But then fate had finally intervened on his behalf: Up ahead by the entrance gate, the black Mustang pulled into the single-lane driveway of the parking lot, the blue and red lights within its black front grill staccato-flashing. With a loud chirp the siren sounded as the muscle car skidded to a sideways stop, blocking the BMW's exit.

Shannon jumped from his car, holding his hand up, stopping the European man's exit, and pulled the gun from his holster.

"Please step out of the vehicle," Shannon yelled.

But the man was already complying.

"Did you send those photos?" Shannon

continued shouting.

The European stared at him in confusion.

"I sent them," Nick said as he ran toward Shannon, coming to a stop beside him. Paul Dreyfus came jogging up, winded, and exchanging angry glances with his blue-shirted associate.

"What kind of sick joke do you think you're playing?" Shannon said through gritted teeth.

"I assure you, Detective," Nick said, "this is no joke."

"Where did you get them?"

"You have to bear with me," Nick said, his hands raised in a pleading fashion. "In the trunk of that car is a stolen mahogany box that belongs to Shamus Hennicot, the owner of Washington House in Byram Hills."

Shannon stared at Nick for a moment before turning his attention to the man standing next to his BMW. "Do you mind opening your trunk?"

Without a word, the man hit the button on his key fob, releasing the hood. Shannon walked around and saw the clean trunk, empty but for a single two-by-two dark wooden box.

"Okay, so he has a box in his trunk," Shannon said. "What the hell is it?"

"My name is Paul Dreyfus," Dreyfus said, approaching Shannon. He held out his wallet, displaying his driver's license. "I work for Shamus Hennicot; my firm handles the security systems for Mr. Hennicot, including Washington House."

Shannon took and read Dreyfus's license, matching the face to the picture on the license. He turned to the other man. "And you are?"

"Zachariah Nash. I am Mr. Hennicot's personal assistant, I oversee his estate."

"And you are who?" Shannon finally asked Nick, his temper rising with the confused situation.

Nick was speechless at the revelation that the European, Nash, the one who had given him the watch, worked for Hennicot.

"Do either of you know this man?" Shannon asked, alluding to Nick.

"No," Dreyfus said.

Nash shook his head.

"My name is Nicholas Quinn." Nick regained his composure and focus and turned to Dreyfus. "An hour from now, your brother steals Shamus Hennicot's collection of weapons, diamonds, and that box."

Dreyfus, Nash, and Shannon stared at Nick, exchanging glances as if they were in a shared dream with a madman.

"Not this box," Dreyfus said softly, taking a step toward Nick as if entertaining his crazy notion.

"That's the box Sam steals from Hennicot's safe," Nick said. "I'm sure of it."

"The box in the safe at Washington House," Dreyfus continued, with an almost bedside manner, "it's a duplicate, an empty prototype."

"What?" Nick's eyes filled with anger.

"My brother will not get his hands on this box or what's inside it, I assure you."

"Why didn't you just tell him you already stole it?" Nick said, his voice straining, his words making no sense in this hour before the robbery had even occurred.

"Excuse me?" Paul Dreyfus said. "I didn't steal this."

"The box in the safe was a decoy, then?" Nick asked, already knowing the answer.

"Who are you?" Dreyfus's face became overwhelmed with confusion.

Nick's mind was teetering on the brink of a nervous breakdown. He had formulated a plan, one that he thought was nearly foolproof, but now, with the revelation that Dreyfus and Nash were working together, that the box in the safe was a fake . . .

Nick stared back, not knowing how far to go, how far to push the issue before his last ounce of credibility was lost.

"Two hundred and twelve people die on Flight 502 later this morning. My wife dies on that flight because of your brother, because he was after whatever is in that box. Why didn't you just tell him it was empty?" Nick could no longer separate the future from the past.

"What the hell are you talking about?" Paul Dreyfus asked.

"I'm sorry," Shannon said to Dreyfus. He looked at Nick as if he was an outpatient from an asylum. "Mr. Quinn, why don't you come with me?"

Shannon took Nick's arm.

"I'm not crazy," Nick erupted, tearing his arm away from Shannon, approaching Dreyfus. "Has anyone seen Hennicot's weapon collection? You did his security, you designed the system to protect everything? Has his weapons collection ever been made public?"

Dreyfus stared at him. "No."

"Up until an hour from now, has the security system you designed ever been compromised?"

"No," Dreyfus said with a shake of his head.

"Spanish swords, Sri Lankan daggers, Ottoman sabers — so no one is aware that

470

Sultan Murad V's custom Colt Peacemaker etched with religious symbols — Catholic, Jewish, Islamic, Buddhist — is in a display case in Hennicot's little basement fortress?"

Dreyfus stared at Nick, his face impossible to read.

"You were just there, Paul," Nick said addressing him as if they were old friends. "Was the case intact?"

Dreyfus nodded. "What are you getting at?"

"The fourteen remaining silver bullets that were custom-made, each personalized before being loaded in the chamber, they had a saying on them in Arabic . . ."

". . . May you be forbidden from Paradise," Dreyfus said slowly.

Nick reached into his pocket, pulled out his closed fist, thrusting it in Dreyfus's face, finally opening it to reveal a handful of the silver bullets.

"What the hell is going on?" Shannon said.

"Look into my eyes, Paul," Nick implored, ignoring Shannon. "I am not crazy. I trust you, I understand you're feeling the betrayal by your brother. But he needs to be stopped now, before the robbery. He screws everyone, he comes here, to you, he steals your plane and causes this."

Nick reached into his pocket and pulled

out Marcus's letter. He tore the *Wall Street Journal* page out and shoved it into Dreyfus's face.

Dreyfus took the printout and became lost in the horrific image of the scorched field, the tail section of the smoldering plane prominently displayed. He scanned the other news stories, the stock closing numbers . . . and finally the date and time of the printout: July 28, 4:58. He continued to stare at it as if it would somehow change.

"Do you see it?" Nick said.

"The time?" Paul said slowly, as if trying to comprehend the impossible.

"No," Nick said as he pointed across the tarmac at the North East Air jet sitting just outside the gate being prepped for flight. "The tail section, the N-number."

Dreyfus looked at the AS 300 jet outside the main terminal, at the large red and blue corporate logo on the white tail section. His eyes drifted down to the registration number, the unique identification required to be displayed on all aircraft: N95301.

It took Dreyfus a moment before looking back at the paper in his hand, at the image of the blackened wreckage, at the white tail section prominently displayed, its logo clearly visible, as was its N-number: N95301.

"Your brother steals what he thinks is the real box from Hennicot's safe. He comes here to see you. He steals your plane and causes all of that," Nick said, pointing at the picture of the devastation. "And he dies along with everyone else."

"What is that?" Shannon said, pointing at the printout.

But Dreyfus didn't respond, his eyes ping-ponging between the photo and the plane across the tarmac. He finally looked at Nick and without a word, handed him back the paper.

Nick tucked it into his pocket, knowing he had just won an ally.

"Your brother's flight just got in from Philly," Nick said. "He's being picked up right about now."

Nick turned to Shannon. "Your partner, Ethan Dance, is working with Paul's brother, Sam, along with Brinehart, Randall, and a cop named Arilio to rob Washington House. He kills my wife." Nick paused, bracing himself for revealing Shannon's future. "And he's the one that kills you."

"That's it," Shannon shouted, grabbing Nick and spinning him around. He quickly cuffed him and spun him back to stare into his eyes. "You're talking like a madman."

"I'm not crazy," Nick pleaded.

"Yeah? Where the hell did you get those pictures you sent to my cell phone?"

"The pictures I sent you are date stamped. One hour and fifteen minutes from now. Dance shoots you in the gut and tucks you in the backseat of his car *where you die.*"

"Detective?" Dreyfus said, trying to interrupt.

"How the hell would you know that?" Shannon railed at Nick, ignoring Dreyfus.

"The same way I know that Dance is a dirty cop, the same way I know about the St. Christopher medal in your pocket," Nick said. "You and Ethan both graduated from St. Christopher High School in Brooklyn. You're cousins and he got you your job."

"How the hell . . . ?" Shannon glared at Nick.

"Did you look at the time stamp on the pictures?"

"Why the hell would I look at the time stamp?" Shannon erupted. He stood there a moment thinking . . . he reached into his pocket, withdrew his cell phone, and flipped it open. He thumbed through to the first picture.

And finally looked at Nick. "How is this possible?"

Nick turned to Paul, his eyes pleading. "You know what your brother is about to do, that's why you traded boxes. You saw what happens, you saw the tail section. Tell him, dammit!"

Dreyfus looked at Nick, trepidation in his eyes. He looked toward Nash, who nodded in approval.

Dreyfus turned to Shannon. "My brother is arriving at this very moment on a flight from Philly —"

"And your partner," Nick cut in, "is picking him up."

Shannon stared at Nick and Dreyfus, his eyes awash in confusion. He looked off into the distance, though he was focused within his mind. After a long moment he reluctantly reached into his car and thumbed the radio.

"Lena," Shannon said into his walkie-talkie.

"Good morning to you, too, Shannon," Lena's staticky voice came back over the radio.

"Have you seen Dance this morning?"

"He left here a little while ago, right after you."

"Do you know where?"

"Did you lose your partner again, Shannon? Why don't you just call him?"

"I don't want to do that," Shannon said, rushing her. "Can you get a fix on his car?"

She paused a moment.

"You're kidding, right?" she finally said.

"No, I'm serious."

"He's with you at the airport. Isn't that where you are?"

"Where at the airport?"

"Jesus, Shannon, you're like a half mile apart. He's at the main terminal. Would you like me to come out there and introduce you?"

Dance sat in his Taurus outside the main terminal of Westchester Airport, primed and ready. He had awakened this morning knowing that he would finally rid himself of the burden of Ghestov Rukaj. But even more than paying off the bounty, he would be pocketing over $15 million once he took care of Brinehart and Arilio. Randall would live — he looked at him as the overweight uncle who knew his deeds but never tattled. He was one of the few people he actually trusted in life, but the others were simply a means to an end.

And then he would disappear. Amsterdam would become his home. He would live out his life as far away from this place as he could, happy, content, with no more worrying about money or his survival.

He had cut it down to the wire. Rukaj and

his men were relentless, contacting him, visiting him, reminding him of his pending demise come midnight if he failed to come up with the money.

He and Sam Dreyfus had run the scenario countless times over, planning for contingencies, for mistakes. They ran it on paper, in discussions, Sam had even made a computer model. They planned it down to the second. The job would take less than fifteen minutes.

They were well prepared, well protected, and nothing could stop them.

Sam Dreyfus walked out of the main terminal of Westchester Airport, stepping into the warm morning sun. He was a mix of emotions, knowing that he was heading down a path he could never return from, but he kept his mind focused on the dark wooden box, kept his thoughts fixed on the rewards he would soon be reaping. He headed straight to the green Taurus parked in the arrivals area, his brown, neatly parted hair fluttering in the slight breeze.

"Everything on schedule?" Sam said with a smile as he got in and slammed the door.

"My three guys will meet us there at exactly 11:10," Dance said.

"You have my stuff?"

Dance nodded.

"I need to make sure everything is in order."

Without a word, Dance pulled out of the arriving passenger pick-up zone and pulled into the area reserved for TSA and police.

Dance popped the trunk and they both got out of the car, walked around, and looked inside.

Sam unzipped the first duffel bag. He pulled out a silver box with a red half dome atop it, flipped it on, and checked the LEDs ensuring the high-spectrum, wide-angle lasers were functioning and had enough battery for at least fifteen minutes. He'd made them himself, all twelve, from a schematic he had found in Paul's files. He didn't know who had created their unique design, but he did know Paul was trying to formulate a countermeasure to their function that he could incorporate on future jobs.

Sam followed suit with each of the remaining eleven boxes and moved on to the three black laserscopes. Attached to five-inch tripods, they were similar to the laser sight on a gun, with a single high-intensity beam that could be seen in harsh sunlight, allowing him to focus them at the various exterior cameras.

There were two small, matchbox-sized

devices, magnetic interference emitters, which he rolled about in the palm of his hand, flipping the tiny buttons on and off.

He finally checked the glass cutter, the simplest tool in the bag but the one with the most reliability. No electronics, no electricity, lasers, or high-tech circuitry, just a small diamond tip and a suction-cup-equipped metal bar.

Sam's cell phone rang. He quickly answered it tucking it against his ear.

"Sam," his brother, Paul, said. "Don't say a word."

"Yeah," Sam said with a fake smile as he closed the trunk, walked back, and got into the car.

"I'm at the private air terminal," Paul said. "I already opened Hennicot's safe; I have the box."

Sam said nothing as his blood began to boil.

"The man you are with, Detective Ethan Dance? When all is said and done, he will shoot you and you will die." Paul's voice had an icy tone. "Think about what you are doing, think about what you're going for. I know it's not the antiques or diamonds, all you want is what is in this box. Well, you chose the wrong partners. I'm holding it in my hands right now. If you want it, you come to me."

Without a word, Sam closed his phone. Dance got back into the car and pulled out into the flow of traffic.

"We need to go to the private air terminal," Sam finally said.

"Why," Dance asked.

"We have a problem."

"Shit," Dance said as he pulled out his gun. "We haven't even started yet."

"What's that for?" Sam asked, looking at Dance's nine-millimeter.

"To take care of the problem."

At 7:00 A.M., when Paul Dreyfus learned of what Sam was about to do, he had called Shamus Hennicot, even though he was implicating his brother, and explained what was about to happen.

Shamus told him not to be concerned with anything except the box and that he could do whatever it took to obtain it before it fell into Sam's or anyone else's hands. He told him to let them take the weapons and the diamonds — they had no meaning to him and were all insured.

Paul had known Shamus for five years now. He had designed the security for all of his homes around the world: for Washington House in Byram Hills, for his wife's cottage on the coast of Maine, his château in Nice, the rarely visited bungalow on his private island in the Maldives, and his summer home on the ocean in Massachusetts. Paul and Shamus had become more than friends, more than confidants, sharing stories of the heart, the loss of loved ones, the private revelries of success. Shamus gave him wise business advice and direction, but only when it was asked for.

Paul had told him of his brother Sam and the never-ending trouble and anguish he created, but it was always Shamus who reminded him that family is the most important of things, a bond that cannot be broken. It is family that knows our true selves: our wants and needs, our fragile egos and faults, not the façade we display to the world. He reminded Paul that he was Sam's only connection to his youth, the one who knew him before the harsh realities of life, before drugs, alcohol, and rebellion.

It was two years ago when Shamus had asked him to construct the box. He told him that he needed to lock away family secrets, to secure them in an impenetrable location that no one could access, but that at the same time the contents must remain mobile.

Paul did not ask what was to be stored away, what was to be hidden from the world, but Shamus insisted on divulging the mystery. And he went one step further. He asked Paul to be part of a triumvirate, along with his personal assistant, Zachariah Nash, and himself. They would be the three who would know the contents of the box and control access to it.

Paul spent a year on the box's design, constructing prototypes that he tested under the harshest conditions, finally arriving at the finished product: a one-inch titanium case wrapped in fire-resistant Nomex and three layers of Kevlar, an idea usurped from NASA space suits designed to withstand all manners of temperature, pressure, and assault. The lock was a second generation of his octagonal key design. Three slots for three eight-sided keys whose insertion was to a specific lettered coordinate on each key. A combination that had over three thousand possibilities between the slots, the keys, and their eight positions. Sheathed in African mahogany, the box's appearance was like that of the finest pieces of furniture, while its endurance and impenetrability were on par with the most secure recesses of the White House.

Paul got off the phone with Shamus, raced to the airfield, and flew straight to Westchester in less than an hour, his small private plane able to fly in air corridors too low for commercial traffic.

With full access and no need to be concerned with video cameras, Paul had jumped into the waiting rental car, gone over to Washington House, and taken the box from Hennicot's safe, replacing it with the empty final prototype he had created during the design phase.

Dance drove his green Taurus up the single-lane entrance into the large parking lot of the private air terminal. The lot was adjacent to a sea of planes that were situated in a parallel line to afford access for their owners when they arrived. The bevy of jets all faced the byway strip, the causeway onto the main runways of the airport proper.

Dance drove up to and parked between a BMW and a blue Chevy Impala that were parked in spaces adjacent to a small, sleek white plane. A dark mahogany box sat on the hood of the BMW as if it was some kind of trophy on display.

A thick man with neatly groomed gray hair stood next to the BMW, his hand upon the box. His shoulders were strong, his gaze intense, fixed upon Sam in the passenger's seat. A second man, taller, polished, a country-club type, sat in the front of the

483

German-made vehicle, the door open, his feet resting on the blacktop.

"Wait here," Sam said as he got out of the car, slamming the door behind him.

The two brothers were polar opposites in many respects. Sam's skinny, slight frame stood in sharp contrast to his brother's bulky build; where Paul had gone gray, Sam's head had yet to know that color; where one was confident and successful the other was twitchy and nervous, knowing that his well-laid plans were completely shot, as evidenced by the presence of the object of his desire sitting on the hood of the BMW.

"What the hell have you done?" Sam whispered in an almost animal-like voice.

"You're kidding, right?" Paul snapped back. "You break into my files, you plan to rob not only my best client but someone who is one of my closest friends."

"Fuck you." Sam's bloodshot eyes squinted in resentment.

"Good answer."

"Don't talk to me like I'm a child," Sam shot back.

"I never have," Paul said. "Did it ever occur to you that maybe it's your misperception of life that leads you to that conclusion?"

"Don't talk to me about life."

"Right, your life is so bad —" Paul's body language spoke as loudly as his words "— you'll destroy everyone else's to feel good?"

"Fuck off," Sam exploded.

"There you go again with that brilliant vocabulary. You're sloppy, foolish, and reckless. Do you know how easy it was to figure out what you were doing? To fly up here and take this box from the safe before you could get near it?" Paul ran his hand along the smooth surface of the wooden lid.

Sam's breathing became labored with anxiety.

"Look, tell me what you want," Paul said as he patted the box. "Is it the money, recognition, or is it just this box?"

Dance stepped from his car and approached Sam. "You want to tell me what's going on?"

"Wait in the car," Sam said.

"Who is this?" Dance waved a finger at Paul as he looked at the box atop the BMW. "And what's up with the box?"

"It's nothing," Sam said.

"Right, it's nothing," Dance responded.

"It's between me and my brother."

"Brother?" Dance said in surprise. "What the hell is going on?"

Neither Dreyfus answered, both caught

up in their mutual anger.

"Who are you?" Dance said, looking at the man sitting in the car.

Suddenly, a black Mustang shot up the driveway into the parking lot, screeching to a halt in front of Dance.

"Hey, Dance," Shannon said calmly as he got out of his car.

Dance turned to his partner, his eyes looking about for anyone else, as if he was expecting someone.

"Everything all right?" Shannon asked as he followed Dance's gaze.

Nick stepped from the passenger seat of Shannon's car and walked around the vehicle.

"I've got a bit of an issue here; nothing I can't handle," Dance said, putting on his false face. "What brings you here?"

"I've got some people making some awfully strange accusations."

"Some people?" Dance asked, looking at Nick.

Nick glared back at him.

"I don't particularly like false or unfounded accusations." Dance paused. "Isn't it off-base to question *your* superior?"

"Just tell me what you're doing here," Shannon said, running his hand through his black hair, "so I can get back to dealing with more important things."

"It's personal, Shannon, so leave now before we have an issue." A hint of anger rose in his voice.

"Yeah, it's personal," Nick mocked him.

Dance turned to Nick. "Who the hell are you?"

Nick stood quietly staring at the man who had wreaked havoc on his life.

"He said you were going to kill his wife," Shannon said accusingly. "Do you know what the hell he's talking about?"

"Listen, Shannon," Dance said, as if speaking to a child. "Internal Affairs already has a file on you. One phone call and you'll not only go down but end up in a prison where the inmates hate cops."

"Boy, you really think that scares me?" Shannon said, stepping forward, his chest expanding in anger. "I know I'm clean and I know you're not. Enough of your bullshit."

Dance laughed, mocking Shannon. "We'll chat later. In the meantime me and my friend have an appointment to get to."

Dance turned to Sam and motioned for him to follow him back to his car.

Sam just stared at him, the moment dragging on. He looked back at the box, at his brother standing there, his hand upon it.

"Dance," Sam said quietly. "We're not going."

"What?" Dance spun about as if a knife had been plunged into his back.

"I'm calling the whole thing off," Sam said.

Dance walked right up into Sam's face, breathing on him like an enraged bull. His eyes moved about, looking at Paul, looking back at Sam, looking toward the box on the car.

Without warning, Dance drew his pistol. His left arm shot out, grabbed Paul, and pulled him into a headlock. He jammed the nine-millimeter to Paul's head.

Shannon was like bottled lightning drawing his Glock, aiming it head-high at Dance. "What the hell, Ethan?"

Dance ignored Shannon, grinding the pistol into Paul's ear as he shouted, "What's in the box, Sam?"

Sam looked at Paul, his mind fogged with panic.

Paul remained the personification of calm — he had been in war, he had been in battle, and he knew that cool heads prevailed.

"I didn't wake up this morning with the intention of ending my day empty-handed. Answer me, what the hell is in that box?"

"It's not what you think," Sam said.

"It's enough to screw me over. Is it worth more than $25 million? Is it enough to trade your brother's life over?"

"Put the gun down, Ethan," Shannon whispered.

"I think you better open the box before I kill your brother," Dance thumbed back the hammer of his gun.

"Dance," Shannon yelled. "Goddammit, put down your weapon."

"Can you handle the blood on your hands, Shannon?" Dance twisted Paul so he was a shield between him and his partner. "You talk a big game, but can you make the shot, are you that confident that you can kill me? If you miss, can you deal with the guilt of collateral damage?"

Nick remained still, a silent observer to the unfolding anarchy.

Shannon stared into Dreyfus's eyes, seeing a man who knew no panic, whose mind was calmly looking for solutions, for escape.

A Chrysler Sebring shot up the drive, coming to a screeching halt behind the standoff. Johnny Arilio leaped from the car, his gun leading the way, pointed straight at Shannon. Randall emerged from the driver's seat, slowly drawing his pistol and aiming it at the other side of Shannon's head.

"It pays to have friends," Dance said.

Shannon gripped his nine-millimeter tighter, knowing that if he gave it up, the man in the crook of Dance's arm would be dead in moments.

"I'll tell you what," Dance said. "Lower your weapon, toss it away, and I won't shoot everybody here, beginning with the man in my arms."

"You wouldn't —"

Dance fired his weapon into the tarmac, sending a shock through everyone.

And the moment spun into chaos.

Nick stood his ground, staring at Paul Dreyfus and Dance's gun, which once again was held against his head. Sam was in a full-on panic, his skinny arms shaking as his eyes darted around frantically searching for salvation.

"The next one will land in flesh," Dance said. "Mark my words, Shannon."

Shannon stared at Dance. Knowing the truth to his statement, he finally relented, placing his gun on the ground and pushing it ten feet out of reach.

"Hey, Randall," Dance said. "In the trunk of my car are some police-issue zip-ties. Get them and secure everyone."

Arilio waved Nick and Zachariah Nash over to stand next to the Mustang. Randall grabbed the plastic restraints from Dance's trunk and quickly zip-tied their wrists in front, sitting them down against the muscle car.

Arilio turned to Shannon, pointing his gun at his chest.

"You guys just made the biggest mistake of your life." Shannon's eye burned with rage as they secured his wrists.

"Just cooperate, Shannon, and sit your ass down," Arilio barked as he pushed the detective down next to Nick.

"See what you have done, Sam?" Dance said as he looked at the three prisoners, turning his attention back to the man he held in a headlock, then finally back to Sam Dreyfus.

"You're not backing out on me." There was a hint of fear in Dance's voice. "I've got commitments, promises to uphold."

Dance stood there controlling the moment, thinking . . .

"This your brother's plane?" Dance looked at the white Cessna on his left. "You know how to fly?"

Sam reluctantly nodded.

Dance turned his attention back to Paul and drove the gun into the side of his head, grinding the barrel into his ear.

"So, we have a choice. A choice where

everyone here can live or die. And it's all up to the Dreyfus brothers. The fate of you all rests in their hands."

Out of nowhere, a yellow Labrador retriever emerged from the woods, running by. He suddenly stopped, his head jerking back and forth, looking at everyone.

"We have a choice between box number one." Dance tilted his head at the mahogany box that sat atop the BMW, ignoring the inquisitive dog. "A choice where you can all live while Sammy boy flies us out of here with our prize, or we can go ahead with the theft of Washington House, a choice where, sadly, we'll have to kill you all before we depart here to relieve Shamus Hennicot of some antiques and diamonds."

The dog suddenly started barking, coiling back on its four legs as if it could sense danger. The incessant loud bark intermingled with a low growl.

All eyes were on the dog when all of sudden, without warning, Dance shot it.

With a screaming yelp, the dog flinched and ran away, but within twenty feet, it slowed and teetered about, its eyes confused and pleading, before it collapsed dead on the ground.

"You cruel bastard," Nash said.

"Hey, I wouldn't want it to delay our

departure," Dance said, half serious before turning to Sam. "Now, unless everyone here wants to die like that dog . . . one of you please open the box."

Sam and Paul remained silent.

"Open it," Dance screamed, squeezing Paul's neck tighter with his arm.

"I can't," Paul said. "It requires three separate keys." Paul pointed toward the three keyholes. "I only have one."

"Where are the other two?"

"With Shamus Hennicot," Paul said.

"Where is he?"

"You don't have a chance of getting the keys from him. He'd let us all die before you got into that box."

"Well, then, he made your choice. I can live with that. I'll just kill you all now, go get the diamonds from his house, and stop with all of this bullshit."

Dance ground the barrel of his gun into Paul's temple and drew back the hammer —

"You son of a bitch. Leave him out of this," Sam said, stepping toward Dance.

"Didn't you think about the consequences when you started down this road?" Dance yelled at Sam. "You said you wanted out of his shadow, now you want to protect him?"

"I was the one who wanted the box, my brother had nothing to do with this."

"Well, if it required three keys, how were you going to get it open?"

Sam couldn't meet Dance's eye.

"Boy, you are the stupid one in the family, huh? You have no idea how to open it?"

"I would have figured it out."

"Then figure it out now," Dance shouted, the veins in his neck distending with his rage.

Sam turned and looked at the box.

"What the hell is in it?" Dance asked. "So help me God, it better be worth millions or I promise, you'll all die here today."

Without warning, Sam spun about, his arm flying through the air, punching Dance in the side of the head.

But the blow barely fazed him, and he quickly responded, aiming his nine-millimeter. Sam retreated in fear. And without hesitating, Dance pulled the trigger.

The bullet exploded from the barrel, hitting Sam in the knee, sending him tumbling to the ground.

"That was stupid," Dance said. "You're lucky I need you, otherwise that bullet would have hit you somewhere fatal."

Sam rolled about the ground clutching his blood-soaked knee.

Dance tightened his grip about Paul's

neck and dragged him backward. He aimed his pistol at the box atop the BMW, firing off a quick shot.

The heavy box skittered along the car roof as the bullet barely split the side corner.

"Don't bother," Paul said. "I designed it. It's got a bulletproof, fireproof titanium core."

Dance pressed the barrel back in Paul's ear. "You designed it? Then you open it or die."

"I can't."

"Then you'll be the first to go —"

"Dance," Nick called out as he rose to his feet. "Look at me."

Nick glared at the detective. He had seen Dance's future and what he was capable of. He had killed Julia in cold blood, and Marcus and Dreyfus and McManus and who knew how many others. And while Nick had moved the pieces around on the chessboard, while he had played with fate, nothing would change the evil that was in Ethan Dance's heart. The corrupt cop would go on killing, ending lives for his own purposes.

"You want your money?" Nick said. "Killing him won't open that box, but I've got something far greater. Worth more than you could ever imagine."

Dance stared at him.

Dreyfus's words echoed in Nick's mind, *"perception of value,"* and Marcus's *"the greedy mind, the double-down, double-or-nothing, win-a-thousand-go-for-two attitude."*

"Let him go," Nick said. "And I promise, I'll prove it to you."

Nick held his trussed arms out as he walked over to Dance and stared into his eyes.

"Let him go, take me instead, and I'll give you something that will grant you more wealth than you could imagine."

"Fuck you."

"If it doesn't meet your needs, then you can kill me in his place."

Dance continued staring at Nick.

"Tucked in a shoe in your office is a St. Christopher medal given to you at graduation. Your mother had it engraved, *Miracles do happen.*"

"How the hell did you know that?" Dance said.

"Do you believe in miracles, Dance?" Nick asked. "Cut me loose," Nick said as he held up his zip-tied hands. "And I'll show you a miracle that can make you richer than you could ever imagine."

Julia looked at her watch. It was 10:55. She

496

pushed her Lexus to over eighty miles per hour. Once again, despite her best intentions, she was running late. She was thanking God that Westchester Airport was a regional terminal, a facility that she could actually run through and perhaps make her 11:16 flight.

The conference call had gone on longer than she anticipated, the other attorneys on the call feeling compelled to argue over nothing in order to justify the extra hour of billing. Julia hated attorneys like that. Their conduct created a global hatred for her profession.

She hit the speakerphone on her cell and dialed her voicemail. Nick had tried her twice. She was sure he was calling to apologize for their fight this morning and regretted that he had beaten her to the punch.

Of course, he could also be calling about dinner with the Mullers, making one last-ditch effort to get out of it.

"Julia," Nick's voice echoed in the car. "It's me. Do me a favor, do not get on that flight to Boston. I don't care why you're going, I don't care if you get fired, do not get on that flight. I have a terrible feeling, I can't explain it. Just do what I say. Call me when you get this."

Julia listened to the message. Nick's voice

was so urgent, so pleading. Though he didn't apologize for their fight. Not that that mattered. But . . .

She couldn't understand how he'd found out she was going to Boston. No one knew except her, Dr. Colverhome, and Jo, and neither of them would ever tell Nick.

It wasn't the first time Nick had tried to talk her out of flying. She had canceled a business trip last February based on his fear of a snowstorm in the middle of the country, and of course there were no problems, all flights arrived intact and on time. It wasn't as if he were crying wolf; it was just his way of saying he couldn't live without her.

Even when Nick was mad at her, it never diminished his love, his caring, his worry. She loved Nick with all her heart, but today, she loved him even more.

He'd had a tough week, a tough month with work; she could hear the stress in his voice. He needed a surprise, a life affirming moment. And what better way to do that than a romantic dinner for two at which she would explain that dinner would soon be for three?

She didn't care if she had to run a world-record sprint through the terminal, she would make her flight. She was even more determined now.

"Come with me to my car." Nick pointed at his Audi fifty yards away on the other side of the parking lot near the exit. "I can offer you not only something of far greater value, but also a way for you to get out of here without anyone knowing where you went."

Dance removed a knife from his pocket and cut Nick free from the zip-ties about his wrists. "Pick up the box."

Nick lifted the surprisingly heavy case off the roof of the BMW.

Dance tucked the gun into Nick's back, pointing him toward the blue Audi, leaving Paul kneeling over his brother's bleeding leg. Shannon and Nash remained bound and sitting upon the ground under the watchful eyes of Randall and Arilio.

Arriving at the Audi, Nick placed the box on the hood of his car and held his hands up in a gesture of surrender.

"First look on my front seat," Nick said, pointing into his car.

Dance opened the door to find the gold and bejeweled Colt Peacemaker on the seat. He lifted it out, staring at the weapon.

"I'm sure you know what that is and where it's from."

"Do you have the rest?" Dance said in shock. "Do you have the diamonds?"

"In my inner jacket pocket arc two letters," Nick pointed toward his pocket.

"Slowly." Dance motioned to Nick to remove them before placing the barrel of the gun squarely in the center of Nick's forehead.

Dance laid the Peacemaker on the roof of the Audi as Nick pulled out and handed him the first envelope. He looked at the blue crest before quickly opening it and reading the two sheets.

Nick slowly withdrew the watch from his pocket and held it out.

"A watch," Dance said as his eyes flicked between the gold timepiece and the letter. "Are you fucking kidding me? Do you think I'm a fool?"

Dance scanned the letter from Nash again. "What kind of bullshit is this?" Dance jammed the gun harder into Nick's head.

"Read the next one," Nick said calmly, handing him Marcus's letter while tucking Nash's letter back into his jacket pocket.

Dance began to read.

"Look at the last sheet," Nick said. "The printout from today's *Wall Street Journal*."

Dance read it through, confusion creasing his brow.

"Look at the date and time," Nick said. "That's eight hours from now."

"A kid could have made this with Photoshop."

Nick slowly reached back into his breast pocket and withdrew his cell phone, flipping it open.

"What are you —"

"Relax," Nick said as he flipped it open, pulled up the picture of Dance's car, and handed him the cell phone.

Dance thumbed through the pictures of his car, stopping at the image of his trunk. He stared at the golden weapons, the knives and swords, and the bag of diamonds, his eyes finally falling on the Colt Peacemaker, the same gun that rested atop Nick's car.

"What kind of trick is this? That stuff isn't in my trunk. I just looked into it a few minutes ago."

"It's no trick," Nick said calmly. "You're looking at the future."

"How is this possible?"

"Bear with me a moment. If the letters you read are the truth, think of what you could do."

And Dance's mind began to work.

"Manipulate the past, know the outcome of lotteries, horse races." Nick appealed to his greed. "Use it wisely, and you could amass a fortune."

"Why would you give this up? You would trade all of this for that guy's life?" Dance pointed his gun back toward Paul Dreyfus.

Nick nodded.

Dance smiled. "No," he said, shaking his head as the pieces came together. "That's what Shannon meant about my killing your wife, that's what these letters are about. I do it in the future and you've come back to stop me."

Dance looked around. And stared at the watch.

"Holy shit," Dance said in realization.

As Dance became lost in his thoughts, Nick looked about the parking lot, down the driveway toward the road.

"I know who your wife is," Dance said. "Hennicot's attorney, right?"

Nick said nothing.

"If I take this watch," Dance smiled a cruel smile at Nick as his thumb moved about the golden case, "who's to say I still won't kill her?"

Nick's heart began to pound, the blood coursing through his body, filling him with fury.

Dance looked again at the watch in his hand and it was all the distraction Nick needed.

Nick snatched the Colt from atop the Audi and holding it like a hammer drove it into Dance's temple. Nick's left hand grabbed and twisted the Glock from the detective before he could react and tossed it aside. He raised the Peacemaker again and drove it down against Dance's nose.

Tossing the gun aside, Nick pummeled Dance with all his rage, all of his anger and frustration, his fists a blur of wrath directed at the evil soul before him.

Despite all of his strength, despite all of his experience on the street, of fights and killing, Dance was no match for the passion-fueled onslaught being released from Nick's soul. Nick had seen his wife die, experienced her death too many times, in too many ways, and all of it brought about by this man.

Nick finally stood, leaving the broken and battered detective writhing on the ground.

Nick spied the gold watch, his passport for the day, gleaming in the sunlight. He picked it up and tucked it into his back pocket.

Then he picked up the ornate pistol, reached into his pocket, and withdrew a silver bullet. He flipped out the cylinder and dropped the .45 slug into the gunmetal chamber. He flipped it back and gave it a spin.

He looked at the gun, at its intricate design, at the golden finish that shined in the midmorning sun, giving the impression of a holy aura about the weapon. Nick thought of the Arabic lettering upon the bullet casing, *May you be forbidden from paradise*, hoping that the phrase had some magical property of actually weighing down the soul so it could be dragged into hell.

He laid the gun against Dance's head.

"You're going to kill me to avenge a murder I haven't even committed yet?"

Nick drew back the hammer, clicking it into place.

Dance stared up helplessly into Nick's eyes.

As Nick looked at the bloodied cop, a man who had shot his wife, had killed his best friend, killed Paul Dreyfus and Private McManus, set in motion the crash of Flight 502, Nick realized he was looking into the heart of evil, looking at a man who saw humanity as his pawns, a man who was without morals or compassion.

And then a crushing realization coursed through his body, as if the three sisters of fate were holding him back. For none of those things, none of those deaths had yet occurred, they were all in the future, a future that was no longer fixed but left to chance.

But as Dance's eye burned up at him, Nick saw the coldness, the lack of a soul and knew this man would visit darkness upon others throughout his life.

"You can't do it, you can't pull that trigger, can you?" Dance said.

Nick's eyes softened.

"You know what, if I killed your wife in the future —" Dance paused as if he was about to apologize, but that possibility quickly passed as a mirthless smile creased his lips "— she probably deserved it."

With those words burning in his ears, with all reason gone from his mind, Nick wrapped his finger about the antique pistol and . . .

. . . pulled the trigger.

Shannon stared up at Randall and Arilio standing next to the Chrysler Sebring, watching Paul Dreyfus wrap a makeshift tourniquet about Sam's leg. The two dirty cops exchanged whispers.

Shannon sat up against his Mustang next to Nash. He had quietly dragged the zip-tie against the blacktop, shaving it, compromising its integrity. He took a glance at the far side of the parking lot where he saw Nick and Dance begin to fight. Without further delay, Shannon drew his arms apart, twisting, stretching the zip-tie, ignoring the pain as the plastic cut into his skin, until it finally broke.

Randall and Arilio caught sight of Nick beating on Dance, but they were too late.

Shannon sprang to his feet, and his fist caught Randall square on the nose, exploding it in a crimson mess as he stumbled back against his car, dazed and confused. But Shannon continued moving toward him, unleashing two massive body blows into Randall's soft belly, sending the middle-aged cop to the ground barely conscious and in agony.

As he turned, he knew Arilio would be a far different opponent, younger, faster, angrier, and still holding on to his gun, which was now aimed at Shannon's head.

"Shannon, back off or I'll kill you where you stand."

Shannon didn't answer. He had never understood why people in fights, in life-and-death situations, felt compelled to talk.

With a sweep of his rising left arm, Shannon deflected the gun up and away from his body as he wrapped his hands about Arilio's wrist, twisting the police-issue Glock and compromising the cop's ability to effectively use it.

Arilio's instinctive reaction was to battle for control of his gun, which was exactly what Shannon was counting on. Arilio twisted his wrist while grabbing at Shannon's arm, trying to free his weapon. Shannon's right fist cocked back and unleashed his fury into Arilio's throat, stunning him, sending his hands to his damaged esophagus. Shannon tore the pistol from the cop's hand, all the while continuing a massive succession of blows to Arilio's head and body. The cop had no chance, as his hands had instinctively wrapped his throat trying to catch his breath. And within ten seconds, he was disabled upon the ground.

Dance was still alive. The gun's hammer had fired against an empty cylinder.

"You can't kill me, can you?" Dance said, taunting Nick, who stood above him holding the Colt Peacemaker.

"It was never my intention," Nick said as he looked down the drive at the approaching car.

The black Mercedes limo drove up the drive behind Dance, pulling to within a few feet of where he lay.

"There are some people who are better equipped for that sort of thing." Nick looked up as the rear door of the black car opened.

Dance turned his head and saw the two large men emerge from the driver and passenger doors of the black stretch Mercedes. Their shoulders were wide, each wore a short-sleeve button-down shirt. Imposing pistols rested in shoulder holsters on the left side of their bodies.

Without a word they walked past Nick, reached over, and effortlessly hoisted Dance to his feet.

Dance's face went white with fear.

"No way," he screamed. "I said I'd pay you tonight."

A short man emerged from the rear of the vehicle, his good eye squinting in the bright sun while the milky one was wide open, oblivious to the glare.

Dance ripped his arms away from the two bodyguards, threw his shoulders back in defiance, and stared at Rukaj. "You said I had till midnight."

"I got a call a little while ago." Rukaj looked at Nick before casting his eyes back on the cop. "I was told you had no intention of paying me, that you were going to fly out of here this morning."

Nick began taking small steps backward, moving away from the Albanian and his two-man wrecking crew. He had lifted Rukaj's number from Dance's phone near the end of the eleven o'clock hour, finding the cop's cell on his dead body. Nick knew it was the last call Dance had received, and he had seen how terrified the caller had made him. He dialed Rukaj just after 10:00 A.M., knowing that the Albanian would pay a personal visit if he learned he was being lied to and betrayed.

Dance stood, flanked by the two hulking guards, and glared at Nick. "You son of a bitch. It was all bullshit: the watch, that box. It was all a trap, you bastard."

And without warning, Dance spun about, ripping the pistol out of the driver's holster, and in a fluid motion, he continued his momentum spinning toward Nick and firing a single shot.

The bullet hit Nick in his right side, the force of the nine-millimeter bullet knocking him off his feet.

The bodyguard grabbed Dance's arm, twisting the gun from his grip, snapping his wrist in two with a loud crack. The two guards each took an arm, pulling them outward, sending Dance into agony.

Rukaj walked over and knelt over Nick. He laid his hand against the wound, seeing the blood bubbling through his shirt. He silently stared into Nick's pain-filled eyes before exhaling and rising to his feet. He turned back and walked up into Dance's face.

"I came here to scare you, Dance, not to kill you," Rukaj said in his thick accent. "If you were going to run you had fourteen months to do it, you wouldn't wait until the last minute. But now . . . You just shot a man, most likely killed him." Rukaj stared back at Nick lying upon the tarmac, blood pouring from his side. He caught sight of the dead dog, lying in a pool of blood twenty feet away. "Did you kill the dog, too?"

Dance stood there like a rag doll, his arms being torn apart by the two bodyguards.

"Sometimes in life," Rukaj said, "we don't realize how one simple action, one single mistake will affect our future."

Rukaj nodded to his bodyguards, who twisted Dance's arm even harder, sending him into a crippling agony.

"You're useless to me now," Rukaj continued. "A cop committing murder doesn't play well. They'll hunt you, and I can't afford you leading them to me."

Rukaj pulled out his knife, its polished metal shimmering in the morning sun. "I don't do many favors, and I certainly won't get in the habit of it, but I believe your slow death will allow more than a few people to go on with their lives."

Dance looked back and saw Shannon and Paul Dreyfus fifty yards away sprinting madly toward them.

Rukaj laid the blade under Dance's eye, trailing it down his cheek. "Time to pay up."

Dance's eyes filled with terror as the bodyguards pushed him into the back of the Mercedes. Rukaj took one last look at Nick and, without a word, climbed in and shut the door.

And the limo pulled away, driving out of the parking lot, disappearing around the corner, leaving Nick to die.

Julia raced through the main entrance to Westchester Airport, her foot burying the accelerator of the Lexus. She looked at the clock: 10:58. She was determined to make it, she wasn't about to let her plans for the evening, her plans for surprising Nick, disappear because she was late for a flight.

As she zipped past the private air terminal she couldn't help wondering what the unmarked police cars with their flashing lights were doing.

And then up ahead, racing toward her, were two TSA cars, the lights upon their roofs spraying the air with their red, white, and blue strobes. An ambulance could be seen in the distance coming her way. She hoped whoever they were racing to was all right, that it wasn't a matter of life and death.

But her curiosity quickly waned as she thought of Nick and the baby inside her. She couldn't wait to surprise him tonight.

Nick lay on the ground, blood pouring out of his right side. Paul Dreyfus arrived and knelt, tearing off his own shirt, applying it to the large exit wound at Nick's back, trying to stem the bleeding.

"Oh, man," Dreyfus said, trying to make light of the severity of the situation. "How are you?"

"Ouch." Nick tried for humor, but it slowly faded. He had no idea what the bullet had pierced but whoever said being shot didn't hurt had never been shot. It felt as if he had been hit by a rocket, the tip of which had passed through his side.

The blood loss was enormous, pooling out beneath him on the black tarmac. His eyes began to drift as he grew ashen.

Suddenly, Nick's body seized up, his limbs rigid, his jaw clenched. And then he fell limp.

"Shit, we've got cardiac arrest. The blood loss is too much," Dreyfus yelled as he started CPR. "I really need a —"

But Shannon was already there, ripping open the AED, the police-issue automatic external defibrillator that was in his trunk. He turned it on. A subtle beep began growing as it built up a charge.

Dreyfus ripped open Nick's shirt. He tore the cross from his neck, dug through his pockets, removing the etched silver bullets, his keys, his cell phone; in the rear pocket he found the watch. He pulled out the antique, knowing its value, and placed it in his pocket, making sure he had cleared all the metal from Nick's body.

Shannon passed the electrode pads to Dreyfus, who affixed them to Nick's chest, his failing vital signs already being interpreted by the machine.

"Three, two, one," the electronic voice called out. "Clear."

And Nick's body arced up in shock as the pulse was sent through his heart's electrical system, fully stopping it so the body's natural process could restart it.

But Nick's body didn't respond. The AED began its ascending whine again, building up a charge.

"Three, two, one. Clear."

513

Nick rose again, before settling back down.

His heart restarted. His breathing was faint, but it was there.

"Where the hell is the ambulance?" Dreyfus shouted.

Nick's eyes opened to half mast, looking up at Dreyfus.

"The jet," Nick said, weakly.

Dreyfus took his hand and dangled the keys to his Cessna in front of Nick's half-closed eyes. "There'll be no plane crashes today. You just hold on."

Nick struggled to speak. "My —"

"Try not to speak." Dreyfus tried to calm him.

"My watch?" Nick whispered.

"No worries, it's in my pocket. I'll hold on to your stuff till we get to the hospital."

"What time is it?" Nick's voice was barely a whisper.

"What?" Dreyfus leaned an ear to Nick.

"The time," Nick struggled to say.

"It's 10:59," Dreyfus said, looking at his own watch. "Don't worry, the ambulance should be here any minute."

It didn't matter. There would be no plane crash, Julia would live, she was out of danger and Dance sat in the rear of Rukaj's limo on the way to his death.

Nick's heart slowed.

The world grew numbingly cold, and he felt a chill he had felt eleven times already, every hour. He had the same metallic taste in his mouth, but he knew he was not dancing in time anymore. The watch was gone, out of his reach.

But as he thought on it, it didn't matter. He'd removed Dance from the fateful moment, and without him there would be no plane crash in Byram Hills. Julia was safe, Marcus was safe, everyone was safe. He looked at the price of fate, trading his life so they could all live, and in his mind, the sacrifice was more than worth making.

He had become the focal point of time. Because he had been shot, Rukaj chose to kill Dance, making it impossible for him to endanger Julia, Marcus, Paul and Sam Dreyfus, Shannon, and McManus. Nick's actions here in the last five minutes, culminating in his death, would reverberate through the lives of countless people, most of whom would never even hear of Nicholas Quinn. People would get on planes, go on vacation, head off to business meetings, never realizing how close to death they had come.

But above all, most important, Julia would live.

He only wished he could see her once more, to hold her, to tell her that he loved her one last time, to apologize for getting caught up in the race of life, never appreciating the value of time, never living in the moment or understanding what was truly important. For in the end he was leaving her alone, leaving her with nothing.

From the edge of his vision, it began to creep in, a darkness that obscured his sight in spite of the bright morning sun. It muted the sounds around him, enveloping him in a heavy blanket, until the world finally went black.

And Nicholas Quinn died.

CHAPTER 13

July 28
10 P.M.

Julia sat in the uncomfortable metal chair, her eyes bloodshot, and cried out. It was after 10:00, and a moonless night sky blanketed the world.

She had arrived in Boston on schedule and taken a cab to Dr. Colverhome's office. Seeing the remarkable vision of life on the screen filled her with a new emotion. She was a mother, her and Nick's child was alive and growing within her, and in seven and a half months would emerge to find parents who would love it unconditionally.

But then, as she was leaving the doctor's office, her cell phone had rung.

Marcus's voice was unnaturally calm.

He told her that Shamus's jet was awaiting her at Logan International to take her immediately back to Westchester Airport where Marcus would be waiting to take her to the hospital.

The entire flight, her mind couldn't focus. How could one life be entering her world as another was being taken away?

Julia rose from her chair and stood over Nick. Seeing him wired and tubed, the steady beep of the heart monitor ringing constantly in her ear reminded her how close death really was. Nick had yet to awaken and she feared, despite everything the doctors said, he never would.

Nick was encased in darkness, lost in an abyss of despair. He kept seeing Julia dead on the floor, Marcus killed right in front of him, bodies tethered to the bottom of the Kensico Reservoir. He saw planes falling from the sky, fireballs, and black, acrid smoke rising up and filling the air. He saw the bodies of the dead, hundreds of them; he was stuck among them, aimlessly wandering, as their voices whispered in his ear.

And then Julia was there, filling his vision, her face whole and perfect, calling to him, coaxing him up, drawing him toward heaven.

And he opened his eyes to find her staring down at him, her eyes tear-filled and bloodshot.

"Hi," he whispered.

And she hugged him, all of her anguish at almost losing him pouring forth.

Julia finally stepped back and Paul Dreyfus stepped in, looking at his eyes, checking his vitals. "Glad to see you made it."

Nick smiled as his awareness slowly returned.

"This guy saved your life," Shannon said, emerging from the corner.

"I haven't pulled someone back from the brink since Vietnam," Dreyfus said. "The AED did most of the work."

"Don't listen to him," Shannon said. "He worked on you a long time to bring you back."

"I don't know how long." Dreyfus smiled as he palmed something from his pocket. He took Nick's hand and slid it to him surreptitiously. "But you do lose track of time when you're trying to save someone."

Nick knew instantly what Dreyfus had given him; once again in his hand, the familiar feel of the watch was somehow comforting, like a blanket to a child.

"Hey," Marcus said. He was leaning against the wall, towering over the moment.

"Hey." Nick could hardly get the word out, glad to see his friend alive and in one piece.

As he stared at everyone around him, Julia and Marcus, Dreyfus and Shannon, he felt as if he had just returned from Oz, his head filled with an impossible story that no one would understand.

But then he saw it, sitting on the table next to him: the dark mahogany box.

"Listen," Shannon said as he patted Nick's leg. "Brave thing you did today."

"Thanks," Nick said.

"I'm glad you're okay." Shannon walked to and opened the door. "I need to be getting home though, I've got to take on a new partner tomorrow, this punk named Brinehart, probably have to knock some sense into him. Listen, Nick, your friend Dreyfus filled me in a bit, but you still owe me some explanations. In the meantime, though, take care, get some rest."

And Shannon walked out the door.

"Thanks for coming down," Nick said to Marcus.

"Come on," Marcus said as he leaned over his friend, a devious grin on his face. "I'd take a bullet for you. And I don't say that to just anyone."

"Look, I know you're glad to see me," Nick said. "But your eyes are dancing with something else. Did you fall in love again?"

"You won't believe this," Marcus said, glad he could let out the building head of steam within him. "This young guy, Jason Cereta —"

"Cereta?" Julia asked, dumbstruck at hearing the name. "Blond guy, twenties?"

"You know him?"

"We flew to Boston together this morning."

"Really? Small world," Marcus said, trying to continue his story. "At any rate, he called a few minutes ago. Sharp as a tack, crafty as the devil, charming as all hell, kind of like a younger version of myself with hair." Marcus ran his hand over his bald head. "Just not as handsome.

"He ran off on his own to Boston today," Marcus continued, "and put my dream deal of owning Halifax Skis together. I'll have to hire a whole new team to deal with this coup but it will be worth it."

"Marcus, you need to do me a favor," Nick said, sitting up in the bed. "I know a guy. Just got his MBA, he's in the National Guard."

"Military guy, I like that."

"He's already had enough death in his life. You need to hire him."

"Without an interview?" Marcus said in surprise. "What's his name?"

"McManus. Private McManus."

"What a perfect military name his mother

521

gave him. Does private have any other first name?"

"Smartass. It's Neil."

Marcus rubbed the back of his head. "It gives me such a headache taking chances on new guys, but if you say so, he's as good as hired."

The heavy pine door to the room swung open, and an incredibly old man entered. He walked with a long dark mahogany cane, the head of which was a carved elephant's head, the walking stick supporting his slow, shuffling gate. His hair was white, his pale skin wrinkled, seeming two sizes too large for his skeleton. But the eyes . . . The eyes were sharp and focused.

He was accompanied by Zachariah Nash, who wore his crisp doubled-breasted blazer and white, pleated linen pants. Nick recognized Nash full well as the man who had given him the watch, who had set him on his journey.

"Nick," Julia said, pointing at the older man, "this is Shamus Hennicot."

"Nicholas," Hennicot said with a bow of the head. "I'm so glad to see you alive. And I would like you to formally meet my attaché, Zachariah Nash."

Nash tilted his head to Nick, as if he were meeting him for the first time. Shamus turned briefly to Paul Dreyfus and gave a subtle nod of recognition.

"Julia?" Nick took a deep breath and licked his lips. "Do you think maybe you could get me a Coke or something?"

"Of course." Julia smiled. She turned to Shamus and Zachariah with eyebrows raised in question.

"Nothing for us, dear," Shamus said.

"I can't believe you came down for this," Julia said. "It means so much to me."

"I understand you flew with my wife, today," Shamus said with a warm smile. "Pleasant flight, I hope."

Julia appeared confused.

"Petite, gray-haired, talks a lot . . ." Shamus prodded her.

"Katherine? That was your wife?" Julia asked in surprise.

"She spoke so highly of you," Shamus said warmly.

"I had no idea . . ." Julia replied with confusion.

"Which makes your charm all the more special."

"I'm a bit hungry myself," Marcus said to Julia as he walked across the room and opened the door. "I'll go with you."

Alone with Dreyfus, Nash, and Nick, Shamus pulled a chair over and took a seat right next to Nick's bed.

"You have an amazing wife, Nicholas, you're very lucky."

"I know," Nick said.

"And she is even more lucky to have someone like you," Shamus continued. "Only a man whose heart is filled with such love would not abuse the power that you hold in your hand."

Nick finally opened his fist to reveal the watch that Dreyfus had placed there.

"Julia's death, my wife's death, were all my fault," Shamus said with regret. "Sadly, time has robbed me of my youth. If I were a younger man, I would never have tasked you, burdened you with such an impossible journey.

"I'm too frail, too weak, to endure the leaps and machinations of time. My mind no longer has the clarity of thought to step backward and place the world back on its proper axis."

"But wait," Nick said in confusion. "Did the plane crash occur?"

"No," Shamus said.

"The burglary?"

"No. Ethan Dance disappeared into the limo of a man named Rukaj, and he hasn't been heard from since. Detective Shannon arrested Horace Randall and John Arilio on a multitude of charges after they held him and Nash hostage at the airport this morning."

"What about Sam?" Nick asked as he looked at Paul Dreyfus.

"Sam has gone away for a bit," Shamus explained, "to think things through. Paul wanted him arrested, but I wasn't about to see his brother go to jail. The two other cops already have Internal Affairs issues, their karma is catching up to them. But I thought Sam deserved another try at this thing called life."

"If nothing occurred," Nick paused, "then how come you remember everything?"

"I don't," Shamus said matter-of-factly.

"How do you know then?" Nick asked.

Shamus held up the letter that Zachariah had given Nick back in the interrogation room and pointed at the small strange lettering along the bottom. The lettering he never could fathom.

"It's an ancient offshoot of Gaelic, I wrote

that part myself — *to* myself, actually, the way you had your friend Marcus do it. We think alike, you and I," Shamus said with a smile. "I explained to myself about Julia's death, about my wife's death, the plane crash, the robbery, and how they were all intertwined around this box." Shamus patted the mahogany box on the table.

"I specifically noted why I had sent Zachariah to you and my intentions, knowing your love for your wife."

Shamus pulled out the printout from the *Wall Street Journal,* the crash of Flight 502 in the center photo. "But seeing this, seeing the wreckage of the jet my wife and your wife were on, hearing what you said to Paul about Julia's murder, about the robbery, filled in the rest of the details."

Nick turned to Zachariah. "What do you remember?"

Zachariah simply smiled. "Just your bravery at the airport."

Nick turned to Dreyfus. "What about you?"

Dreyfus took the printout of the *Wall Street Journal* from Shamus. "Once I saw you had this page eight hours early, I knew what was in your possession. And I knew that if you had it, if you were riding time backward, then it was given to you by Shamus."

"With the thought of power," Shamus said, "men's hearts darken, with the vision of wealth, morals and values crumble, but that all becomes secondary to love."

Hennicot pulled out a key. It was octagonal, created by Paul Dreyfus for his exclusive use. Dreyfus pulled out an identical one, as did Nash. Each inserted his respective key into the locks on the three sides of the wooden case that sat on the table next to the bed and turned.

Hennicot lifted the lid to reveal a velvet core that filled the interior almost to the rim. Within its center was a single three-inch circular recess, the exact size of the gold watch.

And it all became clear.

"It was found by my grandfather," Shamus said. "Stolen, I believe, from a man in Venice, Italy, who had stolen it himself from the Martinots in France. It was how grandfather made all of his money, slipping back and forth through time, manipulating fate. His empire was built upon it. An empire whose growth continued with my father. Both were men of greed who lusted for power without grasping the consequences of their actions.

"When it was passed down to me on my father's deathbed, I promised myself that I would never fall prey to the lust that had consumed them. I made it my goal to use it only to do good in the world. But I soon learned that good intentions could lead to disastrous consequences, so I tucked it away, refusing to make use of its abilities. Instead, I made it my purpose to distribute the billions acquired by my forefathers, acquired without regard to the end results of their actions, or the effect their travels had on the world.

"Who knows how our fateful interactions affect one another? If a butterfly flaps his wings in China, does it beget a war in Europe? The what-ifs of fate are endless: If Queen Isabella had not financed Columbus, if Hitler had won the war, if Einstein hadn't written to Roosevelt urging him to develop the atomic bomb. Who are we to know, who are we to decide, who are we to be playing God?"

"But if you knew how dangerous the watch was, why didn't you destroy it?" Nick asked.

"We are all fallible, Nicholas. No matter how noble we imagine ourselves to be, we each think of ourselves as righteous in our actions and beliefs, strong and of steadfast character. I thought I could resist its temptation, only making use of its ability in the most dire of circumstances."

"And your wife's death was such an instance," Nick said in understanding.

"Actually, Nicholas, it was your wife's death that was such an instance."

Nick tilted his head in query.

"You leaped through time to save Julia. You would walk through the fires of hell and back if it meant she would live. Well, I know that level of love. I knew through your travels, seeing the death around you, you wouldn't just stop your wife's death but my Katherine's and everyone else's on that fateful flight."

Shamus held up the letter Nash had given him and pointed to the Gaelic writing. "Hearing of Julia's death, I sent Nash to you with the watch and this letter. It is one thing for my wife to die in the plane crash; it's another for your wife to die innocently as the result of my failure to properly dispose of this thing. I love your wife like a daughter, Nicholas, and when I die, when my wife dies, my estate will fall to Julia, but let's keep that between us." Shamus smiled, patting Nick's hand.

"If you would be so kind," Hennicot said as he tilted the mahogany box toward Nick.

Nick looked at the gold watch in his hand, flipping open the cover, reading the engraving one last time: *Fugit inreparabile tempus.* He closed it and placed the watch in the circular velvet recess of the heavy mahogany box.

Dreyfus took the box from the table and closed the lid, turning each key and removing them, handing one to Nash, one to Hennicot, and tucking the last into his pocket.

Hennicot took hold of his elephant's-head cane and stood. "Thank you, Nicholas, for being who you are."

Hennicot shuffled toward the door to leave, Dreyfus and Nash right behind him.

"What are you going to do with it?"

"No worries. Paul and Zachariah are taking a little sailing trip in the western Pacific over the Marianas Trench. It's almost seven miles deep there."

Dreyfus and Nash nodded to Nick as they followed Shamus out the door.

Julia walked in, Coke in hand, along with a pack of Orcos. "Breakfast of champions." She popped the Coke and handed it to him while she opened the blue wrapper on the Oreos.

"I sent Marcus home, he was making a play for the nurses; you know how he gets after making some money, the whole world is beautiful in his eyes." Julia laughed. "I saw Shamus in the elevator. Did I ever tell you what a great guy he is? I love him like a second father."

"He feels the same way about you," Nick said as he stuck a cookie into his mouth, washing it down with a swig of soda.

"If I left my job," Julia said slowly, "we'd be okay, right?"

"We might have to cut things back a bit but that's fine with me."

"I don't care if we live in a shack as long as we're together. I'm just thinking it's time to focus on things besides money."

"Funny you should say that," Nick said. "I don't think we'll have any money troubles going forward."

"How do you know that?" Julia asked.

"I got a little glimpse of the future." Nick smiled. "Now, about starting that family," Nick pulled Julia into his arms, kissing her deeply.

"Funny you should say that." Julia sat on the bed and laid the two gift-wrapped packages in Nick's lap, the teddy bears smiling up at him.

"Presents?" Nick picked up the first gift. "Mmm, feels like a book."

Julia smiled, barely able to contain herself.

"Do me a favor, open the other one first?"

Nick felt like a kid. "What is this, Christmas in July?"

"Better," Julia said as she took hold of Nick's hand squeezing it the way her mother used to squeeze hers when she was a child.

Nick tore open the wrapping paper on the other gift,

   pulled out the frame,

   and . . .

Epilogue

Shamus, Zachariah, and Paul Dreyfus stood in the parking lot of the hospital holding their respective keys. The two mahogany cases were the sole objects in the open trunk of the BMW. The locks on each had been released. Both cases were custom-designed and built by Paul; the box on the left was the final product, while the one on the right, identical in its construction, was the prototype.

Shamus reached out and lifted the lid of the dark wood case on the left. The dome light of the car's trunk was absorbed by the black velvet compartment of the open box. Dreyfus reached into the case and withdrew the gold watch, staring at it, admiring it.

Nash's brow furrowed in curiosity, as if he were a child who had just witnessed Houdini conjuring a rabbit from thin air.

"If that's the watch we prevented from being stolen," Nash stopped himself as he looked upon the closed mahogany case on the right, "what did Nick have?"

"The watch you gave him," Shamus said, as if it was obvious.

"But I never gave it to him," Nash said.

Shamus smiled. "Actually, you did, just not in our time line."

Shamus lifted the lid of the case on the right, the one they had just carried down from the hospital room, and placed in the trunk of the car. Laying his cane against the car, he reached in and withdrew an identical gold watch.

"This one?" Nash pointed to the watch in Shamus's outstretched hand.

"This is the watch that you gave Nick," Shamus said. "The one that he used to prevent a horrible future, the one that he used to remove the reason to ever give him the watch in the first place. They are one and the same, a paradox brought on by violating the laws of physics."

"So, you're saying . . . ?"

Shamus flipped open the watch cover to reveal the engraving. *Fugit inreparabile tempus.* "It's identical, down to its smallest particle, as if it were the offspring of the original timepiece."

"So, does this mean . . . ?"

The three of them looked back and forth between the identical watches.

Shamus finally looked up . . . "Now there are two."

ACKNOWLEDGMENTS

Life is far more enjoyable when you work with people you like and respect. I would personally like to thank:

Gene and Wanda Sgarlata, the owners of Womrath Bookshop in Bronxville, NY, for their continued support and friendship.

Peter Borland, for your inspiration, guidance, friendship, and enthusiasm. I'm beyond thrilled to be working together. Judith Curr, the most forward-thinking professional in the publishing world, and Louise Burke, for her unwavering support and belief. I could not be in better hands. Nick Simonds, for keeping it all together. Joel Gotler, for once again doing the impossible. Mike DeLuca, Alissa Philips, Meredith Finn, and everyone at New Line Cinema, for creating the initial excitement.

And heads and shoulders above all, Cynthia Manson. First and foremost, for being such a good friend. Everything else aside, it is a rare day when we find a true friend in this world, and finding one to work with is magic. Thank you for your innovative thinking, your continued faith, and your unlimited tenacity.

Thank you to my family: Richard, for your creative, intellectual mind, your strength of character, and sense of humor in the face of adversity. Marguerite, for your tenacious approach to life, your warm, caring heart, which reminds me of everything that is good in this world, and your never-ending sense of style and beauty no matter how dark the day. Isabelle, for your laugh that fills my soul, your sense of adventure, and your constant curiosity about the world around you.

My dad, for always being my dad and the voice of wisdom that forever rings in my ear.

Most important, thank you, Virginia, for putting up with my upside-down work habits. You are my muse, my laughter, my joy; you are the reason for everything good in my life. Your beauty, smile, and personality inspire every word I write. You have given me life, you've given me hope, you've given me love. You make my heart dance.

ABOUT THE AUTHOR

Richard Doetsch is the bestselling author of two previous thrillers, *The Thieves of Heaven* and *The Thieves of Faith*. He is also the president of a national real estate company based in New York, where he lives with his family. Visit him online at www.RichardDoetsch.com.

The employees of Thorndike Press hope you have enjoyed this Large Print book. All our Thorndike, Wheeler, and Kennebec Large Print titles are designed for easy reading, and all our books are made to last. Other Thorndike Press Large Print books are available at your library, through selected bookstores, or directly from us.

For information about titles, please call:
(800) 223-1244

or visit our Web site at:
http://gale.cengage.com/thorndike

To share your comments, please write:
Publisher
Thorndike Press
295 Kennedy Memorial Drive
Waterville, ME 04901